PENGUIN BOOKS
The Glass Room

Born in Vermont, Kate Holmquist followed her heart to
Dublin at twenty, landing on her feet, eventually, as staff
journalist with *The Irish Times*. She has also written for radio
and theatre and has worked as an actress and dancer in
Paris. She lives with her rock musician husband, three
children, three dogs, four cats, assorted fish, a gecko and
a tarantula. Her previous book, *A Good Daughter*, was
published by Raven Arts Press in 1991.

The Glass Room

KATE HOLMQUIST

PENGUIN
IRELAND

PENGUIN IRELAND

Published by the Penguin Group
Penguin Ireland, 25 St Stephen's Green, Dublin 2, Ireland
(a division of Penguin Books Ltd)
Penguin Books Ltd, 80 Strand, London WC2R ORL, England
Penguin Group (USA) Inc., 375 Hudson Street, New York, New York 10014, USA
Penguin Group (Australia), 250 Camberwell Road,
Camberwell, Victoria 3124, Australia (a division of Pearson Australia Group Pty Ltd)
Penguin Group (Canada), 90 Eglinton Avenue East, Suite 700, Toronto, Ontario, Canada M4P 2Y3
(a division of Pearson Penguin Canada Inc.)
Penguin Books India Pvt Ltd, 11 Community Centre,
Panchsheel Park, New Delhi – 110 017, India
Penguin Group (NZ), cnr Airborne and Rosedale Roads, Albany,
Auckland 1310, New Zealand (a division of Pearson New Zealand Ltd)
Penguin Books (South Africa) (Pty) Ltd, 24 Sturdee Avenue,
Rosebank, Johannesburg 2196, South Africa

Penguin Books Ltd, Registered Offices: 80 Strand, London WC2R ORL, England

www.penguin.com

First published 2006
1

Copyright © Kate Holmquist, 2006

The moral right of the author has been asserted

All rights reserved
Without limiting the rights under copyright
reserved above, no part of this publication may be
reproduced, stored in or introduced into a retrieval system,
or transmitted, in any form or by any means (electronic, mechanical,
photocopying, recording or otherwise), without the prior
written permission of both the copyright owner and
the above publisher of this book

Set in 13.5/16 pt Monotype Garamond
Typeset by Rowland Phototypesetting Ltd, Bury St Edmunds, Suffolk
Printed in Great Britain by Clays Ltd, St Ives plc

A CIP catalogue record for this book is available from the British Library

ISBN-13: 978-1-844-88092-8
ISBN-10: 1-844-88092-3

For Ferdia, Sienna, Bessa and Finn

Each day I live in a glass room
Unless I break it with the thrusting
Of my senses and pass through
The splintered walls to the great landscape.

'Each Day I Live in a Glass Room'
Mervyn Peake

PART ONE

I

On the morning of her thirty-seventh birthday, Louisa Maguire awoke to an embrace. Someone had climbed into her bed and snuggled up against her warm, sleepy body. But it was her son, not her husband, whose silky limbs entwined with hers.

'Ssh, only a nightmare,' Louisa whispered, as he buried his face in her neck, wetting it with the tears he was determined to hide.

'It's okay, you're safe now,' she murmured.

As Milo relaxed into sleep, Louisa thought, some day he won't be so little. Some day he'll be a man and hide everything from me.

Through the rippled glass of the old window, she watched apricot and lavender light swell from the horizon and waited for night to slither away, leaving her exhausted. She pulled the duvet higher, careful not to cover seven-year-old Milo's face. It was in mid-May, the reluctant Irish summer hovering.

Her body ached with winter and Louisa wanted to feel the hot American sun, imagined herself lying on a beach, bathed in the light from an azure sky. In her mind's eye, she had the sand-speckled brown legs of a girl starting out, rather than a woman wishing she could start again.

Then she remembered: *thirty-seven today*. So, what's the problem with thirty-seven? I'm still in my mid-thirties – just about. If fifty is the new forty, then thirty-seven is the new twenty-seven and forty – *forty!* – is years away.

By the time she was forty, everything could be completely different. Better.

Would be if she let it.

I

I should get up and put on a load of laundry, do some ironing, make the most of the time instead of lying here brooding.

Thirty-seven today.

I don't feel any different. Still waiting for my life to make sense. If this is what thirty-seven feels like, then I might as well have stayed seventeen.

Louisa sighed. Turning thirty-seven wasn't the problem. It was turning thirty-eight. The long slide.

She watched the light transform from apricot to pink and from lavender to blue, light growing slowly, like a child in the womb. The view from her bedroom window, perched above Dublin Bay, was the grey-green expanse of the sound and, beyond it, Dalkey Island with its Napoleonic tower and tumble-down stone house, eroded by long-ago hurricanes. Dalkey Island, where Ben had promised to bring her but never had. On the rocky coast, there would be black seals lounging and Risso's dolphins scooping the air, so picturesque that tourists stopped to point their cameras, thinking, this is why we came to Ireland. *Erin go bragh.*

Louisa hadn't come to Ireland willingly. It had reached out and grabbed her, sucked her in, given her vertigo and so confused her that it had been thirteen years now and she had never been back to the States. Ireland meant Ben, coming and going: ferry service reliable except in rough weather, except in rain, except when you really needed him.

'I don't know what you're going on about. It's nothing personal,' he had said. It was his philosophy.

She never knew what Ben was up to in New York, LA, London or Berlin, chasing money for another one of his 'projects'. The next documentary or low-budget art film was always going to be 'the one'. It sounded glamorous, but the only red carpet Louisa had ever been on was the one at the Savoy where the locals heckled you because you weren't famous: 'Hey love, those boobs real?'

That dress had been a mistake. Afterwards she had given it to Elvie for dress-ups and watched her daughter fill out the top with two Valencia oranges. Not melons. Enough said.

Ravishing, unbiddable, nine-year-old Elvie, the little girl Louisa might have been, and trusting Milo, two years younger, were the two things she'd done right.

Thirty-seven today.

Yikes.

She needed to talk. Get out of her head. Becca would be awake, already off the treadmill and getting ready to prepare a client for confrontation on the early-morning news. Careful not to waken Milo, Louisa disentangled one arm from her son and reached for the phone by her bed.

Becca's voice cut through Louisa's angst, as Louisa had known it would.

'Hey baby doll! My mouth's full of mango. What's up?'

'You know,' Louisa whispered.

'Go on. You can tell me,' Becca whispered back theatrically.

'I didn't plan my life – it planned me. Ben planned me. And now it's too late. What's the point?'

'Jeez, Lou-eez. You sound like a Swedish art-house film from the 'sixties. Go back to sleep.'

'I think I'm having my mid-life crisis early.'

'Listen up.' Becca had returned to her usual throaty bark. 'There's only one crisis you're having. You're at a turning point, not gunpoint – and it's scary – but it's good to be scared. Feel the fear, babe. Stop thinking about it and just walk through it. Do what you have to do. Then get a lover –'

'Thirty-seven, Becca!' Louisa interrupted. 'A lover can't turn the clock back.'

'That's news to me. Anyway, I don't remember you going on like this at thirty-six. Age isn't what this is about. Where *is* the bold Ben, by the way? Bringing you breakfast in bed? Giving you a cuddle? Wrapping up a nice little present for you to wear on your finger?'

'I wish,' Louisa said. 'He came in late. He's probably asleep in his study.'

'Hmm. Thoughtful of him to give you some space. So you're alone then, are you? What are you *wearing*?'

Despite herself, Louisa laughed and smothered it in the duvet so that she didn't wake Milo.

Becca sighed. 'That's my girl. Listen, if I could make you seventeen again, I would. If only to seduce you. But you'd make all the same mistakes. What am I saying? There are no mistakes, only –'

'Catastrophes?' Louisa offered.

But Becca had been distracted by business on the other end of the line. She muttered to her minions in media-land, 'Chinese walls, right? Separate entrances, separate rooms, separate exits.'

'Sounds just like my marriage,' Louisa murmured, but Becca didn't hear.

When she spoke again, it was only to bark, 'Gotta go, baby doll. Stop taking yourself so seriously. Nobody's going to die. That's always the bottom line. Happy birthday, babe.'

As the line went dead, Louisa knew not to take the brusque sign-off as a rejection. She imagined Becca with her bosom puffed out and her long red nails poised like the talons of an eagle as she gripped a scared-bunny in a business suit and whispered, 'Feel the fear, babe.'

There was nothing to be afraid of. Insolvency, loneliness, the corruption of the body, the long slide, death. Nothing to be afraid of at all.

Louisa wanted to leap out of bed, smash the window and scream out across the bay, 'Feel the fear. Bring it on!' It felt good, smashing glass, even if only in her imagination.

As Milo breathed softly beside her, she remembered when he was a baby and she had got up at night to make sure he was still alive. Even now, feeling his pulse beneath his translucent, child-skin made her feel both protective and terrified. 'Are

4

hearts set to beat a certain number of times? Like alarm clocks?' Milo had wanted to know.

Louisa took a deep breath, closed her eyes and exhaled slowly to calm herself. She put her arms around Milo, trying to steal some of his peace for herself. Lulled by her son's steady breathing – the ticking of a clock – she drifted into sleep.

Two hours later, she cringed into wakefulness, eyelids too heavy to open. Rustling of cellophane at the end of her bed alerted her to Ben's presence. Cellophane meant flowers. Red roses probably. One dozen or two? Two dozen would mean Ben's guilt-meter had topped the scale. Thirteen years of marriage and still he couldn't remember that she hated red roses – scentless, senseless and commercial.

Cellophane crackled again as she felt him lay the bouquet on her abdomen. They weighed nothing. She feigned sleep. Her eyelids quivered.

'Happy birthday, darling,' he whispered.

How like Ben to produce a ray of sunshine when she least expected it. How like an Irish summer he was. Charming at the best of times, infuriating at the worst. Ben sat on the edge of the mattress by her foot and made the bed-frame creak. Beneath the earth's crust, the continental plates shifted imperceptibly.

'Lou?' He rested his hand on her bare foot.

She kicked involuntarily, clipping his nose.

'Ouch!'

'Sorry!'

He was still such a handsome man, even holding his nose, Louisa thought. Better-looking, even, than when they had first met. Age suited him. She took in his longish dark hair, still like a teenager's even though he had ten years on her, the strong dark brows, the determined cheekbones and then – as he tipped his head back to stave off a nosebleed – his slightly crooked nose with that little bump she used to kiss, the craggy skin tanned from his travels, rugged.

'Happy birthday,' he said again.

She'd forgotten her lines. Ben's crooked grin and crinkled eyelids hid the emptiness she had come to expect. He'd rather be somewhere else, with someone else, if only he'd the grace to admit it.

Louisa wriggled away from Milo and sat up, ran her fingers through her hair and took the flowers. Ben reached into his pocket and pulled out a small box.

'For my *paparazza*,' he said softly, holding it out to her.

Paparazza. Little sparrow. His pet name for her.

Louisa felt sick. Typical of Ben to launch an armistice on her birthday, when he knew she'd be feeling vulnerable. 'You shouldn't have,' she said, meaning it.

'Why not? I forgot last year, so I'm making it up to you.' His roughly lilting Dublin accent had once melted her. She let him take her hand. 'I do still love you, you know, despite your moods,' he said.

'Moods?'

'I can tell by the way you open your eyes in the morning. You're one of those people who wake up expecting the worst. Sometimes I wish you'd email me an emotional weather forecast. Hurricane warning, tornado warning – whatever. I never know how you'll be when I come home.'

'Is that so?' How *dare* he suggest that she was the moody one when it was all she could do to hold her little family together while Ben wandered. She suppressed her rage for Milo's sake. Still asleep, he mustn't awaken to a storm. That was marriage for you, one moment of barely registered surrender followed by another and another, eroding you minute by minute until, more than a decade later, you didn't know who you were anymore.

'Open your present,' Ben said, putting the box in her hands.

Louisa held it in her open palm. Silver paper, silver ribbon and a tiny silver card, all provided at no extra charge by a pretty shop assistant, she imagined, with whom Ben had flirted in his non-committal way.

Suddenly Milo sat up. 'Happy birthday, Mum! I have a present for you too. I hid it downstairs in the dirty-washing basket!' Milo beamed with satisfaction as Ben let out a booming laugh. 'The last place she'd look, hey lad? Come and give me a hug. I haven't seen you for ages, son.'

But Milo didn't move. He was awkward with his father, who was more often away than he was at home.

'You go down and find it, Milo, and I'll be along in a minute,' Louisa said. 'Then we'll make breakfast.'

'Pancakes?'

'Of course! Now skedaddle.'

Milo ran off on his mission and Louisa became aware that the television was on at full volume downstairs. Elvie was watching her favourite Saturday-morning nature programme.

When mating, the male dolphin forgets everything, including breathing; it is the female's job to push him back to the surface. When she emerges to the surface, there is usually another male there waiting for his chance. She may accept him, or go off in search of her preferred mate . . .

Louisa laid the unopened box on the pillow beside her.

'Lou, baby, why are you being so difficult?' Ben looked disappointed.

Louisa pulled up the duvet over her breasts. Her white linen and lace nightdress had been washed so many times that it was nearly transparent. 'Ben?' she said tentatively.

Ben seemed bored already. His attention span had never been great. 'Yeah?'

'I want a divorce.'

She watched his face change from bemusement to anger in an instant. The mattress sagged beneath him as his head dropped into his hands.

Louisa had expected some response and, when she got none, her anger drained away. Just as well, with the children down-stairs. Ben sniffled and she realized that he was weeping.

7

Suddenly, she wanted to comfort her husband. She knelt up on the bed and put an arm round his shoulders. 'I didn't think you'd be so upset,' she said softly.

He turned to face her, a single vein standing out on his forehead. 'Not upset? My wife is cutting me off like a – a –' He shook his head.

'I can't do this anymore, Ben,' she said gently. 'You act like you don't live here. You treat this house like a hotel. I'm not your concierge.'

'Who's your speechwriter?' Ben stared at her.

'You can't just fly in from – from –'

'Working my arse off for a yoghurt commercial in stifling Barbados,' he interjected.

'Poor you.'

'I was trying to earn a living.'

'I suppose the money will go towards your next "project" and we won't see any of it.'

'So I'm not rich enough for you, is that it? Since when did you care about money?'

'Look, it doesn't matter where you were or what you were doing. And it's not about money either. The point is that you're always somewhere else. Even when you're in the same room. You can't just fly in and plug into your wife and children like we're some sort of life-support system on call for your benefit. And when you're here, you don't want to be. I know you don't. No matter what you say.'

'Who are you to know what I'm feeling?'

'Exactly!' Louisa said, her voice brittle but still restrained. 'I've been married to you for thirteen years and I never know what you're feeling. You never know what I'm feeling.'

Ben attempted to take her in his arms.

'Ben, let me go.'

'Becca worked you up to this, didn't she? She thinks I'm a loser, right? The problems started when she came into your life. Well, Becca's successful only because she's a carpet-eater.'

'That's disgusting!'

'She's as macho as they come. You're not like that, Louisa. You have this home and two beautiful children. Why can't you be happy with that?'

'I *am* happy with that,' Louisa said, pulling at a fingernail she'd bitten. '*You* are what is making me *un*happy.'

Ben tried to get her to look at him. 'If that's true, you haven't given me one good reason why.'

'You're unfaithful.'

He tightened his grip. 'I thought you'd forgiven me for Nina. She was a colleague. It got a little out of hand. Why are you dragging her up now?'

'Nina? That's the first I've heard of her. I was referring to Vanessa. And Carla . . . who else have I left out? There were always ten of us in this marriage, Ben.'

She sounded so restrained, she marvelled. Why couldn't she get hysterical or throw things and make witty putdowns like they did in films? Take scissors to his clothes? Pour acid on his DVDs or into his smug, ageing face?

Because she didn't love him enough to hate him.

'*Paparazza*, you don't know what you're saying,' Ben murmured, kissing her between her breasts. 'It's been too long, babe. I know what you need.'

Chemistry, pure and simple. That was what had made her follow him to Ireland.

Louisa felt his hand slip beneath her nightgown and caress her back as his lips grazed her collarbone.

'No!' she pulled away. 'This is not how it's going to be. Let me go.'

Ben's eyes widened. 'You're forty today. That's it. Now Louisa's forty she wants to change the rules. Change me. I was never good enough for you, was I?'

'I'm thirty-seven.'

'Who is he?'

Ben's eyes lit up at the prospect of a rival. What was it

about men that they couldn't countenance plain rejection? They preferred a battle.

'You've always been a romantic,' he went on. 'Whoever he is, he's not worth wrecking our marriage over. You've said as much to me, many times. And you were right, Lou. I've told you this before. I don't mind who he is, just as long as you tell me about him. I just don't like to see you sneaking around. It's tacky.'

'Is that so?' Louisa raised an eyebrow.

'Look, marriage is marriage and a bit of fun is just that. When can I meet him?'

'You've just proved my point,' Louisa shouted, frustration getting the better of her. 'If you loved me you wouldn't want to *meet* him, you'd want to kill him!'

Ben tried another tactic. 'How can you do this to the children?'

It was a low punch, but Louisa had been expecting it. 'My children haven't got a father. They've got an occasional uncle. Us being divorced will be better for them because you'll have to make a formal commitment to them with regular visiting times in your busy schedule. They'll see more of you than ever before.'

'You've been planning this for a long time, haven't you? Pretending you still cared about me while all along you were plotting to –'

'Don't go there, Ben,' she interrupted. 'It's over. Accept it.'

Elvie's voice, musical and light, arrived in the room before she did. 'Mummy! Happy birthday!' Glowing in the sunlight now pouring through the window and proudly holding a gift, Elvie took a running jump on top of the roses.

'Careful, sweetheart! They have thorns!' Louisa warned her.

Milo was close behind with his offering, lingering in the doorway. 'Come on, Milo,' she said. 'I can't wait to open it.' The birthday ritual, she hoped, would prevent her and Ben bickering in front of the children – at least for now. She felt like an actress as she opened the presents – first the ribbon, then the paper, then shaking the box to guess what was inside. Elvie had made her a necklace of glass beads. 'Oh, Elvie! Very Bohemian chic!' Louisa remembered seeing a few of the same beads on their child-minder Mary's kitchen table. She recalled fingering one absently as Mary told her to look into her fractured heart. Louisa dropped the necklace over her head, then got out of bed to admire it in the mirror above her dressing-table. 'Elvie, the colours are perfect!'

Elvie looked up at her proudly. 'Like the sea, Mary said.'

Milo had made her a small, wooden bird-box that he had painted himself, with bright flowers on the sides and a yellow sun on the roof. 'You're to hang it in the garden. A bird will build a nest in it.'

'It's wonderful!' Louisa exclaimed. The children would be fine. Better than fine. Their lives would hardly change at all.

Elvie stood on the bed and hopped up and down.

'Elvie, cool it,' Ben said. 'It's not *your* birthday.'

'Ben!' Louisa admonished him. Then, 'It's okay, Elvie. Daddy's a bit tired from travelling.' Louisa pulled her daughter close. 'I love you.'

'Why couldn't I be born a dolphin?' Elvie's serious little face was full of longing.

'Maybe in another life,' Louisa answered. 'Maybe next time.'

This seemed to satisfy Elvie, but Louisa was tired of wishing for another life.

Milo asked, 'Will you be a dolphin too, Mum?'

'We'll be a dolphin family,' Louisa said and pulled the children close.

Over their shoulders, she glimpsed Ben glaring at her with a hostility she was relieved to see exposed.

2

An hour later, the children were dressed in mismatched clothes and Louisa was in her standard work uniform of tailored, fawn trouser suit and crisp white shirt – her dark blonde hair tied up in a messy chignon. They walked along the seafront to Mary's, breathing in the green seaweed scent of a fresh tide.

'Does Daddy still like us?' Elvie whispered.

'Of course he does.'

'Do you still like Daddy?'

'Of course I do,' Louisa lied.

'Do you love Daddy?'

Uh-oh. 'In my own way,' Louisa said, finally.

Milo was stern, as he dawdled in their wake. 'What's the difference between like and love?'

Louisa considered this. 'Like is for friends and love is for family,' she said. That was too simple. Love wasn't a feeling; it was something you showed in the way you treated people. It wasn't token presents and red roses. It wasn't sexual chemistry or even having children with a man. Maybe it was this: walking a familiar path, your children's hands snug in your own while you tried to figure out what love was.

Louisa knelt on the footpath and looked up into the children's worried faces. 'I know you heard Daddy and me arguing about grown-up stuff this morning, but we both love you and we always will.'

They found Mary in her front garden bending over a flowerbed with a trowel in her hand. 'Look, guys! Worms! It feels so much like spring today that I decided to do a little gardening. Want to help?'

'Yes!' the children shouted.

Mary turned to Louisa. 'You run inside, you two. I want to talk to your Mum for a minute.'

Louisa watched with relief as Milo and Elvie tumbled away.

'You look a bit pale,' Mary said, taking off her gardening gloves and putting them in the pocket of her jacket.

'I did it,' Louisa whispered. 'I told him I want a divorce.'

Mary beamed with surprise. 'Fantastic!' When Louisa didn't respond, her face became concerned. 'How do you feel?'

'Numb,' Louisa said. To be numb is to be strong, she thought.

'When did you tell him?'

'This morning.'

'You're shaking. Come in for a cuppa. Don't drive in that state.'

'I'm running late. We'll have a chat when I come back this evening. Do me a favour, though, and keep an eye on the house. Text me if he's not out by six.'

'I'll help him pack.'

Louisa walked back to her own house, where Ben was waiting in the open doorway possessively. Her car was parked outside. All she had to do was get in and drive away.

Ben was having none of it. 'This isn't like you. Are you having a breakdown or something? Maybe you need to see a sex therapist.'

'It's always *my* problem, isn't it, Ben? Well, I wash my hands of it. It's *your* problem now.'

She opened the car door.

'Louisa, wait. Listen! You're right – I've been too preoccupied with my own problems. I'm thinking of starting therapy myself. I'll do some inner child work.'

'For God's sake, Ben. It's not your inner child you need to get to know. It's your inner adult. Pack your bags and be gone by six. Call me in a few days and we'll make arrangements for you to see the children.'

'But this is my mother's house! *My* house!'

'Not anymore. Your mother is dead. This is the family home

and the children and I are entitled to remain in it. Do you want us homeless? Is that it?'

'But what about *me*?'

He looked so lost.

'You're going to a hotel, even if I have to pay for it myself.'

Ben spat, 'You and your credit cards! You're so middle class, you know that? You'd be nothing without me. What were you when I met you? You could hardly get out of bed in the mornings.'

Louisa refused to play his game. 'It's quite nice being middle class. I can pay for you to cool your bloody arse in a hotel for a week. So, how about it?'

Ben took his time to consider this. 'OK, I'll go. Book the Monroe. I'll be on my mobile if you need to talk.'

Louisa was surprised. She'd expected him to put up at least the semblance of a proper fight. But that was Ben all over – maybe he'd been acting all along. 'One week at the Monroe. After that, you're on your own. No more hand-outs.'

She got into her car and started the engine. One week at the Monroe – nine hundred and fifty euro. Getting rid of your husband – priceless. She sped along the coast road, feeling like a bit-part actress whose role as long-suffering wife in a Ben Maguire Production had ended, leaving her middle-aged and washed-up. She would never retrieve the last thirteen years. But she could make up for lost time.

Louisa Maguire, wedding and portrait photographer, gave her clients images of themselves as they wanted to be seen – confident and happy, with the polish of an expensive American advertising campaign. She had arrived from New York in 1993, just as Ireland was beginning to transform itself from a country of staunch Catholic conservatives into a society dominated by the neo-liberal *nouveaux riches*. In Celtic Tiger Ireland, people were no longer suspicious of success, and, instead of emigrating to get rich, they were living the American Dream at home. And who better to document it than an American photographer? Although Louisa had once harboured higher aspirations, she didn't mind doing weddings and portraits of bonny babies. After all, that was how Dutch painters had made their livings centuries before, churning out portraits that reflected their clients' prosperity. Louisa Maguire, photographer, had introduced Dubliners to high-quality black-and-white portraits in life-size formats shot with her beloved Hasselblad, which they hung on their walls like works of art. She was expensive, but that was part of her appeal.

Weddings were the other mainstay of her business. She shot them in documentary style, always telling the story of the day in a way that showed the fairy tale, but also caught the uniqueness of each occasion. Digital cameras were far easier to use than the analogue cameras she preferred, but the old-fashioned method had a timelessness and depth that digital couldn't match. And there were few things she enjoyed more than spending hours in the darkroom, fine-tuning a thousand shades of grey until she got a picture exactly right. Black and white was more evocative than colour, which stripped people of the dark sides that made them interesting.

So what if Ben thought she was an overpaid hack? She could support her children and give them the stability she had never herself enjoyed. That had been her priority.

Louisa drove into Dalkey village and pulled up in front of her studio. Her assistant, Paul, was waiting for her. 'Hey, what's up? You're late,' he said, as he loaded Louisa's middle-aged Volvo estate with equipment, then stretched himself out in the passenger seat.

She would tell him eventually, but not yet. For now, Louisa wanted to drive without having to think. Sensing her mood, Paul put music on the CD-player, sat back and closed his eyes. She found her way to the M50, then gunned the engine as she headed west, determined to make up time. Speeding along the highway that circled the city, she felt regret at the paving of

Ireland: they were passing high-tech factories, warehouses and shopping malls, which made the outskirts of Dublin look like any European suburb.

'You ever visit the cairns?' Louisa asked Paul.

'The wha'?'

'The Bronze Age tombs in Meath. They're five thousand years old. There's one you can actually go inside, if you borrow the key from the people at the Big House. I'll never forget crawling down there. It was like going back to the very beginning. I had an eerie feeling that I'd been there before.'

'You Americans and your history. I thought you hated all that sentimental diddle-eye-doe aul' Oirlan' nonsense,' said Paul.

'I do. I'm not talking about Oirlan'. I mean the real place underneath all that sentimental nonsense.'

'If I can't see it, I'm not interested. We're photographers, Lou. Surface is what we do.'

'I know it.' Too well, she realized.

They left the M50 and headed north on the N25 into countryside that was like a green quilt with grey stitching made stone by stone with muscle and sweat. The earth beneath held buried treasure – bronze goblets, gold torques, wisps of fabric and even human bodies preserved in the peat-rich soil. This was the Ireland she loved, although she usually kept her thoughts to herself. She didn't want anyone to suppose she was just another daft American looking for her roots. The only roots Louisa was interested in were her own dark ones.

Paul seemed thoughtful. 'I grew up in the flats. Father unemployed in the 1980s and drinking himself to death. Didn't see a cow until I was sixteen years old and it frightened the bejasus out of me. The only grass was on the football pitch. Give me concrete and glass, any day – Hey! Slow down!'

'I hate to be late for weddings,' Louisa said. 'It throws me off my rhythm.'

Beside her, Paul rearranged his lanky frame. 'Weddings are like wars, these days. They don't start until the press arrive.'

Louisa skirted a slow-moving lorry, barely missing a car coming in the opposite direction. After the confrontation with Ben, she felt so detached from her body that she didn't even experience the usual pleasant surge of adrenaline. 'Have you ever thought about what would happen if you crashed the car and died instantly?' Louisa asked.

'No.' Paul gripped the dashboard with one hand.

'Maybe you don't die. Maybe you just shift gears a little into another dimension. In this life, you crash, but instead of dying you change lanes into a parallel life where you just keep driving. You never know you died. Everything is almost the same, just slightly different.'

'Are you trying to freak me out? What did I do to you? Jaysus, woman. You're not a Volvo estate-type at all. You should be driving one of those huge four-by-fours that all the women have now.'

'I'll think about it,' Louisa said. 'Although I always fancied a little sports convertible.'

Maybe she'd get one now. Why not? This was her turning-point from martyrdom. She would be in the driver's seat. She'd had enough posh weddings in her conservative suit. She didn't like leaving the children with Mary at weekends when other families were doing things together, and the portrait business was easily big enough now to keep her busy during the week.

For the second time that day, she decided to act. 'I think I'm losing my touch with the wedding thing,' she said.

'Since when?'

'Since now. Right this minute. How would you feel about taking it over?'

He twisted as far in the passenger seat as his seatbelt would allow until Louisa could see him in her peripheral vision. He was looking at her as though she was dangling a baby off a balcony. 'I wish you'd tell me what has you so rattled,' he said.

'I want to spend more time with the children at week-ends. Here's my offer. We're so busy that we're turning down commissions. Our waiting list for portraits is six months long, a year for weddings. If we don't do something about it, some photography chain with high-speed digital and a slick computer printer is going to start offering an inferior product that could still take some of our business. So, I think you should take over the wedding side of things, while I concentrate on the portraits. If we need to hire an assistant or two, we will.'

Paul considered what she'd said. 'So we won't be working together anymore, side-by-side, like.'

'And as part of my new business plan, I want to make you a partner. I don't want the clients to think that when they're getting you for a wedding, they're getting a second-best stand-in, because that's not what you are. So, whaddya say?'

'You've thought this through,' Paul said.

'The time seems right.'

'You're thinking we'll be Malone Maguire, then?'

The hint of mischief in Paul's voice hid his deeper feelings, Louisa knew.

'Maguire Malone,' she said. 'I'll get a solicitor to write up the contracts. The only question you have to ask yourself is, do you want to be the business partner of a neurotic, over-achieving American perfectionist.'

Paul laughed. 'I thought neurosis was an American trait. Just like all Irish are self-deprecating. We Irish always put ourselves down before someone else does.'

'And the Americans diagnose themselves before someone else does.'

She thought of Ben and his 'inner child'. He'd become more American than she was.

'You said it, I didn't. But if you're up for it, I am too. It's sudden, but it feels right. No-one could say we were entering this marriage without a long engagement. I suppose my only doubt is that I wouldn't want business to ruin a beautiful friendship. And I'll miss –' Paul seemed lost for words as he looked out the passenger window, then at Louisa, '– this.'

Louisa smiled. 'I know what you mean. Two for the road and all that. Remember the time we got stuck in fog down in Laois and had to share the only B-and-B room we could find?'

'I thought you'd engineered it.'

'How could you? We both slept with our clothes on.'

'Hmm. All I thought was married woman, my boss, not a good choice.'

Louisa laughed. 'You really figured I'd planned it? Louisa Maguire can make the sun shine, with her top-of-the-range lighting equipment, but fog she doesn't do.'

It had been an adventure, the pair of them working together to build up Louisa's business. Paul had been a shy, scrawny twenty-year-old when Louisa had taken him on to do work experience. She'd only been twenty-nine and had never had an employee before. Just getting Paul used to keeping regular hours had been a challenge. And feeding him his lunch had cost her, once she realized that it was the only meal he was getting. He had come to her through a government-sponsored agency that was training young people from 'disadvantaged areas'. Louisa wasn't a do-gooder. She knew that an assistant, on work place-ment, would not cost nearly as much as a trained professional. Paul had come for three months' training and stayed eight years, learning as he went along. At first she'd had trouble understanding his thick Dublin accent but he had grown up, filled out, acquired mid-Atlantic vowels and was veering now towards cocky. There was nothing more he could learn from her and she was glad that she could pay him enough to keep him. She had known it was only a matter of time before he went out on his own unless she made an effort to hang on to him.

They drove in silence for half an hour, listening to the music, until Louisa felt Paul stealing glances at her.

'Are you sure you're all right?' he asked, eventually.

'Why wouldn't I be?' she answered.

'You seem a bit . . . I don't know. Flummoxed. It's not like you. Hang on – exit coming up. Then it's winding pot-holed lanes from here to Eternity. Bollox to the countryside, anyway.'

'From here to eternity could take less time than you think.'

'Eternity is the name of the house we're going to.'

'Oh, my God. They named it after a perfume?'

Paul laughed. 'Loadsamoney, you know the score. The FOB is big in land and construction, from the bog to the castle in one generation.'

'The American Dream fulfilled in the fine county of Meath,' Louisa said.

Louisa and Paul had begun to use acronyms like FOB (Father of Bride) as a way of labelling pictures efficiently, but it had turned into a running joke. There was the MOB (mother of bride), BOB (brother of Bride) and SOB (sister of bride), a term which was often rather apt. They were always on the look-out for the more exotic species, such as SLOB (spurned lover of bride), SLOG (spurned lover of groom) and SLAP-PER (spurned lover at pains to put everything right). Louisa had even unwittingly photographed a groom embracing a CLOG (current lover of groom), which she had discovered only after the negatives were subpoenaed in a libel case. Most dreaded was the MOBILE (mother of bride insisting on late entertain-ment), who expected them to photograph the revels until all hours, when a tearful cousin would be singing 'Danny Boy' off key. Eventually she had become established enough to write a time-limit into the contracts, explaining, if challenged, that she preferred to photograph the guests earlier in the day, when they were at their best.

There would be things she'd miss, though. Every wedding was special to the couple and their families. Each bride wanted to do things absolutely right and most were fairly stressed out. Having your picture taken all day in those circumstances increased the tension, unless the photographer, at least, was confident and relaxed.

'What's the weather forecast?' Louisa asked Paul.

'Like it always is. Variable, partly cloudy with scattered showers, or cloudy with scattered showers and sunny spells. My boss is a control freak. Next question?'

Louisa smiled. 'Bride's name?'

'Tara.'

'Groom's?'

'Kyran.'

'MOB?'

'Siobhan. FOB is Bryan, BOB 1's named Jack, BOB 2 is Jamie, plus enough bridesmaids and groomsmen for a seven-a-side rugby match. Four grandparents, twelve aunts and uncles, numerous cousins and various VIPs, including – believe it or not – the minister and his new girlfriend. The whole shebang.'

Louisa was unfazed. 'Great.'

After another half-hour of twisting country lanes, Louisa felt an almost overwhelming need to catch up on the sleep she'd lost the night before. 'Are you sure you're OK?' Paul asked. 'You're looking a bit fragile. I could handle today by myself. It's a big wedding, I know, but if you want to drop me off and go home, I can get a taxi back.'

'No, thanks. The last thing I want is to be moping around feeling sorry for myself.'

'I see Eternity!' Paul said, making them both laugh as they rounded a corner. It was on a hill before them, a vaguely Lutyens-style mansion in Portland stone, the size of a country house hotel.

'Are they turrets?' Paul asked.

'Apparently. What's written on those white flags?'

'T & K on that flag. S & B on the other one.'

White roses were planted along each side of the cobbled drive and the grass surrounding the house was so perfectly green it might have been Astroturf. 'Those roses shouldn't be flowering yet, not with the weather we've had. They must have been dug in already blooming over the last couple of days,' Paul said.

'Maybe they're fake,' Louisa said.

'I think they're real. See the petals on the ground?'

'Fifty euro they're fake,' Louisa said.

Directed by a burly security guard in black tie, she parked her Volvo at the side of the house. The guard mumbled something into his earpiece. Next thing she knew, a pair of French windows were heaved open by a woman who was spilling out of a strapless, pink taffeta gown, with a glittering diamond tiara on top of her bouffant, platinum hair.

'I'm Louisa Maguire.' Louisa held out her hand as she stepped into an entry hall the size of a country church.

'I know who you are, of course,' said the woman. 'I'm Siobhan – we spoke on the phone. Welcome to my wedding.'

3

When photographing a wedding, there was one golden rule: find the queen bee and tame her. The queen bee was sometimes the bride, but just as often the MOB and sometimes even the MOG. Louisa had even seen maids of honour taking charge – even to the extent of entertaining groomsmen in a cupboard, but that was another story.

Siobhan led Louisa and Paul through the foyer, where a giant gold Buddha surrounded by arum lilies held court. People in white uniforms scuttled about with trays of food, armfuls of flowers and stacks of spindly gilt chairs.

Louisa was finally beginning to feel the familiar rush. The best part of the work had little to do with actually taking pictures. Her clients didn't want to be photographed as they really were but as they wanted to be, so the real skill was to figure out what image of themselves they expected to see in the final pictures. After that it was a matter of directing them into playing their roles, without making them feel self-conscious. She had to make a contrived, formal event look uncontrived – all the while keeping her eye on the time. That took talent and a kind of intuition on which Louisa prided herself.

'I imagine you'd like some pictures of Tara getting dressed for the wedding,' Louisa said.

'Yes!' Siobhan exclaimed, as though this was an inspired idea.

'Is she upstairs?' Louisa asked, assuming that the bride would be in her bedroom with her bridesmaids.

Siobhan looked stricken. 'Should she be?' Siobhan asked.

'Not at all. There's no rulebook, despite what people think.'

'Oh. Good. It's just that we couldn't fit the dresses up the stairs. So she's in the leisure complex. We've turned it into a salon for the morning.'

Laden down with equipment, she and Paul struggled to keep up with Siobhan but nearly bumped into her when she skidded to a stop by a pair of castle-sized carved oak doors. 'These were reclaimed from an architecturally significant convent in –' she opened them. 'Bryan? The photographer wants to know where you got the doors.'

Louisa couldn't have cared less where the doors came from. She went through them to discover the FOB. His top hat lay on the edge of the snooker table, but he cut an arresting figure in his formal white shirt with a silver-and-gold brocade waistcoat. She readied her camera, made a quick check with her light meter and chanced it.

The FOB leaned over the table and potted the white ball.

Click.

The ball plopped into the pocket.

Bryan didn't seem to have noticed the flash and this was just the kind of picture Louisa loved to take. Other photographers would pose the family in an attempt to create an 'informal' pre-wedding shot. But Louisa worked by stealth. When Bryan was dead, his children would say: 'That was Dad.'

Siobhan put an arm around her husband, her head barely reaching his armpit. 'Happy the day's finally arrived?'

Click.

'I'll be happy when I've paid for it,' he said.

Louisa liked the way Bryan was loaded but hadn't forgotten what it was like not to be. Siobhan, she suspected, was the aspirational spendthrift, guiding Bryan towards his status as lord of the manor.

They kissed.

Click.

Then Bryan reached into his pocket and pulled out a box, which he presented to his wife. 'A souvenir of the day,' Bryan said, rolling his r's like a Kerryman.

Louisa decided he'd waited for her to arrive before he bestowed the gift upon Siobhan, who was now opening the box.

Click.

'Diamonds!'

'For *my* bride,' Bryan said. 'Thirty-five years ago today.'

Under his breath, Paul muttered to Louisa. 'Hasn't she enough?'

Bryan added the enormous glittering ring to the collection on Siobhan's fingers.

Click.

Siobhan leaned in close to him, gazing up into his eyes.

Click.

Thirty-five years was almost as long as she had been alive! Siobhan and Bryan were a long-running love story, so wholesome that it was almost perverse. They must be no more emotionally sophisticated than children to be so entranced with each other after so many years.

Bryan put a finger under Siobhan's chin and kissed her lightly on the lips. Then he said, 'You're more beautiful today, than you were the day we married.'

Click.

Louisa stepped away from the couple, eager to get going with the rest of the pre-wedding pictures. With her back turned to Siobhan and Bryan, she caught Paul's eye.

By the snooker table, Bryan and Siobhan only had eyes for each other.

Louisa leaned in to Paul and whispered, 'Do you think it's for real?'

He shrugged and whispered back. 'Maybe they're the Viagra poster couple.'

Louisa cleared her throat, 'We'd better make a start. There's a big wedding party to shoot!'

Siobhan straightened her tiara and floated out through the oak doors, which were carved with angels that might have been mistaken for cherubs.

Along acres of marble flooring, then across another acre of the freshly laid lawn, then through a formal garden that made Versailles look like waste ground, Louisa followed until they arrived at the leisure complex, where Tod Neville, the wedding planner, was waiting for them.

'Tod the Nod,' Paul whispered, referring to the way Tod used wedding planning as a means of social climbing.

Louisa had never got on with him because she hated pretension. Resplendent in a blue-grey silk suit, Tod was wearing his trademark white gloves, which he insisted on wearing to keep the bride 'clean'.

Louisa pursed her mouth and executed the obligatory air kiss, before showing Tod who was boss. 'Another stunning wedding, as usual. While you're up to your ears doing your usual magic, Tod darling, Paul and I will quietly do our thing.'

She stepped inside an oversized Victorian-style conservatory that contained an indoor swimming pool, surrounded by more marble floors and Greek goddesses on pillars, through which they passed to a bar, gym and then a botanic garden containing a fair chunk of rain forest. Here, a classically inspired Jacuzzi was the centre-piece and, around it, a flock of bridesmaids with upswept hair and tiny bikinis were balanced like tentative birds, dangling their manicured toes in the water as they sipped from glasses of champagne.

Out of the corner of her eye, Louisa saw Paul was focusing on two of the girls, who posed like beauty queens, stomachs in chests out.

Click.

'There's the money shot,' she muttered to herself.

The bride, Louisa guessed, was the girl whose dark hair was elaborately threaded with pearls. She looked pensive, gazing up at a white dove that was banging against the glass ceiling in a bid for freedom.

Click.

'Those pigeons are such a nuisance!' Siobhan cried. 'They're defecating in the pool! I told Tara that it would be far more sensible to let go balloons at the moment of union, but would she listen to me? And now some of them have escaped.'

She clapped her hands. 'Ladies! Out of here at once and into the bar, all of you. If that bird poops on someone's hair, I don't know what we'll do!' The girls fluttered into the bar.

Click.

'Tara! Last chance to use the toilet before you become Mrs Pilkington!' Siobhan shooed her daughter away.

Louisa left the bride to her privacy and followed the rest of the wedding party. Most brides liked to have a few mischievous pictures to keep outside the official wedding album, and this scene of the girls crowding into the bar to get dressed would be perfect. The dresses – which were, indeed, enormous, Louisa noted – were hanging on a rack, ready to be donned at the last minute. As the first girl raised her arms and wiggled into her frock, it became apparent that the inspiration for the designs had come from Cinderella, the old Disney classic, if not the early-1950s New Look. The boned bodices were tightly fitted with diaphanous silk draped across the bust, then repeated in filmy, puffed sleeves that rested just below the shoulder. The massive skirts were hooped and Louisa saw a problem.

'Paul,' she said softly, 'the skirts are so wide that the girls are going to have to stand about two metres apart. We'll need a wide-angle lens to get all seven of them into a picture.'

'I'm on to it,' Paul said. 'I'll go up to the roof. I think there's a sundeck. You arrange them on the grass, and I'll shoot them from above.'

'Off you go,' Louisa said, wishing she'd thought of it. She could see the picture already: the girls arranged on the lawn in a circle, the skirts making pools of colour with the girls' faces gazing up like flowers. It was a strange sensation, though, to yield control to Paul, even though she wanted to.

Louisa took Siobhan aside and explained the plan, hoping that she would help her corral the girls. When they were ready, giggling and gossiping, Louisa stood back and called Paul on her mobile. 'How's that looking?'

'Top stuff,' he answered back.

'Who's the cute guy?' Louisa heard a pink Cinderella whisper.

'I saw him first,' said a blue one.

'Do you think he'll be stayin' on for the afters?'

'Your idea of "afters" or mine?'

Paul did look well in a suit and the one he'd chosen today, navy with a white shirt, set off his sandy hair. He had filled out, now that he was coming up to twenty-eight, and Louisa felt proud of him.

Pink Cinderella nudged her friend. 'Is he your husband?' she asked Louisa.

'No!' Louisa answered before she realized that she was still wearing her wedding ring. She twisted it off and put it into her pocket. Then lifted her camera again.

'She wants him for herself,' Blue Cinderella whispered.

The light was perfect and in Louisa's black-and-white version, the scene would look like vintage *Vogue*, the dresses strictly narrowing the girls' waists, making them stand a little straighter, and the hoops keeping them at a distance from one another, so that when they wanted to kiss or chat they had to bend forward prettily, like ballet dancers. No-one would have guessed that beneath the elegance there were bellybutton piercings and tattoos.

Click.

Then the girls cheered. Expecting to see the bride, Louisa glanced up from her lens and found that their eyes were on Paul.

Click.

'Oh, Romeo,' shouted one.

Paul was shooting away: the girls' good-natured teasing had given him the chance to get some spontaneous facial expressions. His disappearance provoked a disappointed chorus. A few seconds later he was back with flowers in his hand, which he must have picked from the roof garden. She could see him wrapping something around the stems to keep them together – gaffer tape, she suspected, which they always kept on hand. Once it had been used to hold the bride's dress up. Paul held the bouquet aloft, and the girls stilled. Then – click, click, click went Louisa's shutter – Paul flung it down to them.

Tod appeared in a panic. 'They're going to destroy their couture!' The girl who had asked Louisa if Paul was her husband caught the flowers. Now she blew him a kiss – click.

Suddenly, the girls were surrounded by dressers and make-up artists who tidied hoops, hair and lips while Tod supervised. Then their bouquets arrived on a golf-cart and he handed them out. There was a collective gasp.

Click.

The bride had appeared in a dress that was as full and extravagant as the others – but with its bodice beaded with a fleur-de-lis of tiny pearls that also cascaded down the front of the hooped skirt.

Click.

She is the most beautiful bride and this is the most beautiful wedding party I've ever seen, Louisa thought, which was out of character for her – because she had long been immune to the extravagant emotionalism of weddings.

Her own wedding had been nothing like this. It had been quiet, small, private – all those words people use for weddings that cost little with few guests. This wedding, with its enthusiasm and excess, seemed to embody a collective belief in love against the odds.

Thirty-seven today.

Louisa found herself thinking how different her life would have been if, like Tara, she'd had the back-up of a home and parents and money – would she have married Ben? She probably wouldn't even have met him.

Louisa pushed away the memories and took the bride aside for some photographs in the botanic garden. When Tara – who should have been a spoilt bitch – kissed her mother on each cheek – click – Louisa couldn't see through the lens. Blaming the humidity of the glasshouse, she polished the lens with the shammy she kept in her camera bag, then realized it was her eyes that had misted over.

Paul was at her side again. 'I'll take over,' he whispered, 'I need to do as much of this wedding as I can.'

He was right. From now on he'd be doing them on his own.

Louisa watched him and wondered what was going on in his mind. Did he tell himself stories like she did? Read his subjects' lives in their faces? Was photography, for him, a kind of secret voyeurism, as it was for her?

Not that she could imagine Paul projecting hidden desires on to Tara, who was so buoyed up by love that she appeared to float an inch or two above the ground. The white jasmine in the background was a nice touch, Louisa thought, as Paul moved the girl to stand in front if it, and look up at one of the fugitive doves.

There'd been nothing like that at Louisa's own wedding. Louisa remembered the humid heat of an oppressive Manhattan August. Sweating through her sheer 1940s dress, she had barely been able to keep up with Ben as she stumbled after him. The Louis Quinze heel of her second-hand pumps caught in the hem, ripping the fragile fabric, and she had shouted, 'I know you're in a hurry to marry me, but slow down, will ya?' The groom, in a new, white linen suit that had cost more than her vintage dress, barrelled ahead. 'If we don't get there by three-fifteen we'll lose our place.'

Louisa had clutched her wilting bouquet as she caught sight of her reflection in a shop window. Tendrils of hair tumbling on her shoulders, skin glowing, mouth bruised with kisses. She had ignored Ben's rudeness as he hustled up the stairs of the courthouse, leaving her behind. All that mattered was that they adored each other. They had stayed in bed until the last possible moment. Eventually she had showered in cold water and sat naked, doing her damp hair while Ben watched lazily from the bed. 'I wish we could marry in the nude,' he had said.

'There's probably some place in Vegas where you could,' Louisa replied. She shook baby powder over herself so that the dress wouldn't stick in the heat. 'You take a cold shower and within a minute of drying off, you're hot and sweaty again.'

'That's how I like you,' Ben murmured.

When she pulled the musty old dress over her head, she smelt decaying silk and rosewater, which had clung to it from its previous owner. The delicate white tea-gown had an under-slip of bias-cut silk, the dress itself a cloud of silk organza printed with tiny ivory flowers so subtle that they were barely visible. The bodice was pin-tucked and closed with dozens of tiny pearl buttons.

'You sure I don't look like Miss Havisham?' Louisa asked.

'More like Daisy Buchanan, floating across the lawn of Jay Gatsby's Long Island estate.'

'I feel like I'm missing white gloves and a hat.'

'No,' Ben said, 'you look beautiful as you are.'

'I love you so much.'

'Come here.'

She told herself that finally she felt safe in the way she had longed for.

'Are you absolutely sure there's no family member you wanted to have there?' asked Ben.

'If my mother knew that I was surrendering to the male chauvinist institution of marriage she'd turn in her grave,' Louisa said lightly. There was Aunt Alice of course, out in the Hamptons, but Louisa never mentioned her to Ben. She and Alice had nothing to say to one another.

'It's a good thing you're not marrying a chauvinist, then, isn't it?' Ben said. It was one of Louisa's favourite traits in her husband-to-be: he didn't take life seriously and would rather laugh than analyse.

At City Hall, they met their single required witness on the

steps – a mate of Ben's from Dublin – and the civil ceremony was over so quickly that Louisa barely had time to register it. It wasn't quite real, somehow. He put a ring on her finger. She put a ring on his. They kissed, crushing Louisa's wilting freesia between them.

As the city clerk pronounced them married, Louisa felt like a parachutist heading for the ground. She braced herself to feel the earth meet her feet.

'I love you, Lou,' Ben whispered in her ear. Then he folded their marriage certificate and put it in his breast pocket, like the title deed to their lives.

'You're the best thing that ever happened to me,' he said.

Their honeymoon was one night in a small, viewless room at the Plaza. It was meant to be romantic but instead seemed rather claustrophobic. Their wedding portrait was a picture Louisa had taken on the timer, the camera perched on top of the hotel-room TV. She and Ben, already drunk on the champagne that would take them months to pay for, sat on the end of the bed and made faces into the lens.

Click.

'If you ever leave me, I'll die,' Ben said.

In the morning, her dress was a write-off, balled up on the floor like discarded tissue paper. She didn't remember it until that evening when they were back in their tiny studio apartment, preparing to fly 'home' to Dublin. The Plaza had no wedding dress in their lost-property office, they told her when she called.

Now Louisa was struggling to breathe in the glasshouse, which was suddenly stifling.

'Louisa?'

Paul had come down from the roof garden with camera bags on each shoulder.

'Hey,' Louisa said, panting. 'I suppose we'd better get to the church.'

'Louisa, what's wrong?'

Everything. 'You know women,' she said, as a tear ran down her cheek, 'always crying at weddings.'

'Never you,' Paul said. 'Sit down while I get you a glass of water. You look like you're about to faint.'

He directed her sit on a bench and pushed her head between her knees.

'Oh my goodness, is she pregnant?' It was Tod – the last person she wanted anywhere near her at this moment.

'It's very warm in here. She's taken a turn, that's all.'

Louisa was glad her face was hidden. No-one could see the tears that wouldn't stop falling. Her shoulders heaved and Paul muttered something to Tod, who turned on his heel and sped off.

'Oh my God, Paul. My last wedding and I've blown it. Ten years of hard work and my reputation is ruined.'

Paul smiled. 'Don't be so melodramatic. You're not well. I've asked Tod to organize a car to take you home.'

'No!' Louisa whispered. 'I don't want to go home. That's the last place I want to be!'

Paul knelt down beside her and raised her face so that he could look her in the eye. 'Being partners means no secrets. You've been weird all day, Lou. What's happened?'

Saying it aloud would make it real. 'It's not a big deal. It was coming for ages. I don't know why I'm blubbing, really I don't.'

'It's Ben, isn't it? What's he done this time?'

Louisa nodded. 'I've told him I want a divorce.'

'But that's marvellous!'

'I wish you wouldn't say that. It doesn't feel it.'

'No, of course not,' Paul said. 'Let's get you out of here into the fresh air.'

He brought her to a bench in a rose-arbour, from where she could see into the marquee that had been set up on the lawn for the reception. Waiters in white gloves – Tod was reviving the white glove industry single-handed – were putting the finishing touches to glittering table settings on white

33

tablecloths topped with flower arrangements that echoed the colours of the bridesmaids' dresses and draperies that covered the marquee walls. Crystal chandeliers, fairy lights and enormous candelabra promised to create a magical night-time scene.

'Louisa!'

Tod was waving smelling salts beneath her nose, while Paul stood anxiously behind him with a brandy glass. Louisa took the brandy and found herself staring at Tod's shiny black shoes, which had platforms discreetly built in to compensate for his lack of height. A wave of unaccountable empathy swept over her. 'Tod, it's been fantastic working with you all these years.'

Tod was unmoved. 'That's it. I'm calling a doctor.'

'There's no need,' Paul interjected. 'It was the heat of the glasshouse, that's all.' To Louisa, he said, 'One of Tod's assistants is going to wait with you until the car can take you home. I'm going to have to leave you, though – I need to get over to the church.'

'Go on Paul, I'll be fine.'

Looking more like a war correspondent than a wedding photographer, Paul ran across the lawn, head down, Tod behind him. The minister's helicopter landed on the croquet lawn.

4

Louisa was grateful for the silence in the back of the luxurious car, one of many that Tara's family seemed to have at their disposal for the day. Beside her, on the seat, was a white petal she had picked up from beneath the rose bushes lining the drive. She'd lost the bet. It was real. She fingered it now, thinking of Ben's red roses and of Elvie, who would have enjoyed seeing the girls in their pretty dresses. She blinked away the tears' then reached into her pocket for a tissue. Instead she found her wedding ring.

As they were about to cross the Boyne, she tapped on the glass separating her from the driver. 'Please stop!'

He slammed on the brakes and steered the car to the verge at the entrance to the bridge. He was probably thinking she was about to vomit. She opened the heavy car door and dashed on to the bridge.

'You all right, miss?' the chauffeur called, sounding alarmed.

When she reached the middle, she looked down into the turbulent waters, took a deep breath and flung her wedding ring into the depths.

'It's over,' she told herself. 'Goodbye *Paparazza*. Hello Louisa.'

Then she returned to the car.

'That feel good?' the driver asked.

'As good as it *can* feel,' she said.

'There's a mini-bar if you want some champagne to celebrate whatever you just did. I saw nothing, you understand.'

He was well used to seeing nothing, she thought, as her mobile phone rang.

'Hi, Becca.'

'You did it!'

'Did Mary ring you?'

'You're brilliant! Tell me everything!'

Louisa recounted her confrontation with Ben, and Becca laughed when she told her that she'd put him up in a hotel. 'Whatever it takes, girl. Listen, how will we celebrate?'

They agreed to meet at Mary's later that evening and, cheered by Becca's praise, Louisa allowed herself some champagne. It took courage to do what she had done that morning, even if she had taken her time about doing it. Anyone might have thought that pressing the eject button on an errant husband like Ben was a no-brainer. Only Louisa knew how hard it had been to relinquish the only stability she had ever had. That's saying something, she thought, me believing that Ben and I were stable. I suppose we were, considering what I was used to.

She raised her glass to the magic of starting anew, hoping that the girl who had moved continents in an attempt to sort out her life would get it right this time. If only she could find the original Louisa, the woman whose margins hadn't been blurred by trying to be what others wanted or needed, or even thought they wanted . . . She saw a tall, skinny girl, pretty in an ordinary way, wearing a little black dress 'borrowed' from a department store. She saw a free spirit who was telling herself that she had joined her modelling friends on the jaunt organized by the 'high-class' escort agency for a laugh and a few hundred dollars, a tough city girl following the tradition of relying on the out-of-towners in a tight spot. Arm candy, glorified waitress, aspirant artist, man-fodder, ordinary no-hoper, just another girl not unusual enough to be a *real* model, not that she cared in the least about that.

Little Lou had no illusions that she cared to recall. She was no Holly Golightly having Breakfast at Tiffany's – beautiful girls were never redeemed by princes; they just married them for their money.

That night, Louisa had hidden her camera in her bag and

was hoping that, when the party reached a certain stage of intoxication and inertia, she could take some pictures, without anyone noticing, of what modelling was like from the inside out. It might make an interesting coffee-table book. The way some women were willing to function as objects and live entirely on the surface fascinated her as a photographer. To sell herself in this way – on whatever level – a woman had to be constantly aware of how men saw her. She had to think like a man. Market herself as a man would market a woman. The pictures would be part of her Master's thesis at NYU, along with a diatribe on the image of woman in Western art as repeated in pornography. Her thesis supervisor had loved the idea.

As she leaned against the wall in a private suite at the Plaza that night, Louisa was approached by an elderly man in a white suit with skin like tanned leather stretched tightly across his skull. 'You don't look like the usual type,' he said, blinking lizard-like.

Her height had her looking down on his skeletal pate where shaggy white hairs grew like badly tended ferns. She could see the ridges where his skull plates had knitted together in infancy.

When he told her his name, she recognized him as the mogul behind countless soap operas and game shows – *Will to Live*, *Lovers and Strangers*, *Gamble of Your Life*. At the end of every programme, there was always the refrain, 'A Milton Goodbody Production'. It was repeated day-in, day-out, so often – she had thought – that all American life could well have been 'A Milton Goodbody Production'.

So Louisa smiled sweetly at Milton Goodbody, amazed, in a way, to discover that he actually existed. If innocent was what he wanted, innocent she would be.

'You're flirting with me. You want me to be your sugar daddy?' he asked.

'Another Milton Goodbody Production, you mean?'

He gave her a wink. 'You're smart – definitely not like the others.'

He'd got that right. 'I bet you use that line on all the girls,' she said.

'Come with me,' Milton said with practised kindness. His hand was cool but greasy. 'Let's get away from these idiots.'

She followed him to an adjoining bedroom. He leaned over a mirrored table, surprisingly lithe for an eighty-year-old, and took a packet out of his pocket. Cutting lines of powder with a silver razor-blade, he looked over his shoulder at her briefly. Blade held aloft. 'Keeps you young,' he said.

Louisa sat on the edge of the bed. She hadn't come to the party for cocaine, but if he was offering . . .

'So where're you from? Nebraska?'

'Do you want me to be from Nebraska?'

'No, baby. I want to know where you're from.'

'Manhattan,' she said.

He laughed hoarsely. 'I would have thought a New Yorker would know better than to come to a place like this.'

'What's a nice girl like you . . . ? I'm sure you can come up with something better than that,' Louisa said boldly. Men like him enjoyed being bossed around.

'I'm just telling you what I see. Look at that button nose. I bet your people came over on the *Mayflower*.' The way he said it, it felt like an insult.

'The problem with old money is that it's so old no-one can find where it's hidden,' she said.

'What's your name? And don't say Krystal.'

She decided to be truthful. Maybe the old lech could throw some *real* work her way – as long as it wasn't nine to five. That would be death. 'Louisa Stone.'

'Good name. Solid. I could buy and sell you, sweetheart.' He touched her face with one reptilian finger. 'So young. You need a little guidance.'

He could have been the kindly old doctor in one of his own soaps, the way he smiled at her. But he pointed to ten neat lines of pristine snow and told her to go ahead.

She took the rolled up twenty he offered and leaned over the table.

'Sit down,' Milton said, patting the bed beside him. 'I want to know all about you.'

He didn't just want her body. He wanted her soul. She'd met his type before.

'What's your favourite film?' he asked her.

'*La Dolce Vita*,' Louisa replied, as the sublime pleasure of the rush lifted her out of her body.

'*La Dol* – my favourite film of all time. See? We have something in common. Although its message is somewhat bleak . . . Must be why I like it. Listen, what do you think of a remake with John Travolta in the Marcello Minestrone part?'

'Mastroianni.'

'Don't correct me. You can't pronounce it either.' He grinned to show gleaming white Hollywood teeth too big for his mouth. 'You could play the – who was it? Ursula Andress? Her character, anyway.'

'It was Anita Ekberg. And I have no interest in acting.'

'Anyone ever tell you that you look like her?'

Louisa tossed her hair. She wasn't falling for that one. 'My favourite character is Maddelena, the whore with a heart of gold who kills herself after confessing all to the cad. And don't go flattering me. I don't look like *her* either.'

He moved closer to her, close enough for her to smell his sickly breath. She knew that scent, a bit like overboiled cabbage and sweet perfume, the way her mother had smelled. She jerked away.

'What's with you?' he asked, unzipping his pants. 'Go stand there and give me a little more of your amateur film analysis. You're the teacher and I'm the pupil. Do a slow strip while deconstructing Fellini. That's a real turn on. I'd pay extra for that.' He lay his wallet next to the cocaine. She eyed it hungrily.

'Go on. Feel free.'

Except this wasn't freedom.

*

As the drugs went round and the party descended into orgy, Louisa again became invisible with her camera. Ever the alert voyeur, she observed with a cold eye that made her pity herself a little less and despise herself a little more.

As she was getting ready to leave, she peeked in on Good-body, half-expecting to find him dead. But he was using a naked girl as a bed. The girl's dress had been torn away, exposing her breasts. Another man pulled her head back by the hair, while white-suited Milton turned suddenly, saw Louisa and winked.

Click.

The picture, Louisa had thought – she had artistic pretensions in those days – was a perverse take on Titian's 'Rape of Europa'. Although the girl was skinny, rather than Renaissance plump, her boiled-egg eyes rolled back in her head in the same way. The sated beast gloated as he leaned against her, drunk on power.

Click.

'You planning to blackmail somebody?'

She turned to see a man at her shoulder. Cheeky grin. Boxer's shoulders. Face like a film star's. An actor from one of Milton's soaps?

Ice-blue eyes. 'Hiya, pet.'

He seemed above it all, just as she was.

She leaned back against the wall to make herself a little shorter. 'Hi.'

'So, my little *paparazza* – cocaine and Kodak. Winning combination.'

Paparazzi. Flock of sparrows. Fellini had coined the description in *La Dolce Vita*. Maybe it was a sign. Or maybe he was Security, rather than an actor, and had spied on her and Milton. That happened, the minions wanting a piece.

She put her camera behind her back. The man reached for it and grabbed it by the strap.

'A Leica. Nice.'

'Please don't take the film,' Louisa said. 'It's for my Master's thesis.'

'Hey. That's a new one. Whatever you're into, you know? There's a market for this stuff, I imagine. Unless you're working for Goodbody. You are, aren't you?'

She smiled. 'I thought maybe *you* were.'

She grabbed her camera back and he caught hold of her hand, sending a bolt of electricity up her arm and in the vague direction of her lips.

'You're not getting away that easy, pet.'

'You English?'

He laughed. 'Ben Maguire. Film-maker. I was tryin' ta slewder a shit-load of development money out those jackeens. Maybe we could use your pictures to put the screws on them.'

'That accent – you're Irish,' Louisa said.

'I can't help it. It's genetic.'

He grinned at her slyly, totally confident in himself. He made her feel sexy because *he* was sexy, unbearably so. He was fit with a burning energy, yet also laid-back in a confident way – a wild-man who would hide you away in his little thatched cottage forever, if not a suite at the Plaza.

In about five seconds flat, Louisa's heart decided that Ben wouldn't hurt her – unless she begged him to. And she had a way, she knew, of bringing out the sadistic tendencies in men. If they couldn't have her completely, they punished her.

The elevator arrived. 'So, where will we go for coffee? I can't afford this place.'

Just my luck, Louisa thought, to get picked up at a million-aire's orgy by the one guy who can't afford a coffee in the Plaza.

In an all-night diner on Lexington, Ben asked her to marry him.

He had to be joking.

His Irish accent turned her on. (Imagine! And now she was living in Dublin surrounded by it. Nothing special about it at all.)

'So are you not a whore, then?' Ben said. 'I just need to know before I bring you home to mother.'

Ben's accent made the word 'whore' seem courtly and romantic. In his mouth it was a seventeenth-century word, a literary word. He'd probably never met a girl like her before. A real-life New York doll.

They'd gone back to his flat, which had only a gaudy flower-patterned futon in the corner. Louisa could still see the flowers – ugly brown and orange daisies that filled her vision when she lay down. But she had felt safe when Ben pulled the blankets over their heads to keep out the cold.

Only in the morning did she discover that they'd made love surrounded by four other sleeping bodies and that only the blankets were keeping out prying eyes. In the morning, when the bodies had left for work, she and Ben had the place to themselves.

Before she left, after that first night with Ben, she retrieved her camera.

Click.

'Souvenir, huh?' Ben said.

Then Ben produced his wallet. 'So. How much?'

'You couldn't afford me. Let's call it a freebie,' Louisa joked. She kept up the game. She was hardly going to see him again. She so much wanted to see him again.

'You're going to love it,' Ben had said when they arrived in Dublin, jet-lagged, one early morning in August. 'Wait until you see the views.' Ben's mother had died shortly before Louisa met him, leaving her house to her only child.

Dark, depressing and dire. That was Louisa's first impression of the two-storey-over-basement mock-Georgian house, built by Victorians in granite faced with cement. The front wall had since been painted a tone of aquamarine usually used in swimming-pools and was now peeling. The houses flanking it were restored and painted buttermilk, one with a red door, the other blue. Ben's house – *our* house, Louisa reminded herself

– was worse than shabby by comparison: it was positively neglected.

A faded panel on the gate-post gave the house's name: St Agnes's. It was more suited to a convent than a home. Not the sort of place in which she might expect to spend endless days and nights in thrilling intimacy.

Louisa turned away from the house and waited for Ben, who was helping the taxi man unload their bags and boxes on to the footpath. Some contained Louisa's 'photographic archive', as Ben had called it when a Customs officer asked. The prints and negatives were all that she possessed. If she died, an art archaeologist could reconstruct her life based around them. Louisa shivered in the thin dress that had been perfect for a Manhattan summer's day, but was completely inadequate against the chill sea air of Dalkey in August.

Ben carried her across the threshold, catching her dress on a loose nail and tearing it. She blinked against the darkness and took in the odours of camphor and mould and dead mammal. Her heart sank in disappointment. When Ben put her down, she could feel the icy tiled floor through the soles of her sandals. She nearly tripped on the frayed carpet and scrabbled at the wall to regain her balance, knocking down a ceramic vessel that hung at elbow-height.

'That's for holy water,' Ben said, slapping her bottom. 'Ten Hail Marys for ya'.'

He marched ahead and Louisa followed him into a high-ceilinged room dominated by a dark brown and green marble fireplace. The heavy, Victorian wooden furniture was ornately carved and knick-knacks covered every surface – kittens and saints, mostly. The dim room had the air of an unattended jumble sale. She could just make out a crucifix on the wall beside a photograph of the Pope. William Morris wallpaper – mainly greens and golds with an aggressive pattern of magenta tulips – heightened her claustrophobia.

Have nothing that is not beautiful or useful.

Morris's edict had been ignored in this room.

'You can feel the sea.' Ben drew the dark green velvet drapes to reveal a bay window hidden behind greying lace curtains. Louisa focused on the intricate pattern of vines and flowers woven through them.

Click.

'You can see Dalkey Island,' Ben said.

The delicate lace seemed to be held together by dust. As she drew her hand away her nail caught on a thread and a patch of lace fell apart in her fingers, powdery as a moth's wings.

'I'll bring you there some time,' Ben said.

Louisa tried to follow his gaze but all she saw behind the lace were windows filmed with salt.

Louisa felt his hand on her shoulder, then his arms around her waist. He kissed her neck. 'Welcome home, babe.'

The state of the house was irrelevant, she told herself. Solid and protective, Ben was her real home. He whispered, 'Come upstairs.'

Climbing up the gracious staircase with its elegantly turned spindles Louisa started to see the potential. Take down the curtains, strip the wallpaper, paint everything white. It wouldn't cost much. In Manhattan, a period property of this size would cost millions. She caught a glimpse of a claw-foot bath in a tiny room at the top of the landing as Ben led her from one bedroom to another. More velvet, more lace, more heavy furniture, more suffocating dust. He didn't seem to notice the mice scuttling away to their nests and the spiders twitching in their webs.

There were wash-basins in all the bedrooms. 'Mother ran it as a B-and-B for a while after I left home,' Ben said. 'Slap-up fries every morning.'

'I hope her ghost won't disapprove of muesli,' Louisa said.

Louisa thought of grim-faced business travellers with leather cases, and backpackers giggling under the sheets so that the proprietor wouldn't hear their love-making. The house had that feel to it. No misbehaviour allowed.

The first time they made love in the house, all Louisa could think of was the gallons of emulsion she'd buy at the first opportunity. She would make a clean, new life with her paintbrush.

5

Mary's door was open on the latch. 'Anybody home?' Louisa called.

Mary came bustling out, covered to the elbows with flour. 'So soon? What happened? Don't tell me the bride scarpered – or was it the groom this time?'

'The photographer, for a change.'

Mary held herself a little straighter. 'I'll put the kettle on.'

They were interrupted by the children running in from the garden. 'Mum! We have a surprise!' Elvie squealed.

'A cake!' Milo chimed in, and was rewarded with a kick from his sister.

'It was meant to be a surprise,' Elvie sputtered at him.

'I *am* surprised!' Louisa said, stepping in to separate them. 'Can we have it now?'

The children looked at Mary, who nodded. 'Don't worry,' she whispered to Louisa as they went into the kitchen. 'It's edible.'

After choruses of 'Happy Birthday' and 'For She's a Jolly Good Fellow', the children brought their fudgy slices of cake and plastic cups of milk to the Wendy House at the bottom of the garden. Louisa and Mary sat at the kitchen table with mugs of tea, trying to resist a second slice.

'How did Ben take it?' Mary asked.

'He tried to lay all the blame on me at first, but when I refused to play along, he gave up, like it wasn't worth his while to pretend any longer . . . Do you remember, Mary, aeons ago, when you told me to light a candle to St Agnes every Friday if I wanted Ben to stay faithful? I thought you were some sort of Bible-basher.'

'The look on your face,' Mary said, watching the children through the kitchen door. 'I was just being wicked.'

'I tried it a couple of times – and disproved your hypothesis.'

Mary laughed, her cosy face brightening. She had that lovely, pale Irish skin that grows freckled and rosy with age and her hair, once red, was now a curly brown shoulder-length halo, making her seem younger than her fifty-five years. 'The first good look I got at you,' she said, 'you were sitting on the front steps of the house with a shawl wrapped around you like a beautiful young widow waiting for her sailor to come home, while the rest of us were in T-shirts and shorts. I couldn't decide whether to wrap you up or knock some sense into you. I remember thinking, Where are the poor girl's parents? If one of my daughters ends up marrying a man like Ben Maguire I don't know what I'll do.'

'You'll be patient and be there for her, just as you've been for me. I asked you to teach me how to make soda bread, remember? Hadn't a clue what a rasher was. That domestic phase I went through in the beginning, thinking I could make everything right if I had Le Creuset saucepans. I still remember carrying them home from Clery's on the bus. They weighed a ton. It was such a novelty, though, having a house of my own. I look at the twenty-somethings now and think, I never had my twenties. I went straight to my thirties. I became Ben's age – not that he was old, only a decade or so older. But thirty-four seemed so grown-up to me then.'

'And now?'

'Now I see that he was always the child.' Louisa shook her head at her own self-delusion. 'You must have thought I was so naïve, even for twenty-four.'

'Naïve? Never. Hopeful, I'd say. You wanted to make it work and no-one can fault you for that.'

Louisa watched as Elvie and Milo ran in and out of the Wendy House, Elvie bossing her brother around.

'She's a real little mother, isn't she?' Mary said.

'You've been a fantastic second mother to them,' Louisa said. 'And to me.'

'I'll hear none of that. *You* are your children's one and only brilliant and talented Mammy.'

'Will I be as good, though, now that I'm single and working?'

'What's new about that? You've always been a single, working mother – except with all of the responsibility and none of the benefits. I know divorced fathers who spend far more time with their children than Ben does.'

'I suppose so. I'm hoping that now he has to plan about spending time with the children, he'll actually be a better father.'

'Don't expect too much and you won't be disappointed,' Mary said.

'The early days we were together were the happiest of my life.'

Mary took Louisa's hand in her own. 'That's the best way to think of it, love. Bitterness destroyed many a good woman.'

'I just want the divorce to go as smoothly as possible, for the children's sake. I'm determined not to let Ben use them as ammunition.' Thinking of how Mary had raised six children on her own, getting them through school, then university, Louisa was amazed at what women were capable of when they had no-one but themselves to rely on. Mary's husband, Louisa had gathered, had simply disappeared, although there were days when she would find Mary stuffing a letter into her pocket, or reading the deaths column in the London *Times*, and she would wonder how much she really knew about his whereabouts.

'Yoo-hoo! Where is everyone? Where's the birthday girl?'

It was Becca, dressed in white and filling the room with her seductive signature perfume and armfuls of flowers.

'Hiya!' Louisa called, stood up and was enveloped in one of Becca's luxurious hugs. 'I'm so proud of you,' Becca murmured into her ear. 'Do the kids know?'

'Not yet.'

'Chinese walls, then. But, if you ask me, they won't be able to tell the difference.' Turning to Mary, she said. 'Hello Mother Earth. Did we ever think we'd see the day?'

'We lived in hope.' Mary looked at Becca's cream leather shoulder bag. 'What's in there? The usual body parts or did you bring us some champagne?'

Becca pulled out two bottles, set them on the table, then stood back to admire Mary's figure. 'My goodness, are you on the Zone? You're tiny in those jeans.'

'I borrowed them from my daughter,' Mary said, pleased.

Louisa chided herself for not having noticed Mary's weight loss. She hoped she wasn't ill. 'You're always so covered up in those lovely ethnic things you wear – but look at that figure! I hope you're going to take me up on that offer of a studio portrait of you and the children.'

'If I can get them all together in one place at the same time!' Mary said.

Becca was opening the champagne with one of Mary's blue and white checked tea-towels, easing out the cork with a slow hiss. 'Aah,' she said. Mary produced three juice glasses – hers wasn't the sort of home where champagne and wine were on regular offer. 'I think we all deserve this, don't you?'

Becca poured the champagne, handed round the glasses and said, 'To Louisa, for finally making the break. Look at you! Early this morning, you had that desperate note in your voice – like saying the D-word would kill you. Now, twelve hours later, you're a changed woman! You're free! I really wish I could have seen the look on his face. I've been wanting to have a go at that womanizing bastard for years.'

Louisa proposed a second toast. 'To Becca and Mary, for listening to me moan on and on . . .'

'And on,' Becca added.

'Sure, you weren't that bad,' Mary said. 'It was a difficult decision to make.'

Becca was aghast. 'Whaddaya mean? Difficult *not* to make, I'd say.'

Louisa felt triumphant. 'I made a second major decision today, by the way.'

Becca sipped champagne. 'Be still my heart. No baby-steps for you, then?'

'I'm giving up the wedding business.'

A worried look passed between Louisa's two closest friends.

'No, I'm not going AWOL, if that's what you think. Paul's becoming my partner. He'll run the wedding side of the business, while I stick to portraiture.'

Becca sighed with relief. 'That's a great idea. Delegate, develop, diversify. But don't take on too much too soon. Promise?'

Mary leaned forward at the table.

'You're doing your Mother Confessor pose,' Louisa said.

Becca struck the same attitude. One of them on her case was bad enough, Louisa thought, but with the two of them together she didn't stand a chance.

'What happened at the wedding?' Mary asked.

'I had a wobbly moment,' Louisa said. 'I was taking pictures in the conservatory of the dewy young bride, tropical plants flourishing, doves fluttering around and I went weak at the knees. Paul took over and sent me home. End of story.'

'I knew I shouldn't have let you go to work today,' Mary said. 'You can't push away feelings the way you do and get away with it for ever.'

Becca was thoughtful. 'Break up with husband and torture self with dream wedding. I can think of better ways to die.'

Louisa defended herself. 'Look, I'd made a commitment and I'm immune to weddings, you know that, but something got to me. The family were real salt of the earth – despite all the ostentation. You should have *seen* the dresses –'

'You cried because the dresses were tackier than usual. I get it,' Becca said.

'Ssh,' Mary admonished her, then turned back to Louisa. 'Go on.'

Louisa looked into the bubbles in her glass, searching for the truth – *her* truth. 'It wasn't the romance thing that got to me. It was the mother and daughter. The mother – Siobhan – was pushy and a bit over the top, but all she wanted was for her daughter to have the dream wedding *she* had never had. And the daughter – big shock – *appreciated* it.'

'Next you're going to tell us the daughter had only six months to live, right?' Becca interjected. 'And the groom was selling his kidney to save her?'

'Let Louisa talk,' Mary said.

Louisa would have twisted out of her seat if Becca and Mary hadn't each put a gentle hand on her forearms. 'I'm confused,' she said. 'I can't find the right words. I know I did the right thing yet I feel . . . empty. And I've got a pain in my stomach that just won't go away.'

Mary nodded. 'Where do women run when their marriages break down?'

'If they haven't already got a lover in the wings,' Becca added.

The answer to Mary's question pierced through the pain. 'Home to mother,' Louisa said softly. She shrank back in her chair. 'What a bitch.'

Becca and Mary sat quietly sipping their drinks, as relaxed as mother spiders with meals waiting in their silky traps.

Louisa's mother, Amanda, had sat like this with her women friends, talking – or not – about sex and women and love and men and . . . Louisa searched her memory, mothers? Wasn't that one of the things Amanda never talked about as she and her acolytes lay languidly in their sheer Indian smocks, bells on their skirts, sipping Californian Chenin Blanc from pale-green gallon bottles? Thirteen-year-old Louisa, unseen and unheard at the sawhorse table that did triple time as study desk, artist's bench and ironing board, would half-listen to her mother's master class in womanly woes as she tried to concentrate on her algebra. Amanda always had time to talk about sexual politics, but never to listen to her daughter's problems, so

Louisa's solution had been not to have any. As she grew older, she told herself that Amanda's head was in the clouds. She had lacked the nurturing gene. The bitch. If I could talk to her now, I'd give her a piece of my mind. Anger surged through Louisa then, taking her off-guard. It was as though the anger she couldn't feel at Ben, was boiling over now.

'I respect your theory, Mary, but my mother is the last person I'd be running to. All Amanda cared about was releasing herself from oppression. And I was part of that oppression. If she were alive, she'd be too busy organizing some protest or other to take any interest in me, or my children. One of my earliest memories – I must have been four years old. That's right, because I was in kindergarten and I'd been sent home early. She was crying about Bobby. Saying his name over and over again and weeping . . . Bobby . . . Bobby . . . And by then he was five years dead! As though it was her own lover who had died. Her bitterest tears were always for people she'd never met.'

'Bobby Kennedy?'

'Who else?'

'Men – the men that mattered – were always unobtainable. I'm not talking about the ones who were there in the early hours of the morning, grunting and groaning.'

Suddenly Louisa was lying on her mattress on the floor behind a battered antique Japanese screen that Amanda had retrieved from a skip on Park Avenue. She was trying not to hear the drawling voices, unable to sleep because the man in the apartment seemed to fill the space from ceiling to floor. If he smoked, Louisa would pull up the covers as far as her mouth and nose, determined not to inhale that overwhelming feeling of *him*. She would cover her ears with her pillow so that he couldn't invade her head. If her mother forgot to pull the curtains round her bed, Louisa would suppress the urge to use the bathroom, not wanting to see the things she wished she couldn't hear. In the semi-darkness, the room invaded by the artificial city light,

Louisa would gaze at the screen, with its elegant Japanese ladies hiding shyly behind fans on one panel, wise men with long beards strolling in another. It was a peaceful world created from mother-of-pearl and richly coloured lacquer. A visual lullaby that helped Louisa imagine herself somewhere else far away from her own confusion. She would never have a boyfriend if this was what it meant – falling over yourself, sneaking around, crying out when he was there, weeping when he left.

Louisa sipped her champagne, while her friends waited. 'Amanda was "liberated", remember that word? Women's Lib meant sitting around talking about sexual politics and abortion and looking at your genitalia in a mirror. It meant having lovers and acting like it was all so *free*. Amanda never said as much, but there was always a kind of floating agreement between us that motherhood was part of the oppression. I never even called her "Mother". It was "Manna", as soon as I could talk. I used to see other people's mothers fussing over them and feel sorry for them. I suppose I couldn't admit to being jealous. Amanda used to make me feel grateful for being alive. She even said it to me once, "You were almost aborted, you know." I may have shouted back, "I wish I had been!"'

Mary's face was thoughtful as Becca topped up their glasses. 'Mothers and daughters do have terrible rows, say things they regret. That's normal,' she said. 'Ask my daughters and they'll probably tell you I've said worse.'

'You? Never! You're not capable of it,' Louisa said.

Mary let this pass. 'What you're trying to say, I think, is that your mother got you into this mess.'

'Too right,' Louisa answered. 'She was completely irresponsible. It made me independent too soon. She always had to be centre stage. "My Art", she used to call it. I had to suffer for *her* art. *She* never seemed to suffer for it, not really. I was there to prop her up – as was everyone around her. The way we lived – mother-daughter Bohemian hippies on the East Side, me her ragdoll shadow . . .'

'Sounds just like the media types in Notting Hill, if you ask me,' Becca said. 'Hardly under-privileged. Didn't your mother have a trust fund?'

'A small one. The hippie version of the dole.'

Becca laughed. 'Birkenstocks don't come cheap. Oh, the innocence of it – thinking the world was ever going to change. Aren't we still in the 1950s in Ireland? My mother was forever going to Mass and asking God to forgive her sins, of which she had committed very few – unless having a lesbian daughter counted.'

Louisa patted her hand. 'You're right. We haven't moved on one jot from the 1950s. In fact, we're worse off. Mothers then had a certain status. Today we're always made to feel inadequate and guilty, never good enough. At least Amanda's generation didn't buy into that. They saw putting yourself first as a good thing.'

Becca took Louisa's hand. 'You're a really good mother, Lou. You've nothing to feel guilty about.'

Mary turned away to glance out of the kitchen window towards Milo and Elvie. 'They do leave you, you know,' she said, 'and they don't look back. It may be a mistake to put your life on hold for them.'

Louisa thought she saw a shadow of regret in Mary's face. Mary's life was so full, with her grown-up children coming and going, friends filling her kitchen, Milo and Elvie treating her house as a second home. She would never want to give all that up, but it was true: Elvie and Milo would leave Mary, eventually – and leave Louisa alone. 'I'll shoot myself for saying this, Mary, but I don't want you to feel that Milo and Elvie are holding you back. If it's ever a question of your loyalty to me and my children keeping you from anything you really want to do . . . I don't want you to play the martyr, yeah?'

Becca and Mary laughed. 'You're off message, Lou,' Becca said. 'This conversation isn't about Mary, it's about you. Yes, your mother was odd, but there must have been something good about her, to have made you who you are.'

'Why are we talking about my mother? She's been dead twenty years. She would have told me to dump Ben ages ago. If she'd met him, I would never have married him.'

'I thought you said she didn't care,' Becca said.

Mary shot Becca a warning look. 'One question, Louisa. How old was your mother when she died?'

For a moment, Louisa could hardly breathe. 'Thirty-seven.'

Mary nodded knowingly. Louisa was angry again. 'I'm freaking out about my mortality, is that what you think? I'm going to die at thirty-seven because Amanda did? Your mother's dead, Becca's mother's dead, my mother's dead. We're the dead mothers club. I'm over it.'

Mary reached across the table and touched Louisa's fingers.

Louisa let out a deep sigh. 'Thirty-seven today. I never even saw myself as getting this far.'

Becca's voice was soothing. 'Amanda's script is finished. It's time for you to write your own.'

Louisa voice rose in frustration. 'What self-help twaddle have you been reading? I've never sacrificed my children, or even Ben, to gratify myself the way she did. I've built up a solid business and I keep everyone else's show on the road. Sure, I'd love to be doing art photography and leaving the children to drag themselves up, but I'm not.'

'No being-the-irresponsible-artist for you, right?'

'Obviously.'

'That's what we mean. You're so busy trying to *not* be your mother, that she's still writing the script.'

Louisa's head was whirling. 'Can we talk about something else? All this champagne and navel-gazing is making me dizzy. I'll think about it tomorrow.'

'OK, Scarlett. You do that. Let me know when the Confederates arrive. In the meantime, I've got some good news of my own!' Becca said.

Louisa and Mary waited expectantly.

'My little brother's coming home tomorrow! To stay!'

'Is Gill speaking to you again, then?' Louisa asked.

'He's grown up, decided to stop resenting me for acting like his mother. And I've decided to stop resenting him for the fact that I had to be his mother after our parents died. I've promised to be a big sister only from now on, no longer a mother surrogate.'

'Big sisters are worse any day!' Mary said.

'I haven't seen him in a couple of years,' Louisa said.

'Neither have I. We had a long talk on the phone the other night.' There was a faraway look in Becca's eyes as she gazed out over the garden. Then she snapped back. 'His rebellious years are over. He wants a truce.'

'I'd hardly call humanitarian relief work in Africa *rebellion*,' Louisa said.

'He could have been anything – a doctor, a barrister . . .'

'A communications consultant, perhaps?' Mary suggested playfully.

'Listen, I started out as a nobody in a cheap suit organizing beer promotions. After my mother died, I had to leave school so I could support Gill. I studied at night. I went everywhere, met everyone, schmoozed until I was sick so I could make a name for myself and earn enough in PR to put Gill through boarding-school and university. The boy lacked for nothing. I'm proud of him for spending the best five years of his life in Africa. Really I am. But now he's coming back, I want him to make the most of himself. If he wants to be a human-rights lawyer, fine. Or even get a medical degree and go back to Africa as a doctor. I have no problem with helping Africa, *per se*, I just think that for Gill it's been an excuse for drifting.'

Louisa stifled a theatrical yawn. 'You worked your fingers to the bone for that Third-World-rescuing eco-crusader and does he appreciate it? You sacrificed your own needs and grew up too fast so he could stay a child a little longer . . . Your mother's early death was the making of you, if you ask me, no offence to your mother. By the way, you forgot the part about how, on her deathbed, your mother made you promise that Gill would become a doctor and win a Nobel Prize for curing cancer. Maybe you need to throw *that* hoary old script out of the window.'

Becca gave Louisa one of her trademark killer looks, then they both looked down at the table like two school-chums caught pulling each other's hair by the teacher.

'Nice one, Lou,' she said.

Mary chuckled. 'Takes one to know one, hey Becca? You two are so alike that you might have been separated at birth. You've been working off the same script, practically page for page.'

Mary sat back as Becca and Louisa's eyes met, each challenging the other to give in first.

'You're two of a kind, the pair of ye.' She turned to Becca. 'Give Gill a bit of space. Put a roof over his head, feed him, give him spending money, let him have friends round. Don't organize his future, his thoughts or even his wardrobe. Just be there for him, like you and Louisa are for each other.'

Becca propped her forehead on her hand. 'I was kind of hoping he might be there for me for a change.'

Louisa laid a hand on her shoulder, but Becca pulled away. She almost asked her what was wrong, but then she saw hurt in Becca's amber-flecked eyes. If she didn't put a stop to it, it would ruin their friendship. 'Sisters?' she whispered.

For Becca, enduring sisterhood was the consolation prize and they both knew it. 'Sisters,' she answered with a smile.

Mary surveyed them. 'Before we even think about opening a second bottle of champagne – and I'm not sure we should –'

'I hate that word – *should!*' Becca broke in.

'– I'm going to make us some omelettes. And I've got soup ready. You two *should* eat.'

'I can't imagine a better birthday feast,' Louisa said.

Mary handed Becca a mixing bowl, two forks and a carton of eggs. 'Beat those for me. Hey, my daughters say there's a club in Leeson Street they call "Grab a Granny". It's full of horny wrinklies – that's any woman over forty, girls – and toy boys looking for one-night stands.'

'Nobody wants a woman with two kids,' Louisa said.

'Try six kids,' Mary said ruefully.

Becca considered this. 'Don't be so negative. Men have children too, you know.'

'Yeah,' Mary responded, 'and their wives have thrown them out for being a waste of space.'

'Imagine this,' Louisa giggled. 'A woman goes through a traumatic and lonely marriage with a complete bastard of a man, divorces him, finally gets her act together, goes out on the town and meets –'

'Ben!' Becca laughed.

'You read my mind!' Louisa was still giggling. Then she became serious. 'What if it's me? What if I end up with another Ben without even knowing?'

'We won't let that happen,' Mary told her.

'Typical Louisa,' Becca groaned. 'You haven't even been out on the town yet as a single woman, and already you're plotting how you'll cope with future disasters. You're projecting into the future, again. Keep one leg in the future, one in the past –'

'And you piss on the present!' Mary and Louisa said together.

'Exactly.' Becca was cracking eggs. 'It won't come to that. If anybody messes with my girl, this is what I'll do to his head.'

And with that, she crushed a shell between her manicured fingers.

6

The following Monday morning, revived after an easy, aimless Sunday with the children (and still no call from Ben), Louisa opened her studio and prepared to lose herself in work. The light-filled modern space was decorated like a gallery with some of her favourite portraits. It always surprised her clients. Hidden behind the original village shop-front, which was in keeping with the rest of the busy little main street, the airy studio with its twenty-foot-high ceiling was new. High windows angled the northern light and prevented direct sunlight from interfering with Louisa's complex lighting designs. For certain effects, she could seal off the windows at the touch of a button, plunging the studio into complete darkness. A winding metal and glass stairway led up to a minstrels' gallery, where Louisa kept an office for herself, while the darkroom, changing room, toilet, baby changing room, file room and props room were tucked under the gallery just off the main space.

It always gave Louisa a thrill to open the door. The studio was the only place that she felt belonged truly to her – mortgaged to the hilt, but hers none the less. She went straight up the winding metal and glass stairs to her office, where the answering machine was blinking. She pushed play and scanned her diary.

The messages reeled off.

'Hiya. This is Trish Cooney – from the wedding? I'd like to come in and see the portfolio with a view to buying some of the pictures. You can call me . . .'

'Hello. This is Chloe Mitchell. I met you on Saturday at the wedding. Pink dress? You liked my hair – at least you said you did. Whatever. I want to come in for a portrait . . .'

'Paul, how are ya? This is Casey, who else? Call me. You have my number.'

They all seemed to be bridesmaids from Tara's wedding, with rather similar schemes for getting to know Paul better. Louisa smiled to herself. He had never had this sort of reaction as her assistant. She'd have fun playing the messages back for him.

The women's voices, each with its own style of seduction – cute, curious, commanding – were so alive. Louisa felt she was eavesdropping on something more intimate than a phone message. What must it be like, she wondered, to have that confidence, to be out there in the world on the pull, lusty enough to ring up a man with a transparent excuse. She felt younger just thinking about it.

If divorce was going to change her life, it would involve more than just getting Ben out of the picture, since he'd never really been in it in the first place. That morning she had brought the children to school as usual, opened her studio as usual, and was now losing herself in work, as usual, with little to look forward to but an unremarkable evening after the children were asleep. So far, life as a single woman had been a bit like a car crash, with her life replaying itself in slow motion, except that the final impact never came. She suspected that it never would. Acceptance would filter through gradually. One morning she would wake up and realize, without knowing precisely how it had happened, that she had created a brilliant new life.

I should call him and arrange a date for him to see the children, she thought. For the children's sake. I'll be bright and breezy and suggest next Sunday, avoid anything personal. It will be rather nice, actually, to have a Sunday afternoon to myself.

She called the Monroe Hotel, thought better of it and hung up.

I don't want Ben to think I'm using the children as an excuse to contact him. He'll only try to wheedle his way back. I should be seeing the solicitor about this – isn't that what women do? I have to talk to him anyway, about arranging the partnership for Paul.

She dialled the number.

'Murphy, Pearson and O'Brien.' The voice was bright, efficient, young and female.

'Hi. This is Louisa Maguire. I'd like to make an appointment to see Mr O'Brien, please,' Louisa said.

'Does he know what it's in connection with?'

'It's personal.'

'Of course. Could you give me some idea?'

Louisa took a deep breath and exhaled. It shouldn't be humiliating, announcing to a complete stranger that she was divorcing. The receptionist probably dealt with that sort of call all the time.

'I need to discuss my divorce. I also need a contract drawn up. I'm taking on a new partner.'

'Fine. You'll want to sort out the divorce before you start thinking about the pre-nup,' the voice said.

'Excuse me?'

'Your new partner will have to wait until your divorce is sorted out.'

'Why?'

'Well –' the woman seemed lost for words.

Louisa laughed. How easily she laughed today. 'My new *business* partner. Not my new husband. I'm never marrying again, thank you very much.'

The woman was cool. 'Famous last words. You have no idea how often I hear them. Forgive me. Let's look at the diary. Mr O'Brien can handle the business contracts, but for the divorce you want a family lawyer. Ms Pearson is our specialist, but she's in court all day, every day this week. Would next week do? Wednesday at four?'

Please don't let Ben and me end up fighting it out in court.

Louisa flipped through her desk diary. There were portraits booked back-to-back that Wednesday, but Paul would be available. 'Wednesday at four. See you then,' Louisa said.

Nine days to wait, she thought, as she flicked back in her

diary to see what today held in store. There was a First Holy Communion portrait, then a head-and-shoulders for a company report, a mother and baby portrait followed by a newly engaged couple – the very thought of that one made her sick. Seeing people in love was starting to hurt so much that she had cried while watching *The Little Mermaid* with Elvie the night before. She went back downstairs to collect the files.

She opened the metal fire door of the file room and heard the climate-controlled unit whirr reassuringly as the light switched on automatically. The wide, flat portfolio drawers were light silver steel and opened to reveal an archive of vibrant family life – a sort of alternative universe where everyone was happy and good-looking. Some of them actually were. Many were not. So she cast spells with her camera, creating family fictions that masked any ambiguity or doubt. When they saw the finished portrait, she could see how relieved they were to have pulled it off. But if her clients knew that this was the contract, for the photographer to make them appear certain, when they were uncertain, or happy when they were not, they never spoke of it. Did they appreciate the way she subtly guided them towards arrangements of faces, shoulders and limbs that gave an impression of cohesion when ties were fragile? Louisa had long ago learned that her clients often had no idea how tentative they seemed with each other. Accustomed to using words to hide their feelings, rather than pictures, they were usually uncomfortable faced with Louisa's impassive lens. Her job was to make them appear at ease.

Composing happy families was a game she had begun to play in childhood, she now realized. Funny that, how, making a decision about Ben was like sloughing off a withered skin, so that memories of who she had been before Ben, bobbed up from beneath the surface.

'I need pictures, Mannie,' seven-year-old Louisa had called as she came in from school, the key to the apartment on a ribbon round her neck. Milo's age, that's how old she'd been.

'Hello, bestest friend,' Amanda sang in her baby voice, laying down her pencil and turning to see what Louisa had brought home with her. This day she had two apples from the whore in 1B – that's what Manna called her – but Louisa liked her.

'Where's our family album?' she asked, giving Amanda a peck on the cheek like she'd seen children do on TV.

'Haven't got one,' she replied suspiciously, then picked up her pencil and returned to her drawing, one of thousands that were never good enough, but never discarded either, so that they piled up in the corner as high as the ceiling.

'Everybody has a family album, the teacher said.'

'We haven't got a *family album*. How *bourgeois*.' Amanda hated anything *bourgeois*: it was a word like a giant-sized junk bin into which Louisa threw a growing pile of experiences denied. Shiny black patent Mary Janes, a lunchbox handed to her on the way out the door, hot dinners at the table, vacations, kids' movies and popcorn, knowing more about your father than that he was probably one of Amanda's Californian friends passing through on the way to India . . . Santa Claus.

'It's time you knew,' Amanda said, one Christmas Eve when Louisa was still young enough to be hoping for a Suzy Home-maker Oven because Manna's was broken. *It's time you knew.* Amanda's lessons began when she'd been drinking and had no-one better to talk to. 'This is very, very important so remember it always. Promise me you won't forget?'

'I promise.'

'Cross your heart and hope to die?'

Louisa crossed her heart, but only mumbled 'hope to die' in case saying it might make it happen.

'Okay then. Growing up is about stripping away your illusions, one by one.'

Louisa tried to think of an illusion. 'Like magic?'

'Exactly. Society is always deceiving us with magic tricks. Now, don't interrupt.' Amanda took Louisa's face in her hands.

'The first thing you learn,' Amanda said, 'is that there is no Santa Claus.'

Big deal. She'd known that already, Louisa thought.

'Next you learn that there is no God,' Amanda continued.

Louisa tried to nod, but her face was immobile in Amanda's grip.

'Then you learn that there are no adults.'

'Not even you?'

'Not even me. Not even teachers. Teachers don't know everything. You know more than they do.'

Amanda released Louisa and went back to her drawing. Louisa got out her homework. 'If there are no adults,' she asked her mother, 'then why do we grow up?'

'You have to figure that one out for yourself.'

Louisa often wondered why she had to figure out so many things for herself, while her mother seemed to know so much more than everyone else. Amanda liked being different, but Louisa hated it. Being different meant that only the teachers seemed to like her. Good grades didn't make her popular, but at least they made her superior. Being 'above average' or even 'excellent' might give her a chance at 'normal' one day.

The family album was important, no matter what Amanda said.

Besides, that popular girl with the shiny, new black Mary Janes had boasted that her family could trace their family back to the royal family in England.

'That's genealogy,' the teacher had said.

Louisa knew that her mother liked big words. 'Genie-ology, then. Have we got that?'

'What are you talking about? You're blocking my light.'

Amanda had a thing about light.

Louisa tried to remain patient – that always worked best with Amanda. 'We're doing family trees in school. I have to get as many pictures as I can of all the people we're related to.'

Amanda put down her pencil.

'Teacher says everybody's parents had parents, Manna. The tree has to have relatives hung off the branches.'

'No.'

'Haven't I got a Grammy?'

Amanda held her arms out. 'Come here, baby. It's you and me. Just us. Aren't we so lucky to have each other?'

So Louisa had improvised. Everyone at school, including her, had already painted a large brown tree trunk with a worrying number of branches. Louisa had started out making a tree with no branches, since she had only one picture, of Amanda, to put on the top. She had no pictures of herself. If they existed, she hadn't found them in the cardboard boxes Amanda never unpacked. But when the teacher said her tree was only a trunk, Louisa had had to make branches like everyone else's. She dreaded the day when she would have to hang the photos on her tree.

She was saved from the embarrassment of being the only child in the class without family pictures when someone died in the apartment upstairs and all their personal effects were put out on the street. While Amanda chose a lamp, some dishes, a small table and a few other things that they hardly had space for, Louisa dug until she found a photo album. She knelt on the pavement on 63rd Street, flipping through the pages, careful not to let the old photos of people in First World War uniforms and extravagant hats fall out. She felt protective of them already.

They were perfect.

When the day came to hang their pictures on their trees, Louisa's was packed with photos of people she had never met and never would. She watched what the other children were doing out of the corner of her eye, as was her habit, and noticed that old people were generally grandparents, younger to middle-aged ones were aunts and uncles and the children were cousins.

Louisa picked the faces she liked best, arranged them according to age and made up names for them. 'Aunt Jane. Uncle Sam. Cousin Hermione.'

When it was finished, the teacher looked at Louisa's family tree for a long time, then said, 'You have a very large and imaginative family tree, Louisa Stone.'

'Thank you,' Louisa said, half-believing that she, indeed, had unearthed a very large and imaginative family.

It took Louisa a moment or two to realize that the coffee had brewed and that Paul was calling from the lower floor. 'Hey Lou! You alive up there?'

She leaned over the polished metal rail, 'Hi! How'd it go on Saturday?'

He ran up the stairs and into her office. 'What are you smiling about?' he asked.

Louisa punched play on the answering-machine and sipped her coffee. His face reddened. 'Nothing happened, I swear.'

'Nothing yet,' Louisa said. 'You'd better book them in on separate days unless you want to see hair flying.'

'Don't leave me alone with any of them.'

'I thought you were well able to handle yourself,' Louisa said, teasing him.

'You have no idea what they're like! I'm not a piece of meat, you know.'

Louisa resisted the urge to give him a motherly hug, lest he think she was after him too. 'Poor lamb.'

She suspected that being mauled by bridesmaids wasn't his real worry. 'You weren't expecting to be working alone on Saturday. I dumped you in at the deep end and you rose to the occasion.'

Paul's shoulders dropped. 'They came at me in a pack at the reception. And there was a bit of MOBILE going on.'

Louisa paled. It had been a mistake. Paul hadn't coped.

'Were you drinking with them?' she asked gently.

'God, no! You know I wouldn't! It was Siobhan. Launched herself at me when I was packing up to leave. I was pinned up against the wall with that lethal tiara poking up my nostrils. Then Bryan turned up, gave me a dirty look, lifted her over his shoulder and carried her away.'

Louisa was dumbstruck. Siobhan, the perfectly married MOB with a FOB who adored her, getting pissed and throwing herself at Paul? She began to laugh. 'It's fantastic! The best thing that could have happened! I'm always doing that, seeing the family I never had in the people I photograph. The mother I wished I had, the brother I thought would protect me – it's madness! If you ever see me doing that again, shoot me.'

'What if Bryan thinks that I'm to blame and refuses to pay the bill?'

He was talking like a businessman now, which pleased Louisa.

'He'll pay. It probably wasn't the first time that Siobhan let her hormones get the better of her. He probably took her straight upstairs and gave her a good seeing to.'

Paul's eyes widened.

'I know,' Louisa said. 'Like imagining your parents in bed.'

The doorbell rang with the first clients of the day: a mother in a business suit with her plump eight-year-old daughter, whose long, blonde tresses had been arranged in an artful tumble of curls that must have taken hours. They were followed by a man holding a plastic dress-bag aloft in one hand and a make-up case in the other. The mother gave Louisa and Paul a brisk wave and ranted into her mobile phone.

Louisa immediately set about putting the child at ease. 'Hi! You must be Samantha. Doesn't your hair look pretty!'

Samantha chewed a thumbnail.

The mother barked, 'Samantha! Take your thumb out of your mouth!'

Great, Louisa thought. Make the child even more self-conscious, why don't you? 'You've got a lovely colour, Samantha. Have you been on holiday?' she asked.

67

Samantha shook her head.

Fake tan, Louisa realized. It was First Holy Communion high season, and everywhere you looked at weekends there were bronzed mini-brides.

Samantha fingered the diamond cross at her neck.

'Mummy give that to you?' Louisa asked.

Samantha uttered some words at least. 'No, Daddy.'

The man spoke up. 'I'm Max. I'll be doing the styling.' He held out his hand.

Louisa shook it. 'That'll be an easy job. Samantha's so pretty already,' she said and winked at the little girl.

Children's skin was naturally reflective and make-up made them look dead. Louisa would have to be firm with Max.

She guided Samantha to the changing room where she could put on her dress, Max at her heels, while the mother kept talking to the wall. The child was going to need help with the dress and, while Louisa was happy to give it, she knew that most mothers liked to do it themselves. 'Excuse me, for a moment,' she said to Samantha and strode over to the mother. 'Mrs Dillon?' she said, putting out her hand.

The mother cut the phone conversation. 'Sorry about that,' she said. 'Don't you sometimes wish that people could cope without you? The sky's hardly going to fall in –' Her mobile rang again and she answered, 'Eileen Dillon, Dillon Investments.'

Louisa turned away to see Max rushing towards her. 'She doesn't want me dressing her and it's my job!' he complained.

'I have a daughter myself, Max,' she said. 'Don't worry. I'll handle it.' She went to the dressing room and knocked. 'Do you need help with your dress, Samantha?'

The door opened a crack and Louisa slipped in. Several thousand euro worth of Vera Wang was lurching about as though an animal was stuck inside it. 'Samantha?'

'I tore it! Mother will kill me! I had to diet for this dress!' The poor child was panicking.

'Stay still and I'll get you out of there.'

'I can't breathe!'

Louisa tugged the dress down until it hung the way it was supposed to. She grabbed the needle and thread she kept there for emergencies and fixed the seam where Samantha had ripped it. 'Not a word to your mother. She'll never notice.'

Samantha looked relieved, and even a little pleased as she scanned herself in the mirror. She covered a delighted little smile with her hand while Louisa pinned the veil over the child's curls, then said, 'We'll go out now and take a few pictures. I want you to think about the nicest day you've ever had.'

'Like at the dentist?' Samantha asked.

'It won't be that bad,' Louisa said.

'OK, then, I'll try. I can't remember all the catechism, though.'

'You don't need to today. This isn't the ceremony, just the picture.'

'I know, but Mummy said I was supposed to be speaking it in my mind, so I'd look all holy.'

'Do me a favour,' Louisa said. 'Try not to look too holy. But don't tell your mother I said that, OK?'

'I wouldn't worry about her. She's an atheist.'

On the set, Louisa had her work cut out trying to keep Samantha in a prayerful pose, blue eyes cast heavenwards, while Max interfered. 'Just a little lip gloss,' he pleaded. 'Maybe some powder.'

Louisa whispered, 'Lip gloss, if you insist. But no powder. The poor child's skin will end up like the bride of Frankenstein's.'

'But her cheekbones need shaping!' he hissed.

'The light will do that.'

Hunkered down safely behind her Hasselblad, Louisa took refuge in the only place where she felt she had some control over the uncontrollable world. Some day Samantha would be a grown woman looking back at these pictures and Louisa wanted her to be able to say, 'I was so pretty then.'

The shoot flew by and Louisa barely had time for a glass of

water before the next client swanned in, a company CEO seeking a portrait for the firm's annual report. He mistook Louisa's attempt to put him at ease and began to flirt: 'It's a fantasy of mine to pose nude. If you're ever looking for a model . . .'

'Don't do nudes,' Louisa said. His vanity reminded her of Ben.

When the shoot was over, Louisa asked, 'Paul, would you handle the next shoot? I need a breather. I'll see you after lunch.' She couldn't get out of the studio fast enough.

7

In her old waxed jacket, with a mizzle of rain beading on her face, Louisa marched down Dun Laoghaire pier, leaving her car parked on the seafront road. The pier jutted for a mile into the harbour like a beckoning finger. One mile out, another mile back, with only the steady beat of her own footsteps to keep her company. Just the thing to clear her head.

The pier was always busy with walkers, mostly women and retired men at this time of day. While men tended to walk alone, the women were more likely to be in pairs, leaving snippets of conversation to drift on the wind.

'She says she didn't know.'

'She must have known.'

'I said nothing.'

We know what we want to know, Louisa thought.

The day was mild enough for a few mothers to be out with babies in pushchairs. That was me once, Louisa recalled. Her days had been taken up with feeds, naps and bed-time baths. When the midwife had put newborn Elvie into her arms, Louisa marvelled that something so beautiful could have come from her. She had been amazed by Elvie's natural acceptance of her as her mother, suckling within minutes of her arrival. It was the first and only time in her life that Louisa's body had been in tune with the love she felt.

Stop thinking, Louisa told herself. Just walk. One foot in front of the other. She watched the yachts, lined up like toys in the harbour, saw the ferry arriving back from Wales trailing a white super-wave that cut the bay in two.

Cut in two – that's how I should be feeling at the prospect

of getting divorced, she thought. But how can I grieve for a split that happened long ago?

Before Ben, she had been a student, putting herself through university on academic handouts, student loans and waitressing jobs. Louisa had protected herself from the harm love caused by experiencing it through her camera, framing and refocusing until the picture became her own. Any man she met seemed to have his own inner viewfinder, determined to see what he wanted to see in her and she had learned to hide behind it. By watching herself, as they watched her, she could stay safe. She was photographer and photographed.

She had met only one man – Blyss – whose cynicism matched her own, a married lawyer with rich brown skin that smelt of the forest floor. He was charming yet impersonal, sensual yet cold. He wouldn't hurt her, she knew, because he wouldn't ask her to expose her heart. With him she could be anyone she wanted to be, and he felt the same. Role-play released him from his responsibilities and released her from having to feel. Like Louisa, he got off on watching himself – in mirrors, pictures, Louisa's eyes. And he was generous, as long as she handed over the negatives.

They only spoke of each other in the third person.

'What's the bitch whore doing now?'

'She's going down on him and then she wants him to come all over her face.'

'She's a bad girl. He won't give her what she wants until she –'

'Fuck off.'

It was silly, in retrospect, like viewing stills from the worst porn film ever made. Yet beneath their fragile bravado, Louisa and Blyss were making the only connection that they were capable of. When he wanted to divorce his wife and marry her, she cut him off. She'd had higher expectations of marriage – even though she hadn't been quite sure what these were.

As Louisa walked the pier, the old feelings bubbled up: I

want him to fill me up until I explode. I want him to punish me like I deserve to be punished. I want him to make me feel something. Anything at all.

That is what Louisa felt.

This is the sexual liberation my mother told me about.

That is how she justified it.

Sex is insignificant. I can be like a man. Take pleasure where I find it, like Amanda taught me. Taking control of sex means taking control of life.

So why had she yielded control to Ben? Sought the happy ending even though she knew that endings were never happy? Louisa learned at her mother's knee that it was stupid to want true love, yet she seemed programmed to want it anyway.

Stop it, Louisa! she warned herself again. One foot in front of the other. Nearly at the end of the pier now.

'Louisa!' The voice came out of nowhere. 'Louisa?'

She turned. A good-looking young man in an anorak and an ethnic cap was looking at her as though he had just discovered that the woman he had stopped wasn't who he'd thought she was. He smiled in a friendly, non-committal way and Louisa smiled back. She knew him, but how? A past client? One of the children's teachers? The man pulled off his cap.

'Gill? I don't believe it. You're only just back, aren't you?'

'Yesterday,' he said. 'I'm sorry, you were in another world. I probably shouldn't have stopped you. I just wanted to say "hi".'

'Hi,' Louisa said. Go on, Louisa. Be friendly – give him a little hug. This is Becca's brother, not a stalker. 'It's really nice to see you!' Louisa said, holding out her hands, which Gill took. 'You've changed – I didn't recognize you at first. You're so . . . so . . .'

'Please don't tell me I look all grown-up. That's what Becca said.'

Louisa had just stopped herself short of saying exactly that and felt bound to correct Becca's *faux pas*. 'It hadn't occurred to me!' In fact, Gill was the same, but different – like young men who have spent time in the army.

Having stopped her, he now seemed to have nothing to say. They stood looking at the sea, until Gill said, 'OK, if I walk with you?'

'Sure.'

They chose a good pace, matching stride to stride. 'So, what have you been up to?' Louisa asked.

'Trying to adjust. Every time I come back to Dublin, things have changed so much I hardly recognize it. Everybody's living at hyper-speed.'

'I suppose life in Zimbabwe is slower?' Louisa said, trying to connect with him.

'*Slow?* If you call having your home torn apart by government troops slow, then it's slow. Yeah, dying is slow. At least, it never comes fast enough.' Now he reminded her of the idealistic teenage Gill, always knowing better than his elders. Instinctively, she tried to mollify him, 'What you've been doing out there is amazing. Very few people would put their lives on the line as you have.'

'I suppose a little bleeding-heart concern isn't so bad as long as people keep writing cheques,' he said, watching a raucous flock of seagulls harass an incoming fishing-boat.

Really, he was impossible. 'Maybe you're the lucky one, being able to do something about your ideals. Real-life may seem cushy back in Dublin, but it's still real life.'

'Right. Whatever you're having yourself,' he said, with the offhand arrogance she knew from Becca.

The anger she'd been walking to avoid ran full-steam across her good intentions. 'Gill, if you plan to start a new phase in your life here in Dublin I suggest you knock that chip off your shoulder.'

Gill laughed at that. 'That's what Becca said.'

'She adores you,' Louisa said. 'She was so happy that you were coming home. I know she wants things to work out this time, so whatever your views of the rest of the Western military-industrial conspiracy, go easy on her.'

'You want to go for a coffee?'

He must be lonely, Louisa thought. But so was she, so she smiled and said, 'If you don't mind associating with a cheque-writer, why not?'

Unaccountably, she found herself wishing that she was wearing lipstick.

Half an hour later they were chatting like old friends. It helped that they had Becca in common, but it seemed more that Gill had needed to talk to anyone who would listen. Louisa could have watched him talk all afternoon but told herself she was doing Becca a service by helping Gill through the debriefing process. She listened attentively to his descriptions of suffering and cruelty that she hoped she and her children would never experience. She wondered if Gill had had a girl-friend out there.

It was hormones, she reckoned – divorce hormones. Now that she was free, her dormant libido was pleading to be allowed out to play. She certainly couldn't ask the girlfriend question. She didn't want Gill to think she was interested in him, even though her interest was purely maternal, and, in any case, he was talking now about the order of nuns he'd been working with. She wondered, did some nuns break their vows and have sex? If priests did, nuns could too. She imagined Gill with a nun, night having fallen outside their primitive mud hut, the interior lit by candles . . .

'So what do you think?' Gill asked.

What did she think about what? Her mind went blank. She's heard none of what he's been saying. 'Run it by me once more, I want to make sure I give you a considered answer. And thanks for asking me. I'm flattered you would think so much of my opinion – an expert, like you.' Please, give me a clue, she begged the froth at the bottom of her cup.

Gill was mystified. 'That's kind of a long answer.'

Louisa decided to be straight. 'I'm sorry. I was so moved by your descriptions of life in Zimbabwe that my mind went off-track to what it must be like to be one of those poor Aids mothers.'

'Right so.' He stood up, and for a moment she feared he was going to storm off in a huff, but he said, 'I was only asking if you'd like another coffee? I'm going to have one. Maybe a slice of cake too.'

Louisa sat up straighter. 'Oh! No thank you. But you go ahead.'

Louisa arrived back at her studio refreshed, just in time for the afternoon booking with the engaged couple.

'You're looking better,' Paul said. 'The air did you good.'

'Sometimes that's all it takes,' she said.

'Come here,' he said.

'Hmm?'

He was leaning forward, looking at her mouth very closely. 'You've got chocolate on your chin.'

'Oh – sorry.' She licked a finger and tried to wipe away the dab of cake Gill had insisted she share.

'Don't apologize to me. Do you want to take over? The blissfully happy couple are in the changing room. I could use some time in the darkroom, if you don't mind.'

'Go ahead. In the changing room, huh? Checking their hair, I suppose. Maybe if I leave them alone for a few minutes, I'll get them with a post-coital glow.'

'You sure it was only chocolate and fresh air?'

Louisa felt almost bubbly. Two hours of undivided attention from a man had transformed her view of the world – which was pathetic, she knew, but thrilling. When the engaged couple emerged in their weathered jeans and well-fitted white shirts, Louisa felt a buzz of excitement. She knew she would do them justice. She closed her eyes for a moment. Sometimes she thought of her camera as a time-machine, pulling together her subjects' past, present and future. She could see the loving young couple moving from passion to politeness to truce.

In this portrait, though, they would always be young and in love, no matter what happened afterwards. In a few decades' time, they could look back at how passionate they had been.

That night, when she was ready for bed, Louisa went downstairs to lock the front door, shoving it with her shoulder until the lock caught. She glanced at the holy water dish, which she had long ago reattached to the wall, out of respect for Ben's mother. She was tired.

Upstairs, Elvie was sitting on Louisa's bed. 'What's this, Mum?'

Ben's box had been sitting unopened at the bedside. 'A present,' Louisa said.

'Who from?' Elvie demanded

'A . . . friend,' Louisa said.

'Aren't you gonna open it?'

'You open it,' Louisa said, knowing it would give her daughter pleasure to carefully untie the silver ribbon.

Elvie took her time, then wrapped the ribbon around her wrist like a bracelet and gave the box a little shake. 'It rattles,' she said. 'What do you think it is?'

'A snake?'

'Very funny.' Elvie lifted the lid and drew out a gold necklace, an elegant design of sparrows in flight, arranged tail to wing.

My little paparazza.

'Aah,' Elvie held the necklace up high, almost as if waiting for the birds to take off.

He chose it instinctively, without a second thought, not knowing what his faithlessness has done to me, she thought. A man who can choose the perfect gift while caring so little is dangerous. He didn't love me, only the role I played.

Louisa fastened the necklace round Elvie's neck. 'Keep it safe for me, OK?'

Elvie touched the gold against her skin. 'But it's yours, Mum.'

'Think of me when you wear it.'

Elvie put her arms round Louisa neck and held her. 'I love you, Mum.'

'Me too,' Louisa said. And thank you, Ben. You bastard.

8

Louisa was taking an unhealthy interest in shoes – stilettos, kitten heels, boots, sandals. She tried on pair after pair, amazed at how feminine her feet appeared now that they'd been liberated from the sensible flats, trainers and cowboy boots she always wore with her jeans.

Standing in a shoe shop named Soul with her jeans rolled up to her knees, Louisa considered a pair of cream leather slingbacks with a killer heel that made her feel leggy, confident, in control. I could clip along without a bother in these, she thought. Next she tried walking in high-heeled, red sandals. The only time she'd be able to wear these was flat on her back. 'That's the point,' the shoes seemed to say. 'And how will you ever know if you haven't got me in your wardrobe, just in case?'

She took them off, then tried on tarty black sandals masquerading as boots with thongs that criss-crossed all the way up her calf. *With a little black dress . . . What am I thinking? I'll never wear any of these. These are seduction shoes.* In the mirror, she turned her legs this way and that. The effect of having the pressure of her body focused on her toes, the lengthening of her Achilles tendon, the adjustment in her lower back as she worked her stomach muscles to stand up straight in the shoes. She felt like she was waking up to how her body might feel if . . .

If . . . she walked about the shop, wondering if she could manage the distance from a taxi into a restaurant in the shoes. Possibly. The sales assistant stood patiently by. Sod it, Louisa thought, rolling down her jeans and putting the cream leather sandals into their box.

The sales assistant looked at her expectantly. Louisa tried to be offhand. 'I haven't bought shoes in ages. I'll take all three pairs.'

It was the day of her first appointment with the family lawyer and she had decided to take time off and go shopping in town. She'd started with a cut and highlights at the hairdresser's, then found herself detained in a chic little lingerie shop, where she bought matching bras and panties in six candy colours. It wasn't until Brown Thomas, though, that Louisa wondered if she was right in the head. A new wardrobe seemed imperative. She wanted to become unrecognizable, even to herself.

But for whom was she dressing? She'd flirted a little with Gill, but he was too young. He'd hardly be interested in her, and, even if he was, he was too much the sensitive, new man type when she wanted a certain degree of experience. No heart to break would be ideal. She would play without paying.

Her arms ached with dresses – a classic jersey wraparound that made her figure look almost girlish, a summery white linen top and skirt, a cream linen suit (hence the cream leather shoes) and an outrageous black sleeveless frock with a glittering diamante empire waist and a plunging neckline.

I'm nurturing my self-esteem, she told herself, as the credit-card machine demanded her pin number. I'm doing this for myself, no-one else. *I'm spending an obscene amount of money.*

Louisa had forgotten how to dress like a woman. It was so much less hurtful not to care. She thought of the effort she had once made on the nights when Ben was home, with make-up and red lingerie Ben had bought her, even though it didn't fit. Becoming desirable for Ben had been like a project – Louisa trying to cajole him into loving her again and Ben half-hoping it might work.

Wife. She hated the word. *I will never be a wife again.*

On the way back to her car, it occurred to her that she would feel a lot more confident dealing with the family lawyer if she was wearing the cream linen suit. And the shoes.

But where would she change? And if she was going to all that trouble, shouldn't she be meeting someone for lunch?

She punched speed-dial. 'Becca, have lunch with me.'

'I'm all yours, babe.'

'I'll meet you at your office. I want to change.'

Twenty minutes later, Louisa had pulled her car into one of the spaces beneath the building where Becca had recently opened new offices. 'Recent' meant about three years previously and Louisa couldn't believe it had taken her so long to call in. She went through the bags, took out the new cream silk undies, the new cream suit, the new cream shoes, the new silk stockings and a packet of leg-wax strips she'd picked up in the chemist, then headed up in the lift to Becca's offices.

The receptionist gave her jeans and corduroy jacket the once over. 'May I help you?'

'Becca Lynley's expecting me.'

'Have a seat.'

Louisa sat down on a turquoise leather sofa to wait, straight across from a businessman who looked like he was waiting to be shot. Almost immediately, Becca appeared. 'Louisa,' she said primly. 'Please come in.'

Becca's corner office, with floor-to-ceiling windows, over-looked the new Dublin, where massive cranes loomed over the cityscape. 'Remember that little place you started out in? A couple of prefabs in an office park?' she said.

'How could I forget? We used to put buckets out when it rained and hide them when clients arrived. You've never seen the new studio, have you?'

Becca brought Louisa into a small, windowless conference room with walls of tan leather. Then she pressed a keypad so that one wall parted to reveal a wide window with a view of what looked like a nightly news programme studio. 'It's just like the real thing,' Becca said. 'Gets clients used to the idea.' At the presenter's desk, a young woman sat grilling an interviewee while another woman watched. 'We can hear them as well, if you want, but they can't see us. I like to keep an eye on how everyone's doing.'

She pressed a button and the interviewer's voice, berating her subject, came into the room.

Louisa was shocked. 'People pay you to rip them apart?'

'I do the same thing as you do Louisa. I observe critically, then repackage.'

'But I'm a photographer. I don't psychoanalyse people. I leave them as they are.'

Becca shrugged. 'In the real world, the media are hardly so sympathetic. I've yet to find a client who didn't believe he or she deserved to be deconstructed and put back together again. Anyway, you can pay all kinds of people to tear you apart – psychotherapists, life coaches, marriage counsellors. Rarely is it useful. It exposes people even more. I teach people how to hide themselves behind a professional, convincing face. Anyway, you said you wanted to change. I'll show you to my dressing room. You can take a shower if you want, but don't mess up your new hair. It takes years off you like that.'

The dressing room was equipped with toilet facilities and a white velvet sofa. 'For my power-naps,' Becca explained. 'I'll leave you to it.'

Louisa took her new clothes out of the bags and laid them on a chair, then undressed quickly, balled up her jeans and shirt with the serviceable Marks & Spencer's underwear and stuffed them into the bin.

Her French silk lingerie felt as delicious as it looked and when she saw herself in the mirror, she couldn't help but stand a little straighter. *Maybe if I'd done this before my marriage would have worked out . . .*

Next she got out the wax and had a go at her shins. 'Shite!' she screamed.

Becca poked her head in. 'What's going on?'

Louisa held up the wax. 'Self-torture.'

Becca laughed. 'What are you like? People usually do that

before they come in.' Becca had left behind her professional self in the observation room. 'Let me do that. It hurts more when you do it yourself.'

On her knees, Becca propped Louisa's leg up on another chair and went to work.

'Bloody hell. Becca, you're ruthless!'

Becca tore off another swathe of winter's growth.

'Ouch!'

'It'll be over in a minute. Nice undies, by the way.'

'Thanks.'

When she was finished, Becca ran a hand down each of Louisa's legs. 'Smooth as a baby's,' she said huskily.

Louisa slapped her hand. 'Away, hussy. Take a call while I finish getting dressed. I want to surprise you.'

Ten minutes later, dressed in her cream suit, shoes and silk stockings, Louisa felt like a lady who lunched. She and Becca settled themselves at a local French place, which just happened to have three Michelin stars. They ordered mineral water, since Louisa wanted to remain clear-headed for her appointment later, and studied the menu. Something was on Becca's mind, which, Louisa knew, was a far deeper place than Becca usually let on. Becca was a woman who deserved to be completely loved – her strong character had a vulnerable side that only those closest to her were allowed to see. Becca needed a woman who could stand up to her, but be gentle too. Becca wasn't the type to lose her heart easily, but when she did it was so total that Louisa found it frightening – closer to obsession than attraction.

Becca's eyes seemed to be on the menu and her thoughts far away. 'Stop looking at me funny,' she said suddenly.

'I wasn't.'

'You were. Scallops or lobster?'

'Both?'

'That's my girl.' Becca turned to the waiter, who had appeared at her side as if he was psychic. 'Lobster and scallops for two. And a bottle of Chablis.'

The waiter inclined his head towards the menu with a quizzical expression, but Becca said, 'Stuff the menu. Tell Chef that Becca Lynley asked for scallops and lobster. Whatever he serves up will be fine.' She looked up at Louisa. 'I hate pretentious French menus. They never mean what you think they do.'

Becca always threw her weight around when she was worried. Louisa sipped her water thoughtfully. 'Becca, what's wrong?'

Becca gave her a searching look.

'You're miles away,' Louisa added.

'I'm sorry. I've developed an obsession that won't go away. I'm embarrassed to talk about it, although I shouldn't be.'

'You're in love,' Louisa said.

Becca gave her a cynical look. 'No, unfortunately. It's worse than that. I want to have a baby before it's too late.'

Poor Becca, Louisa almost said, but stopped herself in time. 'That's not embarrassing. It's natural. And you'll have a baby, if that's what you want.'

The waiter brought the wine and Louisa accepted some, despite her previous resolve. This was going to be a glass-of-Chablis conversation, especially with Becca in victim-mode – a side she let no-one but Louisa see.

'To the future,' Louisa said.

Becca was inscrutable. 'Easy for you to say. First, I need a partner who also wants a baby. Second, I need to find a way of getting pregnant – and don't go suggesting I have a one-night stand with a member of the opposite sex. That was Gill's valuable idea.'

'Sweetie, a relationship and a baby don't happen overnight, even for a man and a woman. Meet somebody, then consider donor insemination or adoption or IVF – there are plenty of solutions.'

Becca's hand was shaking as she lifted her wine glass. 'You think I decided this only yesterday? It's been on my mind for ages. But it's a head wreck knowing that even if I carry the baby

84

myself, the baby's father will be a stranger. I don't believe in buying sperm off the Internet. It's so cold.'

'I know. But think of the advantages – a genetic profile, for instance.'

'What am I to tell the child?'

'You're jumping the gun, big-time. Fall in love first. Isn't there anybody at all you're interested in?'

'Maybe. We'll have a proper night out soon, now that you're on the prowl. I'll fix it so we bump into her. You can tell me what you think.'

'My opinion is hardly important,' Louisa said.

'It is to me. Oh, God. I just want to scream! And the mood I'm in, Gill's driving me crazy. The sooner he finds a purpose in life the better.'

'He's only been home a week! And he hasn't a notion what you're going through.'

'He's a man.'

'I noticed.'

'But not an ordinary one.'

The thought of his quizzical face as they talked in the coffee shop made Louisa smile.

'I can't explain it, Lou,' Becca went on. 'Gill and I just hit each other the wrong way.'

'He's really fond of you and glad you're there for him.'

Becca gave Louisa a sly look over her wine. 'He told me you two met.'

A second waiter appeared with a basket of home-baked bread. Becca was about to wave him away, then asked Louisa, 'What's the latest diet fad? Can we eat bread again, or what?'

'We eat whatever we please. Whoever wants me, can take me as I am.'

'Well said.' She ran a professional eye over Louisa's outfit. 'You're gagging for it, aren't you?'

'I thought this was rather well-tailored and tasteful.'

'It would be if you were wearing a blouse under it.'

'Forgot to buy one.'

'Uh-huh . . .'

They sat back as the waiter delivered the first course, four perfect scallops, each crisp on the outside and lusciously pale pink within.

'If you found out you had only six months to live, what would you do?' Becca asked, suddenly.

Louisa put down her fork. 'I'd spend every day like it was my last with my children, and at night have the best sex ever.'

'See? Children again.'

'If I didn't have children, I'd have the best sex ever. For six months straight.'

'I have to be in love,' Becca said.

'Love is definitely not what I want. Love makes you crazy. For a few seconds of euphoria, you spend months of anguish knowing where it's all going to end. I'd like to have sex with a man I like, no strings attached, once or twice a week, no expectations.'

'That's impossible.' She was staring over Louisa's shoulder. 'Don't turn around,' Becca said.

'OK, why not?'

'Take another sip of wine,' Becca ordered.

Louisa obeyed.

'Ben is behind you. They're coming this way and I want you to remain serene. We're going to be friendly and polite. Let me do the talking.'

Becca stood up graciously. 'Ben, darling,' she said, holding out a hand to avoid the usual air-kiss. Now Louisa turned. Ben was dressed like an MTV presenter and had an impossibly leggy young blonde at his side. Louisa couldn't keep her eyes off his shirt, which appeared to have had tiny holes burned into it.

'And who is this gorgeous little thing?' Becca asked.

'Becca, I'd like you to meet Lucy Carling. Lucy, this is Becca Lynley. And this is . . . ?' Ben gazed helplessly at Louisa and swept back his hair with his free hand.

86

Louisa took Lucy's hand. 'I'm Louisa Maguire. Ben's wife.' Then turned to Ben, 'This is rich, you dining out in splendour. I hope you're not using my credit card again. And if not – well, I'm glad to see you're flush . . . unless Lucy is paying.' Louisa beamed at Lucy, whose baby-doll crinoline appeared to have been purchased in Mothercare.

Ben wasn't given to stuttering, but he did then. 'You're – looking – well, Lou.'

'Splitting up is the best thing we ever did. But I'm still expecting that call from you! The children are getting impatient.'

Ben avoided Lucy's eyes by staring at his feet, which, Louisa noticed, were shod in high-tech runners more suited to a Brooklyn homeboy than a forty-seven-year-old Irishman. 'Tell them I'll see them soon.'

Clearly Lucy was desperate to escape: she directed a look of unconcealed panic at Ben.

'We won't keep you from your lunch,' Ben said and the pair walked away.

'Well played,' Becca said.

Louisa sat down and sighed with satisfaction. 'I do hope she likes children.'

Having faced Ben in public, Louisa was undaunted by the prospect of meeting with the solicitor. She saw O'Brien first to discuss the business partnership contract, and enjoyed the admiration in his eyes as she crossed her stockinged legs demurely. Later, he brought her down the hall to a meeting room where Stella Pearson was waiting. 'Louisa, good to meet you,' she said, and shook Louisa's hand. A row of gold bracelets on one of Stella's tanned wrists tinkled. 'Do sit down. Will you have coffee or tea?' she asked, and selected a fresh notepad from a pile on the table.

'Coffee, please.'

Stella picked up the phone and asked her secretary to bring it. Louisa's heart was in her mouth. The coffee, the notepad, the sympathetic expression on Stella's face and the box of tissues close at hand, were telling her that this interview was going to be more difficult than she had anticipated.

9

Louisa had never lost the joy of seeing a picture emerge from the white contact sheet in the developing tray. The effect of chemicals on paper, bringing forth the play of light that she had captured with her Hasselblad days earlier, was magical — only light and shadow blending to create a human face. To see a moment in time that had been held on film, re-emerge in ghostly form on paper at the moment of her choosing, never failed to mesmerize her.

Perhaps it was because people weren't solid objects to a photographer. They were no more than light reflecting off skin, hair and clothing in one millisecond of time. Once captured, this recording of light was forever static — not in flux as life was. So pictures were always of the past, never the future. Yet, as she developed the portrait of a newly married couple, she conspired with light to create in their faces the future they believed in — even if it was just an illusion. The picture would last, outlive the marriage perhaps, remain hidden away to be found by someone else and until everyone who loved the couple enough to want a picture had died. And then, the picture would be worthless.

If she could peer through the viewfinder for a reliable portrait of her own future, she was afraid of what she might see. What scared her most was the prospect of never having the time to explore her art, to create photographs that might be worth something to people who didn't know the subjects. Photographs that were worthy in themselves.

Her Aunt Alice, whom she barely knew, was a superb painter. Her images were abstract, sensual and unsettling — not reassuring, as Louisa's were. If Alice knew what Louisa was doing she'd pour scorn on it.

Best to remain on separate continents, Louisa thought.

She was unusually meditative in her darkroom that morning. It was a refuge where no-one could get to her until she decided to turn on the lights.

Paul knocked on the darkroom door. 'Mary's here!'

An hour had passed without Louisa realizing it. Mary had phoned her that morning to say there was something they needed to talk about. In all the time she had known Mary — years measured in her children's ages — this was the first time ever that she had formally requested a chat. Louisa had been dying to tell her about her meeting with Stella Pearson, but, as soon as she heard the anxiety in Mary's voice, she knew that would have to wait.

She washed her hands and emerged, blinking, into the brightness of the studio. Mary was a dark shape sitting on a sofa by the window. 'Hello, sweetie,' Louisa said, bending to kiss her cheek.

Mary seemed bone-tired and her face had lost its usual calm. Her weight loss had revealed a shapely figure, but had made her face sharper. She would have to talk to her about changing her hairstyle.

Louisa held out her hand and helped her get up. 'Come on, let's go for a bowl of soup. It's that kind of day, isn't it? You'd think it was November, not June.'

Louisa took her coat down from the rack, gave it a shake and pulled it on. 'You'll close up for lunch, Paul?'

'I'll use the darkroom for a while. Bring me back a sandwich, yeah?'

'OK.'

Louisa and Mary walked silently into the rain, then down the street to a bright, modern pub that was furnished like someone's living room. They found a sofa in a corner and claimed it. Louisa helped Mary out of her coat, then took off her own and hung them on a nearby coat stand. Then she sat down again and picked up the menu. Mary would talk when she was ready.

'Two bowls of soup and a plate of bread?' Louisa said.

Mary nodded.

Louisa ordered then sat back and waited. 'Whatever it is, we'll handle it, OK?'

Mary's eyes were welling with tears. Louisa handed her a napkin.

'I don't know how to say this. It's the last thing I want to dump on you,' Mary choked.

Louisa remained as steady as Mary had always been for her. 'Are your children all right?'

'They're grand.'

Mary leaned forward with her hands bracing her knees. 'I'm just going to tell you straight. Please don't be shocked and promise me you won't say anything to anyone. My children don't know yet.'

'You can count on me, you know that. And your children will be fine.'

Mary took a deep breath and smiled. 'Here goes.'

Louisa held her breath.

'Remember, last Christmas, when the children clubbed together to give me the laptop?'

Louisa nodded.

'I started surfing the web.'

'I didn't know you did that.'

'Doesn't everybody?' Mary said. 'Please don't think I've lost my mind because I haven't. I was in a chat room with some old friends from school – they're all over the world now. And you know how small the world is especially if you're Irish. I chat with other women in my Loreto girls circle – that's what we call ourselves, after the school. We were chatting about old boyfriends. I posted a message describing Tony, and a few days later one of my friends – Sinead, in Melbourne – said that Tony was out there and had become quite successful. He'd emigrated many years ago, after he'd finished his education, then married an Australian girl but she'd died. She asked me would I like to get in touch with him, and I said, why not? So, next thing I know, there's an email from Tony and the minute I read it! – well, I don't know. You shouldn't be able to fall in love with someone all over again just by looking at words on a screen, but I did. He phoned and we talked. A lot. Every night. We still do. The bills are drastic. At this rate, I said to Tony, it would be cheaper for one of us to get on a plane and he said, "I'm sending you a ticket." So that's the story.'

So Mary was leaving her and the children to go to Australia. 'But you don't know anything about him. He could be a complete disaster,' Louisa remonstrated.

Mary looked at Louisa as though she'd anticipated this. 'Sinead's checked him out. I've got everything there is to know about him. Even his credit rating, believe it or not. Sinead, the pet, actually got on a plane to Sydney and went to meet him in the guise of having to be in town on business. She took a picture of him for me. See?' Mary handed Louisa a digital shot that she'd printed off her PC.

Tony was fit, tanned and had an open smile. About sixty, Louisa reckoned.

'He's attractive,' Louisa said. 'What does he do?'

'He's a pathologist.'

Why can't I be happy for her? 'You mean, he goes to crime scenes and cuts up bodies?'

Mary giggled shyly. When she next spoke, she sounded like a starry-eyed schoolgirl revealing her first crush. 'He's a hospital pathologist, not a forensic pathologist.'

Louisa made a heroic effort to look delighted. 'Nobody deserves this more than you, Mary. I'm so happy for you.'

'I haven't been able to sleep thinking about how I was going to break this to you,' Mary said. 'I know asking for six weeks off over the summer is a lot.'

Six weeks with the children off school! 'It's owed to you, Mary. I just hate to see you go. Milo and Elvie will be – I'm so, so, sorry. I want to be happy for you. But I'm terrible at faking things. I don't want you to go to Australia. I can't imagine living in Dalkey without you a few doors down the road. I'm a selfish bitch, but that's just tough. You, Mary, deserve all the happiness you can find and I really hope things work out with Tony.'

'Whoa, girl. I'm only going for a visit. It's just that it's such a long way and I want to travel all over Australia and even see Hong Kong. It will be the trip of a life-time for me. Even if things don't work out with Tony, I'll have an amazing experience. I can't leave my own children and emigrate just like that. I'll just go to see him and keep my sensible hat on and try to figure out if it's all too good to be true. I could meet him and find that there's no attraction anymore. At worst, I'll have a brilliant holiday.'

Please, Louisa prayed secretly, please let it be no more than that. 'When do you leave?' Louisa asked.

'In two weeks' time.'

It took Louisa the full two weeks to come to terms with Mary's bombshell. It was far worse than her marriage breaking up. Losing Mary felt, ironically, more like losing a spouse than losing Ben had. She had grown to take her so much for granted that the idea of her not being there was shattering.

'Your wife has finally flown the coop. I bet she won't be back,' Becca said, as they moved furniture in Becca's living room to make space for an antique Georgian desk she'd bought. They'd said goodbye to Mary that morning, Louisa dusting Mary with fairy glitter and Becca handing her a packet of condoms at the departure area in the airport in their vain attempts to be light-hearted. They'd cried all the way back to Becca's, where the children had remained with Gill.

'I can't believe she's done it. It's a bit crazy to be going after a lover you haven't seen in thirty-five years,' Louisa said in the car. 'What if she's disappointed? What if he's horrible to her? She'll be on the other side of the world.'

'I think it's wonderful. Say you had six months to live, isn't that what you'd do?'

'I suppose. Although I'd hate to waste my last six months on a guy who turned out to be a no-hoper. I mean, isn't it a trifle worrying that he couldn't find anyone in Australia? It's a big country.'

'Mary knows what she's doing,' Becca said. 'Everybody needs to have at least one mad adventure in their life.'

'But Mary of all people.'

They were both so unsettled that, when Becca had an impulse to start rearranging the furniture in her living room, Louisa rowed in. Now Becca leaned on the Georgian pillar desk, sweating. 'What do you say? Will we try it against that wall next to the fireplace?'

'Then we'll have to move the credenza.'

'I've been meaning to vacuum behind that thing anyway.'

'If you say so.'

This was the fourth piece they'd moved. Gill was in the kitchen with the children, baking pizzas, and the smell of yeasty dough and home-made sauce was making Louisa hungry.

The credenza was hard to shift. 'Will we ask Gill to give us a hand?' Louisa asked.

'No. He's already pissed off at me for making him move bookshelves around in the library.'

They'd managed to move the heavy sideboard a couple of feet away from the wall when Becca changed her mind. 'Let's put it back. I've got used to it here.'

'Aren't you going to vacuum behind it, then?'

Becca poked her head around the back of it to look for lost objects. 'Hang it. I can't be bothered.'

When they had put the credenza back in its place, Becca said, 'You know what these things were for, don't you?'

'Haven't a clue.'

'Tasting food for poison before it was served.'

'You're joking. It's a pity it doesn't work on men.'

'Yea, but consider that the taster was risking death. I'm going to the kitchen to get us water before we both faint.'

Louisa stretched and half-lay across the back of the sofa, which faced the fireplace. Her eyes rested on the portrait of Becca above it – a mad experiment. Becca had wanted Louisa to photograph her in a recreation of Manet's 'Olympia', but, rather than having a servant in the background delivering a bouquet, Becca wanted to be surrounded by flowers. She reclined on her side on a chaise-longue. The flowers were exaggeratedly bright colours – clashing reds with pinks and oranges with greens. In the midst of it, Becca was a porcelain goddess with red lips and platinum tresses. It was one of the few portraits Louisa had ever agreed to do in colour and then only because Becca begged her too.

'When I'm an old lady I want proof of how gorgeous I was. I was born in the wrong century. I have the body of an odalisque so I want to be depicted as one,' Becca had insisted.

Her white skin shimmered in the picture, a woman in full command of her powers. This was a woman to be worshipped.

'Something happens when women photograph other women, doesn't it?'

Louisa jumped. Gill was standing behind her, holding out a glass of iced water.

Louisa nearly dropped the slippery glass as he handed it to her, then steadied it by holding the bottom with the napkin Gill had provided.

'Thanks,' she said, then took a long, thirsty swallow.

'When men photograph women, they just see sex,' Gill said.

'Is that what you see?'

'I think that's life. I think when men look at women, camera or no camera, they see sex. When a man starts looking beyond that, you know he's really interested.'

'Really.' Louisa was intrigued.

'I'm not saying that the picture of Becca isn't sexy, although she is my sister. What I see is so much more . . . a kind of power. Power over death, perhaps?'

'Manet's Olympia was a courtesan so celebrated that she could no longer be bought. That was the general idea. A woman who doesn't need men. I'd like to do more nudes. Just for fun.' It was supposed to be fun, she realized, not just hard work. 'My photography has become too routine. I've forgotten why I started doing it in the first place – before I earned a living from it, I mean.'

Becca was back now, all business. 'Let's try the window. You'd better get back in the kitchen, Gill. Milo and Elvie are playing volleyball with the pizza dough.'

Gill hurried off, as Louisa considered the wide half-moon of space in the bay window. 'I think there would be glare, Becca. You might get headaches. And you wouldn't be able to see your laptop screen.'

'You have the wrong idea, Louisa. I'm not actually going to use the desk. I just like the idea of having it. I'm going to store my life there, you know – all those scraps you keep in shoeboxes. My scraps are better than most.'

'Why didn't you just say that in the first place?'

They hefted the desk over to the window. 'This is displacement activity. We're definitely going out tonight. If Mary can find love, we can.'

'Pizza's ready!' the children called.

Gill leaned in the doorway. 'You know, if you leave it there, you'll have to keep the curtains drawn all day long. Otherwise the sun will destroy the wood.'

'Know-it-all,' Becca muttered under her breath. 'I'm leaving it there. The sun never shines in this damned little country, anyway.'

Louisa and Gill exchanged a look, both knowing that if anyone else had imparted such useful information to Becca, she probably would have heeded it. Gill and the children went back out to the kitchen, followed by Louisa, while Becca went to her cellar for a bottle of wine. Louisa took a look around the finished room, thinking of how much she'd love to have such beautiful things herself, then went out to the kitchen.

'Please never let me help Becca move furniture again,' Louisa whispered to Gill.

He grinned. 'What? Don't you like playing dolls' house with a real house?'

'This *is* Becca's dolls' house, isn't it? It even looks like one from outside. I'd never thought of it that way.'

'You just try moving one little ornament this way or that and see what happens. The woman's compulsive.'

'Tell me about it.'

Becca came in with the wine. 'This looks cosy.'

The pizza was delicious. 'You're a fabulous cook, Gill,' Louisa said, through a slice topped with tomatoes, feta cheese and spinach. The children were eating a simpler version with tomato sauce and buckets of mozzarella.

'I enjoy it,' Gill said, cutting two more pieces for the children. 'It's the sort of thing you can do without having to think.'

'You know,' Becca said. 'There's a huge demand for good chefs. You could do a course at the culinary school and start your own restaurant.'

Louisa knew Gill's views on his sister's career advice. And Becca must have noticed the look that Louisa and Gill shared because she added, 'OK, I'll keep my mouth shut.' She turned to the children. 'How about we watch some films in the library this afternoon? We'll have ice-cream and chocolate and stuff.'

'Yeah!' the children cheered.

When they'd eaten as much pizza as they could, Louisa and Gill stayed behind in the kitchen to tidy up. 'If I don't leave this place looking like the centrefold of an interiors magazine my sister will freak,' Gill said.

'She's lived on her own for a long time, so she's set in her ways, that's all,' Louisa answered. She was sweeping flour off the floor. 'We'd better give this a mop.'

'See what I mean? She's got to you, too.'

'If you don't want me to help . . .' Louisa put away the broom and headed for the door, just to see how he'd react.

'Please stay!' Gill said. 'I mean, I could use some help.'

'I'll load the dishwasher then,' Louisa said. She began by scraping and piling plates, while Gill scrubbed pots and pans at the sink.

'Will you have coffee?' he asked.

'Love some.'

Gill fiddled with Becca's state-of-the-art Italian coffee machine. His sinewy forearms were nicely hairy, she thought. And she liked a man with his sleeves rolled up.

'This bloody machine,' Gill said. 'You need a degree in engineering to operate it. I can't see Becca in Africa, lugging her own water and sleeping on a dirt floor.'

'You need to be patient with us mortals,' Louisa reproved him. 'Not everyone has your courage — or sisters to bankroll them while they're sorting themselves out.'

Gill bridled at her remark. 'Sort myself out? What does that mean? Become a capitalist like my sister, re-branding people like they're products? Or maybe you think I should re-brand myself. Go a bit more upmarket. Sure, why not? Let's get a focus group together and see what they say. Gill Lynley, aged twenty-seven, unemployed waster. Thanks a lot.'

'Why *have* you got a chip on your shoulder?'

'I haven't.'

'You have.' She stared him down. At least he didn't leave the room like most men did during an argument.

'I'm just feeling . . . a bit lost. Like an alien on Planet Celtic Tiger. I went out with some mates from college last night. All they talked about was cars, property, holidays and pulling birds — not a phrase I like. The women sort of interview you — what car have you got, do you own your flat, how many other flats do you own, where were you on holiday last, who are your parents. I felt like a prize bull. I am not a good prospect, apparently.'

Louisa sensed there was a bit more to it than that. 'Any particular girl give you the cold shoulder? Or was it just every girl in the pub?'

Gill's eyes darkened and Louisa could see him pulling the shutters down. He turned back to the coffee machine and managed to get two cups of espresso out of it. He handed Louisa hers, then drank his while leaning against the counter and glumly staring at a fridge magnet that said, 'I am a goddess'.

'Gill, listen. Adjusting back to whatever this life is that we call normal can't be easy. We all grow away from our friends, I suppose. And young women don't appreciate experience these days. You'll meet like minds, I'm sure. It just won't happen overnight. As soon as you've got your teeth into something new, you'll find a new circle of friends.'

Judging by his expression, Gill didn't think much of this. 'Dublin has changed so much, I don't know if I can stomach it. It's become a city of envy.'

'Don't leave us just yet. Doing another geographic isn't going to solve the problem. You take yourself with you – believe me, I know.'

Gill smiled at this. 'I wanted to ask you a favour.'

'Go ahead,' Louisa answered.

'I did a lot of photography in Africa, some of it digital, but the pictures I care about are analogue. Black and white. I've got rolls and rolls to develop. Can I borrow your darkroom?'

Louisa's immediate instinct was to find a way to put him off. 'Do you know how to use one? Mine's got a bit more techy since you saw it last. Paul's a sucker for fancy equipment.'

'All I know is what you showed me last time I was back . . . and . . . if it's a hassle –'

Becca was her best friend and Gill, who was great with the children, was fast becoming part of her life too. He had promised to babysit that evening while she and Becca went out for a girly night, which was generous of him. Elvie and Milo were going to sleep in one of Becca's guest bedrooms, which had a four-poster bed, an en-suite bathroom and satellite TV. And they'd taken to Gill as they hadn't to anyone in a long time. Gill must have been great with children in Africa, she thought. He had a way of treating them as equals while still gaining their respect.

'It's not a hassle,' Louisa replied. 'As long as you don't mind keeping it to the occasional evening and weekend. Paul and I will bring you up to speed. He's better at explaining things, though. I learned everything I know by trial and error but he's actually got a degree in photography.'

Gill dipped a sugar lump into his coffee. 'You're funny, the way you put yourself down. I remember when you were with Ben. In Zimbabwe the women always sit on the floor and the man gets the only chair in the room. You were like that, except it wasn't the chair that Ben had. It was your entire life.'

Louisa was beginning to feel sorry she'd said 'yes' to the darkroom privileges. 'Lecturing me isn't going to change the past.'

'I'm sorry. I'm just glad that you're over him. You look younger than when I saw you last. You were always a looker, but now you own yourself.'

He thought she was a looker. Hmm.

'Ben Maguire has no idea what he's lost,' Gill added.

'Thanks,' Louisa said. 'All ego-boosting gratefully accepted. Becca's paying you to say these things, I presume? Will I bring some coffee into her?'

She had to get out of there. He was annoying, full of himself and too gorgeous for words. He'd find a young idealistic female his own age. She'd put manners on him soon enough.

10

'Are you sure I'm not mutton dressed as lamb?' Louisa asked as she stretched her legs out of the taxi, stepped across a streaming gutter, then wobbled forwards on her new black stilettos with the leather straps that criss-crossed from ankle to knee.

'Would you rather be lamb dressed as mutton?' Becca asked.

A doorman built like an oil-tanker placed a practised arm beneath her elbow. 'Steady miss, watch the kerb,' he said.

Becca had fallen so hard for Louisa's new black cocktail dress that Louisa had insisted she wear it. She had decided she felt more comfortable in one of Becca's racier suits – a jacket with a neckline so wide it was nearly off the shoulder and a waist that laced up like a corset. It kind of went with the shoes – hard to remove, Louisa thought wickedly. The skirt fitted snugly, then turned up at the hem like an overturned nasturtium. Flirty and just the right length for the knee-crossing.

Gill had whistled when he saw them gussied up and ready to take on the town. 'Dangerous women,' he commented. 'I'll stick to playing Monopoly with the kids and an early night.'

Louisa teetered along beside Becca through the hotel lobby. They were going to a party for some self-help guru whom Becca was involved with. 'If the party's a write-off we can have fun in the bar. It's the best bar in Dublin – the best heterosexual bar, I mean.'

'You're so kind to make allowances for the sexually challenged,' Louisa said.

As they walked into the lobby of the Four Seasons, Louisa could feel herself being appraised by men and women, who were circling each other like punters sizing up horses at the races. The place was heaving with barristers, money-types and society girls. The men looked mostly married, in clothes that younger single ones wouldn't have been seen dead in.

'Holy g-strings,' Louisa said to Becca, under her breath. 'I had no idea.'

'Welcome to the world,' Becca said. 'Deep breaths now. You're not having a panic attack on my watch.'

They took the lift upstairs to the suite where the party was already in full swing. Becca had insisted on taking their time getting dressed and arriving late.

They paused at the double entrance doors, where a waiter held out a silver tray laden with glasses of champagne. When they had each taken one, Becca raised her glass to Louisa in a toast.

'You are now officially on the market,' Becca said.

We'll see, Louisa thought, wishing she'd taken a practice run in her dominatrix stilettos as she followed Becca into the fray.

'Steady, love.' A rugby-built barrister-type grabbed Louisa's arm possessively. 'Haven't we met?'

Becca rescued her. 'Sorry, Donal, Ms Maguire has people to meet.'

Louisa let her friend pull her away. 'Ms Maguire?'

'You're top totty, babe. Re-*spect*. I'm not letting you talk to the first man who hits on you.'

'I want to go home,' Louisa muttered.

She dawdled uncomfortably every time Becca paused to air-kiss someone and introduce Louisa, who stuck to a traditional, 'How do you do?'

The self-help guru turned out to be a rather threatening-looking ex-IRA political prisoner who, Becca said, was set to make billions teaching middle-class businessmen how to apply terrorist-negotiation skills in boardroom battles. Fresh from a TV appearance, his face was an unsettling shade of orange. Becca informed him that he'd blown the interview, which she'd had on in the background while she and Louisa had been dressing.

'You were way too nice-nice,' Becca said. 'When we launch you in the States you're going to have to work a little harder at frightening people. Come in first thing Monday and we'll look at the tape.'

Leaving the hard man deflated, Becca marshalled Louisa through the crush to an oasis marked 'reserved'. She picked up the sign and tucked it into her bag. 'My exclusive seating area may be reserved, but I'm not,' she said. 'And you're definitely not.'

Louisa caught herself staring at a tiny girl-woman wearing torn, low-slung jeans and a tassled scarf-thing as a bra. She seemed totally out of place. The girl gave Louisa a 'What-are-you-staring-at?' look and Louisa pulled her eyes away. It was a bad habit she'd had since childhood, staring at people's faces as though she herself were invisible. She was way too used to hiding behind a camera, definitely.

'I feel awkward without a camera to protect me,' Louisa said. 'I've got no reason to be here without it.'

'Relax, will you? This is normal life, Louisa. Get used to it.'

It was only then that Louisa realized how effectively she had boxed herself in to a safe, predictable sphere, with Mary and Becca as her touchstones. Even though Becca had spent years trying to get her to go out more, Louisa had always made excuses involving the children. The friendship had flourished in a domestic bubble where there were no outsiders to judge it.

Sitting on the sofa with Becca, she felt exposed.

'Becca!' called a stunning woman in an impossibly tight Gucci dress. 'I really need to sit down. If one more person asks me whether to buy or sell shares in A, B or C – I won't even mention the companies they're talking about – I'll freak. Who's this?'

'Daphne, meet Louisa.'

'How do you do?' Louisa offered her hand.

Daphne raised an eyebrow. 'Just fine. I could use a little something to perk me up, though.'

'Champagne?' Becca asked.

'Not that, silly. I'm on a diet. Listen, I'm just going to check out the scene downstairs and if that's as dull as this is, I'm going over to Plain Jane's. See you there maybe.'

'She talks a good line, but never trust her with your money,' Becca whispered.

People came and went, exchanging gossip and banter with Becca. The occasional man gave Louisa the once-over, but there wasn't one she could actually talk to.

'So you're Becca's secret friend,' a woman purred into Louisa's ear from behind the sofa.

Louisa turned to find a pair of plump red lips near her own and sharp eyes assessing her. 'And you are?' What part of her body didn't the woman have pierced?

'Wouldn't you like to know. Tell Becca I'll text her later. Nice suit, by the way.'

Becca hadn't seen. 'These are all media types,' she apologized. 'Let's go down to the bar and find you a real man.'

'Who was that piercing fetishist?' Louisa asked.

'The one I ignored?'

Louisa nodded.

'That was her. The woman I told you about. So, what do you think?'

'I think she's scary.' Milo and Elvie would think so too. She couldn't imagine her fitting in to their lives. 'But if you fancy her . . .'

'She's history.' The crowd parted as Becca brought Louisa back into the lift, where she relaxed as the doors hushed closed. Becca pushed the button for the ground floor, then leaned forward and lifted Louisa's chin with one taloned finger. 'Why so sad?'

'Not sad, just . . . it reminds me of my old life. I would have been that girl in the scarf-bra, looking for a sugar daddy.'

'You're the one that needs perking up,' Becca said.

When the lift doors opened, Becca led Louisa into the ladies' room, which was packed with women applying lip gloss and adjusting their clothes. Louisa noticed one pop her wedding ring into her bag.

'She'll be well-fucked and home by midnight,' Becca whispered to Louisa when the woman had left.

A cubicle became free. 'Follow me,' Becca said.

'I'll wait for the next one,' Louisa said.

'No you won't.' Becca pulled her into the cubicle and locked the door. Then she closed the toilet lid and sat on it backwards, facing the wall. She took a make-up mirror, a razor blade and a plastic bag from her purse.

'You're not!' Louisa whispered.

'The hell I am,' Becca said.

Becca laid out six clean lines of coke. Then she inhaled two of them without blinking. She stood and breathed in deeply, eyes glittering. 'Nothing like the clean Alpine air,' she said.

Louisa leaned back against the cubicle door. It had been years. 'No thanks,' Louisa said.

'Oh go on, you know you want to.'

'I don't want to,' Louisa said. She hadn't used cocaine since the night she met Ben. He hadn't approved, and she'd transferred her addiction to him, she realized.

Becca smiled. 'I can't believe you're being so mumsy, Louisa. It's only a one-off. You try being *bad*, for once. You might like it.'

Louisa shook her head with all the confidence of a child trying to resist a bag of sweets.

'Have it your way,' Becca said, promptly sniffing up the remains.

Then she stood up and found her footing. 'My God, that's good.'

Becca pushed Louisa against the door of the cubicle and kissed her full on the mouth. 'Now baby, wouldn't you like that with a man?'

Louisa pulled away. The kiss had been pleasurable, but Becca had broken a major rule in their friendship. The kiss hadn't been of the kind girls gave each other in clubs to get men's attention, and there was a wildness in Becca's eyes that scared her. Becca pinned her against the tiled stall and kissed her again, stopping this time when *she* was ready.

'You're freaking me out, Becca. Stop being so weird. Our friendship is way more important to me than a bi-curious one-night stand and you know it.'

Becca crinkled her nose. 'I'm only trying to show you what you're missing, ice queen. Don't you want cuddles in bed in the early morning, someone to reach out for at night? Somebody who finds you so intoxicating they can't get enough of you?'

Becca moved to kiss her again and Louisa felt a warm tingling in her abdomen and her knees went weak. 'Becca, stop.'

'You know you liked it.'

'It's not about liking it. It's just not me. And wanting me, when you know you can't have me, that's not you either.'

Becca shrugged. 'The kissing was purely therapeutic. The kiss of life. Aren't you tired of being in control all the time? Just imagine how it would be with a man. Come on, let's go find you one.'

The bar was fizzing with flirtation, which spilled out into the lobby, where women were dancing provocatively around a piano. This place was the way-station to full sex. The free-sample zone.

They found an empty place by the counter where a forty-something woman with a mahogany tan was holding the hand of a man so much younger that Louisa assumed he was a gigolo. Several men were standing around drinking beer out of bottles.

Becca noticed that Louisa's eyes were on the woman. 'There's something odd about her,' she said darkly. 'She's been young way too long. They call her the youth hostel. They're all drinking on her slate.'

And Becca was Becca again, sharing a joke with her best

friend. Louisa even thought she saw a tinge of remorse in her eyes. She leaned forward, cupping Becca's ear with her hand, and whispered. 'I hear they call her the Dyson.'

Becca looked at Louisa quizzically.

'The vacuum cleaner that never loses suction.'

And then they were laughing as though nothing had happened. They started drinking very dry martinis and Louisa began to feel nicely pissed in a way that almost made her wish for a line of coke. That too, was a feeling she hadn't had in years and she realized, in one of those rare blinding flashes that she usually only got when she was behind a lens or in her darkroom, that she had handed all her appetites over to Ben's safekeeping. She'd lived in Ben's reality, a Ben Maguire Production, just as – if she'd made another decision that night in the Plaza, she might have become a Milton Goodbody Production. So what was she tonight? A Becca Lynley Production? All those years, when Ben didn't want her, Louisa had never risked seeking out another man. Instead, she'd kept Becca around to remind her that she was sexually attractive, knowing it could never go anywhere. Poor Becca.

'I'm sorry,' she whispered in Becca's ear.

Becca took Louisa's hand. 'I'm the one who's sorry. Now smile pretty, babe. Your knight in shining lust is at three o'clock. Don't look!'

There was a tap on her shoulder. Startled, she turned to see a man who looked familiar. Maybe she'd known him all her life, maybe not.

'Hi,' he said, leaning down slightly so that he didn't tower over her so much.

'Hi,' she answered, looking up at him and thinking, This is a good angle. It elongates my neck, stretches my skin, makes me seem younger.

'You on your own?' he asked. *Are you available?*

'With friends.' *No-one I can't dump.*

'I'm Matt. Not with friends.' He smiled.

Louisa held out her hand, 'Louisa.'

Matt took her hand and held it longer than necessary. Louisa turned to introduce Becca, but her friend had vanished.

'Buy you a drink?' Matt asked. 'What are you having?'

Is this how they still do it? Buy you a drink? Society hasn't moved on at all since 1993.

Matt was attractive – mature, athletic, well-groomed with quick eyes that would be able to see a liar at ten paces. He had to be married. 'I've been admiring you from afar,' he said. 'Followed you downstairs from that party. You're not from around here, are you?'

He'd followed her, how thrilling.

His cologne smelt of fresh linen sheets and mown hay.

'Just my luck. A stalker.' She looked down, then up at him from under her eyelashes, letting her body take over, leaving her mind far, far behind.

'A bit sad. I just had to meet you. I'm no good at this kind of thing but I told myself that if I didn't at least find out your name I'd regret it.'

Wow, he was smooth. And she liked his British-public-school accent. 'Now you know my name, what are you going to do with the information?' she asked.

'I'm going to say it slowly, softly and over and over again,' Matt said. His voice rumbled when he spoke into her ear. She could feel it straight down through her body right to her toes.

He picked up their drinks. 'There's more room in the lounge. Will we go there? We might be able to hear each other better.'

She could hear him just fine, thank you. 'Why not?'

Louisa looked over her shoulder once more, to see if Becca was near. Just as she had given up, she saw Becca walking through the lobby with the pierced woman.

Matt found them a sofa by the windows overlooking a spotlit courtyard. Louisa sat down and crossed her legs – not too self-consciously, she hoped. Matt sat beside her. 'So,' he said.

'It's not often that I meet beautiful Americans on my travels in Ireland. What brought you here?'

A jumbo jet, she considered saying. 'I was a sucker for Irishmen.'

'Irishmen had a weakness for you, more like.'

'Not really.'

'So where's home?' he asked.

'Dalkey now. New York originally.'

'Manhattan?'

'You bet.'

'I love New York. I'd move there in a flash.'

'So why don't you?' *Wife and kids in the home counties, perhaps?* She touched her hair because she wanted to touch him.

'My company has interests here.'

He was searching her face for clues. Presenting himself for her pleasure. A *tabula rasa*. I'll be who you like, take me or leave me, he seemed to say.

'I come here once every couple of weeks, just to keep them on their toes. When I'm not here, I'm in London, New York, the Far East.'

'Sounds like a big company,' Louisa said.

'And what do you do?' he asked.

'I'm a photographer.'

Before Ben, she had protected herself from harm with her camera, preferring to see the world through a lens, framing and focusing her environment to give herself the illusion of control. She told herself that, if she ever got involved with a man, he would be someone older who could pay the bills. Intimacy was dangerous so she'd shut herself down from love. Love was the problem. Love was everything that was wrong with her. She wouldn't let it happen again. Matt would bring her back to that comfortable place she was in before Ben, when sex was a way of hiding in the open.

'Photography, that's interesting. You work for a newspaper?' Matt asked.

'No. Portraits. Private commissions, that sort of thing . . . You look relieved.'

'Relieved? Oh no. I just thought, if you were a journalist, you might have difficulty in future fitting me into your schedule.'

He didn't mean it, she knew he didn't.

'If I were to fit you in, Matt, it wouldn't be according to your schedule. This is a once in a life-time opportunity,' she said, suppressing a smile at her own audacity.

Matt glanced at her long legs, encased in the criss-crossed straps. Louisa knew the type. He was just like Blyss, the cynical lawyer, the kind of man who probably liked the sight of himself in the mirror but wouldn't betray her. She sensed he had too much to protect. And she liked that.

'You're your own woman. I'd better be careful,' Matt said, discreetly eyeing her breasts.

'Maybe you should,' Louisa responded, thinking, *Take your time. Enjoy every minute. Like you used to. Pretend you're someone else.*

'I think you're actually quite a careless girl,' Matt murmured.

They were two middle-aged adults acting out a script that Louisa hadn't played in a very long time, yet she remembered every line.

By the time they arrived in Matt's room, she was barely conscious of anything but desire. As soon as they were inside, Matt pushed her against the wall and kissed her. 'I've been waiting all night to do that,' he said.

'Do it some more.' She needed him to make her *feel*, even if it was only desire without hope of anything more. In any case, she didn't want more: *love is the problem. Love is everything that is wrong with her.*

Matt stood back, placed a hand gently on her neck and held her still while he watched her face, reading her, showing her how detached he was.

'*Please* do it some more.'

He smiled at her then and led her to a low, white leather couch and placed her there – black against white – as though she were a pretty object. Taking off his jacket, he stood back and gazed at her again, which Louisa found more erotic than anything he could have said. For a moment, he disappeared into the bathroom. On the coffee table in front of her were a pile of brochures. *Cathedral Square, luxury one, two and three bedroom apartments in the heart of the city. Award-winning design. Private parking, fitness centre, two penthouses available. Ready for immediate occupancy. Mortgage packages –*

'You buying property?' she asked when he returned.

'Thinking about it.'

Louisa sipped from the glass he handed her, but wanted to take off her mad stilettos. She reached down and began to undo the knee-high straps.

He stopped her with his hand, as she had known he would, and said, 'Let me do that . . .'

Fit, isn't he? said the running commentary in her head.

Holding her ankle in his hand, he stroked the criss-crossed leather from knee to toe, then touched her skin in between. 'Pretty,' he said, then slowly untied the strap as though her foot was a precious package. Wrapping his fingers around the arch of her foot, he kissed her toes.

A delicious, throbbing sensation travelled upwards through her body. She instinctively moved forward, to pull his face towards hers. But he wouldn't let her. He had to remain in control.

'Relax,' he whispered, pressing her back against the couch and undoing her complicated jacket. Taking his time. Kissing each inch of flesh as he exposed it with the care she gave to developing her photographs.

When she was unveiled, he undressed in front of her, pinning her to the white sofa with his eyes. But it was himself he was watching – his own performance reflected in her responses, as though he was looking in the reflective side of a one-way mirror with Louisa unseen beyond the glass, watching. It made her feel safe, knowing that he couldn't see her – not really. He didn't need *her*. He had his own heckling voices to listen to – his wife, probably, his fantasy women, perhaps.

When he was ready, he held out his hand to escort her to the bed. She lay down and he began to stroke her.

I'm about to have great sex. This guy knows what he's doing.

And she did.

Matt slept, Louisa couldn't. She'd forgotten how fantastic it was to be made love to. Her own inner voices murmured their pleasure.

I feel like I'm someone else.

This is the real you, baby, this is you.

How could you have forgotten?

Matt moved – he hadn't been asleep, after all.

He brought her more champagne and kissed her again, dragging her down into the fire.

'Hey!' His breathing was hard and fast.

She opened her eyes to see him looking into hers. 'You OK?' he whispered.

'Yeah,' she said.

He snaked within her, holding her gaze and then – for a split second that felt like an eternity but wasn't – they were everything to each other. True lovers.

Strangers.

In that dark and timeless place again where she could be anyone.

'This is how it was meant to be,' Matt said.

Flattered, Louisa knew he believed it, even though she couldn't.

11

Early next morning, just as the swans were beginning to stir the water on the canal, Louisa drifted back to Becca's in a taxi, knocked gently on the door and collapsed against a fleecy bathrobe so soft she could have fallen asleep on it then and there. Gill had been waiting.

'Show me a bed,' Louisa said, as she stumbled across the threshold. 'Did the children miss me?'

'They dropped off shortly after you left and haven't stirred since,' Gill whispered.

Louisa nodded sleepily. 'Where can I drop myself? I'm wrecked.'

'So I see. Have a good night?' Gill's voice was cool. 'Or shouldn't I be asking?'

'Forgive me father for I have sinned,' Louisa said. 'Just point me in the direction of a bed.'

'Mummy, wake up! Daddy's on the phone!'

Louisa struggled to focus. Her gluey mouth needed water.

Elvie's fingers were prying open Louisa's eyelids.

'Mmm . . . Ouch!' Louisa said.

'Wake up!'

Elvie held the phone to her mother's ear.

'Hello?' came a voice from outer space. 'Hello?'

'Yeah?'

'Baby, where were you last night?'

Thirty-seven-year-old woman. Ready for immediate occupancy. Mortgage –

'Lou? Are you there?'

Matt . . . his sharp suit with the handkerchief in the pocket.

'Is anybody there?'

Ben. Keeping tabs on her. He had a sixth sense.

'What's up?'

He wanted to see the children. About time.

'I called at the house last night and it was dark as a tomb. I got worried.'

'You were supposed to ring me to make an arrangement.'

'I know. Listen, I'm flying out today on a job. Give me your solicitor's address, will you?'

'Stella Pearson. She's in the book. Get your solicitor to contact her. You have got one, haven't you?'

'If that's the way you want to play it.'

Elvie was on the floor, going through Louisa's make-up bag, and Louisa realized that she shouldn't be having such a conversation in her hearing. 'I've got to go, Ben. Call me when you get back.'

She disconnected and pulled a pillow over her head.

Milo came in and sat beside her. 'Is Daddy coming home? Patrick's daddy never goes away.'

'Your Daddy has to work abroad, Milo. He still loves you, though.'

This massaging of Ben's reputation couldn't go on forever.

Elvie was silent, smearing her mouth with lipstick. 'Elvie, give that back to me.'

'No.'

'Elvie, it's mine.'

Elvie rubbed the lipstick so hard on her mouth that it broke in half. She looked defiantly at her mother, mouth and cheeks bright red.

Louisa lost it. 'Elvie! If I've told you once I've told you a thousand times!' She got out of bed and grabbed the lipstick from her daughter.

'You stink,' Elvie said.

She took a deep breath. She needed to take a shower and calm down. She needed lots of water and painkillers to stop her head pounding.

'I'm sorry, Elvie. I shouldn't have shouted.'

'You're a liar.'

'I'm not.'

'You are. Daddy's not gone away for work. You and Daddy are getting divorced.'

Milo's face turned white. He knew what divorce meant. Several of his friends' parents were separated or divorced.

Louisa knew she had waited too long to talk to them, but she had hoped to do it together with Ben, the way the experts advised, which was idiotic when she thought about it. When had she and Ben ever cooperated on anything, especially where the children were concerned?

'Milo, Elvie: sit on the bed for a minute.'

She certainly hadn't intended to have the big talk when she was hung-over. She sipped from the glass of water that Gill must have left for her on the bedside table.

The children stared at her.

'Daddy and I love you both.'

Milo and Elvie looked at each other for support.

'Daddy and I will always love you.'

Milo blinked.

'But we have decided that because we're unhappy with each other – not with you – it would be better if he lived in his house and I lived in mine. You aren't going to have to choose between us, though. Nothing much will change. You'll still live with me and Daddy will come visit. You might even see more of him. One day you'll visit Daddy in his house.'

'That's divorce,' Elvie said. She turned to Milo. 'Told you so.'

Milo looked confused.

'This is going to take a while to understand. I'll always

let you know everything that is happening. There'll be no surprises, OK?'

'But I like surprises!' Milo said.

'That's not what I meant. Nothing is going to happen about the divorce without you knowing about it. You two are the best things that ever happened to Daddy and me. It's not your fault we're getting divorced.'

Elvie screwed up her mouth. 'Good speech, Mum. Sounds like what Amy's mum told her.'

Louisa tried to pull Milo on to her lap for a cuddle, but he shrugged her away.

'Let's do something nice today,' she said. 'You think of something.'

Elvie piped up. 'The zoo!'

'The zoo!' Milo chimed in.

'Done,' Louisa said.

'Can Gill come?' Milo asked.

'If he has time,' Louisa said. 'He may have things to do.'

'I have time,' Gill said, appearing in the doorway with a cup of tea for Louisa. 'Sorry about the rude awakening, Louisa. Your mobile was hopping and the children couldn't resist any longer.'

'Get up, Mum,' Elvie said. 'You look a wreck.'

Two hours later, in clothes she had borrowed from Becca, Louisa felt a new lightness in her body, which was still tingling from the night before, as she and Gill followed the children around Dublin Zoo.

'Did Becca say anything about who she was with?' Louisa asked Gill, who didn't seem too bothered that his sister had decided to stay out for the day.

'The animals in Dublin are just like the people,' he remarked.

'Wild?' Louisa asked, thinking of her own behaviour the night before.

Gill shook his head. 'Caged. There's no freedom, especially

for children. You can't miss something you never had though, can you?'

'I'm not so sure,' Louisa said. 'Certain things can feel like they're missing, even though I've never experienced them.'

'Such as?'

'Don't ask me to explain.'

Milo and Elvie were dashing around, making faces at deadpan gorillas. She lifted her camera and focused on Milo.

Click.

'You're never without that camera, are you? Even when you're hung-over,' Gill remarked.

'Will you stop it? I went out for the night. I'm sorry you don't approve.'

'That's not what I meant.'

Gill had no life, that was why he was following her around the zoo when he could have been off doing whatever it was twenty-seven-year-old men did. He pulled at her sleeve, stopping her in her tracks. 'I'm sorry. I just don't want to see you acting crazy like women do after divorce. There are lots of men out there who'll take advantage of it, but you're better than that.'

'Thank you, Gill. Now, can we drop it?' Gill kept close to her as she stepped up the pace. She was feeling a burst of energy now and her body felt young and alive. She wanted only to feel it, though, not think about it. 'Listen, Gill, you've never been married, never had your heart broken.'

'I thought you wanted to drop it?'

'I do.'

They walked on for a few minutes, like a couple having an argument. Elvie and Milo disappeared and reappeared, while Gill and Louisa kept enough distance from them to give them the illusion of freedom.

'Do you notice that no-one dares talk to children these days? People weren't so paranoid when I was a child,' Louisa said, as a way of making peace. 'When I was Elvie's age, I had the run of Central Park. It was right at the end of our street – sixty-fourth and Fifth. Some children play in their gardens, I played in the park.'

'Would you let Elvie do that?'

'No way. I used to feel sorry for children who were kept on a leash by their parents. "Don't run or you'll trip and fall." "Sit down and eat your ice-cream before you drop it." They reminded me of the parents in storybooks or on TV.'

Elvie and Milo disappeared around a corner and Louisa and Gill followed them. They nearly lost them in the crowd around the seal pool, then saw them peering through the railings at the occupants.

'It was the same for me,' Gill said. 'Our mother was too ill to keep tabs on me when I was Milo's age. After she died, Becca gave me more freedom than a mother would. Boarding school clipped my wings, though. You couldn't get away with much there.'

'I still think my kids have more leeway than most. I'm not a clean-clothes, clean-face, clean-thoughts mother. We're quite relaxed at home, which is why I'm dreading having to hire a nanny – if I can find one. I like my privacy.'

Gill stopped for a moment. 'I've been wanting to ask you something. I need some work, but a nine-to-five job is the last thing I want right now. Can I apply for the nanny job?'

'I never thought of having a man look after the kids. But the children are mad about you. And you speak English . . . They're a handful, though. They need a routine, or they get stroppy. And you do understand it would be temporary, just till Mary gets back.'

'Sure, that's the idea.'

'OK, then.'

'Easy as that?'

'Easy as that.'

Louisa, with one less problem to worry about, ran up the hill after Elvie and Milo. 'Hey!' she shouted, camera at the ready.

Elvie turned, hair flying, face full of excitement. Milo twisted so far round to see his mother that he was nearly horizontal.

Click.

My children.

'When did you start taking pictures?' Gill asked.

'It was a gift,' Louisa said, taking out her light meter and holding it out beneath an overcast sky. 'From an old lady I made friends with in the park.'

The bird-lady had been as much a part of the furniture as the bench she sat on. Same bench, every Sunday afternoon, throwing crumbs as bird-ladies do and making soft chuff-chuff noises in her throat.

Gill was curious. 'A gift?'

'She used to offer me crumbs to throw. She was like someone's great-grandmother who had got left behind in the park. I used to pretend she was mine.' She took a swig from her water bottle.

'Go on,' Gill said, shielding his eyes so that he could see Louisa better.

'Sometimes she called out strange poetry as she threw crumbs, like street people do.' Louisa put on an old-lady voice: '"I'm a vamp! Not tramp",' making Gill laugh. 'I thought she was a hundred years old. She would tell me stories about Theda Bara and Clara Bow and MGM. I had no idea then who those women were. Later, I realized she was talking about her life in New York and Hollywood during the twenties and thirties. I used to understand very little of what she said. She would talk about the "silents" and I thought she meant silence at first. Only later did I put it all together, that "silents" were a form of "pictures" that were replaced by "talkies". The talkies had brought about the bird-lady's fall from fame many, many years before. When she was still a young woman. Her beauty had literally died with the silents. Language — spoken language, as opposed to visual — that was her enemy, really.'

'That's incredible,' Gill said. 'Did you ever find out who she was?'

'I hadn't the wherewithal. I was only nine.' Louisa put on her old-lady voice again. '"You'll never see my pictures. The nitrates are crumbling to powder."'

'Nitrates?'

'The film reel was called a "nitrate". It decomposed after a couple of decades.'

Gill was captivated by the story. 'Self-destructed. Her career was gone and she didn't even have pictures to remember it by.'

'I know,' Louisa said. 'I can see her withered lips now, so wrinkled that her dark red lipstick would bleed into the surrounding skin, making her mouth look frilled. Her crooked eyebrows were drawn in with pencil. I can almost hear her talking – "I was a vamp, an angel, a southern belle." I made a rhyme out of it when I played hopscotch or skipped rope. "Vamp, angel, southern belle. Angels go to heaven and vamps to hell. Baby in a carriage for the southern belle." She used to give me money to buy pretzels and hot nuts. One day, the bird-lady brought a leather-bound album to show me. Stills of herself that she had gathered decades earlier. Hypnotic, round eyes lined with black kohl. Finger-waved dark hair, sometimes long, sometimes not. A real natural beauty. Massive eyes – innocent in some pictures, wicked woman in others.'

'Which pictures did she like best?' Gill asked.

'The wicked ones of course. "Kiss my shoe!" she would say, when a picture pleased her more than the others.'

'Kiss my shoe?'

'Same as kiss my arse, nowadays. Much more polite, really. I was fascinated by those pictures, and I wanted so much to take one of her myself that I hankered for a camera. One Sunday afternoon, to my surprise, the bird-lady gave me a brand-new Leica. It must have cost a fortune. It was even loaded with film. She said to me, "I had them load it at the pharmacy. Madison and sixty-fifth. You bring it there and they'll develop it for you. They won't charge you. I had a word."'

Gill's face was animated by Louisa's story. 'That's amazing.'

'I fell instantly in love with the entire process, from the moment I figured out how to position the viewfinder. And then . . .'

Louisa raised her camera, focused on the children, who were quiet now, watching a flock of flamingos.

Click.

'It still gets to me. Clicking the shutter ties me to the moment. Makes me feel that for just a fraction of the second, I've stopped time.'

'Power?' Gill asked.

'Of a benign sort, I like to think.'

She led Gill to a bench, where they sat silently, watching Milo and Elvie, until Gill asked. 'So, what happened when you went to get the pictures developed?'

'True to her word, the bird-lady had paid the bill in advance. I can still remember opening a yellowy-orange envelope and seeing my first set of negatives – which fascinated me as much as the prints themselves – most of which were useless. But a few came out OK. I raced to the park to show the bird-lady, but she was gone and I never saw her again. The pharmacist told me that I could have my photos developed free of charge for as long as I wanted. I hardly questioned it at the time. Children don't question magic, do they? The bird-lady, whoever she was, affected my life more, probably, than anyone I've known before or since.'

'Strangers do that, sometimes,' Gill said.

The thought of Matt, the perfect stranger, brought a rush of euphoric recall that made her catch her breath. She closed her eyes and lifted her face to the sky, where the sun was trying to break through the clouds.

'The man last night,' Gill asked, 'was he a stranger?'

He was reading her mind again. 'What makes you think there was a man?'

'The way you move today,' Gill said. 'And you're talking in the nostalgic way women often do afterwards.'

'Is that so?' Louisa wondered how many women had told Gill long stories. 'I suppose you men put up with pillow talk in the hope of second helpings.'

Louisa and Matt had hardly spoken at all. There had been no post-coital sharing of confidences. She had merely drifted out of the hotel room and back into her life feeling as if she'd been woken up inside. She wanted to be back in that bed now, where only gestures mattered.

'You must think I'm a typical man,' Gill said, finally.

Louisa turned to Gill, who had laid his arm across the back of the park bench – she could have rested her head on his shoulder if she had wanted to. 'Have you never slept with a stranger?' she asked.

'Aren't all lovers strangers?' he replied.

'You think so too, huh?'

He didn't have to answer. Gill wrapped one arm around Louisa and gave her a squeeze, as though he understood her loneliness. She wanted so much to rest her head on his shoulder – even to kiss him. But she knew this was only because he was there. He wasn't the dream lover she missed, the one she couldn't put words on.

'You're wrong about me never having had my heart broken,' Gill said.

'I'm sorry. I shouldn't have said that.'

'And I'm sorry for acting jealous,' Gill said.

A new desire turned in the pit of Louisa's stomach, her body having risen from the dead with Matt the night before. Her body wanted to take Gill on, while she stayed safely behind a window looking in.

'I need to talk to you about something. It's going to upset you.'

He was going to accuse her of leading Becca on, wasn't he? Just as she was leading him on now. Louisa watched her children chase each other around the flamingo enclosure, the bright plastic-pink of the birds. What could he say that would possibly upset her?

'Becca's not in a great frame of mind at the moment – maybe you noticed?' Gill said.

Louisa recalled Becca's kisses the night before, the confession in the restaurant. 'You mean her obsession with having a baby? That's painful.'

Gill seemed to think about this for a moment. 'It's not about having a baby. That's just a reaction.'

Louisa could feel the blood draining from her face and Gill's arm tightened around her. She focused on the children. Elvie had found a feather. 'A reaction to what? What's wrong with her?'

Gill was sombre. 'She thinks you're going through too much at the moment to be able to deal with anymore. And I'm not sure that's the case. You strike me as the type who can handle quite a lot.'

Louisa was on the edge of the bench now, leaning forwards to Gill. 'Tell me what's wrong, Gill. Let me decide what I can and cannot handle.'

12

The hospital smelt of disinfectant and death, funeral flowers and fear – the same as New York Presbyterian all those years ago. She was thirty-seven now, not seventeen. This wasn't the same place, the same woman, the same disease. Becca would not be like Amanda, cowering as she collapsed in on herself, her body withering as her abdomen grew, giving the impression of a nine-month pregnancy . . .

They can cure cancer now, Louisa reassured herself. Be positive and upbeat, for Becca's sake. She negotiated a labyrinth of lifts, stairs and corridors until she found her friend's room.

'I don't see why I can't have my mobile phone and laptop,' Becca was saying in her most authoritative manner. 'I'm not going to lie around and watch TV all day.'

Louisa smiled to herself and knocked gently on the door.

'Come in!' Becca called.

Louisa stepped in the private room, a pot of hyacinths in her hand, to see a nurse adjusting a drip by Becca's bed. Becca opened her eyes and her face went through a range of emotions, from distress, to anger, to resignation – ending in a beaming smile. 'Girlfriend!' she called. 'Welcome to hell.'

Louisa kissed Becca on the cheek. 'It can't be that bad.'

'They're trying to institutionalize me. No mobile phone. No laptop. Apparently I can have an iPod. I haven't got a bloody iPod. Get me one will you?'

'Sure thing.'

'And no weepy music.'

'I'll sort it out. What time's your surgery?'

'Later on today. They won't be more specific than that. It's part of keeping the patient passive, isn't it Nurse?'

Louisa exchanged a look with the young woman who had been taking Becca's blood pressure and a sample for testing. 'There's no harm in being passive, Becca. The world's not going to come to an end without you running it.'

'Yeah, yeah. This hospital could use me running it, I'll tell you that. They had me in here for eight this morning. And all I've been doing since then is lying on my backside. I could have got a lot of paperwork done if they'd told me.'

'Relax, Becca. You won't be here long.'

Louisa pulled up a chair and sat down. Becca gripped her hand, and Louisa knew that the macho complaining was for show. 'You're not going to die,' she whispered.

'You psychic?'

'I just know. The majority of women with breast cancer do really well now. It's not like it was back then, OK?'

Becca's eyes were frightened. 'They won't be able to tell me anything for certain until they get the lump out.'

'Don't even think about that. Just stay with me, OK? Right here, right now. We won't let ourselves go trailing off into the past, or getting fearful of the future. What is it you always say?'

Becca was holding back tears, Louisa could tell. 'Keep one foot in the past, and another in the future, and you piss on the present. And this present is worth pissing on. I hate it. I hate the cancer. I hate myself for getting cancer.'

The nurse made a few more notes and hung the clipboard at the end of the bed. 'Ms Lynley. I expect we're talking about surgery this afternoon. But you must keep fasting, got it?'

Becca was combative again. 'They're sadists in this place. No food or water since midnight last night and they expect me to keep going all day. I'm dying of thirst. If my kidneys fail I'm going to sue the hospital!'

The nurse scuttled out of the room, as an image flashed through Louisa's mind of holding a wet sponge to her mother's mouth, trying to get some fluid into her. She had no doubt that similar horrors were streaming through Becca's head too as she thought about her own mother.

To take both their minds off Becca's thirst, Louisa pulled some pictures out of her bag. 'Becca, look! Mary emailed me some pictures of herself with the Australian doctor. What do you think?'

Becca looked closely at the pictures, her face brightening. 'Oh. My. God. He's a cuddly koala bear. Honest-looking, if that's possible. And Mary! She's like a teenager, leaning on his arm. I can't believe it's her, can you?'

'I bet you she can't either,' Louisa said. 'I wonder if we'll ever see her again.'

'Of course we will. She has to come back for her children, unless they all go out there to live with her. Which isn't a bad idea. Maybe we'll go too, Louisa. Whaddaya say?'

Louisa lifted Becca's hand to her mouth and kissed it. 'I love you.'

Becca handed the pictures back to Louisa. 'I'm sorry I couldn't tell you, Lou. I couldn't bear to see the look on your face when I did.'

'I would have felt the same. The dead mothers club, right?'

Becca nodded. 'Life's a bitch.'

'Promise me you won't keep anything else from me, OK? I'm not going to leave you, Becca, not for Australia, not for anywhere.'

'Don't say that.' A darkness drew across her face. 'Gill tells me that he's going to be your nanny.'

'For a while,' Louisa said.

'I can't stop him. He adores you and the children. You're the family he never had, I suppose. And, at a time like this, I'm glad you're there for him. But please, please do one thing for me.'

'What's that?'

Becca held Louisa's eyes with her own. 'Promise me, on your children's lives, that you won't break his heart like you broke mine.'

Louisa looked at her hands. She thought of Becca's desperate kiss during their night out when Becca knew that she would shortly be in hospital and Louisa had shunned her. Gill deserved more than a confused divorcee looking for a bit of action. 'It's just a little crush. He'll meet somebody soon and forget about me.'

'Promise me,' Becca said.

'Heart's honour, I promise.'

Storm clouds enveloped Dalkey like an angry mood when Louisa left the children at home with Gill and headed into the city to meet her solicitor. There must be more to living than this, she thought, anticipating the busy day ahead. They were still waiting for Becca's test results, although it was likely she would need chemotherapy. She would stop in and see her this evening after work. Her night with Matt had made her restless and agitated: she wanted more. And more meant shaking up her life, if it was ever to be anything more than a series of one-night stands. *Maybe I should have left him my number instead of sneaking away. It could have been a tidy arrangement, a lover who comes to town occasionally . . . no demands.*

High winds and rain. Gale warning. She remembered what Ben had said about wishing she'd warned him about her moods. Wasn't she allowed feelings? Her mother had been the same, a vortex of chaos while Louisa held the calm centre. It would be nice to meet someone calm, Louisa thought, so she could go a little crazy for a change.

She parked alongside the Mercs and BMWs in the basement of the office building where Stella Pearson worked. If she'd married a man with one of those, she could have been home with her children now, or playing tennis, or getting her hair done. But no, she'd had to go for the erratic artist. Never again.

Louisa went up in the lift and introduced herself at the desk. Stella didn't keep her waiting. 'The other party has been in touch through his solicitor, you'll be glad to know.'

Louisa noticed, again, Stella's high-maintenance nails and thought, that's what I'd like. Great nails.

Stella went on, 'Please don't be shocked when I unpack it for you. I'm afraid he's taking a rather aggressive approach.'

That woke Louisa up. 'I was talking to him only yesterday. I got the impression he hadn't done anything about it.'

'That's not an unusual tactic. I doubt he would have wanted to dump this on you himself.'

Ben had a tactic? 'Go on.'

'His solicitors are arguing for half of the house, or the equivalent value either way. He owned it before he met you.'

'He inherited it from his mother.'

'That means you move out and he pays you off, or vice versa. And the payment must be made on its current value, which is well over a million, thanks to the property boom.'

'He wants half a million from me? The bastard! Why am I not surprised?'

'In addition, the other party is seeking half of the business. Your accounts are pretty much up to date. I've had a search done to make sure there are no other claims on the business – merely a formality – and there are not.'

'The other party, as you call him, can't have half! It's my business. I built it up!'

'The other party is arguing that he supported you in the early years.'

'He did, my arse!' Louisa shouted, then caught herself.

'He'll have to prove it in court. And he'll have to prove that he has a stake in the company. But that creates another problem. We can't legally set up the partnership between you and Paul until all this is sorted out. Which could take some time. Unless, that is, you want to make things easy on yourself and find a way to buy Ben out. We'll argue for paying the minimum we can get away with, but even making those arguments costs money when you're talking about repeated hearings in the High Court.'

Louisa felt sick. Half of the house, half of the business – that was hundreds of thousands of euro. 'I can't afford to hand him cash so he can live in style with his floozy. What about the children? They need a roof over their heads. Ben never gave a toss about financial security and I haven't seen a penny in child maintenance since he left. He's off having one affair after the next! The man's a reprobate.'

Stella remained calm, showing how well used she was to such hysteria. 'In Ireland, we have no-fault divorce. It doesn't matter if your ex-partner kept a harem. The financial arrangements are determined by legislation and, in some cases – particularly where large sums are concerned – legal precedents. Your case would be going to the High Court and, if necessary, the Supreme Court. I don't know if you want to drag yourself and your children through all of that.'

'I don't.'

'Right. So my advice would be at this point to give Ben what he wants. It's the cheapest thing to do in the long run.'

'I'd have to sell the house! The children and I would be homeless!'

Stella's expression didn't change. 'If you go to court, Ben will have to prove his entitlement to half your business. As for the house, it appears from what I have that you are the main breadwinner. In that case, you are entitled to two-thirds of it. Considering that the children are living with you as well, you may be able to keep the house entirely until they're of age – but the business is another issue.'

Louisa felt sick. She grabbed a tissue and held it to her mouth.

'Do you need to use the lavatory?'

Louisa shook her head. She wasn't going to let Ben destroy her.

'Has he asked about Milo and Elvie? They're well used to him being away, but they know, now, about the divorce.'

Stella sighed. 'The other party hasn't asked about the children.'

'Why ever not?' Louisa had thought of him as feckless, but not cruel.

'Another tactic, I'm afraid. If the other party expresses a desire for contact, they're handing us a bargaining chip. If we initiate contact, we're handing them leverage.'

'But I didn't want this to happen! I won't have my children used as bargaining chips. And Ben isn't "the other party". He's their father!'

'I'm sorry.' Stella picked up another file, thicker than the first, and opened it to the top page. 'This all sounds cold and calculating, I know. And it's not what I like to see happening, either. You're going to have to put up with it, for the moment, and not let it get to you.'

'I feel like an idiot, reassuring the children that their father loves them when he obviously couldn't care less.'

'You're right to do that,' Stella said. 'You're going to have to be bigger than he is, I'm afraid.'

Louisa questioned her perceptions again. She had lived with a man, loved him and failed to see how callous he could be. She'd wasted her energy propping him up to fulfil her idea of who he was, while all along she had been living with a stranger.

Stella seemed to read her thoughts. 'Divorce brings out the worst in people, believe me. You're actually doing very well. Normally, I'd be sitting here listening to you plot and scheme to destroy him. I'd be the one telling you to think of the children. So don't be so hard on yourself. You have every right to be angry – at *him*.'

'Thank you, Stella. For being so blunt. I'd better go now, if there's nothing else. I have a busy day.'

Stella still had the thicker file open in front of her. 'Actually, there is news, on another matter, which I'm afraid makes all this a bit more complicated. Have you time?'

How could she not have time? She'd have to text Gill to collect the children from school. There was no way she'd be home in time now. 'Go ahead. I'm listening.'

'Fortunately, this matter came to my attention some time after you and Ben agreed to separate.'

Stella was smiling. 'You had an aunt, Alice Stone.'

'How did you know that? I haven't seen her in twenty years.'

'This sort of information tends to find its way to the right place. We have an office in New York, which expedited the search process.'

'Is Alice looking for me?'

Stella's cool, marble face gave little away. 'Your aunt has died, Louisa. You didn't know?'

Louisa had the sensation of being cut adrift and pulled by the current. 'When?'

'A few months ago. I'm sorry to be the bearer of bad news.' Stella's sympathetic manner was well practised.

Louisa had kept Alice buried so deep that she had expected never again to have anything to do with her. 'Why are you telling me this?'

Stella paused for effect. 'It appears that, failing other legal challenges, Alice Stone has left you her estate.'

'She's left me her house on Long Island?' Louisa thought of the huge shingle-style mansion at Amagansett, its paint peeling with neglect. The beautiful beach and the mad summer nights. Voices calling and reflecting off the water, sounding louder in the dark than they ever did during the day. 'She wouldn't have done that. I meant nothing to her.'

'Apparently you did. The estate is not only the house. She has bequeathed you many of her paintings – her own work – as well. And as you can see from the thickness of this file, there is a lot of business to settle where those are concerned. Museums and others – private collectors, investors – are eager to buy whatever they can get their hands on. You can probably name your price.'

'Because a painter's true value is found when she's dead.'

Stella shrugged. 'I guess so. You're going to need good advice, Louisa. And we still don't know who's going to come out of the woodwork and make a claim on the estate. This isn't my area of expertise, but our office in New York has advisers in this area who could handle it for you.'

Louisa's mind went blank. It was all too much to take in. 'Ben's going to be demanding half of all that as well, isn't he?'

'No. You and he both filed for separation before this information came to light. Unless he asks directly, he doesn't need to know anything about it, which is why I suggest that you say nothing to anyone. And I mean anyone at all.'

Alice was dead. Difficult, abrasive, selfish Alice. 'Why me?' Louisa asked aloud. There had to be a sting.

'Only you'd know the answer to that.'

'Alice wanted little to do with me. Why should I want anything to do with this, now?'

'You have a lot to think about. This is all a bit of a shock, I'm sure. You may want to wait a few weeks before doing anything at all. There's no immediate pressure. Why don't we agree, for the record, that I haven't told you about the will. There is nothing in writing to prove that you've been informed. The search for Louisa Stone is still under way.'

Louisa didn't know what to say or how to feel. This wasn't the sort of thing that happened in real life. 'There has to be a mistake,' Louisa said.

Stella overlooked the comment, already tidying the file in preparation for meeting her next client. 'You're welcome to hire any firm you like to handle this estate. Don't think that just because we've got wind of it that we have to represent you. You might want a specialist legal firm that handles art.'

Louisa thought back to her hungry days in New York, when she hadn't dared ask Alice for anything. There was no-one in New York she even knew anymore, much less trusted. 'I think I'd feel on safer ground with you. Bring in expertise, if you need it. I don't want to be traipsing back and forth between Dublin and New York, dealing with people I don't know.'

'Think about it,' Stella said. 'As for settling certain issues with your former partner, you may want to keep in mind that it will cost you relatively little to free yourself of him, compared to your future income.'

'I'll think about it. If I don't kill him first.'

'I didn't hear that.' Stella stood to see Louisa out. 'I'll reply to your ex-husband's solicitors with the sort of letter we use in these situations.'

'And what's that?' Louisa asked.

'Leave it to me. Just give me a shout when you want me to inform the State of New York that Louisa Stone – Louisa Maguire, I mean – has been found.'

Louisa left the office, her head reeling. She had to sit in the car for half an hour to steady herself before she could drive. Stella's pronouncement – Louisa Stone had been found – had shaken her to the core, for Louisa Maguire had never wanted to find Louisa Stone.

That evening, back at home, after Louisa had helped the children into pyjamas, she tucked them into bed thinking how lucky they all were. The idea of losing Becca was so horrible that it grounded her to do the normal things mothers do, tidying away clothes and toys, making sure the children had their favourite teddies in bed with them.

Elvie had brought so many stuffed toys into her bed that she was in danger of suffocation. 'I want a story.'

'*The Cat in the Hat*,' Milo urged from the next room, where he was eavesdropping.

'Come in here to Elvie's bed, then,' Louisa called.

Milo came scrambling in and tucked himself under Louisa's arm. Her voice was soft and rhythmic, sending Milo to sleep before the story was over.

Elvie's eyes stayed open to the last. 'The cat makes things worse before he makes things better, doesn't he, Mum?'

'Life's like that sometimes,' Louisa whispered.

'I like Gill,' Elvie said.

'Me too,' Louisa answered.

She only wanted to be with them, storing up moments for the day they would have to part. The more you love, the more there is to lose, she thought. Nobody tells you, when you have children, that, from the moment they come into your life, you're always waiting to say goodbye.

Louisa got up from Elvie's bed, then lifted Milo and carried him into the next room, loving the fresh scent of shampoo in his curly hair. Everything she loved, it seemed, was a loss waiting to happen. Only a month before, Louisa, Becca and Mary had sat at Mary's table celebrating the end of Louisa's marriage and putting the world to rights. Now Mary was searching for love in Australia, Becca was fighting for her life and Louisa had been too blind to see the storm coming. Or maybe she hadn't wanted to see it, the way she'd ignored Ben's affairs. Like she was avoiding dealing with issues now – like Aunt Alice. How typical of Alice to leave Louisa to clean up after her. All because of that summer, twenty years ago.

Louisa covered Milo with an extra blanket – it was unseasonably cold. Then she went downstairs to the kitchen, poured herself a glass of wine and set up her laptop on the kitchen table to Google Alice Stone.

There were thousands of entries. Interviews, biography, exhibitions, criticism, Buy Alice Stone reproductions.

Louisa clicked on biography.

Alice Stone, undisputed doyenne of American modernist painting, became a recluse at the height of her popularity in the mid-1980s. Strong-willed and audacious, she broke new ground as a woman in what had been a male preserve. Her colourful and erotic work provoked and inspired, making it possible for other women to explore symbolic imagery once regarded as solely male visual language.

Born in 1930, Stone was the eldest child of the wealthy industrialist Tobias Stone, whose fortune was revived following the Depression by manufacturing armaments during the Second World War. After the war, she was sent to art school in Paris, an experience she subsequently dismissed as 'learning to paint by numbers'. A familiar figure in Left Bank Paris in the 1950s and 1960s, she had numerous friends on the art scene, among them Pablo Picasso.

Apparently Alice had been a woman in a man's world and her paintings had won her acclaim among the public, if not critics. The list of her lovers included writers and artists who were household names, but one stood out: Larry Stein, the photographer.

A website showed one of his nude photographs of Alice, in which she reclined outdoors in an Adirondack chair that Louisa recognized from Amagansett. The commentary read:

There is a view that, without the portraits of her by Larry Stein, Alice Stone's work might never have received the exposure it did. Stein's striking studies of the artist were works of art in their own right, prompting interest among galleries and collectors in the subject of the photographs. His photographs of the artist have themselves become icons of that period of modern art and fetch high prices. A nude portrait of Miss Stone, taken in 1964, was sold for $1.1 million recently, after it was discovered that Stein had destroyed all of the original plates before his death in 2004.

Larry Stein. Louisa had met him, but now she couldn't bring his face to mind. She skipped to another website.

Reclusive for the last twenty years of her life, Miss Stone never acknowledged the retrospective exhibitions of her work that were staged across the US and Europe. Her refined and slightly removed style and adventurous imagery have earned her work enduring public popularity and high prices. She went almost unnoticed by mainstream art critics because her originality fit into no known school or trend. Delightful and vivacious company, Miss Stone's home and studio in

Amagansett became legendary in the late 1960s and 1970s as a mecca for young artists.

Louisa clicked from site to site, discovering that her aunt had granted no interviews in twenty years. She had shown no new paintings – the Artichokes series had been the last to reach the public domain.

There was nothing about Alice's family, apart from the reference to her father. The impression was of an eccentric who had died prematurely – and very much alone. Well, that wasn't Louisa's fault. Alice had never made contact. Surely it was Alice, the mature aunt, who should have taken an interest in her orphaned niece.

A news item caught her attention: *Local painter found dead. Foul play not suspected.* She couldn't read on. It was too much to take in. Seventy-six years old and Larry dead two years. He would have been in his mid-fifties, at most – the age her mother would have been now.

All gone.

I am alive - despite Ben.

Then Stella's words came back to her. She decided to tell her solicitor to let the world know that Louisa Stone had been found.

13

Gill and the children settled into a routine, Gill keeping them active with cycling, swimming and fishing, all new for the children. It was like having their very own summer-camp counsellor. Louisa kept her distance, which wasn't difficult, because, as soon as she got home from work, Gill would go back to Becca's to cook and clean for her. Louisa visited Becca during her lunch breaks, always asking her friend if there was anything she needed and always getting the same answer. 'I have a credit card and a telephone. I can have anything delivered.' She even had a wigmaker coming from London. The chemo was stripping Becca of her usual vigour, but she was still running her company from her bed.

Louisa found her life becoming settled, despite her anxiety about her friend. July was quiet and Louisa spent her evenings catching up on laundry and housework, and reading to the children.

At work, her days began as they always had, with Louisa carefully cleaning the infinity curve. 'I'm always telling people to take their shoes off, but people have awfully dirty feet all the same,' she said to Paul in irritation.

'You never complained before,' Paul answered. 'You need to take a vacation.'

Not with Becca suffering. She'd wait until they could all go together.

They were behind on orders, unusually for them. One of Paul's wedding portfolios had had to be completely redone after the bride insisted that the maid of honour be excised from the pictures. From Paul's account, there had been 'words' at the boozy reception. The groom had been implicated.

'Can't you convince her to forgive the girl? We can't just black out her face. This is costing us a fortune.'

Paul was in and out of the darkroom and file room, trying to catch up before setting off for an afternoon wedding. 'Is it me that has you so stroppy? Are you still up for the partnership? My solicitor says he's being stone-walled by yours.'

Poor Paul. She'd been feeling guilty for days, waiting for him to ask about the contracts and not sure what to say when he did.

'I'm sorry,' she said. 'I don't mean to mess you around. My offer still holds, but the legal red-tape on my end is taking far longer than I'd expected it would. There's no deliberate delay. I should have said something before. I have some decisions to make and, well, I'm having difficulty with them.'

'So you're not sure about this,' Paul said, his usual good humour fading.

'I *am* sure. It's just that Ben is trying to get a share of the business. For cash. He's entitled to do it, apparently, as part of the divorce.'

Paul was crestfallen. 'I was afraid of that.'

'It's going to work out, Paul. It's just Ben being difficult.'

'It's what I'd have expected from him. Are you sure he hasn't a little company stashed away somewhere? He hardly seems to be starving.'

'How do you know?'

'I've seen him out and about with that Lucy on his arm. She's a photography stylist, you know. Fashion shoots. Nice girl.'

'I didn't know that. Nor do I care.'

On the way out the door, Paul said, 'Keep not caring. Do me a favour, though. Keep me informed?'

'I'll do that,' she answered, thinking of her Aunt Alice's estate and how claiming it, a process now under way, could change everything for her.

Her mind buzzing, she was loading her Hasselblad in preparation for her first shoot of the day. Paul had booked the session recently after a cancellation had left the morning free and Louisa hadn't had a chance to check the clients' names in the diary. She was just about to do this when she heard an unmistakably shrill New York accent. 'Loo-EEEE-za!'

Louisa looked up to see a tidy thirty-something blonde, chic in white jeans and a pink shirt, with her face pressed to the studio door. Petite, perfectly coiffeured, diamonds on her fingers. A soccer mom from New York suburbia had time-travelled to her studio, complete with husband and twin boys.

'Hi,' Louisa said, opening the door and trying to sound friendly.

'You don't remember me do you?' said the woman.

'I'm sorry, I know I should – but –'

'Amagansett?'

It was Louisa in the time-machine now, being propelled to long days reading on the beach and foggy evenings spent wrapped in blankets in the dunes. 'Annabel? What are you doing in Dublin?'

'It's all Humphrey's fault. You remember Humphrey.' Louisa remembered him all too well, usually to be found with a six-pack, a surfboard and a hard-on, cruising the beach in Amagansett. She'd been repulsed then and felt the same way now, although her image of drunken Humphrey with his wandering hands hardly tallied with the conservative father now standing a respectful pace or two behind his wife. She wasn't surprised they had married. They were born to be married to each other, as far as their wealthy parents had been concerned.

She could see them now, Belly and Hump, two arrogant teenagers with vulgar pet names they relished, sunning themselves on the beach because they had never had a care in the world and never would. Louisa could see Belly, in her pink-and-green-flowered bikini and Hump, hanging around with a beer in his hand. The pair of them were at the centre of a group of young people who had known each other since nursery school, and whose parents before them had been to nursery school together too. Their white Anglo-Saxon protestant world was insular and safe from the beginning and they carried it with them.

'Hey, Loopy-Lou,' Hump said.

Louisa cringed. 'Long time no see.' When he tried to hug her, she pulled back but still felt his sloppy lips on her ear.

'Gorgeous,' he whispered, then his gaze surfed over her from head to toe.

Belly tapped her husband lightly on the arm. 'Oh, Hump, it was Foster she had a thing for, not you. Foster still talks about you, Lou. You do remember him, don't you?'

Why had she forgotten? 'He's well, I trust.'

'Peachy. As I was saying, Hump's setting up the European operation of his company here in Dublin. He could have had someone else do it, of course, but you know Humphrey!'

Yes, I know Humphrey. Wish I never had, though.

It seemed impossible that her single summer at Aunt Alice's Bohemian palace in the Hamptons should suddenly materialize just after Alice had died and left her the estate. She wasn't used to being contacted by old friends in any case, having sliced her former life out of the frame.

'The minute I heard you were here I was determined to have you do a portrait for us. Everyone seems to have one. Tell us what to do,' Belly said.

Louisa directed her to the infinity curve.

'Great to see you're doing so well. Nice little country, huh?' Hump said. 'Where can I put my jacket?'

'Let me take it,' Louisa said.

Mrs Humphrey Smith loaded her own Burberry and those of her children into Louisa's arms. They were quite the Burberry-check family.

'Love the scarf,' Annabel offered. The silk voile shawl was a guilt-present that Ben had bought her on his travels. She had flung it round her shoulders without thinking this morning, forgetting it might be in the way while she was working. Louisa took it off and folded it. 'Thank you.'

'I can't wait to tell Foster that we met!' Belly crowed as Louisa arranged them for the portrait. Belly was practically vibrating with excitement. 'It goes to show: you never know, do you? People come and go, then they come back! Oh my, you *are* looking divine. No wedding ring I see.'

Whatever she's on I'll have some, Louisa thought.

'He's single again, you know,' Belly said.

'Again?' Louisa asked.

Foster, aged nineteen in her memory, had died in Louisa's heart when she left Amagansett after that summer. To discover that he was still alive and even talked about her, that for twenty years they had existed in parallel universes, was disorienting. 'Tell him "hi" from me,' she said automatically.

'Is that all? Why, you broke his heart!'

Hardly. Years ago, for her own survival, she had erased her memories of Foster. The first love of her life. That's all he had been. A practice-run for better loves to come.

'Any children, Lou?' Humphrey asked.

Preoccupied with lighting, she ignored him.

'A sore point?' Annabel pouted a little.

'No,' Louisa said, adjusting a reflector. 'I have two.'

'You never come to Amagansett,' Annabel added. 'Your children would love it.'

'I haven't been to Amagansett in twenty years,' Louisa said pointedly.

'Surely you can find time for old friends.' Humphrey spoke like a man used to sitting at the head of the board of directors.

Annabel's eyes were like saucers. 'You're not on the run or anything, are you?'

Louisa laughed. 'What would I be on the run from?'

Humphrey rounded on his wife with a glance so effective that she said, 'Sorry. It was meant to be a joke.'

To avoid any further awkward reminiscence, Louisa focused

on husband, wife and their adorable twin boys: the perfect American family on the infinity curve. Belly had dressed her men in tastefully worn blue jeans and crisp white shirts. With their gene pool, they looked like an ad for Ralph Lauren. You could nearly smell the Hamptons seashore on their pampered skin.

Louisa focused on the adults Belly and Hump had become: Mr and Mrs Humphrey Smith of Amagansett and Manhattan, and family. They emanated unshakable self-belief and generations of money, just as they had twenty years before. And it still intimidated her, just as it had then.

Belly came from a long line of women who had never been fat or poor, or liked to think so. Hump inherited a lifestyle that was about managing wealth rather than creating it. Their parents had been the types who believed that society began to disintegrate the day people stopped bothering about the social register.

Louisa made some final adjustments, then stood back. 'I think we're set.'

The twin boys were frightened, as children often were in this situation, as though the camera might steal their souls. Coaxing the boys along until they relaxed, Louisa casually snapped the Smith family as they really were: Belly in profile ordering Hump to smile, her perky nose pointed at him like a weapon, Hump wearing a superficial smile to hide his annoyance, the boys gazing anxiously at their mother for approval.

They had waited an awfully long time to have children, Louisa thought. They had been together more than twenty years by now – thirty-eight years if you counted their nursery school romance. Louisa had seen the wedding announcement in *The New York Times*: Mr and Mrs Archibald Worthington of Manhattan and Amagansett announce the engagement of their daughter, Annabel Worthington, to Humphrey Smith III. There were always two addresses. Chicago and London. Connecticut and Florida. People like Belly and Hump had multiple roofs over their heads for generations – usually they could trace their pedigree to some castle in Scotland, England or – failing that – France.

And now Dublin. Not their kind of place at all, Louisa would have thought.

'Don't think you have to force a smile,' Louisa said to Hump as he twisted and cracked his neck. 'Let's all take a break for a minute.'

Belly was doing some sort of strange facial yoga. 'Smiling hurts, you know that?'

'Please relax, be yourselves,' Louisa said. 'This isn't a perform-ance. You all look terrific. You don't have to try, believe me.'

When they settled down, the family proved annoyingly photogenic in the way that naturally slim people with great bone structure tend to be. Everything about them spoke prosperity and contentment. They looked at the camera with smiles as fresh and neat as newly minted cash. Butter wouldn't melt in their mouths, Louisa thought. Ireland for them was no more than another adventure, not an escape as it had been for Louisa.

Eventually, Louisa captured the adoration the boys obviously felt for their father, which Hump surely didn't deserve. In her mind's eye, she saw a teenage creep, while through her lens, her professional eye saw a rather handsome, athletic, middle-aged man. In his devil-may-care youth he'd had a destructive untamed energy, but now he appeared more like a benign bear.

'A photographer? You've done well for yourself, little girl. Who'd have thought it?' he said mischievously.

Little girl. It brought back the taste of beer from a bottle with grains of sand on the rim.

She was shooting automatically now, preoccupied and con-fused as the pictures in her head – the present and the past – jostled for attention. While she was changing to a fresh roll of film, Humphrey leaned into Louisa and asked, voice rumbling, 'You don't know of a good PR company, do you? My company is launching itself in Europe and I could put the contract out to tender, but I always prefer word of mouth, don't you?'

Louisa didn't hesitate. 'Lynley Consultants,' she said, then went to her desk and wrote down Becca's number on a slip of paper, thinking, *she'll put manners on him.*

'Now, Louisa. You are going to come to dinner,' Belly said. 'I need your insights into Dublin society. It's nothing like what I'm used to.'

In Amagansett that summer, Belly had initially snubbed Louisa. She was one of those who had excluded her from the clique of girls that fluttered around Humphrey and Foster. Now, she was behaving as though she and Louisa were long-lost sisters. Needs must, Louisa thought.

'It must be lonely for you,' Louisa said, 'leaving your friends behind in New York.'

'Some are best left behind,' she said, sharply, then leaned in to Louisa confidentially, 'I think this was meant to be.'

'How do you mean?' Louisa answered.

Belly gave a conspiratorial smile. 'You'll see.'

And then, with a flurry of jacket-buttoning in the midst of Irish summer, they were gone before Louisa had a chance to ask if it was really true that Foster had never forgotten her, or if Belly was merely being polite. The notion that Foster might have held her in his mind for all those years was as shocking to Louisa as the news had been that Mary had found a lover on the Internet. But maybe it was true that people came back into your life at the right time. Maybe Mary wasn't so reckless after all to believe in second chances.

PART TWO

Louisa leaned her head against the window of the Hamptons jitney, trying not to worry about Amanda. Used to being her mother's shadow on their summer travels, Louisa had never been left out and sent away before. She was aggrieved, even though there had been many times in the past when she had prayed to be released from the cyclone of emotions that was Amanda. Yet, now that she was free, she felt lost: an inner life, with its own rhythms of reflection building to action, was a luxury for Louisa, who was always running like an emergency response squad to attend to Amanda's latest crisis. She had become so adept at handling her mother's moods – the endless sulks, the flash-rages – that she had never had the chance to explore her own feelings and reflect on her own needs. At seventeen, she was already exhausted.

Outwardly, Louisa was breezy for Amanda's sake as she boarded the jitney, which was no more than a bus with a pretentious name. Amanda pressed fifty dollars and piece of paper into Louisa's hand. 'Don't read it till you're on the bus, hear me?' Louisa stuffed them into her jeans pocket, then held her mother close. 'Be careful out there – promise?'

'There's such a thing as being *too* careful!' Amanda retorted. 'Isn't this exciting? You're going to the Hamptons! I spent all my summers there as a child – oh, but you know that. Wait until you see the house! Right on the ocean!'

As the bus pulled away, Louisa kneeled on her seat and craned her neck to see wild-eyed Amanda crying as though they would never see each other again. Amanda really knew how to milk it. Look: already her mother was being rewarded with concerned attention from the attractive older man who had dropped off his grandsons at the bus-stop. That was what hurt most, really – Amanda would find someone to take her daughter's place as she gadded about in Goa. Louisa had grown out of the job now that she was no longer a charming child, but a rival to her mother. Just as well, Louisa thought. The sort of men her mother attracted were no-hopers. So, with their apartment sub-let for the summer to raise extra cash, Louisa had had only two choices: take the jitney to the Hamptons and a painter aunt she'd never met, or run away and be homeless.

Amanda had thrown herself into a frenzy of stripping the apartment of their possessions in preparation for sub-letting it while they were away. When the worn Turkish rugs, the carousel horses, the canvases that covered every inch of wall and the flea-market oddities that had made their apartment look like an Aladdin's cave had been expunged, only the most basic furniture remained, looking even shabbier without the backdrop. Their lives packed away and dispatched in the back of a U-Haul, Amanda sat smoking and drinking iced 'tea' while Louisa covered the stains of their lives with a coat of white paint. When Louisa pressed her hand against the window of the bus in a gesture of farewell, she noticed that she still had the patches of white paint on her fingers, and calluses where she had held the brush.

'Are you sure we're just sub-letting, the place is still ours? You have paid the rent?' she asked her mother.

'If we were being evicted, I wouldn't be bothering to do the place up, would I? There's a nice bit of pin-money for us in sub-letting. It will pay for India.'

They had finished the evening before Louisa was to travel to the Hamptons, the apartment so achingly bare that Amanda started ringing all her friends to throw an impromptu party. Louisa's argument that this would destroy all their efforts had no effect on Amanda. 'I'm thirty-seven soon, and you were seventeen when?'

'A month ago,' Louisa said.

'A mother–daughter birthday party then!'

Louisa didn't bother to invite anyone of her own age; she couldn't bear to listen to her friends going on again about how lucky she was to have a mother who acted like a sister. Louisa would have preferred a sister who acted like a mother.

As the sky over Manhattan dimmed to smoggy greenish-violet, Amanda sent her out to buy ice. Louisa was returning with the heavy bags when she saw Amanda hanging out of the apartment window, breasts bobbing beneath her muslin blouse. 'Did you remember lemons?'

She hadn't been asked to get lemons. 'Shut the window. You're letting the heat in!' Louisa called up from the street, then turned and headed for the store. She followed the drip-drip pattern that the melting ice had made on the footpath on her walk home a few moments before. Having retraced her steps, she filled a bag with waxy lemons, asked the Indian who ran the shop to put it on their tab – they didn't officially have one, but she had no money – then returned home to find Amanda leaning even further out the window. 'I love summer!' she called to no-one in particular.

Louisa stopped in her tracks as her mother flung one bare leg over the window ledge, her ankle-length prairie-skirt hitched to her waist. As she straddled the windowsill three floors above the street, she raised her arms and the long sleeves on her gauzy Indian blouse spread like wings.

'*Bella!*' a taxi driver called.

Her mother was drunk already – no ice and lemon required – and the party hadn't even started. Louisa ran back to the apartment, the bag of lemons splitting, the ice bags seeping, unlocked the street door, ran up three flights and burst through the heavy metal apartment door to find her mother sitting giggling on the sill, the window closed behind her, legs crossed demurely, with one hand elegantly balancing a cigarette holder. 'This is what I mean, Manna. You've got to stop this craziness. How can I be sure you'll make it through the summer alive?'

'You can't,' Amanda said, in the saucy-little-girl way she had when Louisa challenged her.

'Very funny. You smoke way too much pot, you know. It's rotting your brain.'

Louisa washed a pail and dumped the ice in it, leaving Amanda to wonder aloud how they would slice the lemons with all the knives packed away. While they were waiting for the guests to arrive, Louisa checked her knapsack once more to make sure she had everything that was important to her. Her bird-lady picture, her camera, her photograph portfolio and her report card – straight As. She thought of the childhood possessions she had deposited in the back of the U-Haul, driven away by 'friends' of Amanda's. She didn't expect to see any of it again – especially the fragile Japanese screen.

'Last pictures, baby,' Amanda called.

Louisa readied her camera while Amanda posed coquettishly, long blonde hair coiled loosely at the back of her head and fastened with a silver clip. Amanda let her hair down around her shoulders, then coiled it up again – hairclip in her mouth. Then, like a woman deciding which path to take for the rest of her life, Amanda coiled her hair up again more firmly – only to let it uncoil again moments later. Her expression by now was far away, the camera forgotten.

Louisa focused on her mother's beautiful, bony face in close-up. She looked like Joni Mitchell, some said. Others thought Cybil Shepherd. Louisa saw a bit of both.

Hair up. Click.

Hair down. Click.

And so on, until – satisfied in some way by this ritual – Amanda took the camera from Louisa and stood her up against the newly blank white wall. 'Smile,' Amanda said.

Click.

Louisa refused, preferring to turn her head right, then left, then straight ahead, in a mug-shot. 'Don't blame me when these are worse than your passport pictures. Have you got your passport?'

'You don't need a passport for the Hamptons, Manna.'

'Are you sure? A woman should always have clean panties and a passport. Smile for me just once, Louisa. Like when you were little, please? Nobody will see these but you and me.'

Louisa smiled.

Amanda handed her back the camera. 'Send me that one when you've had it developed, yeah, baby?'

'Send it where, Manna?'

The buzzer sounded. Hordes of Amanda's friends, friends of friends, acquaintances of friends and acquaintances of acquaintances piled into the apartment. There was no space left but the stairs and the street. Amanda perched on the windowsill, the window wide open again. Women sat cross-legged on the floor and six shared what had been Louisa's bed. They wore strange-smelling 1930s dresses; others had gone punk with spiky short hair. Joints were passed freely from hand to hand, cocaine was snorted in the tiny bathroom.

Among the guests was a new clan Louisa hadn't met before: the women in shoulder-padded suits. These had decided to take on the world on men's terms and were secretly envied by the others because they had started earning real money. One of them cornered Louisa by the kitchen sink. 'What are your college plans, Lou?'

Louisa hadn't got any. The school guidance counsellor had helped her fill in forms for colleges in the city, plus scholarship and loan applications. She had a year left of high school, but the counsellor thought that Louisa's photography portfolio might get her early admission. She had tried to tell Amanda about it, but Amanda hadn't been interested. 'Just sign the forms, Mannie.' With the deadline upon her, Louisa had forged her mother's scrawl.

The party had lasted all night so Louisa hadn't slept. Her eyelids drooped as the bus ploughed through the Manhattan traffic. Her fellow travellers seemed so confident about where they had come from and where they were going – evincing a tangible security with their preppie clothes and designer luggage that made Louisa crave to be one of them.

Remembering her mother's note, she reached into her pocket and unfolded it, wary of what it would say. Some scary poetic rant about love and loss, probably, scribbled in the drunken dawn. She unfolded the paper, read it, squirmed with shame, then quickly folded it up again, hoping it hadn't been seen by the man sitting beside her.

It was a prescription for the Pill. It put Louisa off the very notion of sex. The first question Amanda would ask her in September: 'Did you do it?' And then she'd want all the embarrassing details.

The bus snaked through the perfectly groomed countryside of Long Island, where the right sort of people summered with their own kind. Louisa watched as they progressed from Manorville to South Hampton, Bridgehampton to Sag Harbor. Louisa thought, this must be what the mental map of a secure person looks like. It was so unexpected, this feeling that she was bringing her mother's flaws away with her, that Louisa resolved to grab the chance to 'find' herself, as Amanda would have put it – always searching and never discovering. Maybe Aunt Alice would be motherly and self-composed, the sort who would want to sit down and discuss college choices and maybe even help pay the tuition.

When the bus finally arrived in East Hampton, Louisa felt she'd stepped onto a film set. It was a quaint, white, New England-style utopia, which she recognized from films and ad campaigns, never quite realizing that such a place actually existed. It was so clean, so manicured, so unself-consciously smug that Louisa immediately decided it was the most boring place she had ever seen. No wonder Amanda had told her little about it. In the parking lot beside the bus-stop, Louisa waited while the normal people who knew where they were going evaporated as rapidly as water droplets on the pavements of the city.

Amanda had screwed up the arrangements. No matter how many times Amanda let her down, Louisa always expected her mother to get it right the next time – just this once. She stood with her knapsack. From the few looks she was given, she soon realized that aimlessness was frowned upon. She glanced around for a telephone and noticed that she was being observed by a tall, skinny woman wearing clam-diggers and a white, paint-spattered man's Oxford shirt rolled up to her shoulders. Her sun-etched face was half-hidden beneath a battered straw hat. Leaning against a jalopy that belonged in a museum, the woman could have been forty or sixty. Louisa stared boldly back at her. But when the woman removed her hat and Louisa recognized a version of her mother's high cheekbones and patrician nose, she was sorry. There was a good chance that this brown skeleton was Aunt Alice.

Louisa shouldered her knapsack and walked across the pavement. The woman didn't wave or even smile. If she wasn't Aunt Alice, Louisa could ask her if she knew where Alice lived.

The woman held out her leathery hand. 'I'm Alice.'

Louisa shook it. 'Thanks for picking me up.'

'You'd hawdly find Paradise uthawise,' Aunt Alice said, in one of those Anglo-American accents that skim haughtily across the r's. Then she pointed to Louisa's knapsack. 'Is that it?'

'Yeah.'

'Well, I expect you won't need much.'

They climbed into the car, Louisa placing the precious knapsack at her feet, and when the passenger door wouldn't close, Alice – who smelt of turpentine and gin – reached across and tied it shut with twine. Then she revved the engine and skidded into the road. 'Damnable summa people,' she said.

Abandoning all hope that she had been rescued by the saner sister, Louisa attempted to converse with her aunt. 'So, what's there to do around here?'

'What's they-ah to do? What a question.'

They headed out eastwards on the narrowing peninsula

towards Amagansett, the bay to the north and the Atlantic to the south. Before they reached the tiny village of Amagansett – where, Amanda had said, the painter Jackson Pollock had lived – they turned right, towards the Atlantic, on to sandy, pitted lane that made the car rattle and shake. Overgrown hedges on each side formed a tunnel. Slim branches of privet slapped Louisa's face through the open window. Just when the passage became so narrow that Louisa expected the car to get stuck, she saw something ahead that took her breath away: the almost surreal blue of the Atlantic. Alice changed gear and gunned the engine until the car spat out on to a grassy field that stretched as far as Louisa could see to both right and left, with only the yellow dunes and the ocean ahead. Alice twisted the steering wheel and the car bounced down a track to a 'cottage' the size of a hotel. They came to a halt behind a two-storey barn, which was hung with a giant wishbone that Louisa recognized as a bleached whale jaw. Alice turned off the engine, left her keys in the ignition and slipped out. As the car shuddered into sleep, Louisa struggled to undo the twine that held the passenger door shut. When she had managed it, she clasped her knapsack to her chest and rushed after her aunt to a battered screen door at the side of the house.

'Welcome to Paradise,' Alice said, 'Or not. I always use the kitchen entrance. Some idiot locked the front doh-ah a few years ago and lost the key.' The screen door creaked when it opened and banged when it closed. Louisa's eyes adjusted to the gloom of the cavernous north-facing kitchen.

'In a manner of speaking,' Alice said, her voice echoing, 'this is the only room I really use. My studio is in the barn and that's off limits. You'll find yourself a bedroom upstairs. Feel free to explore, but keep it to yourself. I don't do reminiscence.' And with that, Alice crushed a cockroach with the toe of her taped-together shoe and sloped off to the barn.

Louisa opened the antiquated icebox: tonic water, limes. She searched for a glass in the high kitchen cupboards, found a teacup, rinsed it and got herself water at the sink. Then she picked up her knapsack and meandered out into an enormous hall that filled the centre of the house. At the south-facing end, looking out to sea, was the locked front door. Peering out of a grimy side window, itself a masterpiece of arts-and-crafts lead-work, Louisa thought it a pity not to have that door open all day to the sparkling blue. On both sides of the hall, vast living rooms were filled with antiques and curios, collected over generations from across the globe. A film of grey covered the windows, making the rooms seem dark, even though this was a sunny day.

Louisa turned to the grand central staircase that curled up from the hall to the upper floor and was drawn to a bedroom on the right, facing the sea. Through the windows, she felt she could see the whole world. Louisa wrenched open a window and the sea-breeze ruffled her hair. The surf tumbled in her ears. She scanned the yellow beach – dotted here and there with people lying in the sun, or simply walking along the shoreline. A dog chased waves.

Her back to the window, Louisa scanned the room: there was a carved mahogany double bed, a bench covered with moth-eaten velvet and an overstuffed armchair in faded chintz. The walls were a garden of cabbage roses and peonies. The mahogany tallboy had space for ten times more clothes than Louisa owned and the bookshelf contained a complete set of Audubon guides to birds – some of which, Louisa reckoned, must by now be extinct. A blue-and-white Chinese vase on a side-table was waiting to be filled with wild daisies.

My own room. My own safe place. She could finally appreciate having been cut free from her mother, even though it was lonely. This lovely room was just the symbol of the summer's blank canvas, waiting to be painted. Maybe it was the closeness to the open water beyond the dunes that made Louisa feel optimistic, her life stretching into forever, full of possibilities, now that she had space to breathe.

She lay on the bed, unused to such privacy, and coughed slightly at the smell of mildew that permeated the bedclothes. The waves whooshed steadily, in and out, Louisa closed her eyes and listened until she fell asleep.

'My God I thought you'd never wake up,' Alice said next morning. 'You teenagers are all the same.' She was eating toast with sardines and handed Louisa a plate. 'I have a can of tuna, if you prefer. I generally save that for the cat. There are a few tomatoes in the garden. Might be a bit green, though.'

'I don't mind,' Louisa said. 'I'll just have some toast.' She was starving and could have demolished a more substantial meal, but wanted to be polite. She suspected that Aunt Alice, as skinny as any model she had seen, subsisted on such scrappy fare.

'Good girl. There's some Earl Grey left in the pot. I've got to run. Meeting of the gallery committee. See you later.'

A cat jumped on to Louisa's lap.

'That's Fiendish,' Alice said. 'Keeps the mice down.'

Louisa ate her toast, found an apple in a bowl on the table – which she hadn't noticed the day before – and brought it back with her to the bedroom. She dug into her knapsack for her new bikini, put it on, felt naked, and pulled an old Indian caftan of her mother's over it. White, with colour stripes woven into the fabric near the hem, it smelled of Mannie – patchouli and Ivory soap. Then she went downstairs and out of the kitchen door on to the sun-baked wilderness of grass and through the rampant daisies and Queen Anne's lace. A set of rickety weathered stairs took her down onto the beach. Louisa wished she'd worn sandals to protect her feet from the splinters. At the bottom, a step was missing, forcing her to jump down onto the sand. She found herself nearly alone, but for a few scattered groups of mothers, nannies and shining children. The air smelt of coconut.

There was no-one there her age and everyone belonged to

someone else. She wasn't a daughter, or a wife or a babysitter or a nanny. She baked in the sun for a while, then swam lazily, which made her hungry, so she headed back to the house. She heard laughter and the tinkling of ice coming from the kitchen. Apart from sardines, tonic water and limes, Alice had ice. Louisa pulled open the screen door shyly, unable to see past it as her vision adjusted to the dimness, then stepped on to the mottled red linoleum to find a circus – like her mother's crowd at home, she thought, but a notch or two up. The talk was of art and aesthetics, and gossip about galleries and critical reviews. Alice must have brought the 'committee' home with her.

A drink appeared in Louisa's hand and someone offered her a cigarette, which she took, then put out in the kitchen sink when no-one was looking. She was absorbed into the group, the men making space for her at the table, while the women talked over her head. The men didn't mind that Louisa had little to say, but the women were thorny. Louisa liked the way Alice said 'New Yawk', as if she was Katharine Hepburn and Manhattan was a foreign country where she was likely to catch an exotic disease. 'Haven't set foot in New Yawk in yee-ahs,' Alice said, as though the pavements might sully her toes, whose nails, Louisa noticed, were painted lurid violet.

The manicured toes were in contrast to Alice's daily uniform of over-washed chinos and men's white shirts, so soft from repeated laundering that they were like silk – especially on Alice, whose elegance was assured despite, or perhaps even because of, her lack of attention to her appearance.

At Alice's occasional kitchen cocktail sessions, Louisa learned that her aunt scorned *The New York Times*, believing its arts coverage bourgeois. She took *Le Monde* and the *LA Times* on special order. Before long, Louisa got into the habit of collecting them for her in East Hampton, using an old push-bike she'd found in the garage, parked alongside a 'model 57' Bugatti, a relic of industrialist ancestors who, it turned out, had built the house at the turn of the century. 'Who owned the car?' she asked Alice.

'The dead,' Alice replied. 'Did you know that Koreans believe that the spirit of the dead live on in their cars?'

'Whose spirit should I be looking for?'

Alice wouldn't take the bait. 'You can use my car any time. This one won't get you anywhere.'

'I haven't got a licence yet,' Louisa said.

'Wouldn't worry about *that*.'

So this would be her summer, driving without a licence, days at the beach, sardines on toast, Alice locked in the barn painting, emerging only to refill her glass with gin and tonic and to see her friends once or twice a week. 'What are you painting?' Louisa asked her one evening, when Alice had broken the bank to cook them mussels in white wine.

'What a trivial question.'

Louisa wanted to see – was burning to see. She lingered by the barn door, thinking Alice didn't know she was there, and was amazed at how bright the barn was inside, as though the roof had blown off. At her easel, Alice was by turns athletic and contemplative. One morning she broke the silence. 'Stop spying and come in if you want to see.' Louisa's first full view of the barn's interior – with its high glass ceiling, like in a posh Soho loft – showed that Alice could be house-proud when she felt like it. The studio was beautifully designed – the weathered, wide-planked barn no more than a façade. Canvases were carefully filed on their sides in huge storage units on castors, not piled in a corner as Amanda's were.

Alice pointed Louisa towards the canvas she was working on. 'Go on, it won't bite.'

At first, Louisa couldn't tell what it was supposed to depict. Alice lined a few canvases up by the wall. 'It helps to see the bigger picture.'

Louisa saw the stalks and blooms of artichokes. The tough petals. Artichokes stripped to their furry matt hearts. Alice returned to her current canvas, paint curving and swelling with each stroke. The brush soothed and scratched, moulded and twisted. Rich purples and greens, lavenders, pinks and moonlight yellows arose from her palette. Around the studio, there were actual artichokes in all stages of undress – ready to inspire body parts, dunes and even skin.

'Now tell me, what do you think of Titian, dear?'

Dear? Alice was testing her. Louisa's art history class notes were somewhere in the back of her brain. Did Titian paint artichokes?

'All of Titian's work, or a particular painting?' Louisa asked.

'Let's see. 'The Rape of Europa'. Try that.'

'She's lying on top of Zeus, who has assumed the form of a tame white bull in order to seduce her senseless. You can see the whites of her eyes and she's clinging to Zeus's horn, in a way that's both frightened and lustful. It's just like those rape fantasies men have of women getting what they asked for. But to me, she's hanging on because it's the only thing available. She's died a spiritual death. Then in the clouds above her head, against an orange and blue sky, two cupids are flying away from her. Because after what has happened to her, she can never be loved.'

'My dear, you're still a virgin, aren't you?'

Alice pulled out another canvas, so large that Louisa had to help her heave it out of the rack and lean it against the wall. 'Now look. This is my 'Rape of Europa'. She has succumbed to the aggressive power of the erotic. The horn is a phallus. You've seen my bull series before, I presume.'

The painting was almost completely white – with blemishes and bruises of subtle colour.

'Try to see, Louisa. Don't just look.'

The surface was white on white, a million shades of white it seemed, until the light greys became apparent, and the subtlest strokes of violet and pink. Beneath a veil, it seemed, a human form emerged, then – around it, or above it? – a hulking shape.

'So?' Alice demanded.

'It's a woman and a bull,' Louisa said. 'A white bull, barely visible, like a phantasm.'

Alice raised one elegant eyebrow. 'Imagine, Louisa, that the bull is not inside you, but that you are inside the bull. The bull is everywhere and you cannot escape him, so there's no point in fighting him. You are living within his white rage. He is omnipotent, omnipresent, omniscient. That, my dear, is how Europa felt. Flattered. She had been chosen by a god. Titian is crass, dear. A Sunday painter. If he were around today he'd have a camera instead of a paintbrush, and he'd be painting pretty women on velvet or magazine pornography. Titian's Europa – those white eyes rolling in their sockets. Honestly. Europa was proud to succumb! My painting shows the dominant male energy that women crave.'

She had to be kidding. No wonder she was rarely shown in the city. 'I see,' Louisa said, although she didn't see it that way at all.

'You almost see,' Alice answered. 'I need you to sweep this room out for me please. There's a broom over there.'

And with that, she was gone. Louisa felt like Cinderella as she swept the floor, disturbing dust that filled the air and settled again. So different, Alice and Amanda. Amanda always thinking about painting, buying supplies, sketching, tearing up sketches and sleeping with painters. She was rarely focused enough to *paint* and, when she was, she tortured herself with self-criticism until the only relief was in taking a knife to the canvas and throwing it onto the street. Louisa wondered if Alice had imposed humiliating tutorials in art theory on her sister, destroying her confidence.

Maybe – just maybe – now that Alice had allowed her into her inner sanctum, she would let her into her heart too. There were so many questions Louisa wanted to ask, but dared not: Who were your parents? What happened to the prosperity that built this house? Who is the man in the silver frame in the blue living room, wearing a safari suit and standing with his foot on the head of a lion? Who is the woman in the flapper dress and cloche hat, smiling from behind the wheel of the Bugatti? What happened between you and Mannie? Have you ever been in love? Wanted children?

It was useless. She would go crazy trying to get information out of Alice, every encounter turning into a contest. Late one afternoon, Louisa was bringing Alice her five o'clock gin and tonic when she found the barn empty and discovered Alice reclining nude in her secret sun-trap at the western edge of the barn.

'My body disturbs you?' Alice demanded.

'No. Whatever gave you that idea?'

'You're spilling my drink.'

The constant humiliations were too much. It was best to stay away from Alice. She needed to find someone else to talk to. During her second week at Paradise, Louisa walked further down the beach than usual before laying down her towel. She strove to seem self-contained although not unapproachable. One group of potential friends seemed to gather at around the same time every day on a private beachfront. She couldn't quite hear what they said to each other, but she didn't need to. The body language of the girls, who spoke through movement as they turned this way and that on their towels, and the restlessness of the boys, who were constantly sparring, told Louisa that the girls treated the boys with disdain, while the boys would accept the smallest flicker of attention.

One boy breached the tight circle to tease around the edge of Louisa's towel for a day or two – capturing a volleyball that had been flung too far, picking up a seashell near her foot. Once or twice she had heard the boys goading each other to be first to talk to her. The freezing stares of the girls, when Louisa went in for a swim, told her that the boys were interested. But Louisa would rather have talked to a girl. Those girls ran in a pack, though. Only the boys went solo.

One afternoon the volleyball boy came out of the sea and headed straight for her. He sat down by the edge of her towel, peppering his legs and swim trunks with sand. Beads of saltwater glistened on his tanned back and shoulders. 'Hi,' he said, as though she'd been expecting him.

She supposed she had been. 'Hi,' she answered.

'I've seen you at the tennis club, haven't I?'

'Don't play tennis,' Louisa said, turning back to her book, which she hoped showed enough Alice-like disdain to make her attractive.

'What are you reading?'

'Simone de Beauvoir.' It was the only book that hadn't been thrown into the back of the U-Haul. Amanda disapproved of romance novels; they conditioned women to be subservient.

'French philosophy isn't my strong point,' the boy said. 'You in college?'

Louisa liked that. She still had a year of high school to go.

'No,' Louisa said. 'Miss Porter's.'

'I know girls at Miss Porter's. What's your name?

'Louisa Stone.'

'Hmm. You don't know Sally Penrose, do you?'

Louisa did know her. She was well-off, well-travelled and well-adjusted, which meant she was part of a group of bow-heads who looked down on Louisa. A girl like her shouldn't have been at Miss Porter's but, every time she asked her mother how they could afford it, she'd fobbed her off. 'Doesn't ring a bell.'

'Nice girl. Want a beer?'

'I'd take a soft drink if you have one.'

'Be right back.' Louisa turned her gaze back to her book, but, from the silence in the beach-babes area, she knew that they were watching Foster as if their lives depended on it.

He returned almost immediately, head down, as though he'd made a decision to ignore the clique's reaction. She liked that. He'd taken a risk for her already.

'How long are you here?'

'All summer,' she said, sipping a drink from a cold can that was slippery with condensation. She pressed the icy metal to her forehead.

'You don't sound too happy about it.'

'It's a bit dull.'

Foster turned over on his stomach and looked at her from under thick, brown lashes. 'You haven't met the right people.' His eyes were bright green and his face was perfectly sculpted. Way out of her league. His only flaw was that his nose was freckled and peeling a little from the sun. 'Where you staying?' he asked.

'Paradise, with my aunt.'

'Ah, so you're one of *the* Stones.'

She was taken aback. 'What's that supposed to mean?'

'Sorry. It's just that the others were saying they thought you were a relative of the eccentric painter. Somebody else said, no, you were working there but – well, you don't look like you're doing much work to me. Do you paint? Talent run in the family?'

'You mean total madness and uncertainty? No. I'm hoping it skips a generation.'

Foster laughed. 'So, you don't paint or play tennis. What *do* you do?'

It was Louisa's turn then to look at him from under her lashes. I'm up for anything, she was trying to say without being obvious. Oh, how she wished for the confidence of the bow-head clique with their glossy hair and colour-coordinated Alice bands. 'Not much, really. Read. Swim. Cycle.'

'We'll have to get you out then.'

Was he asking her for a date? Or just seeing how she'd react if he did? 'That would be nice.'

They bantered until they heard Foster's name called. 'Gotta scoot,' he said. 'Tennis tournament. You want to come? I can put your name on the door at the club.'

She knew that scene. Membership was reserved for American aristocracy. Louisa would feel like an outcast in her jeans and shirts passed on from Amanda. The girls, she knew, would be in colour-coordinated Lacoste, all sick pink and vile green. 'No, thanks. That scene's rather bourgeois, I find.' She was shocked at how naturally her mother's words emerged from her mouth.

'Hmm, well, the Stones always were above it all. But you should try rubbing shoulders with the *hoi-polloi*. You might like it.' He grinned.

'I'm not being a snob. I just can't play tennis.'

'Strange. There's a plaque with your family name on it at the club.'

'Must be a mistake.'

Foster looked at her as though he couldn't believe her ignorance. 'You been living in Europe or something? There used to be tennis courts up at your place. Probably still there under all that sand and grass. The dunes tend to eat up the property if you're not careful.'

'What else do you know?'

'About tennis?'

'No, about Paradise.'

Foster smiled. 'A very beautiful girl lives there.'

Louisa nearly groaned. Nice try, but –

Foster was persistent. 'Are you sure you won't come? I've got to play or Dad will kill me.'

'You must be very good.'

'He's got money riding on it.'

Louisa watched Foster lope off. She had just met a boy who knew more about her family than she did.

The next day, Louisa claimed a patch of sand within striking distance of the gang of girls, who lay face down on blankets. One, with breasts like overripe fruit, was swatting away a hunk of a boy who kept toying with the strings on her bikini. When she caught Louisa watching, she shot daggers at her. Louisa turned away and tried to read, sweeping through several pages and hardly taking in a word until she came to 'Sex pleasure in woman is a kind of magic spell; it demands complete abandon; if words or movements oppose the magic of caresses, the spell is broken.' She wondered what it would be like to feel that magic.

She got up and ran into the surf, diving against a wave so that she slipped beneath its current and surged down until she needed air, then surfaced. She swam parallel to the shore, then lay on her back, floating.

Amanda had taught her to swim – just about the only useful thing she *had* taught her, apart from sponging off the bourgeoisie. All over the east coast, there were charming towns in which seventy-five per cent of the houses were vacant most of the time. In the summers, Amanda always had one at her disposal. Sometimes it was Provincetown, sometimes Connecticut or Maine. Living in someone else's summerhouse was a bit like wearing a stranger's clothes. Sometimes Louisa and Amanda did wear other people's clothes – if they'd been left behind in the summerhouses.

Floating on her back, Louisa was enjoying the illusion of weightlessness. She thought of de Beauvoir again: 'If words or movements oppose the magic of caresses, the spell is broken.'

What might those words be? Do you love me, do you care for me, do you need me, do you mind if I fall in love with you? She must be careful not to let Foster think she was as loose as the rest of the Bohemian women in her family – not that she knew Alice was loose, she merely suspected it. Louisa needed a plan to ease herself towards making love with Foster – for she already knew that this is what they would do. Whether it was right or wrong hadn't occurred to her. Living with Amanda required the willing suspension of morality – as well as disbelief. Amanda had always said: 'Morality traps people in their tiny lives and makes them suffer. All we have is the moment, Lou. Never forget that.'

Louisa recorded this in her mental book of 'things to say to comfort Amanda'. It would come in handy in September, when Amanda would be nursing a heart broken by Mr Whomever in India. She thought of Amanda diving into the Indian Ocean, then emerging like Botticelli's Venus on the half-shell. Amanda shining. She'd taken a picture of her like that the previous summer, when they'd been best-est friends. This summer, Louisa hadn't even got a postcard.

'SHARK! SHARK!' The boys' cries cut through the water. Louisa rolled off her back in fright and dog-paddled in the waves. They were splashing towards her now, three wild boys with a girl in tow. 'RESCUE! RESCUE!' The next thing Louisa knew, she was being lifted in Foster's arms and carried from the sea. It was childish and silly, yet Louisa couldn't help squealing, watching herself and thinking, this is the way teenagers are supposed to behave. I'm a teenager.

Foster threw her back into the sea and she plunged down until she hit the sand. She gripped clumps of seaweed and stayed on the seabed, holding her breath, to frighten him. He dived in and practically dragged her out by the hair. 'Sorry! You OK?'

His arms around her, cold and hot at the same time.

Louisa giggled. 'Gotcha!'

They played like children, Louisa forgetting the part of herself that usually hovered above – the wise keeper.

Back on the sand, Foster and the boys gathered around Louisa's blanket, an act, she knew, that was a declaration of rebellion against the bow-head babes. She didn't know what happened amongst the factions when they left the beach in the late afternoons, though she suspected that their beach flirtations were foreplay for riskier games at night.

Foster cracked open a beer and took a long sip, then offered it to Louisa. 'No thanks.' The other girl drank one though, as she wordlessly jostled with one of the boys for possession of her own beach towel.

'You going to introduce us?' Louisa asked.

'Pardon my bad manners,' Foster said. 'Lu, meet Hump, Teddy, Chris and Poppy.' The boys guffawed. Louisa wondered what was funny.

Foster lay back on his towel and Louisa, beside him, on hers. They lay there close enough to touch but not touching, for minutes – hours – Louisa couldn't tell. Eventually, Foster brushed her left hand with his right and left it there, just close enough for her to feel a tingling electricity. The other boys were talking in low voices.

'D'ja see the bow-heads?'

'Excellent. They freaked.'

'They need a chill pill.'

She knew from this that the boys had got the reaction they wanted from the girls by snubbing them in favour of Louisa. And, if it was only a game, she wasn't interested. She sat up and gathered her things, Poppy watching her from behind a pair of Ray-Bans.

'You off?' Foster said.

'Yeah. Getting hungry.'

The boys snickered again.

'I'll walk you home,' Foster said.

Louisa could feel the boys' eyes on her as she and Foster began to walk. She wrapped her beach towel round herself protectively, and Foster smiled at her with perfect white teeth. His feet were perfect too, she noticed, as was every slope and angle of his body. The hairs on his legs had turned blonde in the sun.

Louisa glanced back at the girls, their shoulders pressed together in a circle of perpetual whispering. Louisa knew they were talking about her. She'd had plenty of experience of it in high school. Her mother was too peculiar and Louisa herself too solitary to be accepted on the social scene. She was of it but not part of it. When the headmistress commented that Louisa had done well in her exams, she had added to Louisa's surprise, 'But of course all the Stone girls have done well at Miss Porter's over the generations.' Louisa had felt she was talking about somebody else, someone she might have been and not who she was. Louisa did not know the rules of the society in Amagansett, anymore than she knew why her mother had left home and never gone back.

As soon as they were out of sight, Foster put an arm around her shoulder. It was a revelation, walking along the beach with a boy who seemed to like her. 'Listen, you want to get together?' he asked.

'Sure. Where?'

'I'll come by tonight. There's a beach party.'

They waited until dark, then set off for the beach, walking a quarter-mile along the path that fringed the dunes. Foster carried an old blanket and a knapsack in one arm, and steadied Louisa with the other. On this moonless night, the way was treacherous. The beam from a light-house swept across their path at intervals, making scraggly phantoms of the scrub oak.

When they'd arrived at a far section of cove Louisa had never seen before, Foster whistled. A whistle returned, half-human, half-bird. 'Nearly there,' Foster said softly. 'We have to be quiet. The police come down and scope the beach with a searchlight every so often.'

He gripped Louisa's hand and led her down an even narrower path towards a nest in the dunes, where half a dozen boys were hunkered. An orange dot wobbled like a wayward star as it was passed from hand to hand. Louisa caught the sweet scent of hash mixed with the rotten, low-tide odour of black marsh ooze.

She felt reckless as she sat down in the secret circle where the sand was still warm from the sun.

'You came,' Hump whispered in her ear, his breath hot and yeasty.

As she listened to the banter of boys whose faces she could

hardly make out, she felt privileged to be the only girl in the group: they spoke like boys do when no girls or women were around.

Foster handed Louisa a beer, fizzy and warm. In the dark, she tipped the bottle back too far and it swamped her throat, she suppressed her chokes, took another swallow, and another, until she began to feel pleasantly warm. The beer lifted her out of herself. She felt easy. Foster passed her a joint and she inhaled, like she'd seen her mother do.

Foster laid his hand on the back of her neck, and tenderly stroked the skin behind her ear with one cool finger. She closed her eyes.

'Wanna go for a walk?' he asked.

They stood up, Foster carrying the blanket, and moved away from the group. There was a low comment from the boys and a laugh. Fuzzy-headed, Louisa let Foster guide her to another burrow in the dunes, where he spread the blanket.

The laughter of the boys was still too close. More whistles and other juvenile noises came from the dunes as Foster laid his warm body on hers and kissed her. When she began to shiver with the cold and desire, Foster wrapped the blanket around the two of them.

But the boys were still chattering. 'You sure she's had enough? Let's stir the porridge, man.'

'Let's get out of here,' Louisa said.

'Why? They're only joking.'

'I want to go.'

They walked up the beach towards Paradise. In the dark it was almost invisible behind the scrub pine. 'Tell me more about the Stones,' Louisa said.

'Like what?'

'Like, how did they make their money?'

'The three Ps – property, prohibition and piracy.'

'You're kidding.'

'Story goes that your grandfather – I assume it was him,

anyway – used to run rum right up on this beach. When we were kids we used to dig down at the beach to try to find it. Silly, I know. Your grandfather was quite young then. Making a name for himself, more than anything. He didn't need the money. The family owned mills and factories all over the place. But the real money came from *his* father – gold out west.'

'How do you know all this?'

'Beats me. You just hear talk, that's all. My dad takes an interest in the history of the area. He used to tell me the rum-running stories when I was a kid. But don't assume that what I'm telling you is the God's truth.'

Louisa wanted to believe it was true, if only to have some information that made her ancestors seem like more than ill-defined ghosts. 'So what happened to my grandfather?' Alice and Amanda, little girls on this beach, playing tennis up at the house – it was unimaginable.

'Car crash. Alice was left all this and made Amanda's guardian, since she was nearly old enough to be her mother, anyway. She let Amanda run wild. Paradise was some kind of free love commune for a while. Or so they say. Wild back then wasn't the same as wild now. My dad said that it was a scandal when Alice refused to "come out" and took off for Paris.'

'What about Amanda?'

'I never heard much more about her.'

That made sense, considering that Amanda hadn't been back to Amagansett since Louisa was born.

They reached the bottom of the rickety stairs, Louisa legs aching from walking in the sand.

'You know, when I was a kid we used to come up here at Hallowe'en,' Foster said, the house looming above them. 'We used to dare each other to go inside. Some of the guys would let off home-made explosives, just to see if Alice would come running out.'

'You used to come all the way down from the city at Hallowe'en?'

Foster corrected himself. 'If it was on a weekend. People come down here weekends all year, even Christmas.'

Louisa liked the way Foster put a hand on her lower back, in case she fell on the steps. When they reached the top, she leaned on his shoulder, weak with tiredness and something else. Foster kissed her, lightly on the mouth. Her first kiss. They stood, forehead to forehead, for a moment, then they lifted their faces and kissed some more.

'Do you know the botanical name for artichoke, Louisa?'

Louisa shook her head, her teeth stripping the flesh from an artichoke heart dipped in garlic butter. Alice's first crop of the summer was ready to eat. It was all there was to eat, actually.

'What do they teach you at Miss Porter's?' Alice demanded. '*Cynara*. Cynara as in Cynic with a capital C. Look it up. A "choke" is a thistle flower. Peasant food until Catherine de Medici introduced them to the French Court because she was homesick. She also introduced the fork, by the way.'

Dropping the 'r' in fork, caused Alice to cackle roundly. 'Plenty of that too! I can just imagine her sucking on those tender little leaves, trying to make an impression, can't you? Do you know, she drilled a hole in the wall so she could watch her husband's older mistress have sex with him? Diane de Poitiers was old enough to be his mother. I adore the justice of the older woman winning the battle, don't you?' She looked Louisa up and down. 'Perhaps not. Yet. What do you know, anyway? I don't suppose you have any idea what Diane de Poitiers' secret was?'

'Tell me,' Louisa said, wishing there was more to eat than artichokes.

'Painters depict either mothers or whores, Louisa. But for a man, there is nothing more intoxicating than the mix of mother and whore together – which is what Diane was. Every painting of her depicts a pubescent teenager, even though she was decades older. Plastic surgery without the surgery, you know?'

Alice laughed again and drained her glass. '*Plus ça change, plus c'est la même chose.* Fetch some more ice, will you? If you eat artichokes, you can drink as much fine liquor as you want. They detoxify the liver. They're also a diuretic, good if you're watching your weight.'

'So that's your secret. The artichoke, gin and sardine diet. You should write a book.'

'Artichokes increase bile. Bile, my dear, is what life is all about. Without bile, there would be no art.'

Louisa broke apart a lump of ice with a pick, determined to escape the house in search of Foster as soon as this bizarre audience was over.

Something had Alice on a high. 'An artichoke can be anything you want it to be. It's both male and female with its phallic stalk and its breast-like blossom.'

At that moment, Louisa would have dearly loved an artichoke to be a thick, juicy steak. She was sick of eating them, talking about them – but especially tired of her aunt's pretension. 'Surely, then, when people look at your paintings, the first thing they think is: this is not an artichoke.'

Alice was imperious. '*Ceci n'est pas un pipe, non?* You're a superficial girl. Now remember, when you're cutting artichokes, slice them three inches below the bud. Do it right, and this particular variety flourishes twice.'

'Yes, M'am.'

Louisa wandered down to the beach, but Foster wasn't there. She decided to walk anyway, her feet making little impression on the wet sand at low tide.

'Hey, Lu. Wait up!'

She turned to see the abominable Humphrey, on his own, walking towards her. It was the first time she'd ever seen him without his entourage. 'Hey. Foster sent me to tell you that his parents are making him babysit.'

'Too bad,' Louisa said. 'I'll go home then.'

'Hey, don't be like that.' He sang, 'Here we go loop-de-loo, here we go loop-de-lie, here we go loop-de-loo, all on a Saturday night.' The children's nursery rhyme sounded obscene coming from him.

Louisa turned back towards Paradise, backlit by a sunset. The windows had turned to mirrors that reflected the dying light from the sea.

'One thing I've always wondered,' Hump said. 'What's that room at the top? On the roof. It's not a cupola, not a widow's walk – it's too big for that.' He was looking at a structure made of timber and glass, like a conservatory perched at the apex of the main body of the house.

'I haven't found a door to it yet.'

Humphrey was an arrogant golden boy, nothing like Foster. Some would see him as the better-looking of the pair, but he reminded Louisa of a frog in biology class. If she slit his stomach, stinking matter would ooze out.

'Maybe it's one of those architect's follies,' he said. 'You see all kinds of fancy features on these big, old houses. We've got a widow's walk on ours. Mother says it's not much use for a golf widow.'

Louisa wished he'd go away. When they got to the bottom of the splintering, wooden stairs that led up to the grounds of Paradise, Louisa said, 'Thanks for walking me home. I'll see you around.'

But Hump followed her up the stairs, whistling at the dense grass and hedging run amuck. 'The famous Alice isn't into gardening.'

'I like it,' Louisa said. 'It's more natural, like a meadow.'

'You kidding? The long grasses have ticks.'

Nearly at the kitchen door, Louisa planned to close it in Hump's face. He wasn't a bad person, but she didn't like him.

He was on her heels as she opened the door.

'Good night,' she said.

Humphrey held the door open, reluctant to leave.

'Hey!' The voice came from the garden. Louisa peered out to see Foster sitting in one of a pair of peeling old Adirondack chairs. 'I thought you were babysitting!' Louisa called as she ran to him and sat in the other chair before Hump could get to it.

'What's with the musical chairs?' Humphrey shouted.

'Babysitting?' Foster asked.

'That's what Hump said.'

Foster, eyes narrowed, stared down his friend. 'My parents aren't going out after all. So babysitting's cancelled.' Tension flickered between the two young men. 'Belly's looking for you.'

Louisa and Foster watched Hump go back down the steps to the beach, his legs disappearing, then his shoulders, then his head. They didn't see him again until he was jogging along the tideline.

'Listen, Belly's having a party,' Foster said. 'I want you to come. Break the ice. You girls usually need a bit of a push.'

'I'm not one of the "girls",' Louisa said. 'What was going on there?'

'What do you mean?'

Louisa raised an eyebrow. 'You know.'

'Hump was just sniffing around. He's got a competitive streak.'

'Doesn't that make you angry?'

'Why should it? I don't own you. You don't own me. That's what I like about you. You're different. The girls we know, they think they own us. Sometimes we rebel,' Foster explained. 'They're more like sisters, really. I'm not going out with any of them.'

'I see.' The sort of sisters you had your first kiss with and lost your virginity to, she suspected. 'And Poppy?'

'She's wild. Her father's a rock star. The other girls are jealous. So she hangs out with us.'

'When are you going to grow out of the boys versus girls thing?'

'You're right. It's boring – that's why I'm into you.'

But he didn't want to own her, which made Louisa feel second-rate. She wanted to be owned, she realized, even though her mother would have been horrified to hear her admit it. She kept her eye on the hint of white tan-line that was exposed above Foster's blue shorts; they were printed at one side with 'Yale'. He caught her looking, so she pretended it was the shorts she was staring at.

'You like Yale?' she asked him.

'Great parties,' Foster said. 'You should come up one week-end. Hump and the others – they'll all be there.' He spoke as if she'd been accepted into the group because he'd decreed it. She could see herself letting it slip to the girls at Miss Porter's that she was going to Yale to stay with her boyfriend for the week-end. Her boyfriend . . . She was skipping too far ahead, she knew, but the way he talked, assuming they'd still be friends in the fall, gave her the confidence to believe that maybe Foster was the real thing, some compensation for being holed up in East Hampton while her mother was wafting around India in a marijuana haze.

'I'll have to see,' Louisa said, hoping she was acting like a girl who did not want to be owned.

Louisa washed her hair in the outdoor shower, still in her bikini. Alice didn't seem to mind or even notice that the water in the indoor bathrooms didn't run at more than a trickle. Louisa preferred to shower outdoors anyway, where she could watch the sun setting and turning the ocean pink. As she was towel-ling herself off, she heard a rustling in the dense, untidy hedges and looked up, expecting to see one of the foxes that always appeared at sunset, but nothing came. She wrapped the towel around her hair and headed back indoors.

She padded upstairs to get dressed, which was a joke because all she had were denim cut-offs that she'd fashioned into shorts from old blue jeans, the caftan and a totally unsuitable hippie skirt Amanda had given her to go with her boring T-shirts. Her choice of shoes was blue rubber flip-flops or white canvas sneakers. There had to be something wearable someplace in this house.

In one of the bedrooms she had explored one rainy afternoon, there was a walk-in closet smelling of cedar and old leather, loaded with clothes trunks that had never been unpacked since somebody's European tour. There might be something to wear in them – it wouldn't be preppie, might not even be this century, but who cared? She didn't mind dressing to shock the bow-heads, as long as she did it with style. Louisa opened the top trunk and the scent of lavender rushed out. Wrapped in tissue paper, there were layers of clothes. She lifted out the dress on top: a strapless party dress in a strong black-and-white pattern of abstract flowers, with a black crinoline under the skirt. She let her wet towel drop and held the dress up to her naked body in the chevalier mirror outside the closet door. She unhooked the side of the dress, then slipped it over her head and twisted to hook it up again. The girl in the mirror smiled at her. A perfect fit. There must be shoes, if someone had gone to so much trouble to preserve the dresses. Curious, she pulled more garments out of the trunk – another two summer dresses, one full-length, white, a real debutante's dress, another in a pink polished cotton, with straps that tied at the shoulder. She hung them in the closet to air, then excavated further to a layer of tennis dresses suitable for a country club dance circa 1966. Someone about her age had lived in this house in the 1960s like a WASP princess, rather than a gypsy.

Digging further, she searched for a diary, letters, scraps of anything that might tell her something of the story. But there were only dresses, as evasive as Alice. On a high shelf in the closet, she found shoes, her eyes lighting immediately on a pair of white ballet pumps. She blew off the dust and slipped one on to her foot. Again, it was a perfect fit. She wound her hair up into a chignon and fastened it with bobby-pins she found sitting in a china dish on the dressing table, as though they'd been left there only yesterday.

She went out into the near-dark summer evening to wait for Foster. She practised walking in the shoes and twirled her dress this way and that. Half-listening for the sound of a car coming down Alice's treacherous lane, she had started to fear he wouldn't show, that the invitation had been too casual.

'Stood up?' Alice asked, coming out of the kitchen with a fresh gin and tonic. 'Or just playing dress-ups?'

Louisa had learned to ignore Alice's caustic remarks. 'That room on the roof, how do you get there?'

Alice sipped her drink. 'Thought you'd never ask. There are steps up to it. The room was an afterthought, so the staircase is hidden behind a panel in the back of the closet in your bedroom. It's locked. Insurance.'

'But what's it for? Whale-watching?'

'Whale-watching! Honestly. It's a glass room.'

'A glass room – obviously. What else?'

'My grandfather was an amateur photographer back in the days before artificial lighting. He liked taking pictures of pretty ladies. The glass room was a photographer's studio, lit by natural light. Portrait photographers had them then, otherwise they had to take all their pictures outdoors. The subject would have to sit very still for about half an hour, while the negative absorbed the image made by the light. It wasn't entirely unusual to build glass rooms on roofs, although I've never seen one perched as high as that. I think it was partly for privacy. The secret door made it hard to get to.'

'I wonder what the ladies thought of that.'

'I used the term "ladies" rather loosely.'

The dunes hissed and Foster appeared in a white shirt that glowed in the darkness. 'Your lover has arrived,' Alice said, at once making Foster seem insignificant and Louisa feel womanly. She had a lover – much better than a boyfriend.

Louisa walked over to join him. 'You look amazing,' he said, taking her hand. 'Come on. It's not far.'

They slipped down the steps to the sand, where Louisa kicked off her pumps. Holding her shoes in one hand, and Foster's hand in the other, she was enchanted by the hundreds of tiny lights shining through the trees from behind the bluffs. 'I had no idea there were so many other houses tucked in here. You can't really see them during the day, can you?'

'People bought houses then chopped up the land into parcels. Dad says land prices around here are calculated by the inch.'

'He doesn't approve.'

'Hates the traffic. All year-rounders do.'

'Like Alice. I didn't know your parents lived here year-round.'

'When they're not in Florida,' Foster answered. 'We're nearly there. Belly's parents are away.'

'She lives this close?'

Foster laughed. 'She's your neighbour. Where did you think she lived?'

'Paradise feels so isolated. I hadn't realized, that's all. Where does Hump live?'

'With her, as long as her parents are away. She won't let him out of her sight. Hump feels like he's been married all his life.'

A scent of cigarette smoke, then voices, told them that a group of people were waiting in the dark. Louisa could smell beer before she could make out faces.

'Hey, Fossor –'

Somebody was drunk already.

Foster escorted Louisa through the gathering, then pushed her ahead of him up a well-maintained flight of beach steps. She stopped, leaned on the railing, swept the sand off her feet and put on her shoes.

'Hey, Fossor. That's cool beans, man.'

At the top of the stairs, Louisa turned to Foster. 'Who were they?'

'Locals. Hoping they'll get into the party later, or that somebody will bring them out beers, anyway.'

'Locals?'

'They live here year-round.'

Belly was on the terrace, a vision in Madras shorts and a pink polo shirt, scooting back and forth on roller blades while holding on to Hump, who was shouting, 'Bums away' every time he gave her a push. The other girls were lounging around drinking cocktails, while a maid arranged platters of finger food on a linen-draped table. 'Fos! Look at me!' Belly shouted, then slammed into a crowd of boys engaged in competitive peanut-tossing.

'Whoa! That's enough,' Hump scolded.

Belly collapsed into a chair and stuck out her feet. 'Get these things off me!'

Foster brought Louisa to her. 'Hey. This is Louisa. Louisa, this is Annabel. Louisa's family own Paradise.'

I wish, Louisa thought. 'Hi.'

Belly stuck out her hand, 'Welcome. I've heard so much about you. Help me get these things off, will you? Hump wanted to give me a car, but his parents wouldn't let him.'

Louisa knelt by Belly's feet in her black-and-white debutante's dress, the skirt whooshing around her as she worked to undo the roller blades. Belly's knees were red and swollen. 'You should be wearing knee-pads with these, you know,' Louisa said.

'I'll never wear these again. I was only humouring Hump.' When the roller blades were off, Belly took Louisa by the arm and began to introduce her. 'Love the dress, by the way,' she said. 'Everyone, this is Louisa, Alice Stone's niece. Everyone knows Alice.'

It was harrowing, being grilled by six natural blondes with perfect teeth and, no doubt, perfect lives. Louisa was glad of the drink Foster handed her. As the terrace began filling up with students, who appeared to be arriving by busload, Belly leaned over and whispered in Louisa's ear, 'I told Hump to invite everyone, but I meant everyone from the club, not the whole of Long Island. I suppose it's time to put the music on.'

Louisa went with her into one of the rooms off the terrace, where Hump and the boys were sprawled out playing cards and looking bored. Foster circled the group, peaking at cards. Belly chose a Madonna album, then began to dance in front of Louisa, who had to sway along out of politeness. Poppy – sitting on a boy's lap – gave them a withering stare.

'Don't mind her,' Belly shouted in Louisa's ear. 'I think her mother did drugs when she was pregnant. Poppy's a bit . . .' She pulled a face, then dragged Louisa into a small sitting room and closed the door. 'Now, Lu. Serious girl talk. Foster's, like, totally into you.'

Louisa smiled.

'So, is it reciprocated?' Belly demanded.

'Yeah.'

'Good. I approve, in case you were wondering.'

Normally, Louisa couldn't have cared less for anyone's approval, but in Belly's world she decided to take her new friend's blessing with good grace. 'Thank you, Annabel, that means a lot.'

'It's Belly, by the way. What do you think of Humphrey? I know he can be a bit . . . But, really, what do you think?'

'He's one hot, fantastic guy,' Louisa said, hoping her lie would be believed.

Belly tilted her head and looked at Louisa askance. 'I know. You can't have him. You'd never do that to me, would you? Anyway, you have Foster. Thanks for the chat. I feel so close to you now. Let's go get some food. I haven't eaten all week.'

Louisa wanted to say, There's no way I'd ever take Humphrey. Not if my life depended on it, but that would have insulted Belly. Better, really, for her to think that Louisa was a little jealous of her catch. Out on the terrace, Belly and Louisa filled their plates with lobster salad, while Belly's ladies-in-waiting looked on with fake smiles. The pair sat at a table by the edge of the terrace, Louisa enjoying every mouthful of her lobster. 'You have no idea how good it is to eat real food.'

'You can take some home if you like. I've heard Alice is on food stamps.'

Louisa wanted to take her up on the offer, then realized how pathetic that would seem. 'You must think I'm as odd as Alice.'

'Not quite.' Belly inclined her head forwards. 'She swims stark naked year-round, you know. Doesn't even use a towel.'

'Doesn't need one. She's cold-blooded,' Louisa said.

'Hump's Dad took up cast-fishing so he'd have an excuse to have a gawk. You know, they say that Alice and Hump's Dad –'

'I don't want to know.'

'It's kind of gross, isn't it? You got to hand it to her, though. They say it's what keeps her so young ... that and the swimming.'

Foster had pulled up a chair and was holding Louisa's hand now. 'Hey, whatever rocks your boat, you know? You can swim naked anytime, Lu, wouldn't bother me.'

Louisa slapped him playfully, looking into his eyes. 'Anything for you, babe.' She could see herself coming back in the summers, becoming even more part of the group. She'd win the bow-heads over, go back to school in September and tell the guidance counsellor she'd do whatever it took to get to university. Weekends, she'd visit Foster at Yale, or he'd come to the city and see her. She couldn't wait to tell Amanda about all this, even if her mother did think the scene was bourgeois. And to ask her all the questions about the Stones she'd never known to ask before.

Foster held her hand, 'Wanna dance?' he said softly.

Next morning, Louisa held her dress up in the kitchen, sponging off the lobster salad she'd spilled on it. 'Who did this belong to?' she asked.

'Mmm?' Alice mumbled, the paintbrush in her mouth clicking against her teeth as she made a pot of tea. She often stumbled into the kitchen, after painting all night, brush in hand.

'Alice? Who did this dress belong too?'

'What dress?'

'The one I'm wearing.'

'How would I know? It's your dress.'

'It's not. I borrowed it from upstairs. There were tennis clothes too. An entire wardrobe somebody left behind.'

Alice met her eye for a second. 'They must have been Amanda's.' She spoke as though her sister was dead.

'Amanda dressed like this?'

'In 1966, maybe. Fashions changed in 1967. The summer of love, or so they tell me.'

'I was born in 1969. So she would have been seventeen – my age – when she wore this dress.'

'No sense then either. A fragrant blossom, waiting to be plucked.'

Louisa ignored the sarcasm. At least they were talking. 'I changed her, didn't I?'

'Don't be so vain, child.'

Louisa imagined seventeen-year-old Amanda struggling to emerge from the shadow of her sister, twenty years older. 'Were you jealous?' Louisa asked.

'Jealous! Of *what*?' And with that, Alice was gone.

That afternoon, Foster met her on the beach again. When they swam together, he pulled her under and kissed her on the bottom of the sea. They broke the surface, still kissing, until Louisa heard the boys shouting at them, egging Foster on. She pushed him away and swam alone for a while, then went back to her towel. Foster stayed in the water, messing with Poppy and the boys as if he didn't care. She closed her eyes and drifted, until she felt cold seawater sprinkling onto her as Foster leaned over her for his towel. He lay down beside her as though nothing had happened.

'Want to come to the club tonight?'

'You and me? Or you, me and the entourage? Maybe Poppy likes being one of the boys, but I don't.'

Foster covered his face with his T-shirt. 'They're my friends, what's your problem?'

Foster lowered his head to the towel and bestowed a surreptitious kiss on her shoulder. Louisa was caught between the sparks on her shoulder and the doubts in her mind. 'Why can't it just be you and me?' she asked.

'If you want to be alone, let's go up to your house,' Foster said.

They spent the rest of the afternoon on Louisa's bed, exploring each other as the curtains at the windows fluttered outward. They held, stroked, kissed, sucked – did everything but . . .

'When?' Foster asked, pulling the sheet over himself in embarrassment.

'Soon.'

Next morning, she cycled into East Hampton with her slip of paper. She would have to wait a month for the Pill to work, they told her. A month! Unless, she would like to try . . . She said she would.

That evening, Foster arrived in a station-wagon and honked the horn while she and Alice were at the kitchen table eating olives and parmesan cheese. Alice was stuck in the middle of preparing for a show. In only a few weeks' time, she was planning to unveil the Artichokes series at a party at Paradise. 'Can I help?' Louisa asked.

'Can you paint?' was the bitter response.

Louisa was in her denim cut-offs with a white lawn and lace Victorian blouse she'd found in a closet. She caught Alice looking at her in a new way, as if she might actually feel something for her niece and was about to let her mask drop.

'Seduisante, innocente, fleurissante,' Alice said, then caught herself and drew her eyes away. Seductive, innocent, blooming. It was the first compliment she'd ever given Louisa.

'Merci.'

'Be in the studio at dawn.'

The blast of a car horn sent Louisa skidding to the door.

'Dawn, don't forget.' Then Alice reached into her pocket, beckoned Louisa back and handed her a hundred dollar bill. 'Your friends smoke?'

Finally, responsible interest. Halfway out the door, Louisa turned, 'I don't.'

'I'm talking wisdom weed, silly girl. Get me some, will you?'

The woman was incorrigible. We eat artichokes and she has a hundred dollars in her pocket to spend on drugs, Louisa thought, letting the door slam behind her. Amanda and Alice were so alike it was frightening.

Foster smiled from the driver's seat and scanned her golden East Hampton legs approvingly, taking her attention away from the back seat of his car, which was packed with boys. This she noticed only when the wolf whistles started. Then Hump came roaring out of a hedge in a red Porsche, with Belly and the girls hanging out of it like Christmas tree-decorations. Great, she thought, the royal guard. Some date. She got into the front passenger seat, which he'd kept free for her – a sign they were together. Maybe she was being prissy. People dated in groups, these days.

'Hang on,' Poppy shouted, her spiky white-blonde head appearing out of nowhere from the back seat. She scrambled out – the boys offering no help as she climbed over them – opened the front passenger seat door and sat on Louisa's lap, adjusting her halter top. 'OK. Let's go.'

Poppy weighed nothing. It was like having a ten-year-old on her lap. Her legs were as thin as Louisa's arms and her bony shoulder jutted into Louisa's chest. 'Ouch!'

'Sorry,' Poppy said, leaning forward a little so that Louisa could see the spider tattoo on her shoulder. Louisa fought the urge to touch it. 'That must have hurt,' Louisa said. 'The spider, I mean.'

'No pain, no gain,' Poppy said, to a chorus of appreciative guffaws from the back.

This didn't feel right at all. How could Foster be so gallant when his friends were dweebs? As soon as they arrived at the club, Louisa broke away from the group, expecting him to follow. Middle-aged couples dressed for the evening, the men in jackets and ties, were getting out of cars and heading for the club.

'What's up?' Foster said.

'I'm not into hanging out with the guys, Foster.'

'I was only giving them a ride. Come on, we'll ditch them.' She followed him into the sprawling club grounds until they reached a service entrance by the kitchens.

'Never eat here. Food's crap.'

'Hey, Fos,' a man shouted. 'I need dishes.'

'It's my night off,' Foster said.

The man laughed, and turned as he did so, following Louisa's legs with his eyes.

'Hey. Watch that *béarnaise*,' somebody shouted.

And then they were in the dining room. Foster walked casually, as if he belonged there. Louisa traipsed after him, aware of eyes on her cut-offs. Black busboys and Hispanic waiters in white jackets bustled about with trays of dry martinis and Tom Collinses, butter, rolls and jugs of water. The women glimmered in the way rich women do, while the men were grown-up versions of Hump and Foster in their white trousers and navy jackets.

'It's Saturday night. The husbands are home,' Foster said in Louisa's ear as they reached the lobby.

'You work here?' she said.

'Dad thinks it's character-building.'

They swept down a short flight of backstairs to a large room, where a mirror ball flung spots of light on the walls. No-one was dancing. The music was so loud that Louisa couldn't hear Foster when he said something. She gave him her hand and he pulled her out onto a terrace, surrounded by rolling green lawns.

'That was a rather roundabout route,' Louisa said.

'We ditched 'em though, didn't we? Stay there, I'll get us

drinks,' he said, not bothering to ask Louisa what she was having.

Out of nowhere, Poppy appeared like a woodland sprite, with her pale skin and spiked white hair. 'Dead and boring. Like heaven for bankers and their banker babies. Wouldn't you rather be in the city?'

Louisa thought of the apartment, filled with strangers now. 'Not really. Too hot.'

'LA, then. Give me a swimming pool any day. I hate the ocean.'

'There's an ocean in California.'

'If you say so.'

Foster returned with the drinks – a beer for him and something brown in a cocktail class for Louisa. 'Sorry, Pops. Didn't know you were here.'

'Forget it.' Poppy seemed used to slights.

Louisa sipped her drink, which tasted rancid. 'What's this?'

'I think it's a Manhattan,' Foster said.

'Can I have the cherry? I'm starving.' Poppy said.

'Take it all.' Louisa handed her the glass.

Foster offered Louisa the beer and she waved it away. He made a sad-puppy face. 'Just hold the beer. I'll be right back.'

Poppy downed the Manhattan. 'Southern Comfort, straight,' she called after Foster.

Louisa went to sit at one of the tables, empty now that everyone was in the dining room.

'I wouldn't do that if I were you. Members only.'

'Aren't you a member?' Louisa asked.

Poppy almost laughed. 'Here comes Romeo. I'd watch him, if I were you.'

Foster appeared with a bottle under his arm and dangling glasses from his fingers. 'Follow me.'

They worked their way down a meandering path to a bench behind the tennis courts, where Foster handed Louisa a bottle of champagne with a flourish. 'It's warm,' she said.

'Fussy,' Foster answered.

Poppy looked from one to the other. 'It's been real,' and she loped off across the grass towards the trees, looking like she knew where she was going.

Louisa took the glass of warm bubbles he offered her and watched the white froth dissolve to gold. 'Was that our first fight?'

'Who's fighting?'

'We are.'

Foster's smooth brow folded into two narrow lines between his eyebrows. 'Come on,' he said.

They got into the car, with the champagne and glasses, and headed back to Louisa's, Foster skimming the car through the green forest as if it was nothing. They sat on the Adirondack chairs, Louisa slapping mosquitoes away from her legs. She stood up. 'You want to come in?'

'The house?'

'Yeah. Before we're eaten alive.'

She led him into one of the parlours facing the sea, where they sat on a dust-sheet-covered couch.

'Now will you have some champagne?' Foster asked.

'Yes,' Louisa said, crossing her legs primly.

'Other girls don't bring you into their houses to drink champagne. Not unless it's a party.'

'I'm not like other girls.'

'I know. You're different – in a good way. Above it all.'

'I'm not a snob.'

'That's not what I meant. You're . . . independent.'

'I've had to be. Poppy says I should watch you.'

'Don't listen to Poppy. She's jealous.'

'You ever date her?'

Foster moved closer to her on the sofa and put his arm around her. 'Poppy doesn't date. She just does, if you know what I mean.'

'How can you stand to be around that?'

'I can't help it if she likes being used. I'm not her psychiatrist. Good grief, Lou, what's got into you?'

'At least you can see she's being used.'

Foster rolled his eyes. 'You got your period or something?'

She was being a bitch, she told herself. But she kind of liked it. She swung her legs up on Foster's lap, and leaned her head back against the arm of the couch. 'I want you to myself, that's all.'

Foster smiled, dipped a finger in his champagne, and drew a line up her leg, from her ankle to the bottom of her shorts. Louisa felt like she was falling, so intense was the sensation. She closed her eyes, while he caressed her legs. He took her glass and put it on the floor with his, then lay beside her on the couch and fingered the lace on her Victorian blouse. He may as well have been touching her bare skin, the way his finger reached her so very lightly as it traced the fabric. He slowly ran his finger around the outline of her breasts, making smaller and smaller circles until she felt ready to scream. 'Come here,' he said.

She opened her eyes to see him looking into hers. Their mouths met, taking on lives of their own, while Foster held back just enough to keep her wanting more. There was something in what they said, about an experienced older man being ideal for your first, she thought until thoughts faded into feelings too overwhelming to name. His hand reached under her shirt and found a nipple, which he touched so gently that she felt a warmth building between her legs.

Eventually, she lay with her head in Foster's lap, gazing up at him. His hand moved to unbutton her shorts but she pulled it away. 'Not yet,' she said. He drew her hand to his zip and she sat up. 'Not tonight. Just this.' They were both naked from the waist up with everything else held back. Of all the things he made her feel, this was the best: her body was her own.

They lay together so long that Louisa began to fall asleep. 'I'd better go before your aunt comes in and freaks,' Foster said.

'Alice doesn't freak. She *is* a freak,' Louisa answered.

'Still.'

She walked him out to his car, her legs like jelly. 'Listen,' he said when they had kissed goodbye, 'I'm on double shifts this week. I won't have a night off for a while. I'll try to drop down to the beach between lunch and dinner.'

'I'll miss you,' Louisa said.

'Maybe I can sneak in after work.'

'Door's always open,' Louisa said.

He got in his car and she watched him disappear into the green tunnel, listening to the engine until it reached the highway and faded away.

Too soon, Alice rousted Louisa out of bed. 'Get to the studio. You're late!'

'No, Alice,' Louisa mumbled.

'Now.'

Louisa pulled on a T-shirt and shorts, made herself a mug of sugary tea, then stumbled outside. Louisa knocked on the barn door, telling herself that she was only being cooperative because she wanted to find out more about the Stones. If she and Alice could be friends, she might learn something.

'Come in!'

Louisa opened the barn door just enough for her to slip inside, and stood in the bright studio. A huge blank canvas had been readied on an easel in the middle of the room, and behind it a *chaise-longue* draped in brown velvet. That was where Alice would expect her to pose, Louisa thought with a shiver of apprehension. But then Alice appeared, stark naked as she had been on the beach. 'Choose your brushes and paint, Louisa.'

'Pardon me?'

'Go on. You can paint me.'

'I can't paint.'

'Who says? Of course you can paint. Anyone can paint.'

Louisa glanced at the arrangement of artichokes near Alice's easel. Their thick stalks and plump petalled flowers distracted her as Alice lay down on the *chaise-longue*, limbering up like a dancer. 'This okay for you?' Everything was on show, taut, ready and brown as a nut.

'This is mad,' Louisa said.

'Good. Go madder.'

Louisa picked up a brush, which almost vibrated in her hand, so imbued was it with Alice's energy. She held it over the palette, which was covered with glistening globs of colour – browns, fleshy pinks and shades of white so subtly different that at first they all seemed the same. She dipped her brush into a white that had the slightest tint of rose, then stood back.

'You have to look at my body. You must see!' Alice instructed.

Louisa wished she couldn't see. Her eye followed the line of Alice's body, which reminded her of an undulating dune landscape. She swept the brush along the canvas trying to reproduce the line, surprised by how sensual the paint felt. 'There. Done,' she said.

'Done?'

Louisa couldn't wait to get out of there. 'Done.'

Alice pulled herself up from the *chaise-longue* and came round canvas-side to view the work. She stared for ages, saying nothing.

'You have an eye,' she said, finally.

'Sure. Whatever.'

'Don't give me that. I just said you have an eye. That's the difference between you and Amanda. You're far more like me.'

Louisa looked at her naked aunt, 'You've got to be kidding. I'm not like either of you. I wish you could see that.'

Alice said. 'Your turn.'

'I can't, Alice. Really I can't.'

'Lie down on the chaise, cover your bits with the rug I left there – if you insist. I'll close my eyes. Okay?' Alice stood with her hands over her eyes.

'Count to one hundred,' Louisa said.

'One, two, three –'

Louisa had nearly slipped out of the barn door, when Alice growled, 'Come back here. Listen, pose for me. I'll give you the key to the glass room. Deal?'

'Deal.'

A few nights later, Louisa awoke in her solitary room to find Foster stroking her. He smelt of fried food because he had come straight from his kitchen job, and of beer because he'd had a couple to give him courage. At first, Louisa was too stunned to realize that Foster was with her in the bed, not just her dreams. Weak with desire, she let him fondle her, then let him take her hand in his own and guide it to the place he most wanted to be touched. She covered his mouth with her own when he cried out.

As Foster wrapped himself round her, his face covered with her sun-bleached hair, Louisa wanted to ask him if he loved her, yet knew that those words would break the spell. Every cell in her body was waiting for the penetration that hadn't happened yet but soon would. It was a lovely feeling, a sensation of being on the edge. It was a moment she could have stayed in forever, made all the sweeter by the knowledge that her body wouldn't let her. She had to have him, and soon.

It had been in Louisa's room all along. She hadn't bothered exploring the closet with the secret door to the glass room because it was packed with heavy boxes, filled with unreadable nineteenth-century books. Now she pulled out the boxes, one by one, discovering, as she got to the back of the closet, that some held photographs and photographic plates. She unwrapped a photograph from the waxy, white paper that had protected it for half-a-century and brought it out into the light. A saucy Edwardian maiden, in black lace-up boots and stockings held up with garters, stood, otherwise naked, her bottom facing the camera, one foot up on a box, her torso twisted so that her pert farm-girl breasts beckoned in profile. Her frozen smile was meant to seem naughty, but came across as clownish. It must have hurt like hell trying to keep that expression without moving for half-an-hour or more, Louisa thought. Then she noticed the riding crop leaning against the box. Eroticism hadn't changed much in a hundred years.

Louisa wondered if her great-grandfather had sold his wares or kept his collection private. Hell, he probably passed them round at his club.

When she'd cleared the way, Louisa put the key into the lock and twisted it slowly, expecting resistance. The lock clicked neatly open, and, when she pulled at the door, a blast of hot air nearly knocked her over. She drew back, gasping in the cooler air of her bedroom, which seemed arctic now, then went up the attic stairs, her body wet with perspiration by the time she reached the top. The heat was searing. Nearly choking, she glanced about for a sash window, pushing at the wooden frames that held the glass. She had nearly given up when one of them gave way. She leaned out the window and sucked at the air, her heart pounding, grateful for the breeze cooling her face. Then she noticed the view. All of East Hampton was laid out like the village of a train set. The ocean lapped beneath her, the patterns of the waves like one of Alice's paintings. The room itself was far larger than she had expected – big enough to live in, nearly. A bench ran along all four sides. She discovered another window that agreed to open and soon, the room became quite pleasant, with the sea air blowing through it. She could bring a mattress up here, and pillows and candles. How amazing it would be to sleep up here . . . to –'

'Louisa!'

She went to the door and shouted down the stairs.

'Who's there?'

'Louisa?'

She stumbled down the stairs into the cavern of the closet,

then through her bedroom and out to the landing. She leaned over the balustrade: 'Foster? Is that you?'

'Alice said I could come up!'

'What are you waiting for?'

He bounded up the stairs and kissed her there and then.

'I've something to show you,' she said, pulling him into her bedroom.

'I'm all yours.'

'The closet.' She escorted him into it, then pushed him up the stairs. 'Keep going until you get to the top.'

Foster stood in the glass room, like a prince surveying his kingdom. 'Wow.'

'Will you help me furnish it?'

'It's huge.'

'Come on.'

They pulled a mattress off one of the beds and dragged it up the narrow stairs, Louisa pulling while Foster pushed. When they had got it in place in the middle of the room, Louisa went back for pillows and a blanket and returned to find Foster sitting on one of the benches, looking out to sea. 'Maybe he used this to spot whales.'

Louisa laughed. 'Not even close. It was built for photography, in the days before lighting.' She dropped the pillows and blanket on the mattress.

'You'd hardly need a blanket up here. It's hot.'

'At night, you would,' Louisa said. 'Want to try it?'

Foster's face was suddenly serious. 'You mean . . . ?'

'I mean. This is the place.'

'Lie down,' he said.

'Not now. Alice's party is on Saturday. I want you to come. We can lock ourselves up here and no-one will know. I want it to be special.'

Louisa could hear the party growing downstairs, car doors slamming as more people arrived, giggling in the halls and shouting on the cliffs overlooking the beach. The cars were parked up and down the main road and the police had already been at the door once, saying the neighbours were complaining that they couldn't pass on the road.

'Tell them to come to the party!' Alice had declared, ecstatic on champagne and attention.

She'd been planning the unveiling of her Artichoke series for days and had hired caterers and bar staff. She'd had her hair done and looked twenty years younger as she sloughed off solitary months of introspection. Guests – too many to count – had arrived from the city and beyond, and the bedrooms were full of people copulating or sharing drugs. Semi-naked women ran up and down the corridors, making Alice's house seem like backstage at a fashion show.

Welcome to the Hotel California, Louisa thought, but at least nobody would notice her disappearance to her private eyrie at the top of the house.

'Is Larry here yet?' Alice kept asking her guests, her voice rising the more she drank. Larry seemed to be the only guest she cared about. The rest were extras. Artists, actors, models, musicians and groupies – the entire party, Louisa realized, was an elaborate backdrop designed for him. More conservative locals mingled among them, like Victorians visiting an asylum.

Delighted that, for once, there was proper food in the house, Louisa helped herself from the lavish buffet. Beautiful people filled every corner, but where was Foster? She squeezed her way past countless revellers, thinking he might be lost in the crowd. She reached the hall as the front door opened. Louisa rushed towards it and stepped out onto the grass, where she stood alone, listening to the giggles and shrieks echoing from the house.

'Hey, pumpkin. Lost?'

A man's voice, warm, intimate and familiar. She turned to see him leaning against the doorway, tossing a key and catching it. 'You have the key to the front door,' Louisa said.

'Comes in handy. Do we know each other?' His silky voice made her want to listen. He left the doorway and walked through the high grass towards her.

'Alice is my aunt.' Better to let him know she had a connection and wasn't just a vulnerable girl who'd drifted into the party.

'Your aunt, hey?'

Louisa was now walking beside the tall, rangy figure, who was dressed in a black linen suit, jacket sleeves pushed up to his elbows. 'I like your dress,' he said, lighting up a cigarette and illuminating his face. For an instant, Louisa could see him clearly. *He's so familiar. I've seen him before.*

'It was my mother's. It *is* my mother's, I should say. She's not dead,' Louisa said.

'You are little Lou,' he said. 'Do they still call you that?'

'You know me?'

'A long time ago,' he said. 'How's Amanda? Is she here?'

'No. India.'

'In-di-a.'

'And you are?'

He sucked his cigarette. '"I am he that walks with the tender and growing night; I call to the earth and sea, half-held by the night".'

Pretentious as Alice, she thought. A college professor on his summer holidays.

'You familiar with Walt Whitman the Wildman? "Press close, bare-bosom'd night! Press close, magnetic, nourishing night!"'

Leaves of Grass. Her mother adored it. Fortunately, Louisa had been paying attention. '"Night of south winds! Night of the large few stars! Still, nodding night! Mad, naked, summer night."'

Alice's voice trilled like a trumpet from inside the house. 'Larry?'

It held an edge of desperation, like Amanda's pleading. 'Larry?'

The man took another drag of his cigarette, the ember lighting up his playful face. 'So you've been educated, at least.'

'Amanda recited it to me when I was younger.'

'Glad to hear it. Meeting you is like seeing her, I think.'

'Larry!' It was an operatic cry now, mixing with the Eagles blasting from the rented stereo system.

'Let's walk on the beach,' he said.

'But I'm waiting for someone.'

'Look at you in your debutante dress. He'll wait.'

She followed him. Couldn't resist.

'Alice at her palace. Wonderland Alice.' His rich voice was one you could fall asleep to. 'How would you describe her, Lou? One word. No more.'

Louisa wanted to impress him for some reason she couldn't articulate. She thought of Alice's early-morning swims, her late-night swims, her glass constantly filled with gin and tonic, her willowy leathery body and her refusal to give in.

'One word,' he said. 'I have all the time in the world.'

The sand cooled her feet when they reached the beach.

'Unquenchable,' Louisa said.

One corner of the man's mouth turned up. 'Yes. Good.'

'Larry!' the voice shrieked again, closer now. Alice appeared illuminated in the grand entrance to the house as though on stage. They could see her, but she couldn't see them. Larry looked at Louisa and put a finger to his lips.

'Larry?'

They leaned against the fence and watched Alice peer into the darkness.

'She can be such a bitch, but a beautiful, unquenchable bitch,' Larry murmured.

Alice looked stunning, but Alice didn't need court painters to give her the illusion of youth, like Diane de Poitiers – the transforming fires were within her. She had become more youthful by the power of her terrifying will and – Louisa realized

– a desire for Larry that was equalled only by the intensity of her devotion to her art.

'She may be a complete bitch, but she's an amazing woman,' Louisa said.

'Larry?' Alice's voice faded as she disappeared from view and went to search elsewhere.

'Why are you hiding from her, Larry?' Louisa asked.

'Not hiding. Gaining the upper hand,' Larry said.

'Why haven't you been around all summer? Did you have an argument?'

'Life's an argument ... She disapproved of some portraits I was showing in Paris. She didn't like the way she looked. *Women.*'

He threw his cigarette on the ground, where it lit some dry grass. He watched it burn for a second, then stamped it out.

'I've never known Alice to feel self-conscious,' Louisa said.

'Yes, but a little self-consciousness is a lovely trait in a woman, don't you think? Lack of humility is intoxicating in its own way, but I like shyness too. I bet you're shy.' He reached forward and tilted her chin with his finger, as though considering how he would light her face in a photograph.

'Not a bit,' she said, pulling away and thinking of the night she had planned with Foster in the glass room.

'Glad to hear it.'

She saw, on another lit stage made by the open French windows in one of the living rooms, that Alice was surrounded by her guests, being kissed, hugged, photographed – and all the while looking over their heads for Larry.

'You enjoy torturing her, don't you?' Louisa asked.

'Somebody's gotta do it,' Larry replied. 'She's got you under her thumb too, I imagine.'

'She hardly notices me. We have little to do with one another,' she answered.

'Look,' he said, 'she has the barn open. Let's go see the

paintings together. I like to see where her head's at before I have to take it off, fix it and screw it back on again.'

They began circling the house through the overgrown grass.

'Lou!' A female voice was calling. 'Lou, wait up!'

She turned to see Poppy, dressed in black, her hair newly dyed electric blue, running towards her, agitated. 'Lou, hang on.'

Larry was prepared to wait. 'Who's that?'

'Poppy.'

'Never seen a blue poppy before.'

'Louisa. I need to talk to you.' Poppy was antsy and distracted, as if the drug she was on didn't suit her.

'I'm kind of busy,' Louisa said. 'Join the party and I'll find you later. Go on – the whole world's in there.'

'Have you seen Foster?'

Louisa was cool, not wanting Larry to see that she was as anxious to find Foster as Alice was to find him. 'He'll be around later. Could be here already.'

Poppy seemed confused now. 'Are you sure he's coming?'

'Yeah. Go on in, if you see him tell him I'm outside, yeah?'

'I'll wait for you here,' Poppy said, planting herself like a sentry on a low garden wall.

'If you want to.'

Larry and Louisa continued their stroll towards the barn, which had been transformed from a studio into a public gallery by Alice and Louisa over the previous two days. Once they were inside, Louisa could see that Larry had one of those ageless, pretty-boy faces. Still, he had to be twenty years younger than Alice, at least. He reached into the pocket of his denim jacket and pulled out a twist of paper. 'Let's light up. Alice's work is better seen from a height.'

When he offered her a drag, Louisa inhaled deeply. Larry was holding smoke in his lungs too. 'What do you say? Do we proceed clockwise or counter-clockwise?' he said tautly, keeping his throat closed.

Louisa still didn't exhale. 'Counter-clockwise.'

Larry exhaled. 'That's my girl.'

The artichokes, when seen together, were all different yet somehow the same. Larry proceeded from one to the next. 'Tell me. Are artichokes a fruit or a vegetable?' he asked. The look on his face, half-serious and half-mocking, one eyebrow cocked high as Louisa's own when she was sceptical, made her giggle. It was absurd the way Alice seemed to see the female body – even the universe – in the grey-green globe artichoke.

'They're flowers,' she managed to say.

Larry was indignant. 'Flowers, you say? She's painting *flowers*? What would Pollock say?'

Louisa collapsed against him, giggling into his shoulder, partly because she was high, partly because she loved the way Larry was including her in the conspiracy to puncture Alice's dignity. Larry whispered in her ear: 'Or is the artist saying, that sometimes an artichoke, is just an artichoke?'

'That's my line!' Louisa said.

Serious again, Larry moved from painting to painting until they came to one that was different from the rest: *Nude*, it was called. Louisa gasped, then reached to Larry for the joint. She took a puff. The long, pale body was stretched across a brown-draped bench, as though its back was broken. She'd had no idea that Alice had been intending to hang the picture so soon.

Larry stood in front of the portrait for what seemed like hours. 'She chose black for the foreground, earthy beiges and browns. Look at the skin – pale as death. You're not pale, are you?'

Louisa didn't know what to make of the corpse-like figure that was meant to be her. 'I reckon she hates me.'

'She has painted you as the opposite of herself.'

Louisa was holding smoke in her lungs again. 'Unfortunately,' she squeaked.

'What is the artist trying to say?'

'No idea,' she exhaled. She thought of their discussion of

Titian's 'Rape of Europa', and Alice's belief that the woman was a willing victim. That's what she looked like in the picture, a pale corpse floating against the darker shades of the canvas. The nude was passively erotic, the opposite of the saucy young girl in her great-grandfather's naughty photographs.

Larry dragged on his joint, then ground it into the floorboards with his toe. 'You must have some idea.' He was a persistent tutor.

Louisa relinquished her pride, if only for a moment. 'It's obvious. She wishes I was dead.' His hand lay on her shoulder so briefly that she might have been imagining it.

'She couldn't have children,' he said.

'Thank God. She would have been even worse than Amanda.'

Larry moved on to the next picture and Louisa followed. 'Has it been so bad?' he asked.

How to describe living in the eye of the storm? What was the point in explaining to a stranger she'd only just met? He was on Alice's side, anyway.

'I asked you a question,' he said.

'Amanda is more like a sister. I never had – a father . . .'

'What difference would that have made?'

'What a question!' she said.

Larry was too close now, the tip of one hand-stitched cowboy boot touching her toe.

She moved away from him on to the next picture, which, she realized, was equally humiliating.

'Now, how do you explain this?' he asked in mock dismay.

Louisa's portrait of Alice, a single line on canvas like a pre-schooler's scribble, was her aunt's idea of a joke. 'Don't ask me to analyse that one.'

'You have an eye,' Larry said.

'That's what Alice said.'

'I would have kept going if I were you,' he added.

'I didn't know how to keep going. I'm not a painter.'

'How do you know?'

'I take photographs.' Louisa surprised herself by confessing her ambition. 'I want to be a photographer.'

Larry looked at her as though he'd never really seen her before. 'A photographer. I'm a photographer.'

'I know. You're Larry Stein. You're famous.'

'Maybe some day you will be too . . . I'm staying for a few days. We'll talk shop. Right now, we'd better rescue Alice before she has the entire house turned upside down in search of me. And you're into this Foster guy, right?'

Larry winked at her. They went back to the house and he pushed her ahead of him through the French windows, into a room where Alice was waiting tensely, her eyes questioning in a way Louisa hadn't known they could. Alice had met her match in Larry, that much was certain. She watched Alice close in on him, then tilt back her head like a girl and gaze adoringly into his eyes. His face was half-smiling and playful, not quite there. Take me or leave me. Slowly, deeply and with the eyes of the guests on them, their mouths joined in a kiss – carnal and wicked – that repulsed Louisa.

She wandered through the house, in search of champagne and, when she found it, she drank from the bottle and closed her eyes, swaying dreamily to the blasting music. Remembering Foster, she clutched the bottle to her chest and picked her way up the grand staircase to the safety of her bedroom. She caught a glimpse of a girl in a white dress in the mirror as she went through the closet and unlocked the hidden door to the dark staircase. Climbing with sure steps, she retreated to her glass room, where she would wait for her lover.

She lit candles for company, thinking of how her glass room must look from the beach. People taking night-time walks would be looking up at Paradise, knowing that the gathering would be the most talked-about party of the season. She stood by the glass, but the candle-light had turned her eyrie into a mirrored room. She could see only herself: a bride in her white dress. She leaned against the glass and cupped her hands around her face so that she could see. The grass beneath was almost black, but in the light the house cast she could make out the place where she had met Larry. Poppy was gone, poor kid. Louisa felt woozy – Larry's hash had been strong. She took a swig of the champagne and wished she'd brought water. Her head spun, so she lay on the mattress and looked up at the moon and the stars. She waited for Foster's mouth on hers, awakening her without words.

Pain. Sharp pain like a knife stabbing her from inside. Beery breath clouding her face, filling her nose. Pain. Pain. Pain. Pain. Rhythmic and persistent. Jesus Christ. 'Fossor?'

He grunted, sweating all over her. 'Baby. You like it. Tell me you like it.' She didn't recognize the voice. Sick from too much drink and in shock, Louisa couldn't identify her assailant. In the part of her mind that was watching without feeling, she realized it didn't matter who he was.

'No,' Louisa moaned, trying to push him off her. Push him out despite the agony.

'That's it, baby, that's it.' Another voice now, crooning in her ear. Screams filling her head.

Retching. Her head about to burst. Then he was sliding out of her, like a freshly caught fish. More pounding now, another man. Piercing so hard she could feel it reaching her heart. She moaned again despite herself. A stranger's voice, husky and rich, came from far, far away. 'You like stirring porridge, baby?'

Pulling her hair out from the roots, holding her head back, filling her mouth with slime.

Screaming. Retching. Screaming so loud her eardrums were going to burst.

Hands – too many hands to fight off – ripping off her dress, turning her over and pressing so that if she resisted her neck would break. Stay alive, some part of her commanded, as she felt her face being pinned to the suffocating mattress. Pain. Pain. Pain. Pain in secret places not meant to be touched.

'Wake up!' Slapping her face. Squeezing her breasts. 'Bitch.' The bottle.

I don't care. I just don't. I can't care anymore. Then another part of herself wanting to cry out, Manna . . . Manna . . .

She hovered in the dark above salt-clouded panes and looked down on the pathetic girl, eyes staring, mouth bloody, limbs thrown like broken twigs, bent backwards, skin white as lard.

Sun assaulted her face, harsh and burning. Sun that desiccated, stripped away, bleached bones. Louisa struggled to escape the merciless light of the glass room in search of water and took the stairs crawling backwards, unable to stand. She limped to the bathroom and found a trickle of water. Her mouth gaped beneath the tap, letting the water run in and out, in and out, afraid to swallow.

'That must have been one helluva hang-over.'

Larry was in the kitchen making breakfast on a tray. 'Want tea? I'm taking some up to Alice. Where you been, kid? Didn't see you yesterday. Reckoned you must have hooked up with somebody at the party and gone off for the day.'

She'd been so stupid, getting drunk and lying up there for the taking. Any of those creeps at the party could have followed her. She tried to focus on the teapot that Larry was filling with boiling water. She'd missed a day. The party hadn't been last night, it had been the night before that.

'Sugar?' Larry asked.

Louisa nodded.

'One or two? Just hold up your fingers.'

Louisa felt like her skull was filled with sand.

'Two, it is, then. You look like you need it.' He stirred sugar into the tea and placed it on the table in front of her. 'Your

203

friend Poppy came by this morning. Bright kid. We talked about Whitman. "Mad, naked summer night", hey?'

Larry left the kitchen with his tray, an offering for the goddess.

Poppy peered through the screen door. 'Anybody home?' When there was no answer, she pulled it open. 'Louisa? That you?'

Go away, Louisa wanted to say. She was no different from the other spent bodies lying around the house numb and wasted from excess. Poppy sat beside her at the table. 'Are you all right?'

Louisa couldn't speak. Poppy tried to get her attention, took her hand – an intimate and feminine gesture that made Louisa feel ashamed, so ashamed to be like Poppy, the groupie without a group. 'Foster wants you to know he couldn't make it to the party. He was trapped in the kitchens at the club. They wouldn't let him off until two a.m. and then his dad made him go straight home. Some fuss over drugs. Parents, you know?' Poppy's blue hair was oily and slick, her eyes alert in her elfin face.

No, I don't, Louisa thought. She remembered the day she'd gone into East Hampton with the slip of paper and the fifty dollars. Please, God, it must have worked.

'Drink your tea,' Poppy said.

The mug was too heavy to hold. Poppy raised it to Louisa's lips. 'Gee, man. You're fucked up.' Then she reached into the pocket of her ragged, slashed jeans and pressed a few Valium into Louisa's hand. 'Take these. They'll help you come down.'

Poppy got a glass of water at the sink and watched while Louisa swallowed the pills, her throat constricted and sore. The water helped.

'Thanks,' Louisa said. Poppy was the last person she'd have expected to appear as ministering angel. 'What – what –'

Poppy watched her.

'I'm sorry,' Louisa said. 'I left you waiting. Forgot. What did you want to talk about?'

Poppy's face seemed to be saying that she knew. She'd always known. Then it closed, just like that. 'Too late now. Forget about it.'

Yeah, Louisa thought. Forget about setting herself up in the midst of her aunt's orgy, advertising herself in her silly white debutante's dress in her fantasy room for all the world to see. Smoking Larry's hashish, drinking too much, passing out. Fool.

'I'm going back to bed,' she said.

'That's a good idea. See you on the beach later? A swim would do you good.'

Ripped, sore and dirty to the core. No sea could cleanse her. 'Yeah, later.' Louisa trudged upstairs to her room, her mother's room, and tried to sleep for ever.

'You sick? Should I call a doctor?'

Louisa shook her head.

'What the hell's wrong with you?'

Louisa ignored him. Larry sat on the bed, waiting, Louisa drifting in and out.

'We need to talk,' Larry said, 'when you're feeling able.'

She would never feel able.

'A guy came round. Foster somebody. Seemed a bit bummed. Is that what this is about? Fight with the boyfriend? Hardly worth cracking up over.'

Louisa wanted no-one disturbing her for-ever sleep.

Larry stood up abruptly. 'You're so like Amanda, you know that?'

Louisa listened to his footsteps – cowboy boots in summer, drumming the wooden floors – until there was no sound left.

Nothing had happened. It was only her body that hurt and now she couldn't even feel that anymore. Couldn't feel her heart. She'd left herself behind, floating high above the glass room until the sun came out to burn her away with the early-morning fog.

*

Louisa decided to get out of bed. She could do this. She could wash in a tepid half-filled bath, then get dressed and brush her bleeding gums. Do something with her hair. Be the body she would have to be if she wasn't going to sleep for ever.

In the kitchen, Larry was sitting at the table with Alice.

'She arises,' Alice said. 'I hope it was a good trip because you've paid the price, haven't you?'

Cold bitch, Louisa thought. They were looking at photographs. Louisa ignored them as she went to boil the kettle and make some tea. Lift the kettle from the stove, walk to the sink, fill it, bring it back to the stove, light the flame.

'You see what I mean, Larry? These are cheesecake.'

'That's not what they thought in Paris. And it's not what they'll think in New York.'

'Paris,' Alice spat. 'Paris is up its own arse. No artists there anymore. Just amateur philosophers writing one boring treatise after the next to impress their friends at dinner.'

Larry's patience was endless, or else he didn't care. 'Maybe others see these pictures more clearly than you do. You take them too personally, Alice. They're not your art, they're mine.'

'Is that so? Ask the girl what she thinks.'

Standing by the stove, Louisa watched the cold blue flame lick the bottom of the kettle and wondered who the girl was.

'Come here,' Alice said.

Louisa obeyed – easier than resisting. Alice handed her a photograph. It was Alice all right, less leathery than usual. More feminine, almost childlike, if that was possible. Coquettish? No, that wasn't the word. And the light – blank, shadowless light.

'Speak,' Alice said.

'You did them in the glass room, didn't you?'

'See?' Larry said. 'I told you the girl has an eye.'

'I said it first. But she may never do anything with it.'

Louisa gagged. 'Sorry.' She went out of the screen door and onto the lawn, leaving Alice and Larry free to give up on her.

*

206

'If the mountain won't come to Mohammad,' Belly called across the lawn. 'Glad to find you in.' She strode across in her Madras shorts and pink Lacoste polo shirt.

Louisa was sitting in one of the Adirondack chairs. Belly took the other. 'I don't know what happened between you and Foster. And neither does he. He's called round twice and spoken to some guy hanging out with your aunt. He gave him the distinct impression you didn't want to see him. A guy can only humiliate himself so much. So I'm here to smooth things over. It can't be that bad. Is it because he couldn't make it to the party? That's hardly worth having a hissy fit over. Foster's a great guy. He's mad about you. I've never seen him so cut up.'

Oh Belly, shut up.

'The rumour is you took some really bad shit. I wouldn't be surprised, the crowd that was here at that party. What was it? LSD? Smack? Do you need to see a psychiatrist? Kelly's dad's a psychiatrist. Maybe a little chat. Informal, you know. He wouldn't report you to the cops, or anything. He's cool.'

Louisa blinked hard behind her sunglasses, keeping her eyes on the deep blue of the ocean. Belly sat where Foster had, playing with her charm bracelet. She'd be gone soon.

'Has Alice called your mother?' Belly asked.

Louisa shook her head.

'You've got to snap out of this, Lou. Summer's nearly over. It's time to get back to real life, you know? We're having an end-of-summer barbecue at the club. You're coming. Don't leave like this. Then you'll be back next summer, yeah? And we'll start again.'

Larry had decided that Alice should keep the sound system. His taste in music was annoying. 'Heartbreak Hotel', what was that?

'You like Elvis?' he asked Louisa, who was at the kitchen table eating toast.

'No,' she said.

Larry stole a piece of her toast. 'Of course you don't. Not now. But some day you will.'

Alice appeared in the kitchen. 'Turn that off. I have to talk to Louisa.'

Great. Let's talk about Alice, shall we?

Alice sat down across the table from Louisa. 'Listen, I've got news. I'm just going to say it out straight because there's no other way. Amanda's in hospital and you need to go see her.'

Louisa's heart was beating so fast she could hardly breathe. 'She have an accident?'

'No.'

'What, then where is she?'

Louisa imagined her mother on a hospital floor in New Delhi.

'New York Presbyterian. Larry will drive you there. So get your stuff.'

Larry gave Alice a harsh look, as if even he couldn't believe how callous she was being. 'What?' she said defensively. 'I didn't know she was going to die so soon.'

'Manna,' Louisa whispered, as she held her mother's hand, memorizing the lines on her fingers and her palms. She wasn't sure Amanda knew she was there. *Please don't let me forget her face.*

Amanda looked at the ceiling and smiled.

'Who's there?' Louisa asked.

Years before, Louisa had asked Amanda, 'What is heaven?'

'It's what you want it to be.'

This was hell, watching her mother slowly die and wanting to ask her so many questions – questions she hadn't even thought of yet and wouldn't think of for years and years. She hated Alice. Hated her with all her heart for playing along with Amanda's charade. Amanda hadn't been in India. She'd been in hospital all summer, being treated for breast cancer that had run out of control because Amanda hadn't wanted to deal with it. Amanda hadn't wanted Louisa to have to deal with it. Self-sacrificing at last.

But the truth was that it was selfish to keep your daughter in ignorance so that you could be spared her pain.

Amanda's eyes lost the ecstatic glow and became vacant.

'Manna!' Louisa tried to bring her back.

Amanda looked at Louisa then, as though she was a stranger. 'Who are you?' her eyes said.

So many questions that her cancer-addled brain couldn't answer now. One demanded an answer more than any other. 'Manna, who was my father?'

Amanda, dying, was beyond such banalities. Then there was a flicker of recognition – 'Manna, please, who was my father?'

A nurse came in, told her to let it go, whatever it was. There was one more thing: 'Alice rang to say she's handling the arrangements. You're not to worry. And you can come back and stay at Amagansett as long as you like.'

Louisa turned to the nurse angrily. 'Forget it. I'll make the arrangements.'

'Louisa, you can't. You're too upset. It costs money.'

'So, what are you saying? Alice isn't upset? Alice has plenty of money? Where is she? Why isn't she here? Tell her she can fuck off.'

'Sssh,' the nurse soothed. 'Your mother may be able to hear you.'

Louisa held her rage in check. 'If you can hear me, Manna, I love you. I'm not angry. I'll be OK, Manna, don't worry.'

In the end, it was all done for her. Alice starred at the antiseptic funeral in the quaint Presbyterian church in East Hampton, her stoic grief already inspiring her to move on from artichokes to another theme, to which she alluded hoarsely in her eulogy, without dwelling on details – as it would have been unseemly to do so at a time like this. Louisa walked, stood and sat, as she was prompted by the funeral director, numb and unable to cry.

She refused to return to Paradise with the mourners, instead taking the jitney back to the city where she found the old apartment and its summer residents, art students who took pity on her and let her sleep on the floor with her knapsack as a pillow.

PART THREE

14

'Are you thinking you might still be in love with him? Is that why you're freaking out?' Becca asked, as waiters cleared their plates and swept the linen tablecloth clean of crumbs that seemed like bits of conversation left behind. Becca held the engraved invitation in her hands and spoke in royal tone. 'Mr and Mrs Humphrey Smith invite Louisa Stone to dinner on September the twenty-ninth at eight o'clock. Carriages at midnight. *Informal.*'

She handed the thick, white card back to Louisa. 'Well, Louisa Stone, you reckon Foster the Beach God of Mount Yale will be there too? Informal, like?'

Louisa traced the embossed script with one finger. 'When I rang to confirm, that's what Mrs Humphrey Smith said. I wouldn't be going otherwise. I can't stand to be in the same room with her husband. He's such a creep.'

'It's brilliant that you're getting back in touch with that part of your life. You weren't born the day you crash-landed in Dublin with Ben.'

'Sometimes it feels that way. It's so long since I thought about that summer. It seems like it happened to someone else.'

Becca smiled. 'If a little part of you is still in love with Foster, be careful, promise? He's only human and so are you. Don't expect too much. It may be that you're not still in love with Foster, you're in love with yourself, or who you were.'

As Becca spoke, the pudding arrived – a Lilliputian collection of chocolate soufflé, chocolate tart and chocolate parfait. Louisa dipped her spoon into the parfait, picked up another spoon and gave it to Becca. 'We said we'd share it.'

'But I want to see you get fat.'

'Cow.'

Becca gave in and tasted the chocolate soufflé. 'I see what you mean. This stuff is Class A.' She took another bite. 'So, you saw Belly in July and this is . . . September. I suppose that's not indecently fast, but fairly quick off the mark.'

'He was coming over anyway. And not specifically to see me. We'll have dinner, talk about old times, and that will be that.'

'Uh-huh.' Becca was sceptical. 'And if that *is* all it is, will you be devastated?'

'I will *not*. Irish people meet old friends and lovers all the time simply by walking up and down Grafton Street. I've merely decided that it's time for me to face up to that part of my life.'

'Searching for your roots?'

'I pulled them up long ago,' Louisa said.

'Impossible,' Becca said. 'Life histories are like those invasive plants that run underground root systems. You have to do a little digging occasionally, or they take over the whole garden.' She lowered her voice. 'Was he great in the sack?'

'We were kids, Becca. It was about more than that.'

'Precocious kids, then.' Becca plunged her dessert spoon into the parfait, disturbing its artful layers. 'Bottom line: did you break his heart or did he break yours?'

'I don't want to go there.'

'Hmm . . . I've known you a long time, Louisa Maguire, and you've never once mentioned this Foster before tonight. Are you sure he meant as much to you as you're saying?'

'What can you say about your first love? Nothing else compares, does it? You're only that innocent once – which is fortunate, I suppose. No-one could survive first love twice.'

'So why are you diving back in there? Foster won't be the man you remember. He'll be twenty years older, for a start.'

'So am I. Twenty years have probably ravaged me more than him.' Louisa wanted to be understood by her friend, if only to better understand herself. 'He holds a missing piece of me that I hadn't thought about until Belly mentioned his name. You know how you bury people that you've known, even though they're still alive? I'm beginning to feel there's unfinished business between us . . . if I bring him back from the dead, part of me will come back too. Does that make sense? Back then, I truly believed that I wasn't good enough for him. I was a hippie child and he was Hamptons aristocracy. It sounds ridiculous, I know. But I'm feeling more secure in myself now, I'm curious, too.'

'Time brings selective amnesia. There has to be a good reason you broke it off with him. Has this Belly person – love the vulgar name, by the way – divulged anything about Foster's life since? Or is the bored *émigré* just stoking the flames of love for her own amusement? Maybe she has a thing for Foster herself.'

'No way.'

'Is he married?'

'A couple of times.'

'Not a good sign.'

'Two or three marriages equal life-time monogamy by American standards.'

'One divorce is forgivable. Two are unfortunate. Three are reckless. Single man? Manhattan? Screwing around? Looking for a third? Be careful, babe.'

'When Mary hopped off to Australia with Dr Koala you gave her your blessing – and I'm not even leaving the country.'

Becca sighed. 'Mary is smart and perceptive, but uncomplicated. You, my dear, are complicated – very. Anyway, you don't need my blessing. You're your own woman.'

'Thank you. As my own woman, I'm meeting an old boyfriend, come what may. Let's not blow it out of proportion.'

Becca smiled indulgently. 'This special summer – how old did you say you were, seventeen?'

'Mmm.'

Becca considered this. 'Huh.'

'Whaddaya mean?'

'That was shortly before your mother died, wasn't it?'

'Yes . . . where are we going with this?'

'Forgive me for mentioning it, but that was the summer that you had that . . . other trauma.'

Louisa put down her spoon.

Becca was cautious. 'Apart from your mother's death, I mean, as if that wasn't enough. You said those bastards had snatched your soul and gave you nothing in return. Remember telling me that?'

Louisa nodded. 'It was nothing to do with Foster. And I punished him. I cut him off. I was so ashamed. Terrified of anyone ever finding out. I was sure a man could never love me knowing what happened. You're the only person I've told.'

Becca held one hand across the table and Louisa took it. 'Shame is a natural reaction, even though it wasn't your fault. You were only trying to survive. You have nothing to apologize to Foster for. I'm sure he could have found you if he'd really wanted to.'

Louisa could feel her eyes growing hot. 'I just wish I could have that time with him again, without the tragic ending, you know? What's so terrible about wanting a happy ending? Or to put things right, at least.'

'It's human,' Becca said. 'It's what keeps us alive.'

They took a taxi back to Dalkey, each woman wrapped up in her own thoughts. Louisa was already thinking through the next twenty-four hours. 'Ben's coming to see the children tomorrow,' she said.

Becca leaned her head against the car window. 'You seem very relaxed about it.'

'Yeah. I have to be. If I'm relaxed, the children will be too – I hope so, anyway. My solicitor warned me that Ben was trying to play games around the whole access thing, but it takes two to play that game and I'm not. The children need their father in their lives, so I've given him a little push.'

Becca squeezed Louisa's hand. 'You're a great mum, you know that, don't you?'

'I'm a good-enough Mum.' She watched the lights of the city strung like pearls along Dublin Bay. When she looked back at Becca she saw that her friend's eyes were glistening. 'What's wrong?'

'What if it comes back?'

Louisa wished she could comfort her. 'It's not going to come back, Becca. The cancer's gone. The surgeon sliced it out, the chemo poisoned it and the radiotherapy blasted whatever was left. And he told you that seventy-five per cent of his patients never get a recurrence, didn't he?'

'So why do I feel like one of the twenty-five per cent?'

'You're scared.'

'Lou, before I die, I want to be in love. I'd die content if I experienced that just once – even for a day.'

'You will, Becca. And it'll last far longer than a day.'

'Ever the optimist.'

Louisa dropped Becca at her house, promising to keep her posted, then headed for St Agnes's, which was so dark and quiet that she knew the children were already asleep. She found Gill lying on a beanbag on the floor of the TV room, listening to music on his iPod while channel-surfing the TV with the sound turned off. She sat on the sofa behind him, kicked off her red stilt-heeled sandals, and rubbed her feet. Gill pulled out his earphones, leaned back and looked up at her. 'Elvie's right. Sometimes things do look prettier upside down,' he said.

'Go away out of that, ya' boyo.' Louisa tucked her legs under her. She liked coming home to a bit of adult company and was in no hurry to send Gill on his way.

Gill turned back to the TV. 'I love it when you talk culchie. It's the American accent does it for me.'

'How many shows are you watching? Could we settle on one of them?'

Gill rose from the beanbag nest and stretched. 'Nothing takes my fancy. I'd better be going.'

'Before you do, there's something I forgot to mention. The children are seeing Ben tomorrow after school.'

Gill frowned with worry. 'Do they know yet?'

'I told them he was taking them out for a treat. I don't know what they'll make of it.'

'Do you want me to talk to them about it?' He seemed eager to be part of this transition in the children's lives.

Louisa was glad that he cared, but one day he'd be gone too. 'They adore you, but I'm their mother. It's my job to talk to them about these things.'

If Gill was hurt, he tried hard not to show it. 'I know I'm not one of their parents, but I do care about them. I spend –' he looked at his watch 'eleven hours a day with them.'

'Go away out of that. I feel guilty enough already. I'll be home by a quarter to four tomorrow, to keep an eye on Ben, so you can leave early if you like.'

'Are you sure about that? Mightn't it be better if I do the hand-over on my own? That way there's no chance of Ben being awkward with you.'

Louisa shook her head. 'I want to show Elvie and Milo that Ben and I can cooperate as their parents, no matter how awkward he tries to make it.' She could tell that Gill wasn't convinced.

He wound the earphones round his iPod and put it in his jacket pocket. 'See you tomorrow then.'

'See ya.'

Louisa closed her eyes and imagined being back at Amagansett again with Foster. His beach boy's sun-burnished skin, his smooth eyelids fluttering as he dozed in her arms, the muscle above his hip-bone that shuddered when she stroked it. She saw him so clearly, that it was like flicking through a sheaf of photographs . . .

'Mummy?' Elvie was shaking her, standing behind the couch in her blue nightgown.

'Oh, hi, love. You OK?'

'I thought you'd disappeared,' Elvie whispered. 'You weren't in your bed. Please don't leave me.'

'Ssh, darling. I'll never leave you.' Louisa held out her arms and pulled Elvie onto the sofa beside her. 'I'll never leave you,' she whispered again. It was a small white lie, but one all mothers were compelled to tell.

15

In the morning, Louisa awoke with a pounding head and a sore back from sleeping on the sofa. The children were already lying on their stomachs in front of the TV, watching the Discovery Channel. *And then she began swimming in a frenzy that carried her clear of the treacherous coastal waters and guided her thousands of miles back with unerring accuracy, even twenty years or more later, to the place that she was born, her home beach.*

Elvie and Milo stretched out their arms and legs and swam, bellies on the floor, heads raised proudly.

Louisa looked at her watch. They were late. She hated to disturb their imaginary world but school beckoned, so she grabbed the remote control and turned off the TV.

'Mummy! You ruined it!' Milo shouted.

'Sorry, love. Time to get dressed now or we'll be way late for school.'

'Is today the day, Mum?' Elvie asked.

'Yes, Elvie. You're seeing Daddy today.'

'Is he going to buy us presents?' Milo wanted to know.

'No,' Louisa said. 'It's not about presents. It's about spending time together.'

'Patrick's Daddy always buys him presents!' Milo said.

'Good for Patrick,' Louisa said. 'Now let's go upstairs and get dressed.'

After she'd dropped the children at school, she stopped at the chemist for painkillers, then went straight to her studio. Paul was there already, processing photographs. 'Morning, button. How's tricks?'

'I have a headache. How are you?'

'Brutal hang-over. Saw Ben again.'

Louisa feigned disinterest. 'Did you?'

'In a club. Dancing his broken heart away.'

'Ben doesn't dance,' Louisa said.

'Tell me about it. His gang of mini-Bens didn't seem to mind, though – all film-school types. Ugly guys with big plans chatting up wannabe actresses who wouldn't be seen dead with them otherwise. Ben was at the top of the pile, having made a film or two. My mates and I are there, like, "What do girls see in older men?" "Money", my mates say. And I'm telling them – as far as I know, Ben hasn't got any.'

'Good luck to him,' Louisa said.

To signal the end of the conversation, she went through the diary for the day.

'Then Gill turned up.'

'Gill? Last night? It must have been late.'

'We had a chat, mostly about photography. I've been giving him a few pointers, as you know. Then he sees Ben, drinking his loaf off, and he's like – really pissed off. Gave me an earful. Gill's not the brawling type, so I wasn't worried it would come to anything. We changed the subject, me thinking we're in the clear. Then Ben comes over, walking funny in these furry Ugg boots.'

Louisa sat down at the desk, letting the diary close on her lap. 'Go on.'

'Ben says to him, "Nice little number you've got there. My roof over your head. My kids. My wife." Gill's sensible. He wants to walk away but as he stands up from the bar stool, Ben blocks him. So Gill says, "I'm the children's carer. That's all." Ben goes, "We'll see how that sounds in court." He's dying for a fight. I try to take Ben aside, but he says, "You little fucker. You're at it with her too." At this stage, everyone's waiting for their chance to throw a punch, you know how it is, and Security are headed in our direction, well – you know how much I like my pretty face. I'm ducking out of there, when the girlfriend comes over, Ben's girlfriend, and pulls the bold fella out of it. He goes off like a lamb.'

Louisa began to wish she hadn't been so optimistic about Ben behaving himself in front of the children.

Paul towered over her. 'So, is it true?'

'Is what true?'

'You and Gill.'

Louisa turned away towards the file room. 'There's nothing going on between me and Gill. We're friends, that's all. I am capable, you know, of a healthy working relationship with an attractive younger man.'

Paul huffed. 'So I've noticed.'

When her afternoon shoots were finished, Louisa dashed home. Gill had Milo and Elvie scrubbed and in their best clothes – both children muted and tense, also a little excited. 'I'll be off now,' Gill said. 'See you tomorrow?'

'Yeah. And thanks.' Louisa would never let him guess that she'd heard about the confrontation in the club. When he'd gone, she sat the children down on the sofa. 'Your father is taking you to see a film, then out for pizza afterwards. Won't that be fun? Then you'll come home again and I'll be waiting right here for you.'

Milo was glum. 'Why can't we have pizza here?'

'Yeah,' Elvie said. 'Gill's pizza.'

'Because Daddy wants some time with you on his own. Remember what I told you? He doesn't live with us anymore. He has his own place now.'

'Is it big?' Milo asked.

'Has it a swimming-pool?' Elvie chimed in.

'I doubt that very much. I don't think you'll see it today. Please try to be good for Daddy, OK?'

Milo and Elvie were silent, eyes locked, sharing their joint predicament. There was a level, Louisa realized, at which they had only each other: they alone were the children of Louisa and Ben Maguire. As much as she was glad to be rid of Ben, the children loved and needed him.

'Will you be lonely?' Elvie asked.

Louisa shook her head. 'It's OK to love Daddy and spend time with him,' she said. 'You don't have to choose between us.'

Elvie and Milo looked at her strangely, as though she'd read their minds.

There was a sharp knock on the door. 'I think that's him – I'll get it.'

But the children had already run on ahead. 'Daddy!'

'Hey,' Ben said, on his knees to hug them. 'You guys ready to rock?'

Louisa stood back from the open door. 'Hi, Ben.'

'Hi.'

Ben glanced over his shoulder: the girl from the restaurant was waiting for them in a cheerleader's skirt, pink boots and a midriff-baring leather jacket. 'Kids, I want you to meet Lucy.'

Long-legged Lucy picked her way forward, with the delicacy of a pony walking on ice. 'Hi, Milo, Elvie. Nice to meet you.'

Elvie looked up at Ben. 'We don't need a babysitter, Dad. You're taking us out with you to see a film, right?'

Louisa bit her lip to keep from laughing, as Ben looked at her pleadingly. 'Nothing to do with me,' she said. 'Hi Lucy. Nice to see you again. I'm glad Ben's going to have your help with these two. Don't let him give them chocolate in the cinema if you expect them to eat afterwards, yeah? They're better off with popcorn. And if Elvie needs the loo, will you go with her?'

'Sure. I love kids.'

Louisa smiled in what she hoped was a benevolent woman-of-the-world way. 'Then you're really going to love these two.'

Lucy responded, 'Real chips off the old block, huh?'

'Can we go to the park first, Dad?' asked Milo. 'I want to show you the new swings.'

'If you like – I think there's time,' Ben answered.

Lucy didn't quite stamp her foot. 'Benny, it's so cold today. Do we have to take them to the park?'

Ben looked back at her sternly. 'If it's the park they want, it's the park they'll get. Right kids?'

It was amazing to see Ben in almost-divorced Dad mode, determined to impress the children, if not Louisa. It might bring out the best in him yet, as Louisa had hoped. As she kissed her children goodbye, Louisa whispered, 'It's going to be fine. I'll see you in a little while.'

Before the farewells could get out of hand, Louisa waved them off and shut the door after them. Having to let her two precious children go off with their father had been harder than she'd thought it would be. She leaned back against the wall for support, feeling her knees give way as she slid down to a sitting position in the hall. *Well done, Louisa. Welcome to the rest of your life. Now what?*

She hadn't been in alone in St Agnes's since Elvie was born and, without the children around her, masking the suffocating deadness of the house, she felt a panic beginning to rise. She had to get out.

Just as she was fetching her handbag and car keys, the front door opened again.

'Lou? You all right?' It was Gill, come to check up on her.

'Grand. Why?'

'I think I left a book in the kitchen. I'll go get it.'

'You've come back to make sure I'm not in bits, haven't you?'

Gill reddened, 'Sorry, I just –'

Louisa wanted so badly to be hugged for reassurance that she feared he might sense it. His generous, knowing body – so close – made her want to cry out for comfort, but she remained still and silent because it would be wrong to encourage Gill's feelings for her. It would ruin their domestic arrangement and – more importantly – she'd promised Becca that she wouldn't hurt her little brother.

She jangled her car keys nervously. 'If I stay here all I'll do is think about the children and Ben letting them walk in front of a bus or something. Want a lift anywhere?'

'I promised to meet someone in Blackrock, if that's on your way.'

Blackrock was as good a place as any for some retail therapy. Her outfit for the dinner with Foster had been on her mind. There were no closets full of vintage clothes at St Agnes's as there had been at Paradise. 'It was Ben turning up with Lucy to flaunt her in front of the kids that bothered me,' Louisa thought aloud as they drove along the coast road. 'I wanted to hang her up by the collar of her little Barbie jacket so I could see her kicking those little pink boots.' She imitated Lucy's whine, '"Benny, it's so cold today. Do we have to take them to the park? Look at my beautiful, long fake-tanned skinny legs, Benny. They've got goose pimples, Benny!"'

Gill was laughing. 'She calls him Benny?'

'Can you believe it? At worst, the children will see Lucy as an incompetent au pair, I suppose. I hope she's good with them.'

Louisa managed to find a parking place near one of Dublin's most exclusive boutiques. She took it as a lucky sign: she was in the right place at the right time, about to buy the right dress for Foster.

Gill put money in the parking machine and handed her the ticket. 'See you Monday.'

'Monday,' Louisa said, then watched him stroll up the road. He didn't rush like other people. She watched as a petite, dark-haired girl met him outside a coffee shop with a kiss on both cheeks and they went in.

Good, Louisa thought. Much better for us both if he has a girlfriend his own age – although she hardly seems his type. She was preoccupied as she walked into the boutique, and didn't notice the solicitous saleswoman until she asked, 'Have you any occasion in mind?'

Yes, Louisa thought, I'm meeting the love of my life whom I haven't seen in twenty years and I want to take his breath away. 'A dinner party,' she said. 'Informal, yet not – if you know what I mean.'

'Something feminine?'

'Very.'

The saleswoman offered her one outfit after the next but nothing seemed quite right. Too girly and she'd seem vulnerable. Too bohemian and he'd think she hadn't grown up. Too seductive and he'd assume she was desperate.

The woman held out aloft a mossy-green silk ensemble that was exquisite in its way, but would make Louisa look like a leprechaun bride. 'What are those?' she asked, drawn to a rack of reliable black dresses at the back of the shop.

She rifled through them. Too tight, no. Diamante, no. Too much flesh – definitely not. She knew instantly when she saw it. 'That one.'

Louisa stood in the mirrored cubicle, avoiding her reflection as she shimmied out of her jeans and shirt and took the outfit off its hanger. The black taffeta skirt rustled up over her legs. Edwardian in cut, it clung to her hips with fabric draped at the front, drawn back into a discreet bustle behind, with layers of frippery, lace and ribbon-trimmed frills – like a skirt in a Manet painting of women strolling in the Bois de Boulogne. The sheer black silk blouse was high-necked with long sleeves, showing glimpses of skin and Louisa's plain black camisole bodice beneath. It was the buttons that made it – dozens of tiny ones, like those on the Victorian linen blouse twenty years ago.

Louisa stepped out onto the shop floor to get a better look at herself in a floor-to-ceiling gilt-framed mirror. There was another woman her reflection: a femme fatale. 'I'll take it.'

The saleswoman held up two other garments. 'These are parts of the ensemble – it's a coordinating range. See the lovely peplum jacket? It goes with the skirt or is perfect on its own with jeans, and the fitted waistcoat that can be worn on its own under the jacket, or with the blouse.' She was so enthusiastic that Louisa hated to say 'no', but she was on a budget. She hadn't inherited Alice's house yet.

Returning to St Agnes's didn't feel desolate when she was carrying such an exquisite outfit, folded in tissue paper in a posh carrier-bag. She went upstairs immediately to try it on again, thinking that she would have to find some high-heeled, lace-up ankle boots to go with it. The thought of Foster taking them off . . .

'Mummy! Mummy!' The children were back.

Louisa clipped down the stairs, lifting her taffeta skirts with her runners underneath, to find a limp Lucy holding their hands at the door.

'Hello my darlings, did you have a lovely time?'

'Look what Lucy bought us!' Milo held up a cross between a robot and a gun, while Elvie pushed ahead of him with a wooden art box filled with brushes and paints.

'How was the movie?' Louisa asked.

'We went to the mall instead,' Elvie said, now taking a bag stuffed with clothes from Lucy. She pulled out her purchases. 'Lucy knows everything about fashion, Mum.'

'Look Mum!' Milo dropped his bag on the floor and pulled out a Darth Vader costume. 'Lucy said not to wear it while I was eating pizza 'cause I'd wreck it. She's gonna be Princess Leia.'

Meanwhile Elvie was eyeing Louisa's new outfit. 'Is it Hallowe'en, Mum?' Lucy suppressed a smirk.

Louisa stared right back. 'Lucy, you really shouldn't have. They'll be expecting this every time,' she said.

'I wanted to. We had brilliant fun, didn't we, guys?'

Except, Louisa noticed, something was missing. Their father. 'Where's Ben?'

'I dropped him off at the flat. He was exhausted.'

'I bet he was. Well, then. You kids run inside while I talk to Lucy.'

Lucy blanched. 'I really have to go.'

'Let Lucy come in. I want to dress up in my outfit for her,' Elvie said.

Louisa considered the prospect of her daughter dressed as Lucy's mini-me.

'Surely you have time for a cup of tea?'

'Thanks. Next time, maybe. I'd really better get back,' Lucy said. 'I'll see you next week, guys. We'll go to the paintball place I was telling you about.'

'See you next week, then,' Louisa said. 'Tell Ben I hope he can drop them home himself next time. He'll have to build up his stamina.'

Lucy skidded off down the path.

Louisa closed the door and went indoors to debrief the children.

Milo was wide-eyed. 'She lets them put little fish on her pizza!'

'No ice-cream, though,' Elvie said gravely. 'She's on a diet.'

I'm surprised she eats anything at all, Louisa thought, holding her tongue.

16

The day arrived, a Saturday, and Gill had agreed to take the children for the afternoon so that Louisa could get her hair done. It was all so thrilling that, as the hairdresser worked, Louisa kept having to remind herself that only a few months before she had been trapped in a stale marriage and hadn't had sex in years. She felt so new that her emotions were very close to the surface, as though the anticipation of seeing Foster had awakened parts of herself that now demanded to be expressed.

'Lovely highlights,' the hairdresser remarked. 'You like the colour?'

'It's very blonde,' Louisa said.

'Subtle. Not too blonde.'

I can be a girly blonde, why not? Louisa thought. I've been acting the mature and reliable brunette for too long.

When she got home, she sat on the edge of her bed in St Agnes's in her black silk camisole and matching French knickers, with the new skirt and top laid out beside her on the bed. She sensed that it would be a decisive night in her life. She warned herself not to expect too much: Foster might be fat, alcoholic and battered by life. Maybe he was a sad case who had to cross the Atlantic for a date.

This isn't a date, she reminded herself. It's an informal dinner with old friends. Forget who Foster was and see him for who he is now.

Louisa put on the lovely blouse, each button taking ages to fasten and bringing her closer to seeing him again. Already, she was seeing the evening as a photograph: herself, confident yet demure, holding out her hand to Foster, who has taken it in both his hands, raised it to his lips and kissed it. Two middle-aged yet youthful adults meeting again after years of separation and disappointment, scarred but unafraid, their intimacy lighting their faces.

Get a grip, girl. He could be a deadly boring businessman who barely remembers you. Life isn't always photogenic. No-one knows that better than you.

Her mobile rang. 'You dying of nerves?'

'Hi, Becca.'

'Play it cool and call me the minute you get home. I'll wait up.'

'Don't! You need your sleep.'

Louisa put on the rustling skirt, then finished off her make-up except for the lipstick. She added a pair of delicate antique silver and jet earrings she'd found in town. Then she brushed her teeth, rinsed her mouth and did her lipstick. This was barmy, feeling like a teenager going on a date when she was a grown woman meeting a man she used to know. She sprayed herself with her favourite perfume.

Gill called up the stairs. 'Taxi's here!'

'Be right down!'

Louisa looked in the mirror one more time. Staring back at her was a thirty-seven-year-old extra from a period drama. She rifled through her wardrobe. There was the wrap-around jersey dress she'd bought months before and worn so often she was tired of it. But he hadn't seen it. And there were the red sandals, the black criss-crossed sandals . . . the cream pumps? White after Labor Day? Nobody paid attention to that anymore. She wasn't in East Hampton now. Louisa took off the beautiful black ensemble, left on the black lingerie and pulled on the wrap-around dress. It hugged her nicely in the right places. The discreet slit where one side of the dress overlapped the other would be effective when she sat down and crossed her legs. She tried it, sitting on the bed. The dress opened to just above her knee if she was careful, higher if she wasn't. Then she put on the red sandals.

'Taxi, Lou!' Gill's voice bounced up the stairs.

'Coming!'

Gill whistled. 'You look great. Love the hair.'

'Thanks. Don't wait up, yeah? You can sleep in the spare room, if you like.'

'Enjoy yourself and don't worry about us.'

Elvie appeared in her pyjamas, then. 'You're going on a date, aren't you, Mum? Will Daddy and Lucy be there?'

That was her world now, Daddy and Lucy, Mummy and fill-in-the-blank. Louisa didn't want Elvie wondering about the strange men in her life, the way she'd worried about her own mother's paramours, so she said, 'I'm meeting friends, Elvie. Nothing romantic.'

'Too bad,' Elvie said.

'Hang on,' Gill said, making a dash for the kitchen. He returned with a damp sponge. 'You've got a bit of chocolate on your dress.'

'Oh no, where?'

'There.' He pointed to her bum.

'How'd that get there? Were you going through my closet again, Elvie?' She reached round with the sponge to wipe off. Now there was a nasty wet patch.

'The hairdryer! That's what Becca does.'

Gill ran upstairs, came back with it, plugged it into the hall socket and took aim. The silk dress dried quickly, but not quickly enough for the taxi man, who stuck his head in the door. 'Last call.'

Gill switched off the dryer. 'See you later, gorgeous. Have fun.'

Louisa's nerves kicked in as the taxi drew away from her door. Her thirty-seven-year-old head was telling her to play it cool while her seventeen-year-old heart threatened to burst. She ran a script through her head. 'I'm a photographer now. Divorced – almost . . . two kids.' That wasn't right. Too much like speed-dating. 'I've never forgotten you either, Foster.' That wasn't true. She had forgotten him. Completely wiped him from her memory, like the pain of childbirth. Nature did that, Mary said, so that you'd be willing to give it another go.

The drive took no time at all – and it took forever. When she finally arrived, the house was as grand as Louisa had expected. An Edwardian brick mansion in Dublin 4 – the Irish equivalent of Kensington, Beacon Hill or Central Park East. She wouldn't have expected any less of Mr and Mrs Humphrey Smith of Manhattan and East Hampton. The taxi pulled into the drive. 'All right, Miss?'

Louisa got out of the taxi, pulled out some cash and handed it to the driver. 'Keep the change,' she said, for luck. Now she would walk from the car to the house, up that flight of granite steps to the front door, ring the bell and then . . . Her mind went blank. As she mounted the stairs, she could see lights inside the bay window of a reception room, a few male heads with their backs to her. Was one of those heads his? The balding one, the grey one, maybe?

Be prepared for anything, Louisa warned herself as she straightened her shoulders, held in her stomach and rang the bell.

'Hello Loopy-Lou!' It was Hump, looking at her as if she'd just jumped out of a cake. 'You get prettier every time I see you,' he said. So charming, so handsome, so reeking of wealth and ego. He made her skin crawl with his gross assumption that all women were flattered by his attentions. Many probably were, but his good looks were those of a demon in dinner dress, passing as a gentleman.

'Humphrey! Hello.' She forced herself to let him kiss her cheek, then he took her by the hand and led her into the hall.

'You are so, so sexy tonight,' he whispered in her ear, his fishy breath mingling with her perfume.

Louisa moved stiffly away from him. 'Where's Annabel?'

And most importantly, where was Foster? Somewhere in this house – just off to the right through that door – he was waiting.

Or not waiting. Merely intrigued, as she was, to see what had become of a memory. He might be distant at first, she warned herself. After all, she had dumped him.

'Louisa!' It was Belly, glass in hand, magnificent in a black, taffeta and lace Edwardian ensemble. Thank God, Louisa said to herself, as she complimented Belly on the outfit she had left lying on her bed. She took this as a sign that if she followed her instincts, everything would fall into place too.

'My, you scrub up well. Doesn't she Hump?' Then Belly leaned forward, stumbling so Louisa had to grab her to stop her falling. 'You haven't lost your figure,' she whispered.

Hump took his wife's drink. 'Why don't you go into the kitchen and check on the caterers?'

She poked him in the chest. 'Bad boy. It's a party!'

'Go.' Hump patted Belly's bustle and sent her off down the dark hallway. He turned back to Louisa with a long-suffering sigh. 'It's always a party. Know what I mean?' His eyes were hard. 'Come in and meet the gang.'

He led her into a comfortably opulent room, richly furnished without being ostentatious – burnished Georgian pieces, antique Middle Eastern rugs on polished oak floors, colours in a subtle palette evoking low-key grandeur. It showed just the sort of understated class that Louisa had expected of Mr and Mrs Humphrey Smith. The women remained seated, while the men stood up to be introduced and Louisa looked from one face to the next, expecting to see Foster. But they were all Irish, Louisa noted. Bankers and accountants – investors Hump intended to impress with his mansion and American hospitality.

'You'll have champagne?' he asked, as a white-coated Filipino manservant waited in the background.

'Yes, please,' Louisa said and wondered where to sit. She didn't dare ask, in front of all these people, where Foster was – maybe she'd misunderstood Belly. Perhaps it hadn't been a firm arrangement after all and Foster had changed his mind. One of the men offered her his seat, a space in the middle of a sofa, with other men flanking her. 'So Louisa, how are you enjoying Dublin?' he asked.

They must think she worked for Hump's organization.

'I'm a photographer. I've lived here for thirteen years.'

'One of us, then. You haven't lost your accent.'

'It's stuck somewhere mid-Atlantic, I'm afraid,' Louisa said.

'Don't apologize,' one of the men said. 'My children sound like you, and that's only from their summer holidays in the States. We're all turning American now.'

A woman said wryly, 'When we want to be.'

Above the fireplace, Louisa noticed, was the portrait she had taken of the Smith family, looking solid and viable, Hump the proud father, Belly sober, the boys beside them.

Hump, his drink refreshed, stood behind Louisa at the back of the sofa. 'Lou is one of our oldest and dearest friends from East Hampton. Our families go way back, don't they, Lou?'

The women became more amenable at the mention of East Hampton and smiled attentively. 'East Hampton,' one of them said. 'We were there last year, staying with friends.'

'I remember,' said another. 'Wasn't your daughter working as an au pair for that chain-store family?'

Hump barged in: 'It's all changed in the Hamptons. Too built up, nothing like when we were kids, right Lou? Most of us are summering elsewhere now – the Adirondacks, Montana, France. East Hampton's still lovely, though, for weekends in the fall.'

What should have insulted the women, impressed them even more. At that moment, Belly materialized, revived. 'Now friends, dinner is served. If you'll follow me.'

The waiter collected the glasses on a silver tray, while the party proceeded to the dining room across the hall. Louisa milled around with the others, reading the engraved place-cards. When all the seats were taken, Louisa realized that Foster wasn't coming. Instead she had been placed on Humphrey's right. A gloom descended and she realized how high she'd built her hopes, while deceiving herself that it was just a chance meeting – a sort of mid-life bonus. It wasn't meant to be. She was a newly single mother of two at an ordinary dinner party with ordinary people. It was salutary, she reckoned, to be plunged into the reality of socializing alone.

Foster's non-appearance made the grilled goat's cheese salad, the boeuf bourguignon and the New Zealand Pinot Noir seem tasteless. Louisa glanced down the shimmering white linen, crystal and silver at the animated faces and saw that the dinner party was quite a success: Belly was keeping the men at her end in stitches – sometimes unintentionally, she saw. There was an eagerness to please in Annabel that she hadn't shown as a girl and a weariness that meant life had knocked her about. The younger Belly would have cowered at this vision of herself.

The waiter came to clear away the main course and spoke softly in Belly's ear, prompting her to announce, 'Dessert and coffee in the drawing room, ladies. The gentlemen will stay here.' Clever, Louisa thought, to separate them so that Hump could pitch for his business while Belly courted the women.

As everyone stood up, Belly came to Louisa and took her hand, 'You're coming into the kitchen with me for a few minutes, Lou.'

The caterers were fussing over the desserts. 'Lovely meal, thank you,' Belly said to them as she brought Louisa through the kitchen and round a corner into a breakfast nook.

'Hi, Lou.' Foster stood up where he'd been eating his own late dinner in peace. 'I'm sorry I was late. Security alert at Heathrow. You know how it is.'

'Hi,' she breathed. Her heart was beating so fast she could scarcely speak.

The shock wasn't that his eyes were still green, or that his brown hair was dusted with grey, or that his teenage body had filled out. The shock was that he was there at all, flesh and bone, instantly recognizable – yet a total stranger.

Belly was triumphant. 'Better late than never. Right, Louisa?

She was looking so sad for a while there, Foss. Excuse my wickedness, Lou. I'll let you two get reacquainted while I supervise the networking.'

They stood awkwardly, not knowing what to say next, and she was glad that he seemed as self-conscious as she felt. He offered her a chair, got another glass and poured her some Pinot Noir, which startled her now with its flavour of cherries. She sat nervously, stunned by how familiar he seemed – more like a lost family member than a former lover.

Foster pushed away his plate. 'Twenty years – you leave without saying goodbye, but now . . . look at you. I guess it was worth the wait. The years suit you, Lou.' Until that moment, she had felt the years crumbling away and her face must have revealed her disappointment because he said, 'I'm sorry, I didn't mean –'

Louisa giggled. 'It's fine. I know what you meant. The years suit you too. Nothing we can do about them, anyway, is there?'

Foster's expression was difficult to read. 'I was amazed when Humphrey told me he'd tracked you down – well, bumped into you, really.'

'It's a small world,' she said, wishing she could think of something more interesting to say. 'Is this your first time in Dublin?'

He smiled a little, as though he knew her question was a way of marking time. Embarrassed, she looked down at her fingernails. 'Yeah,' he said. 'It's not quite what I expected.'

Hump barrelled in then, a cigar fuming between his thick fingers. 'Foss! You finally made it. I'm sorry to tear you away from the prettiest lady at the party, but I need you to meet some people.'

Foster groaned, stood up, ran his hands through his hair and pulled his jacket off the back of a chair. She couldn't take her eyes off him.

'Sorry, Lou. Hump's always mixing business with pleasure. We'll catch up later, yeah?'

Feeling a little deflated, yet buzzing with excitement to have finally connected with her past, Louisa walked behind the two men down the hall. When they turned into the dining room, Louisa followed Belly's high-pitched voice into drawing-room purdah, where dessert and a cheeseboard had been laid out. Freed from the constraints of male company, the women were gossiping. Dazed by her encounter with Foster, Louisa listened without really hearing. When she glanced out through the double doors across the hall and through to the dining room, she glimpsed Foster in conversation and couldn't help smiling to herself, still not quite believing it was really him. He caught her watching him and grinned in a way that made her shiver with delight. He had looked at her as if she was an interesting stranger.

Belly was bleary-eyed. 'Let's join the "lads" now, ladies – isn't that what you call them here? Lads? I just love your little, local expressions.'

Louisa followed the women into the dining room, where she and Foster moved from one group to another until they were finally together. 'It's you,' he said, gently pushing a strand of hair off her forehead, his eyes focusing on her mouth. 'The way I remember you, you were running along the beach in a white bikini, on your way up to your aunt's. I used to watch you climbing up those stairs from the beach to the lawns at Paradise.'

It was hard to get more personal than this. 'Lawns? Tick-ridden fields, more like. And Paradise . . . well, I hadn't thought about that place in a very long time until recently.'

'You forgot about me, too, I suppose. And why not? You could have had anyone.'

That wasn't how she'd felt back then. His face seemed to show resentment – or was it bitterness? Moved to reassure him, she touched his sleeve and felt energy surge between them. 'You were never just anyone,' she said.

Foster cleared his throat. 'Can we catch up tomorrow? It's difficult in the middle of this circus, and, I haven't slept in

237

twenty-four hours with all the travelling. I'm not up to much, I'm afraid.'

For a split second she considered asking Gill first if he could spend Sunday with the children, then decided that, even if he couldn't, she'd find a way. 'I would love to see you tomorrow.'

'Good.'

'I suppose I'd better give you my number. I have cards in my bag.' She'd left her bag in the drawing room and moved past Foster to fetch it. When she found it, she fumbled in her wallet for a card. *Louisa Maguire, Photographer, Castle Street, Dalkey. Appointment Only.* Having the card in her hand was as reassuring as having found a lost passport in customs. She returned to the dining room and handed it to Foster. He glanced at it. 'Maguire,' he said. 'Was Maguire good to you?'

'Not really,' Louisa said.

'I'm sorry,' he said softly.

Guests were heading for the front door now, calling goodbye. From the window, Louisa could the lights of waiting taxis idling on the street.

'So, Louisa Maguire. I'll call you tomorrow morning. We'll have a long, lazy lunch?' Foster's eyes twinkled.

'I'll clear my schedule,' she said playfully.

Belly was in the hall, seeing the guests off. Louisa watched them moving down the path, some talking to each other, others silent and independent, solitary even. When they had gone, Louisa said, 'I guess it's my turn.'

Foster took her hand. 'I know I said I was tired, but please don't go yet.' His reserve seemed to have left with the other guests.

They went back across the hall, where Belly was sprawled across the sofa, her black skirt up round her knees.

'Louisa, darling,' Humphrey sniffed his brandy, 'no more taxis for an hour. But there's one on the way.' Showing uncharacteristic sensitivity, he hoisted his wife off the sofa. 'Come on, time for bed. Let's give the teenagers some privacy.'

As he escorted Belly away, he called over his shoulder, 'Don't forget to turn out the lights.' Louisa wasn't sure if she heard him chuckle.

A fire was burning in the grate, the lights were low and a bottle of champagne had been left behind in an ice bucket. It was the perfect setting and, for a moment, Louisa imagined that she had stepped into another life that she and Foster could have had. She remembered Paul of all people, *slow down, Lou*, and chose one corner of the comfy sofa to sit on.

Foster slipped off his jacket, then sat at the other end, unlaced his shoes and placed them tidily on the floor. His stockinged feet made him seem more approachable. 'You lead, Lou. Because I have no idea what I'm doing.'

They sat quietly, taking each other in. It struck her that they hadn't much to talk about, apart from memories. And if he didn't fancy her anymore, that was fine, she told herself. *You lead.* 'I'm sorry I left you like that. I found out my mother was dying and it wiped everything else from my mind.' It was untrue, but it was plausible. Time and the malleability of memory made it so.

His face relaxed. 'I forgive you,' he said, stretching out a hand to meet hers. 'How could anyone not?'

She took the hand and felt butterflies in her stomach.

'Tell me about your life,' she said, looking away at the fire because holding his gaze made her lips tremble.

'I work. I travel. I live alone. I ask myself what happened. New York's full of guys like me and women too beautiful to notice.'

'You were married, though.' Their hands played lightly.

'My first wife's name was Louisa.'

'You're kidding.'

'Blonde, tall, an actress. A bit like you.'

'What happened to her?'

'She ran off with the vet who looked after our dog.'

'That's so sad!' Louisa was already grateful to the vet for

having got wife number one out of the way. 'And your second wife?'

'Marissa. She was great fun, but she left me for Vegas. She had a gambling problem. I should have seen it. Tried to help her. But she was a professional, she kept insisting. It seemed more like a business than an addiction, at the time. I like a game of poker myself but I can take it or leave it.'

Foster's life hadn't turned out like Louisa had expected. 'All these years I envisioned you living in Connecticut with a Vassar graduate, a couple of kids and a pair of Labrador retrievers. I expected you to have a rather safe, comfortable life, like the one you grew up in.'

'Hmph.' He seemed amused. 'Marissa went to Smith. Louisa went to Barnard. They were smart, beautiful women. I was the lucky one, really. As for Labs – I did have one of those. But what can I say? I got to pay alimony. She got the dog.'

How strange to think of him calling another woman by her name. Did you call her Lou, too? She wanted to ask, but to do so would seem vain. Nor did she want to hear his answer.

'Tell me one person you know who has a safe, comfortable life, Lou.'

'Our hosts this evening are fairly charmed, I believe.'

Foster put his arm on the back of the sofa. 'Not everything is always what it seems.' When he yawned, Louisa noticed the dark circles under his eyes. His lived-in face made him more rather than less attractive. She was relieved to see that he had aged. He moved his arm along the back of the sofa and lazily played with the cushion fringe.

'And you? Married only once?'

'Once is enough.'

'That bad, huh?' Foster said, his gaze warm. 'Belly tells me the split wasn't so long ago. If you don't want to talk about it, that's OK. Some women hardly want to talk about anything else. It's more graceful to say nothing, if you ask me – not that you shouldn't talk about it if you want to. I'm all ears. I mean

– I care.' He lifted one hand to his head. 'I'm babbling. Jet-lag . . . Tell me about your kids.'

'Milo and Elvie are the only good thing to come out of my marriage. Sometimes I'm amazed they're so balanced. Maybe it's an advantage rearing children in Ireland. I haven't got family here – well, you know that – but there's been no shortage of people to love them.'

Evidently, he had been only half-listening. 'You drove me crazy.'

'Not on purpose.'

'That's what they all say. If it's on purpose it's hardly as effective, is it?'

She didn't remember herself that way at all. She'd never been the sort to manipulate a man, but maybe that was how she'd seemed to him. 'Like you just said, not everything is as it seems. I didn't feel like I was leading you on. I've never been one to play the coquette.'

He laughed slightly. 'Did you get the letters I sent you? It's twenty years ago, I know.'

Stunned that he had written to her, Louisa shook her head, not taking her eyes away from his.

'I thought as much,' he said. 'Alice promised to forward them, but . . .' He pursed his lips.

'She didn't. But I shouldn't have – cut you off . . .' Her heart was beating so fast she sounded like she'd developed emphysema.

He was about to speak when the doorbell rang and Louisa knew it was her taxi. She rose to go. 'Tomorrow then. You'll give me a call?'

'You free all day?'

'Sure.'

He followed her to the door. 'Oh, baby.' He said it just as he used to. 'Come here.' He leaned forward and rested his hands on her shoulders, taking in every inch of her. Then his eyes were on her mouth and hers on his, her lips trembling in anticipation of his kiss. They held back for a second as they breathed each other in. Then she slid towards him ... their mouths as hungry as they'd been all those years before.

The doorbell rang again.

'You're still a great kisser,' she said,

'And you still drive me crazy.'

He fancies me! I can't believe he still fancies me!

He kissed her again and she felt herself tumbling back in time. How could it be? They were two middle-aged people, who had been stumbling towards eternity. Now they were moving at hyper-speed in the opposite direction, regaining their youth with a kiss.

'Tomorrow,' she said.

He kissed the tip of her nose, like it was yesterday.

17

St Agnes's seemed to be scolding her, like a worried mother, when Louisa snuck in the door at half-one in the morning. 'Taxis are impossible to get,' she told the house – preparing her excuse for Gill. Not that she owed him any: it wasn't an unreasonable time to come in from a party. She slipped off her red sandals and left them at the bottom of the stairs, then went into the kitchen to put the kettle on. A cup of tea was what she needed now. The kitchen felt cold and looked drab in the dim light of the lamp she always kept on at night.

I can't believe this is happening! the young girl in her head shouted and Louisa wanted to dance for joy. Finally, her life was coming round. After so many years of waiting and trying to make things right – never quite managing it. Always taking the wrong turn and getting lost.

Foster.

She imagined him already asleep in Belly and Hump's guest-room, lips swollen from kissing her. *I can't believe we picked up where we left off, as though it was meant to be.*

The kettle hissed into life, then rocked as it boiled.

'I'll have one if it's going.'

Gill startled her and she jumped.

'Sorry!' he said.

Act normal, Louisa told herself. 'How were the kids?'

'Fine. No problems. They love that *Cat in the Hat* don't they? Why do children like to hear the same story again and again? They must live it in ways we've forgotten.'

Louisa put teabags in two mugs, then poured the water. 'It's reassuring for them, I suppose, always knowing how it ends.'

'Unlike life,' Gill said. 'I stayed up to watch a film, then fell asleep on the sofa. I tried to turn your central heating on but there seems to be an airlock. You should call a plumber on Monday.'

'I'll do that,' Louisa said, thinking, *I'm going to live another life-time between now and Monday.* She handed Gill his tea. 'I hate to ask you this. But would you mind holding the fort for me tomorrow? I've been invited out and I'd really like to go. I'll pay you double.'

Gill slicked his tea with a dash of milk and stirred it with his finger.

'Take a spoon! You'll burn yourself doing that.'

'I'm made of asbestos,' Gill said. 'Hands like sandpaper.' He took a sip. 'Tongue too.'

'So, is that OK?'

Gill seemed to be considering his options. 'Yeah, this once. Can you be back by six, though? I'm meeting someone.'

Back by six. She hoped Foster wanted an early lunch. 'Why don't you spend the night here? You'll get more sleep. I promise to keep the kids away from you before noon. Ben left loads of clothes behind, if you want something fresh.'

Gill softened. 'Don't want to be alone tonight?'

'I just thought it would be more convenient for you, that's all.'

'Did you now? No, I'll have my tea, then bugger off. I like riding my bike at night. Roads are clear and I can let rip. Sometimes I head as far as Wexford and back.'

'You must have a death wish,' Louisa said. 'Didn't anyone ever tell you that motorbikes are dangerous? Especially at night.'

'That's kind of the point. One man and the road. See ya!'

He was so young, she thought. Then she remembered Foster's kisses and felt euphoric. I'm young, too, she thought. 'Enjoy the ride!'

In no time at all, or so it seemed, Louisa was shielding her eyes from the morning sun. In Ireland the light was never right. Autumn and spring, it hung too low and was painful to look at.

In winter, it disappeared and in summer the sun was too high, creating light without heat. In September, as another dark winter approached, she usually felt sombre, but not now. It was high summer in her life.

There wasn't a peep from the children, who had crept into her bed during the night, so she decided to use the opportunity to have a shower. She'd washed her hair and was shaving her legs when Elvie came into the bathroom shouting, 'Mum! Dad and Lucy are here!'

'No!' She'd forgotten that Ben had planned to visit this morning. 'Tell them I'm in the shower and to help themselves to some breakfast. I'll be down in a minute.'

When she was dressed, in jeans and a shirt – no way was she going to let Ben see her in anything that smacked of a Sunday-afternoon date – Louisa blasted her hair with the dryer, attempting to re-create the look the hairdresser had achieved the day before. She looked in the mirror to see her hair sticking out in all directions. 'Mum?' Milo was calling. 'Will you come downstairs now?'

Louisa put her hair in a pony-tail, then scooted downstairs. 'Hi, Ben, Lucy. You caught me on the hop. I see you've got breakfast, though.'

'We made ourselves at home,' said Ben, with no trace of irony. He was holding court at the kitchen table, reading the Sunday papers over a mug of coffee. Lucy was at the stove, boiling eggs. The kitchen window was wide open to let out the smoke from burnt toast. 'Lucy, thanks. You need a hand?'

'I've made a mess of your kitchen. My eggs are either too hard or too soft – not as good as Mum's, I'm afraid.'

Louisa went to the table, moving Ben's paper aside to reveal what appeared to be perfectly boiled eggs in Milo and Elvie's favourite teddy-bear-shaped egg-cups. She was torn between the warm feeling her children's loyalty gave her, and the uneasy knowledge that they'd been deliberately winding Lucy up. 'I'm sorry. They can be a bit picky sometimes,' Louisa said.

Five minutes later, they were all sitting round the table like one of those blended families who, Louisa imagined, lived in places like Notting Hill or Orange County or, most likely, Saudi Arabia. Ben had the smug look of a man with a harem. Well, she wasn't being tolerant for his sake.

Louisa spread some boiled egg on a slice of toast, then sprinkled it with black pepper, thinking how Lucy felt more like a daughter-in-law than her husband's new lover. Maybe that was the problem, she considered, Ben was my child rather than my husband.

'When you bring them back this evening, Ben, Gill will probably be here. Behave yourself and be civil to him. He's only the child-minder. I have to catch up with some work in the studio.'

How easily she lied. She doubted that Ben would welcome her new life as she did his.

When Ben and the children went out to kick a football in the garden, Lucy hung back for a moment and said, 'Thank you for being so cool about all this. Other women in your position would be eating *me* for breakfast.'

'Why?'

Lucy was flustered. 'You know . . .'

Louisa suspected that Lucy wasn't as 'new' as Ben had let on. 'I don't know, actually, and I don't want to. I do like to think that if Elvie were in your situation, she'd be treated well. We women have to stick together, don't you think?'

'That's pretty radical.'

'Call me an old hippie.'

Lucy gave her a dazzling smile, then skipped off, taking Elvie's hand in her own. Louisa watched as Elvie, in little pink fluffy boots, marched along beside Lucy as though they were sisters, chattering away.

Her mobile rang and she jumped to it, then carried it to the front of the house where she wouldn't be heard. 'Hello?'

'Hey, baby. How does the Shrewsbury Park Hotel suit you? Lunch in my suite?'

18

The hotel had an underground car park from which guests could ascend in the lift to the rooms above. It was the perfect setting for a tryst. Besides, the kitchen did delectable sushi, she knew from having photographed weddings there. How clever of Foster, new in town, to know just the place to pick. They should be meeting in a cottage on the beach, of course, but that wasn't possible at short notice. She'd suggest, sometime, that they go to the southern coast of Ireland to a house all their own, then reproached herself for jumping the gun a bit.

She locked the car, checked her lipstick in the wing-mirror and went to the lift in the black criss-cross sandals that bound her from ankle to knee. They reminded her of the one-night stand with Matt, that was true, but that only added to their power. Matt had helped her prove that she could still surrender to her senses. He'd made her feel womanly again and Louisa, full of memories of being seventeen, wanted Foster to meet her as a complicated woman, not a *silly girl*.

That's only Alice talking, Louisa reassured herself.

She was terrified. This afternoon would be about opening their hearts, rather than their bodies alone. And a promiscuous heart was the most dangerous organ of all. *Slow down, Lou.*

The lift rose smoothly and Louisa got out into an anonymous corridor lined with doors numbered like cards in a game of chance. She knocked, then waited. He had said Room 800, hadn't he?

The door clicked. His face appeared and she pulled him to her. She grasped his face with both hands, letting her bag fall to the floor. She kissed him boldly, letting her body take over. This wasn't going to be the sort of encounter where he murmurs

'Do you like it when I do that?' until she moans a little and wonders if he likes it too. This wasn't about the performance of desire as an introductory get-to-know-you session. All artifice, all seduction, all thought was banished as they struggled over to the bed and collapsed on to it, not caring how they looked to one another. They moved as their bodies commanded and every move was right.

Eventually, Foster paused to catch his breath, face buried in her neck. Then he raised it and said, tears in his eyes, 'We could have been so happy.'

She began to sob, as much from joy as regret, releasing emotions held back for years with Ben. He kissed away the tears as he moved inside her again and Louisa lost all sense of where she was and who she was, caring only for the man she was with.

'I feel like I've been waiting all my life for that,' he said.

Louisa smiled and opened her eyes. 'Me too,' she said.

When she woke, Foster handed her a glass of champagne. 'I propose a toast,' he said, then buried his head between her legs.

'Stop!' she giggled. 'Or I'll do the same to you!'

'Go ahead,' he said.

'Let me drink my champagne first.'

'If you insist.'

Belatedly, he began to take off her sandals. 'Have I told you how fetching these look when you've nothing else on? But they're not much for drinking champagne out of.' He took a slug straight from the bottle.

'Next time I'd better wear wellies,' she said.

He laughed. 'I love your funny ex-pat expressions.' He threw one sandal on the floor, then went to work on the other.

'If they're so fetching, why are you taking them off?'

He held her bare foot in his hand. 'Because I want you completely naked and vulnerable.' He kissed her toes. 'And they were digging into my back.' He turned to show her two red marks.

'I'm sorry.'

'No problem.'

He sat on the bed, cross-legged and naked, stroking her body as she lay back on the pillows, sipping her champagne. She felt like a queen.

'Still scared?' he asked.

'Only in a nice way,' she answered. 'But not of you.'

He poured her more champagne. 'What are you afraid of, then?'

'Don't know yet.'

'You haven't gone neurotic on me, have you?'

'Neurotic? It's a nice kind of fear. The sort you feel at the beginning of a roller-coaster ride.'

'I'm glad you think it's just the beginning.' He bent to kiss her soft stomach, then lay his head there.

'I can't believe you're real,' she said. 'This doesn't happen to people, this sort of happy ending. There's always a price to pay.'

Foster looked at her. 'You've become a very dour European, you know that? Whatever happened to your American optimism?'

'I never had any.'

'You had children. You must have thought it was the real thing with Ben.'

'I did and I didn't. In hindsight, I realize that I'd stopped believing in the real thing.'

'Why?'

She'd wanted intimacy with Foster, but even that had its limits. She felt no need to put into words that night in the glass room. Maybe that was the most important difference between Louisa at seventeen and Louisa at thirty-seven. She knew that in bed she and Foster could become one, but outside it, no two people could merge without smothering each other. To share a trauma as intense as the one that separated her from him would ruin things.

She finally spoke. 'I didn't know what the real thing was — until now.'

'That good, huh?'

She ruffled his hair. 'You hungry?'

'Starving. Let's order room service. What do you want to eat?'

'Sushi.'

This amused him. 'What's Irish sushi? A couple of mackerel dipped in Guinness?'

'What were you expecting? Potatoes cooked three ways?'

'And to find you barefoot and pregnant, living in a thatched cottage with a mud floor. I thought I'd have to rescue you and help you re-adapt to civilization, through intensive one-on-one therapy.'

Foster ordered the sushi and beer for him, more champagne for Louisa. She watched him on the phone, engaging with a stranger at the other end of the line. 'I know almost nothing about you,' she said when he had hung up.

'What's there to know?'

'What you do for a living, for example. Annabel mentioned that you're in business with Humphrey.'

Foster got back on the bed beside her and pulled up the covers to keep them warm. 'Hump is in business with Hump. I'm more along for the ride. Hump's the risk-taker and I'm the fixer. I sort of protect him from himself. I'm not a nine-to-five type. I like to be able to do my own thing.'

'That's quite a luxury in this day and age. I don't suppose you ever had to actually earn a living, did you?'

'Let's talk about something else. Money is so boring.'

It isn't when you need it, Louisa thought. But what would Foster and Humphrey know about that? She had an inkling that money was an area where Foster hadn't really grown up, but who was she to judge? 'Children?'

'Haven't got any, which is a good thing in retrospect. But I wish I had.' He caught her eye and held it, telling her without words that if he had children, they'd be with her.

'What else did Annabel tell you about me?'

He seemed slightly embarrassed. 'About you? Not much.'

Not much. What did that mean? But she didn't want to push it. She wanted to be back in the thoughtless place where they didn't need to speak. She put her hand on the back of his neck and pulled him towards her. When room service knocked on the door, they didn't hear.

Louisa woke with a start. 'What time is it?'

Foster wasn't to be roused, so Louisa scrambled out of bed, eventually found her bag under a chair and fished out her phone, which she'd set to silent. Three new messages. All from Gill. 'Shit.' She clicked on her in-box: 6.18 p.m. 'Where r u?' 6.47 p.m. 'U OK?' 7.43 p.m. 'Call me.' She logged out and checked the time: 8.32 p.m.

'He's going to kill me,' she muttered. She wanted to crawl back into bed with Foster and sleep for hours. Louisa started to text back to say – what? Overslept? In the afternoon? Lost in time? Couldn't give a damn about your schedule? She opted for: 'Sorry! Back soon!'

Foster turned in the bed, mumbling, 'C'mere.'

'Foster, wake up. I have to go.'

'Mmm?' He was dead to the world, jet-lag having caught up with him.

Louisa threw on her clothes, cursed her complicated shoes and left Foster a note on the hotel stationery. 'Had to get back to kids – school tomorrow.' That sounded like she was setting him up for a life-time of limiting routine, which she now knew he despised. She settled for 'Thank you for a magical time, you magical man. X Lou', folded it up and left it on her pillow. In the corridor, she took the lift to the basement car park. Nothing felt the same – neither her feet on the ground, her car, nor the road back to Dalkey.

Poised to apologize to Gill, Louisa found Becca at St Agnes's with a face like a mother superior – countered somewhat by her bald head, on which Milo and Elvie had drawn faces in eyeliner and lipstick. The children were in high spirits – almost too high, Louisa saw. She spotted melted chocolate ice-cream and sweet wrappers on the table.

'You guys had fun, I see. What happened to Gill?'

'He had a date,' Becca said. 'I think you knew that.'

Louisa wanted to scoot the children to bed and settle down with Becca for a post-mortem, but her friend was in no mood for that. Becca tied a scarf over her head and took her car keys out of her bag. 'Please tell Gill I'm sorry,' Louisa murmured.

'You tell him,' Becca said. 'If he's still speaking to you.'

'Don't be like this, Becca.'

'Not only are you rushing this thing, you're trampling over everyone else on the way. Just be careful.'

'Becca, I'm really sorry. I'm acting like an irresponsible kid – it's just, oh . . . I'm allowed, aren't I?'

Becca softened. 'Of course you are. And I'd love to hear all about it but I've got an early start.'

'It was amazing.'

'I can see that.'

'I lost track of time.'

'Good on ya', girl.'

'You're fantastic to bail me out with Gill.'

Becca was nearly out the door. 'I know I am,' she called over her shoulder.

Louisa was left to re-immerse herself in a life she wasn't sure she wanted anymore – except for her children, of course. She returned to the TV room to find them in fits of laughter, decorating each other's faces with Becca's ruined make-up. Foster would love her wild, Irish children, wouldn't he?

Louisa was dreamy as she dressed the children for school next morning. Only half-present, she spoke the minimum of words required to shovel Cheerios into them, not wanting to break the spell.

'Mummy, stop acting like a zombie,' Elvie said.

'I'm going to eat you alive,' she cajoled.

'Why are you wearing make-up?' Milo added accusingly.

'And you smell bad,' Elvie added.

Get them to school. Come back, take a shower. Mechanical step by mechanical step, she would walk herself back into her old life, which seemed so sparse now that she wanted to build a new one with Foster.

Eventually, Louisa arrived at the studio in no mood to work – wanting to dump it all in favour of becoming Foster's lady of leisure – to find that Paul had turned the darkroom upside down. Supplies were scattered everywhere, bits and pieces of equipment were marking her white laminate flooring and Paul himself was cursing the ventilation system in the darkroom as he attacked it with a screwdriver and a vacuum cleaner.

'Paul? What's up?'

'Housekeeping. I can't deal with this chaos anymore. Your friend Gill never puts things back where he finds them.' He looked her up and down. 'Is that who you spent the weekend with?'

'Excuse me?'

'You've got that look.'

'What has you in a mood this morning?'

Oh dear, just when she'd been planning to ask him to fill in for her while she spent an afternoon or two with Foster. 'What's your schedule today?'

'Developing the huge backlog of wedding material, what else?'

'We'll do it together,' Louisa said.

'You've got four portraits.'

'On a Monday?'

'It'll be Christmas before we know it. Busiest season of the year.'

'It's time we hired a rookie, don't you think? You're in with those people at the art college, aren't you? Find us a young, hungry, wannabe portrait photographer.'

'Easier said than done,' Paul said. 'They all want to make movies now. Or do weird self-portraits.'

'There's got to be another Paul out there somewhere.'

'Yeah, I've been meaning to mention that. I'm still the old Paul, really, aren't I? My solicitor keeps getting fobbed off by yours on the partnership agreement. You sure you haven't changed your mind?'

'Nothing like that. I told you: it's all tied up with the divorce. I don't want to leave you vulnerable.'

'Divorces take years, Lou.'

'Not mine. Please be patient? I won't screw you over, I promise.'

She heard the doorbell ring, too early for a client. Through the glass, she spotted a bouquet of white roses – at least three dozen. She opened the door. 'For Ms Stone,' said the deliveryman. She took them from him. Ms Stone – she was starting to like the sound of that.

'Somebody spent a bomb on flowers.' Paul remarked when she turned with the flowers in her arms.

'I adore white roses.' She tore the card from the cellophane around the flowers. 'Remember the white bikini? I do. X Foster.' He'd given her his phone number, too.

A woman can flourish a second time, she thought, like artichokes. She was in the late summer of her life, not quite autumn yet. And all the years of waiting had been, in retrospect, a period of ferocious pruning in preparation for being with Foster again. She held the card over her heart.

'Who's the lucky guy?' Paul asked.

'Wouldn't you like to know?' She felt her body lithe and brown in her white bikini.

'Let me take your picture with the roses,' Paul said.

'Why?'

'There's something in your face . . .'

Click.

'Besides, I'm testing out this new digital the suppliers lent us. They swear it's the best yet.'

'You're a devil. And I've got to make a call.' Louisa went to her office. 'Room 800 please, Foster Adams.'

'Mr Adams' line is engaged. Would you like to hold?'

'Would you tell him Louisa rang?'

She hung up. Her legs felt weak, she'd been so close to talking to him. Like a teenage crush.

The phone rang almost immediately and Paul reached for it. 'Yes, who's speaking please? Just a moment.'

Louisa took the phone.

It wasn't Foster. 'Lou? It's Mary.'

'Mary! You sound like you're next door!'

'I almost am. We're in London and we're on our way to Dublin for a flying visit. Can we have dinner? I want you to meet my honey. Call Becca for me, would you? Arrange a meeting of the coven. I'll call you when I arrive.'

'I can't wait!'

'Gotta run.'

Louisa called Becca and they decided to have dinner at Louisa's, rather than a restaurant, so that the children could see Mary.

'Will I ask Foster?' Louisa asked.

'Can he cook?'

'This is serious.'

'If you want to. Why not?'

'But the children. I wanted to prepare them.'

'Tell them he's a friend. They're not going to ask questions.'

'Elvie doesn't miss a thing.'

'Why are you so nervous?'

Because this could be the rest of my life.

'Louisa, you there?'

'Yeah.'

'Good. See you tomorrow.'

19

Louisa kept the card that had come with Foster's roses in her wallet. It connected her not just to him but to the deepest self she had rediscovered. She walked differently, laughed more easily, felt men glancing at her twice in the street.

She wondered, as the lift rose again, if it was true that her white-bikinied younger self was what he saw in her. A seventeen-year-old girl, with smooth skin and limbs that seemed to stretch for ever. A girl who wasn't trapped in a darkroom early in the morning as she developed other people's lives and loves. She closed her eyes and saw that girl instead of the woman who was actually reflected in the bad lighting of the mirror-lined lift. Before there were mirrors and cameras, women had only one way to gauge their beauty: through their lovers' eyes.

Foster's eyes were shining with pleasure and anticipation when she found him waiting for her in the corridor outside the lift. When she saw him, she stopped in her tracks. For a brief moment, they stood still. He was in a cream cashmere pullover, with a hint of a pale blue T-shirt underneath, blue jeans – like he'd just been walking the lawns of his Hamptons estate. He couldn't have been Irish, French or Eastern European. He was confident, polished, open – *shadowless*. That's it, she thought, he's all there with nothing to hide.

He came to her, lifted her up, carried her into the room and, without speaking, he undressed her. She felt the rasp of his jeans against her skin as he refused to wait, dove inside her, not letting his gaze fall from hers.

The circles under his eyes were gone. A few days had passed since they had last made love and he seemed almost a stranger again. She found that exciting.

'You're here,' he said, pausing to kiss her.

'So are you,' Louisa answered, wrapping her legs around him.

'You're shaking.'

'Can't help it.'

He moved inside her and she was on the beach again, the sand polishing her skin.

There was a knock on an inner door, which Foster opened to reveal a living/dining room she hadn't known was there. 'I'll be right back,' he whispered.

She lay there listening to the voices in the other room. She heard the wheels of a serving cart, the clink of dishes, the clatter of a bottle being lifted from an ice bucket and then, seconds later, a hiss. She heard a man say, 'Thank you, sir', then Foster murmured a few words. She adored this new feeling of being cared for.

She stretched out her arms and legs like a starfish, filling the bed, sensing the silk beneath her back.

He came back to her, a glass of champagne in each hand. 'You're a revelation,' he said. 'I think I like this Louisa even more.'

'Come here,' she said.

She grabbed his clothes, tore them off him.

'You take my breath away,' he whispered.

'Tell me about Ben,' Foster said. 'Does he mind you having a man in your life?' They were sitting up in bed, eating sushi. The dinner that had been delivered earlier had been taken away untouched.

'He doesn't know yet. But he has a woman, so he could hardly object.'

'So you think he might?' Foster scrutinized her.

'I don't care if he does. My only interest is in keeping a cordial relationship with him for the children's sake. When you have children together, you can't just walk away as though the other person never existed.'

Foster shrugged. 'I find that once an ex meets another man, she leaves me alone, except for the occasional drunken phone call in the middle of the night – "You're still my best friend. Can we talk about how horrible my new husband's being?" That kind of thing.'

Louisa felt a twinge of disgust mingled with jealousy. 'I can't imagine you married to a woman like that.' She didn't want to imagine it, that he could be so desperate. Why would he marry a needy woman like that? Then it struck her: for the same reasons she had married Ben.

'Aren't all women like that? Stuck on one guy until the next comes along?' Foster asked.

Pins and needles in her hands, made Louisa put down her drink. 'I'm not like that.' She was confused. She didn't know this cynical Foster – and didn't want to. 'I'm not on the rebound, if that's what you think.'

Foster took her hand. 'I'm only trying to warn you that you don't know what anyone's truly like until you've divorced them. I'm anticipating that Ben will try to make our lives difficult. I want to be prepared. Because *no-one* is going to take you away from me again.'

Relieved, Louisa squeezed his hand. Talking was a minefield. She felt so much safer when they spoke with their bodies.

'When your exes give you trouble, do you never blame yourself for having chosen them in the first place?'

'I wish I could say that. But it was the women in my life always did the choosing.'

Louisa recalled what Becca had said, about three divorces being reckless. 'I have no intention of becoming ex-wife number three. If you want to be with me and my kids, I'll be the happiest woman alive. But if this is no more than a brilliant idyll between two grown-up teenagers who used to be mad about each other, that's OK too. Just don't think of me as a dumb broad who's trying to become wife number three, because I'm not. I had a life before you came back to me, and if you go, I'll have a life again.'

Where had that come from? She'd never been so forthright with Ben. Foster's love had made her feel secure.

'You're tough, aren't you? You've had to be, I suppose,' he said – regretting, she knew, their lost twenty years. 'We've both had to be tough. We can't be those two kids on the beach again, not really.'

He was right, of course. 'If only we could change the past, Foster.'

'What do you mean?'

She couldn't say it aloud: if only he had come to her that night in the glass room. They would have had a chance. He might have been her boyfriend, gone back to the city with her then, been by her side at the funeral. 'Alice's party, do you remember?'

Foster's brow creased in pain. 'I stood you up, I'm sorry. I was held late in the kitchens, then my father came looking for me and –' He had the same defensive look on his face that Milo got when he felt he was being wrongly accused.

'Sssh,' she said. 'It's done now.' If Foster had come to the glass room, there would have been no Ben – which would have meant no Elvie, no Milo, no Becca, no Mary . . . no Gill. She leaned back and closed her eyes. Why was *he* popping into her head? She could almost see his disapproving face.

Foster took away the tray of food and laid it on the floor. Then he came back to the bed and lay on top of her, his hands pinning her arms by her sides so that she couldn't move. 'One day, I'll build you a house with your own glass room. We can make love there every night.'

Louisa winced. That was the last thing she wanted. But he didn't know that. He didn't know that part of her at all and never would, if she could help it.

Foster kissed her, stroking her breasts tenderly. She wondered if he'd be so ardent if he knew . . .

He slipped a hand between her legs. She told herself to give in and forget. Then she remembered what he'd said a few days before, during their first love-making. *We could have been so happy* – and began to cry in anger for what they'd lost and would never get back no matter how many times they made love or where.

'What's wrong?' he asked her.

'I'm not used to being this happy,' she said. It was ever so small a white lie. And maybe it was true.

He moved inside her. 'No more talking.'

20

It was only in the taxi on the way home in the early morning that she remembered her supper with Mary and Becca. She'd forgotten to invite him. No matter. She'd be talking to him soon, whispering into the phone while clients waited in the infinity curve. Through the taxi window, she watched the pink and grey dawn shift slowly above Sandymount Strand and saw a lonely soul, carrying a shellfish rake.

When she reached St Agnes's – a dark shadow against the rosy light – she paid the driver, wondering how often he returned mothers to their children with the early bird. It seemed an effort to get out of the car, to walk along the path to her own front door. She hesitated putting the key into the lock, reluctant to be stepping back into her old life when she had left her new one in Foster's bed.

She opened the door and the house was silent with sleeping children. She walked softly through the gloom and heard rustling in the family room, where she found Gill on the floor. He had her personal portfolio spread open and pictures laid out before him like tiles on a chapel floor. He knelt over them in concentration.

Louisa froze. 'What do you think you're doing?'

'I was going through all that stuff under the stairs. Elvie convinced me she had a doll's cradle hidden in there someplace. I came across this. It's yours, isn't it?'

'You had no right!'

Gill began to gather up the pictures, shuffling them like giant tarot cards. 'I'm sorry. I didn't realize.'

Louisa flinched.

'It's OK. Calm down.'

'I *am* calm. Were you up all night with these?' Perhaps that was why Becca had warned her off her brother. He was snooping at half-past-six in the morning.

'I'm an early riser. I didn't want to look at these when the children were around, in case they got fingerprints on them. I didn't mean any harm.'

He stood up slowly. 'You're not yourself. Has something happened?'

She realized she was shaking.

'I'll make you a cup of tea,' Gill said.

She had to force herself to speak softly. 'I didn't get much sleep.'

Gill raked his hand through his blond hair. 'I meant nothing by it, honestly. I was only curious, once I saw the pictures. They're amazing, the way they tell a story. I thought, well, a portfolio . . . I thought you intended it to be shown. I didn't realize the pictures were so private.'

She felt exposed. 'They're not. I just wasn't expecting it, that's all. I'm over-reacting. Sorry.' She put her hands over her eyes.

'They're amazing pictures,' Gill said, again trying to justify his intrusion.

In front of her, in large-format black-and-white matt, a girl, barely past her teens, reclined awkwardly against a dark garbage-bag spilling over with sparkling dresses. Her long hair half-covered her face. She was wearing a tiny vest and a pair of shorts. Her thigh-high boots made her legs seem fragile enough to snap. Scribbled along the white margin at the bottom in black ink, 'Pussy in Boots, 1986'. The photo was signed in the bottom right-hand corner.

Louisa, photographer's assistant, caught hung-over and napping when she should have been working.

She remembered the photographer's face, bullish and angry.

'Don't move,' he had ordered.

Click.

She remembered shielding her eyes against the flash.

Click.

The invading camera.

Click.

'Reload, Pussy.'

Louisa felt an urge to tear the photograph up. She hated the image of her younger self, who had been struggling to make a living as far away from Foster and her aunt's artichokes as she could possibly get.

'He was trying to see into your soul, wasn't he? Whoever he was.'

'You're a romantic. My soul isn't what he was after,' she said lightly.

Gill took this in, then slipped out another photograph. A woman with long hair and big sad eyes, wearing a 1970s peasant shirt over jeans. In her late twenties, early thirties, maybe, sitting at a table listening to a friend, eyes half-alert, a wreath of smoke round her head.

'Amanda Smoking, 1983', was written in Louisa's teenage hand. 'You look just like her,' Gill said. 'Elvie does too.'

Anxiety rocketed through her body as she felt herself transported to the tiny apartment, the lentils and brown rice eaten by candlelight, Judy Collins on the tape-player in the hot, humid Manhattan night, the lingering odour of marijuana.

You can be whatever you want to be, Louisa. Don't give yourself away. Had Amanda really said that? Or had she waited until now, twenty years after her death?

Seeing the picture, she could even remember the conversation. Amanda's friends bantering as they always did, challenging each other with ethical dilemmas. An affair wasn't one woman being cruel to another: it was two women sharing a man. Amanda had thought this ridiculous. 'Would you ever share a man, Amanda? You would. I know it. You have, haven't you?' Amanda had maintained her superior expression: 'I don't have affairs,' she had said, smoke streaming from her mouth. 'I have mind-blowing sexual experiences. I don't believe in loyalty. It kills sexual excitement. It's men who want women to be loyal, not women themselves.'

Strange how certain conversations came into her mind verbatim, as if Amanda was in the room with her. She sat back, pulled her legs up to her knees and felt Gill laying a blanket around her shoulders. She felt so much like the lanky girl lying against the bin-bag that she could feel the sweaty plastic against her cheek. She had an ache in her solar plexus, an ache that had been with her all her life. It was the pain she felt when she held the children close to her in bed at night. The feeling told her that everything was about loss and impermanence, and that there was no point pretending that relationships would last or that anything good came without pain. The lightness of being with Foster had disappeared like a wisp of smoke.

Maybe that's what Gill wanted. 'These pictures are like a diary,' Louisa said softly. 'I would never do something like that to you – read your diary.'

'I'm sorry.' Yet he didn't stop. Instead he caught her eye, silently asking permission before he lifted the acid-free, waxy paper from 'Bride and Groom (Self-Portrait), New York, 1993'. A man and a woman sat at the bottom edge of a bed, looking into the lens sternly, almost as though the seriousness of their commitment had only just hit them. 'A cut-price wedding, one night in the cheapest room at the Plaza and a mattress on the floor, yet I was convinced I was being rescued,' she said, marvelling at her own naïveté. Gill put a hand on the back of her neck and stroked it tenderly.

'Look at Elvie,' she exclaimed. Newborn Elvie, squalling and naked on the bed, limbs rigid, unlike any pictures mothers usually took. 'I used to worry that my cold eye would affect her.'

Gill sifted through the pile carefully, almost as though he knew what he was looking for. 'Tell me about these two,' he said.

'My Aunt (with artichokes), Amagansett, 1986' and 'Alice at her Easel, Amagansett, 1986' brought up memories of Foster and something toxic that she could nearly taste. Alice, sitting at the table in the huge, cold kitchen, slicing the heart from an artichoke with a three-inch blade, her smudgy-glassed gin and tonic just within reach. Alice, in the barn, intent upon a canvas, in her own world.

Louisa sat down amid the pictures spread out on the floor. Gill turned to her. 'I know that Larry Stein's portraits are regarded as definitive, but your portraits tell me more about Alice than any of his. Stein's portraits idealized her. I never believed they were real.'

Louisa sat quietly, feeling raw. 'How did you know about Alice?'

Gill was quick to explain. 'I thought I recognized her. She's Alice Stone, right? The painter? I studied art history in university, you know. And Larry Stein, well, I've been reading a lot about photography. Looking at a lot of pictures. It interests me. You know it does.'

There was nothing Louisa wanted to say, no possible explanation she could give him without revealing too much. He took her silence calmly, sitting with her quietly for a minute or two, before disappearing to the kitchen. While he was gone, Louisa shuffled through photographs until she found her mother in three portraits: 'Amanda Shining', 'Amanda Drawing' and 'Amanda Passed Out Cold'. They said it all: their holidays at the beach, their days in the apartment, their mornings after.

On her knees again, Louisa rifled through her life until she found what she was looking for. 'Foster Adams, Amagansett, 1986'. He lay on a dusty chenille blanket in his swimming trunks in the glass room, eyes closed, like a child. How young he had been then, Louisa realized. His skin was smooth, his stomach muscles hard and his hairless chest high. He was far more delicate than she had remembered.

She wrapped the picture up in its protective paper as Gill

returned with mugs of tea and toast on a tray. 'Come to the table. You don't want to spill anything on the pictures. I'll put them away for you in a minute, before the children wake up. You should go to bed for a while. I've never seen you so exhausted.'

Louisa tried to smile. 'I'm very happy.'

Gill poured milk into their tea. 'I hope so.'

21

She awoke sweating in the middle of a dream and, for a moment, thought she was back in the hotel room with Foster. Her phone rang and brought her back to reality. She answered with a knot in her stomach, knowing by the light in her bedroom that she'd missed her first studio appointments of the day and that the children were late for school.

'Hello?'

'Louisa?'

'Yes?'

'Stella Pearson. Did I wake you?'

Louisa glanced at the bedside clock – nine-thirty. 'Not at all,' she lied. 'It's nice to hear from you.' She needed water and drank from a stale glass left by the bed some time before.

'I have news. Are you sitting down?'

She was lying down, but never mind. 'Go on.'

'I have confirmation this morning of your aunt's estate – and it's far more than the property at Amagansett. That's a house and ten acres, by the way. Impressive in that part of the world, apparently. She's also bequeathed what appears to be an Aladdin's cave of paintings: her work and others. I understand there's a Picasso or two. Some of her work is on loan to museums. Others were stockpiled in a lock-up in New Jersey.'

Stella's update bombarded Louisa's foggy head. 'Wow.'

'Wow is right. You're going to have to hire a curator and secure an agent. There's a bit of a buzz spreading about this so I'm having the New York office contract a PR. No insult to your aunt, but there's a lot of interest in the Picassos. I don't know how word got out, but I suppose it was bound to. *The*

New York Times was looking for you and I've told them your whereabouts are unknown.'

'This is crazy,' Louisa said. 'The woman didn't even like me very much.'

Stella remained professionally cool. 'You're probably wondering about the value.'

'It's crossed my mind.'

She could hear the smile in Stella's voice. 'I don't think you'll ever have to work again, let's put it that way. But, like I said before, it's a huge responsibility. A full-time job, really – at least for the moment.'

Louisa felt torn. The most important things in her life now were Foster and the children. She didn't want major responsibilities or disruptions. 'Is there a deadline on any of this? Can I just hang on for a while and let it all sink in? It's overwhelming, Stella.'

'Of course it is. This is life-changing stuff. You'll want to be keeping your feet on the ground and – like I said before – your cards close to your chest. You have no idea of the problems when news leaks out of an inheritance of this enormity. And Dublin is small. Tell one Dubliner and it'll be on CNN's next news bulletin. That goes for best friend, your lover and your manicurist.'

'But I trust Becca!'

'The famous Becca Lynley? Which one of those categories does she fall into?' Stella seemed to sense her discomfort. 'Hey, I'm not trying to make you paranoid. But, please, you'll be making my life a lot easier, and your own, if you don't show your hand. Chinese walls, yeah?'

Louisa smiled at this, almost hearing Becca's tone of voice in Stella's use of her favourite phrase. 'I keep thinking, why me?'

'Why *not* you? I have to be in court in ten minutes. We'll talk again soon.'

Louisa hung up, shook herself and remembered where she

was supposed to be. She punched in Paul's number. 'Paul, one of the kids is sick. Can you cover this morning?'

'Already am. Good thing I was here. This isn't like you. What's up?'

'Milo's sick,' she lied. 'Nothing serious.'

With that settled, she thought again of Foster. He had to be awake by now. She rang his hotel room, but the desk picked up. 'Mr Adams checked out this morning.'

'Did he say where he was going?'

'No, Madam.'

Odd. She tried his cell-phone. 'Baby, I'm sorry. I'm at the airport. Business crisis. I tried to call you an hour ago but you must have been dead to the world.'

'You're leaving me?' She felt hopelessly child-like.

He laughed. 'I'm not leaving you, babe. I've got urgent business. I'll be back in a week or two.'

'Oh.' A week. Or *two*. 'Why didn't you say anything last night?'

'Because I didn't know last night.' This was a different Foster – the hard-nosed businessman. She mustn't let him know how disappointed she was.

'I'll be back as soon as I can for as long as I can. For ever, if you let me.'

She hadn't been prepared for a sudden disappearance and it rattled her. 'Don't say it if you don't mean it. We're adults. We know that nothing is for ever.'

Louisa knew that they were perilously close to admitting they were in love. Maybe that was what he was running from.

'I was going to call you from New York. I hadn't the heart –'

'Coward.'

'Perhaps.'

She could hear the sounds of an airport in the background. Already she was yearning for him, for his touch and to make love to him. But was that love?

*

That evening, Mary and Dr Koala – whose name was actually Tony – took centre-stage.

'I can't believe it's real, you know? It's like he was waiting there for me, all my life,' Mary confided when Milo dragged Tony out to the garden with the boomerang Mary had brought him.

'If I hadn't seen you and Tony so happy, Mary, I wouldn't have thought it possible. I know my thing with Foster was just a teenage summer romance, but I feel as though he's my best friend.'

Mary glowed. 'I know exactly what you mean. It's weird. I went through a stage of telling myself it would never last and just to enjoy it for what it was. Then Tony asked me to marry him.'

'He did?' Becca and Louisa exclaimed.

'It's so good,' Mary said, 'that sometimes, I almost feel our years apart were worth it.'

'I hope you'll give us plenty of notice for the wedding,' Louisa said. 'I'll be doing the photography.' She'd bring Foster and the children. By then they'd be like a family.

Gill spread the table casually with a dinner of minted couscous and stewed lamb with vegetables and a salad. Louisa had discovered he could cook more than pizza, and was at pains to encourage him. 'What a nanny,' Tony said when he returned from the garden. 'Men don't look after kids or cook in Australia. We're fairly unreconstructed, as Mary will attest. My dead wife used to say that a woman needed a wife if she was married to an Aussie. You've got your wife *and* your man, Louisa. I gotta hand it to ya.'

Louisa looked up at Gill apologetically, but he seemed to be taking this with good humour.

'Pity your Foster couldn't be here, too,' Mary said.

'I know why he couldn't,' said Becca. 'Humphrey seems to be in some sort of financial difficulty. He asked me to plan a launch, Louisa, after you put us in touch, but it's been delayed indefinitely. And I had to put the squeeze on him for my retainer.'

Louisa felt cold. 'So Humphrey contacted you after all? Why didn't you tell me?'

'Chinese walls, Louisa. Business is business and pleasure is pleasure. Foster doesn't seem a bad sort, though.'

'You met him?'

'For about five minutes.'

'He never told me.'

'He probably hasn't any idea I know you. How would he? Humphrey hasn't an inkling you and I are that close. Chinese walls, like I said.'

Louisa was jolted by Becca's secrecy. 'Why didn't you tell me before?'

'Relax, Lou. I didn't want to burst your bubble.'

'I want to know what you think of him.'

'Humphrey? I'd rather not say.'

'Foster!'

'He seems like a lovely guy. I didn't talk to him much. It's Humphrey I've been dealing with. Foster seems more the backer, while Humphrey's more hands-on. Foster seems OK. I suppose I wanted to tell you that.'

Louisa tried not to show her pleasure at Becca's approval. 'I'm glad you think so.'

'I'd trust Tony with my life,' Mary whispered to Louisa over slices of lemon tart. 'And my children's lives. Tony and I won't have children. That's my only regret. Now Gill – he's a bit like Tony. I don't feel quite so guilty about abandoning you all, now that I've met him.'

Louisa put down her fork and hugged her friend. 'I'm glad I've learned to cope without you. And now I understand why you dropped everything for Tony.'

It wasn't until Mary and Tony were leaving that Tony asked Louisa for the name of a lawyer in Dublin. 'We need to get Mary divorced before we can wed,' he said. Louisa got a card out of her bag and wrote Stella's name and number, which she had used so often she'd memorized it.

'Stella Pearson,' Tony said. 'Right.'

When she and Becca had waved them off in a taxi, Becca said, 'You know Stella Pearson?'

'She's my lawyer, like I said.'

'Huh,' Becca said. 'Not a woman you tend to meet in clubs or parties. Keeps to herself pretty much.'

'You know her too?'

'Only to see,' Becca said. 'Now put the kids to bed and let Gill off for the night. You look like you could use some sleep too.'

22

Days crawled and weeks flew, Louisa telling herself that the separation was merely an inconvenience. She admonished Foster for relying on technology rather than sending her handwritten letters and he responded by promising snail mail, which never arrived, and flowers, which did. Slim-stemmed white orchids in a pot, which continued to bloom profusely in the steamy atmosphere of her bathroom where she kept escaping into warmth and bubbles, as if these might somehow bring back the warmth of his arms.

She took the chance of Foster's physical absence to get the studio back up to speed, working so hard with Christmas orders that Paul urged her to slow down once again. 'You're driven,' he said. 'Don't you ever sleep?'

Not much, she could have said, between talking to Foster in various time zones and lying awake at night, willing him to materialize in her bed. It was good for the children, though, to have a period of stability. Louisa hadn't liked disappearing at night, even though they hadn't seemed to notice, thanks to Gill. When she saw Foster again, she would talk to him about how they would adjust – how *would* he adjust, a bachelor, to the demands of an instant family?

She planned to have a chat with Belly about it. Even if she didn't have any insight into his feelings on the matter, it would at least be an excuse to talk about him. Belly had sent Milo and Elvie an invitation to the twins' birthday party. The address confused her. Far from leafy Dublin 4, this address was in Cabinteely: '41, The Manor', it said, sounding suspiciously like an ordinary housing development. She wondered why they'd moved. On the day of the party, she was late, of course.

Expecting to find Belly's drive full of cars, she was surprised to see only one car there. Had she got the day wrong? The time?

'Will there be a bouncy castle?' Milo asked, as they waited at the door in spitting sleet.

He and Elvie had been looking forward to the party and they were in their best clothes, each holding a present for one of the twins.

'It's you!' Belly said when she answered the door, then added, 'Oh my.'

She wasn't her usual tidy self: she was wearing a pair of tracksuit bottoms and a coffee-stained T-shirt – far from the Hamptons chic Louisa had come to expect. 'It is today, isn't it?' she asked.

'Yes, it is! I'm afraid I'm not very well-organized, though.'

'Have you got a bouncy castle?' Elvie asked.

'Elvie, shush,' Louisa said.

'No bouncy castle,' Belly said, letting them pass into the house. 'Please excuse the mess. We've only just moved in. This house is unsatisfactory but –' she had the air of a woman running on empty as she rushed down the hall, picking up fluff from the otherwise clean carpet on the way. 'Clean, clean, clean and you're never finished,' she said.

Louisa was surprised that she did her own housework. She and the children followed Belly through to a small, chilly con-servatory at the back of the house, where the twins were lying on their stomachs, mesmerized by a Playstation game. Elvie and Milo stared up at Louisa. 'I thought it was a party, Mum,' Milo whispered.

'Ssh,' Louisa said.

Belly tried to explain: 'I was planning a proper party, but Humphrey had to dash off at short notice. I never know where I'll be with him. Foster flew in yesterday, kidnapped Humphrey and they flew out again.'

Louisa's heart sank. 'Foster was in town?'

'Didn't he tell you?'

'No.'

'It was only a fleeting visit. He left the boys a pile of new computer games for their birthday and they haven't stopped playing since about six a.m. I don't know how I'll drag them away. I'm so glad you're here! Let's make this festive! Vodka tonic okay for you?'

'A cup of tea's fine,' Louisa said. What was Foster up to?

Belly already had the vodka bottle in her hand. She opened the freezer compartment of the fridge – miniscule compared to the double-doored stainless steel affair in their Dublin 4 kitchen. 'Oh shoot. Out of ice. No – here's some! *And* I have limes too. It's so hard to get limes in this country, have you found that?'

'No, actually, I –'

'Shoot – no tonic, though. We'll have to settle for vodka and lime juice, then.' She poured large shots of vodka, dribbled in some lime and dropped an ice cube into each glass. She handed one to Louisa, then slugged hers down.

The immaculate kitchen was fitted to the highest standard but felt sterile. Louisa realized that on the night of the dinner party, none of the furnishings had belonged to Belly and Hump apart from the family portrait she had taken. Louisa put her glass down on the kitchen counter.

'Sorry, Louisa. I haven't any peanuts or crisps. You call them crisps, right? Everything's so different here. A chip's a crisp and a fag turns out to be a cigarette and a rubber's a condom.'

There was a brittleness to Belly's voice that reminded Louisa of Amanda. 'Not to worry.'

She looked around the kitchen counters, expecting to see a birthday cake, but there was nothing.

Belly handed Louisa back her drink. 'We'll take these through to the drawing room, shall we?'

The family portrait hung over the lifeless fireplace. 'So,' Louisa said. 'Where are Humphrey and Foster at the moment?'

'Monte Carlo? Vegas? Mozambique? How the hell should I know?'

'I see. It must be hard for you, with Hump travelling so much.'

'Oh my, Lou. When wasn't he travelling? He's always been *travelling.*'

Belly sneezed, waving her hand back and forth in front of her face. 'I can't get rid of this cold. I've never felt so bone-cold as I have in this little country of yours. Is it the damp do you think? IS IT THE DAMP?' She was a balloon about to burst, one prick and she'd pop.

'Annabel?' Louisa asked, in a gentle voice she usually reserved for the children when they were ill and unreasonable. 'Are you OK? No, obviously. Forget I asked that.'

She was weeping. 'I can't take it anymore. I –'

Elvie came in then. 'Mummy, I'm bored. I thought you said there'd be cake.'

Belly cringed.

'Later, Elvie.' Louisa explained. 'Give us a few minutes, will you?' She would have to organize a cake somehow. 'Elvie, go keep an eye on the boys. You be nanny. You be Gill.' Elvie ran off, pleased to have a mission.

Louisa turned to Belly. 'I'm sorry, go on.'

'Elvie's right. Our lives are boring. Bor-ing.' Belly's speech was becoming slurred. She pulled a naggin of vodka from beneath the seat cushion and refreshed her glass. Then she leaned forward, 'We're not those girls on the beach, you know. We're past it, baby.'

Speak for yourself. Louisa felt trapped.

Belly was rambling. 'They're brothers, separ-separated at birth. Almos'. Fossor and Hump.' She put her finger to her lips and stage-whispered. 'Mustn't talk about family bzz-bzz. Money, money, money, y' know? Ya *do* know. My own parents – jeesh. D.I.O.R.C.V.E. Many times. I know what it'sh like. Two wicked stepdads and two wicked stepmoms. The full set. Bet you didn't know we were white trash.'

Belly held up her fingers and stared at them, like a child

counting. 'They weren't horrible to me or anything, but they didn't love me. They put *up* with me.'

Louisa sensed that tears weren't far away. 'Why don't I make us some coffee?' she suggested, putting aside her untouched drink.

Belly held out the bottle to her. 'Where's your drink? Have another.'

Louisa picked up her glass, let the other woman top it up, then went into the kitchen and dumped it down the sink. She'd been married to Ben for thirteen years without becoming an alco-bitch. Annabel Worthington Smith was spoiled: she had grown up with all the advantages Louisa had never enjoyed because her own mother had given it all away. Maybe it was better not to come into money until you were nearly forty, rather than frittering it away by the time you were, Louisa realized.

She returned to the drawing room, where Belly was in mid-monologue. 'Why do I put up with Humphrey? He only married me for my money. Lots and lots of money. Where is it now? I dunno. Ask them. Foster snipped my platinum American Express card in two. They don't trust me. They think I'm a shoppa – shoppa – shoppa—'

'Shopaholic,' Louisa said, her head spinning. 'Is that why you moved house? Humphrey cut your budget?'

Belly hiccuped as she poured the dregs of the vodka bottle into her glass. One problem solved, then. 'That was a rental. Like this one.' Belly's eyes were brimming. 'You're so-o-o-o kind. It's verr-ry complicated, Lou. I should gedda divorce. But the lawyers would take whatever's left, just like they did to – to – what was her name?'

Belly's mind appeared to blank. 'I'm in bits – quaint Irish phrase. Describes me perfect-ly. *In bits*. The mother bit. The heiress bit. The-smile-nice-for-the-camera bit. The being-shat on by Humpatee Dumpatee bit. You can't put Humpatee together again. Oh, no.'

Louisa knew there was no point in talking sensibly to her. She was probably in the middle of a black-out anyway. 'Just pack your bags and go back to the States. It's a no-brainer.' And check into rehab, while you're at it.

Belly's face grew fierce. '*You* should talk.'

Louisa recognized this phase of drunkenness from Amanda. Self-pity followed by spite. 'I think you need to drink some water, now.'

'Huh! What about your ex? Rich?'

Louisa shook her head.

'Didn't think so. Jeesh. That aunt of yours taught you nothin'.' Belly's eyes lolled. 'Girlfriend to girlfriend . . . You watch yourself.' She poked a finger at Louisa's heart. 'When your ex gets word of your inheritance he'll come running back –' Belly attempted to snap her fingers – 'just like Fossor.'

Louisa was deliberately vague. 'What inheritance are you talking about?'

'No secrets. Who else would it be but you? Congratulations. You deserve it. You've got class. I always said that.'

So that was why Belly and Hump had been so anxious to pull Louisa into their lives again. Now that she was rich – on paper, anyway – she was socially acceptable. She took Belly's glass away from her and ushered her into the kitchen. 'I'm going to make some coffee,' she said. 'Where do you keep it?'

But Belly was nodding off. Louisa opened and closed cupboards frantically, disturbed by what she had heard. If Belly knew, so must Foster. Being the man he was, he would think it ill-mannered to mention it. And Belly was only working on rumour.

For a moment, Belly revived. 'He'll come running back, Hump will. Just like Fossor. Bees to honey.'

'I'm putting you to bed,' Louisa said.

'Whatever you say. No-o-o funny stuff.'

Belly began to laugh then gagged, her head between her knees. Louisa hoped she wouldn't throw up.

Suddenly, Belly surfaced again – like a soprano springing to life in her dying aria. 'You are such an idiot. Let me enlighten you.' She could no longer focus on Louisa, so her words were addressed to thin air.

'You're drunk. You don't know what you're saying.'

Belly tried to focus her eyes. 'Lemme, enlighten you, Loopy Lou.'

Louisa wished she'd shut up. She took Belly upstairs and laid her on her side in the bed with a pillow at her back, so she wouldn't choke on her own vomit. Soon the woman was snoring like a soldier. She couldn't believe that the woman had such a serious drinking problem and Foster hadn't mentioned it. Maybe he was being loyal, or had never seen her like this. Hump might be in the dark too, considering all the time he spent travelling.

23

When the doorbell rang at eleven o'clock, Louisa was doing housework and the children, who had got up late, were still in their pyjamas, eating cereal and fruit in front of the TV. 'Ben!' she said, surprised that he'd turned up at the appointed time. 'We're not quite ready for you, I'm afraid. The kids still have to get dressed.'

'Sure thing,' Ben said. 'You're looking well.'

Louisa glanced down at her greasy chinos. 'You must be joking. Go through and make yourself a coffee, or whatever. I'll get Milo and Elvie dressed. Where's Lucy by the way?'

'Busy.'

'The children will be disappointed.'

After she'd managed to make the children presentable, she found Ben sitting at the kitchen table, reading the newspaper he'd brought with him. He really was relishing the comfort zone of a tame ex-wife, Louisa thought resentfully. Elvie went over to him and sat on his lap, while Milo stood beside him, looking over his father's shoulder at the sports section of the newspaper. Her resentment disappeared.

Ben, as though suddenly realizing how lucky he was, gathered them both in his arms and squeezed his children so fiercely that Louisa was moved to put her arms round them all. They were a family and Milo and Elvie knew their parents loved them, which was all that mattered. Then she disengaged herself.

'Don't move,' she said, and rushed for her camera. She returned to find the three of them, still in a tangle, smiling up at her.

Click.

'Thank you,' Ben answered.

'Where are you taking them today?'

'Just for a walk to the park, if the rain stops. Maybe a cup of chocolate in the local café. They're beginning to see me as Mr Fun Guy and I've neither the energy nor the funds to keep it up.'

'I was planning to go out. I have some shopping to do and I'm meeting Becca for lunch. You can stay here if you like, I don't mind.'

Ben looked as if he couldn't believe his luck. 'You sure?'

'Absolutely,' Louisa said.

This outward politeness was part of the game. There were vicious exchanges of letters going on between their lawyers. But Louisa and Ben had always been rather good at pretending things were fine, while beneath the surface they were anything but. 'I'm going upstairs to change. Make yourself at home,' Louisa said cheerily.

In the bedroom, she went through her clothes, some reminding her so much of Foster that she hardly dared touch them. The room was a mess because Louisa had turned her back on it. It felt too lonely now that she knew, once again, what it was like to reach out to her lover in her sleep.

'Louisa?' Ben whispered.

'Go away, Ben!'

She hastily pulled the nearest dress on, not bothering yet with stockings and shoes, and ran her fingers through her hair, which seemed to be growing faster lately. Being in love was an anti-ageing remedy, she'd decided. And having an ex-husband lingering outside her door would have the opposite effect. 'What do you want?'

He pushed open the bedroom door. 'To see you alone for a moment.'

'Is there a problem?'

He stepped nearer. 'You're looking more beautiful than ever,' he said.

'It's a bit late for that.' She searched the dressing table for a hair-brush.

'I just want you to know, that I love you and I always will. I haven't been the best husband, I know, but you've been a wonderful wife.'

Louisa was brusque. 'What's brought this on?'

His shoulders heaved. 'I'm so sorry,' he cried.

Louisa was repulsed but tried not to show it 'What's wrong with you?'

Ben's eyes were imploring. 'Lucy's pregnant.'

'How far on is she?'

'A few months.' He was sobbing openly now.

Honestly, Louisa thought to herself. They don't pay me enough.

Tentatively, she put her arms round him. 'Everything will be fine. You're an experienced parent and Lucy's great with kids. It'll all work out as long as you behave yourself. Now, pull yourself together.' *Be a man, for once.* 'The children want to have fun with their father. This isn't the time to start wallowing in self-pity.'

As she peeled Ben away from her, Louisa noticed frayed threads on his collar and for a moment she felt the old urge to mother him. *No you don't! It's only a fashion statement!* He clung to her, his collar loose. He'd lost weight – then she read the label on his shirt. Yeah, it was a fashion statement.

She pushed him away. 'Off you go. The children are waiting. And I'm late to meet Becca.'

Ben's bitterness at being rejected seeped out. 'I don't know what you see in Becca. You're two sockets without a plug if you ask me.'

'Go away, Ben!' Louisa snapped, grateful to be reminded of how repulsive he could be. Poor Lucy, she thought.

She met Becca at the Unicorn in Dublin City, an Italian restaurant where the long, boozy Saturday lunches were reputed to be almost mandatory amongst media types. Louisa was glad that Becca was in the mood again for public outings and looked well, although she'd lost so much weight. No longer soft and voluptuous, she was lean and mean in her superfine black denim jeans and leather jacket. She looked younger without the make-up – although she'd glossed her lips and had her eyelashes dyed, which hardly counted. Her hair was growing back in its natural colour and the short style suited her.

Becca ran her hand through it, as they studied the menu. She remembered Gill making the same gesture. Maybe it was genetic. Milo often slept on his side with a hand tucked beneath his cheek, as his father did.

'You're looking well, Becca. The hair suits you.'

'Better than the old fright-wigs.'

'Short hair makes you look so much like Gill.'

Becca gave her the death stare. 'You saying I look like a butch lesbian?'

It was a trick question. If Louisa said 'no', she'd be pandering. If she said 'yes', she'd be accused of stereotyping. 'You look like yourself. How do you feel?'

'Like I'm not trying to portray a character, for a change. I'm dressing for myself, you know? Not bothering with mirrors. That was the good part about being sick. Lynley Consulting can run without Lynley. I'm thinking of diversifying –'

Louisa interrupted: 'Speaking of your work, how are things going with Humphrey Smith?'

'No idea. Our ways have parted.'

Louisa couldn't hide her sudden fear. 'Why?'

'No big deal. We don't work with people who aren't honest. We don't care what people do or how they do it, as long as it's legal. We're confidential. But we don't deal in bullshit.'

'What kind of bullshit?'

'That's all I'll say,' Becca scanned the menu.

'I'm not living in fantasy-land, if that's what you think. If there's something I should know, you need to tell me.'

'The linguine with scallops sounds good. You choose. How's Ben, by the way?'

Louisa knew there was no point in probing. She remembered Foster saying that Hump was hassling him and that he'd rather have nothing more to do with the project. So what Becca was saying made sense. Becca and Foster were distancing themselves from Humphrey, which was good. She didn't want that man anywhere near her life.

'Lou? I asked about Ben?'

'He came home crying to Mummy this morning.'

'What happened? Britney Spears dump him?'

'Worse. She's with child.'

'Up the pole? The big eejit.'

'He should know better.'

'Not him. *Her*. Why is it that people who don't want babies can have them just like that, and people like me can't? Is she going to keep it?'

'I don't know but from Ben's reaction, I got the impression she was insisting he face the music. It's strange thinking of Ben and Lucy as a couple with their own problems. At least it's nothing to do with me.'

'Hello?' Becca said. 'That child will be Elvie and Milo's brother or sister. You'll probably end up half-rearing it.'

Louisa hadn't thought of that. She put down the breadstick she'd been nibbling. Elvie and Milo with a half-sister or brother. Ben with two families when he couldn't even handle one.

'How's Gill getting on?' Becca asked.

'Same as ever. Loves his work. What can I say?'

'Sometimes I think his job is as much about looking after you as it is looking after your children.'

Louisa stiffened. 'Well, I'm not so sure. I saw him with a girlfriend.'

'Is that so?' Becca was watching Louisa keenly. 'Who do you think it was?'

'No idea. I hope he finds someone. He deserves it.'

Becca laughed. 'He *needs* it. He's a man, Lou, not a saint, and I don't keep tabs on his love life.'

'So there is one, then?'

'Why are you so interested?'

'I'm not. I care about him, that's all.' Louisa was feeling uncomfortable.

'I see. Well, first off. Gill doesn't have girlfriends. He has friends who are women. Whether he has sex with them or not, I couldn't tell you. I'm not going through his pockets or checking for stray hairs on his clothes – unless they're long and blonde.' Becca looked at Louisa pointedly.

Louisa was saved by the sight of Stella Pearson standing in the centre of the restaurant, scanning the tables. She looked different – younger – in jeans, a white silk shirt and a delicious caramel suede jacket. Louisa caught Stella's eye and waved her over. 'Hi! Great to see you, rather than just hear you on the phone.'

'I think I've been stood up and my friend's mobile is off so I can't track her down.'

'Join us,' Louisa said. 'If she turns up late, you can always move across to her. It's nice to have a chance to talk to you in real life, if you know what I mean.'

Stella laughed. 'I do.'

'Stella, I want you to meet Becca Lynley. Unless you know each other already?'

'I know of you, Becca.' Stella gave Becca a curious smile and held out her hand. 'Haven't met you face to face, though.'

Becca stood up and shook it. 'So, how do you know our Lou?'

'I think I told you, she's handling my divorce,' Louisa said. 'But not a word about that because we're all on days off.'

After Stella had sat down, Becca became her most charming self, ignoring Louisa completely.

The lunch went splendidly. They shared dishes, talked about books, cinema and holiday plans – with Becca and Stella discovering that they'd both booked a winter trip to Palm Springs. They knew so many people in common that they were amazed they hadn't met before. Louisa enjoyed seeing Becca regaining her feet on a purely social level, and Stella, with her no-nonsense take on life, was more than a match for her.

When four o'clock came round, Louisa was feeling sufficiently guilty about having left Ben on his own with the children for so long, that she made her excuses and left. Stella and Becca were already making plans to see a new French film at the Irish Film Centre that evening and Louisa got the impression that Becca wasn't disappointed that she couldn't join them. After kissing them both goodbye, Louisa floated out of the restaurant feeling she'd done a good day's work. A love affair was just what Becca needed.

As Louisa rode home on the DART train among the shoppers and commuters, she day-dreamed about Foster meeting the children when he returned. For some reason, she was anxious about him seeing her home. A woman's house might be thought of as a reflection of herself and she wanted Foster to see her as sophisticated and assured. That wasn't the image presented by St Agnes, the patron saint of betrayed women.

Foster loves me for who I am, she reminded herself, not for my decor. Paradise was even more chaotic.

Louisa got off the train at Dalkey. She slipped through the village and along the sea to St Agnes's. Inside, the house was too quiet. 'Hello?' she called out.

The children were watching TV and drawing pictures. They were distant, not offering her their usual hugs and greetings. 'Milo? Elvie? You OK?' They didn't respond. 'Where's Dad?' Nothing. 'Where is he?'

Elvie gave her a withering look. 'They're upstairs.'

'They?' Louisa dashed up the stairs. 'Ben?'

She heard a squeal from what had been Ben's study.

'Hello?'

Silence. Louisa pushed open the door to find Ben on top of a densely fleshed mattress of a woman, with cheap gilt necklaces strung across her fake-looking breasts.

Louisa wanted to vomit. 'Ben!'

As he struggled away from the woman, more annoyed than embarrassed, she shut the door and waited.

Louisa's inner warning system flashed: DON'T FREAK IN FRONT OF THE KIDS.

Ben emerged, zipping up his trousers. 'Hey, Lou. Caught me at it. What can I say?'

'How dare you? The kids are traumatized.'

Ben bristled. 'We were just talking. The kids didn't see anything.'

'I want you to leave,' Louisa said. 'Now.'

'We were only having a chat, Lou.'

'Out,' Louisa said, barely controlling her anger. 'This is my home!' Then she kicked open the study door and said, 'Get out of my house!'

The woman stood up. She hadn't taken off her skirt and straightened it primly. Then she picked up her blouse.

Ben looked from the woman to Louisa and back again. 'Fine. Come on Angel, we're leaving.'

'Angel?'

'That's her name, what's your problem?'

When the woman was dressed, Louisa hustled them down the stairs and along the hall to the front door. She slammed the front door after them and double-locked it, then raced into the family room. 'Are you angry?' Milo said softly.

'Not at you,' Louisa said. 'I'm really sorry, kids. Daddy didn't know what he was doing. It was a mistake. It had nothing to do with you.'

Louisa poured herself a glass of wine and sat on the sofa, half-listening to the children as they went on drawing.

'No, Milo. The tower is where Mummy lives,' Elvie was explaining. 'The apartment is where Daddy lives. You can't put the tower there.'

Milo threw his crayon at his sister. 'I can put it where I want!'

Louisa's heart twisted at the children's play, but she didn't want to show it.

How humiliating, to have to roust him out of bed with his lover in her own home. Except it wasn't, was it? It was his mother's house and always would be, no matter whose name was on the deeds. She'd rid the house of oppressive wallpaper and religious statuary and still Ben's indulgent mother hung like a stench. The house was a love-trough that Ben would keep returning to even if he had to bring a surrogate mother with him. She thought of Lucy – remembered how Ben's ardour had diminished when she was pregnant with Elvie.

She had to get out. 'Kids, we're going out for our supper. Anywhere you like.' Milo and Elvie, immersed in their pictures. 'Come on guys. Aren't you hungry?'

Reluctantly, they got up, put on their shoes and coats and let Louisa lead them to the car. When she had them strapped in, she said, 'Be right back.'

She shouldn't be driving, she knew she shouldn't. She wasn't drunk – Becca and Stella had consumed most of the wine at lunch – but she wasn't entirely sober either. 'No, let's walk,' she said to the kids. 'The village isn't far and the air will do us good.'

They marched along the coast road, Elvie complaining that her feet were cold and Milo dragging a stick along the iron railings of the houses, making a rattling noise that set Louisa's teeth on edge. It was beginning to rain and she had forgotten how dark it was at five p.m. in October. She kept them going with the promise of hot pizza.

'Don't want pizza!'

Cars whizzed by as commuters rushed home to the warmth of their homes. That's where the children should be right now, in front of a fire, not in the street. This is what Ben had brought her to.

They reached the pizza place, which was already crowded with families. They'd better have a table, she thought angrily. Hot, steamy air scented with garlic and herbs embraced them as they went in. The waiters ignored them as Louisa saw that there were no empty tables. They'd wait. Not a problem.

Eventually, a waiter appeared. He walked up to Louisa with his hands in the air. 'You book?'

'No.'

'No book, no table.'

Louisa could handle him. She'd just thrown her husband and his lover out of her house. 'My children are cold and hungry. We won't stay long. Somebody's bound to cancel or turn up late. Give us the first table available.'

'No book, no table. Very sorry. You book next week. *Ciao!* Bye-bye!' He opened the door and saw them out.

'Come on, kids. We'll find somewhere else.'

She corralled them along the road again, wishing she'd brought an umbrella. The children were miserable. This was precisely the sort of disorganized chicken-run her mother would have put her through when she was their age.

'Hey!' a voice called from the road.

Louisa turned to see Gill, his motorbike engine idling. 'What are you doing walking in the rain?'

'Foraging for food,' Louisa said.

'Hang on!' Gill walked his bike over to where they were standing. 'Car break down?'

'No. I thought the walk would do us good. We're nearly there anyway.'

'Nearly where? Pneumonia Valley? Let's get you out of the rain. In here.'

He pushed them towards Finnegan's Pub. Louisa didn't approve of children being in pubs, especially in the evening, but inside a welcoming banquette waited for them in the corner by the fire and there was a tantalizing smell of home-cooked food. The children were wide-eyed as she took off their dripping coats, then her own, and hung them on a row of hooks attached to the wall.

Gill shook the rain off his jacket, then strolled over to join them. 'So, folks, what'll it be? Fizzy orange?'

'Yeah!' the kids said. 'And chips!'

He turned to Louisa. 'You look like you could use something warming. A hot port, perhaps?'

'Sounds good.'

'I'll be right back.'

Gill got up to go to the bar and Louisa followed him. She leaned her elbows on the high marble surface, as Gill ordered. Then he turned to her. 'What's up?'

When she told him what Ben had done, Gill's face reddened. 'I'd like to go over there right now and tear his head off his neck. He's a savage pile of shite, he is. Marking his territory like an animal.'

She had never seen Gill angry. His posture was rigid and his muscles twitched as if he was aching for a fight. It was an unexpected side to him – he was so gentle and patient with the children. 'I'll get Stella to write him a nasty letter and that will be that.'

'If only it was so easy,' Gill said.

'Nothing worthwhile is easy. The sooner I get out of this country, the better.'

'You're leaving?'

Louisa had even startled herself. 'It's an option.'

The publican placed two glasses of fizzy orange, a hot port and a pint of Guinness on the bar. Gill pulled out his wallet and paid for the drinks. 'Just remember, Lou. You can do a geographic, like you did before, but wherever you go, you take yourself with you.' He handed her the two glasses of orange and carried the other drinks over to their table.

Before long, each of them had a plate of steak and chips in

front of them. The children tucked in but Louisa had no appetite and Gill ate hers when he had finished his own. The poor boy was ravenous. She thought of how proud his Mammy would have been to see what her son had become.

After the children had had apple tart and cream, the four of them walked back to St Agnes's. The rain had stopped, leaving the atmosphere crisp. It reminded Louisa of Hallowe'en in the States. She enjoyed walking past other people's houses at night, taking sidelong glances into the cosy rooms. She imagined them as stage sets for other lives she might have lived. If fate had treated her differently.

24

When they got home, St Agnes's looked dark and forlorn. Gill went in first, in case Ben had returned, although Louisa knew he wouldn't be there. The atmosphere he'd left behind was another matter. She felt he'd poisoned her new life, somehow.

'It's freezing,' Gill said. 'I'll light a fire in the front room. The central heating was supposed to click on at five. Don't tell me the wanker of a repairman's blown it again.'

That was another good thing about Gill: he got repairmen to the house when he couldn't fix something himself. While he investigated the central-heating timer, Louisa switched on lights and put the kettle on. She wanted to get the children warm and safe in bed, then have a bath – if Gill could get the boiler working. 'Haven't you got a date tonight, Gill? It's still early.'

'Nothing special.'

'Do you think there's enough hot water for the children to have a bath?' she asked.

'You'd better switch the immersion heater on, just in case.'

'Come on kids, let's go upstairs and get ready for bed.'

When the children were in bed, she read to them for a bit and Milo was soon asleep.

Elvie resisted her fatigue. 'Mum?'

'Yeah?'

'Who do you think she was? Not Lucy.'

'No.'

'Why did he let her in? He was supposed to be playing with me and Milo. Does he not like us anymore?'

'Daddy loves you, Elvie. He just made a bad decision. He won't bring anyone else.'

'Not even Lucy?'

'Maybe Lucy. I don't know.'

'Daddy was very bold, Mum. He left us all alone.'

Louisa tucked her into her bed. 'I'm sorry, Elvie.' She had no idea how much Elvie knew about what Ben and the woman were doing, but thought it better to let the child tell as much as she knew, rather than putting ideas into her head by asking questions.

Elvie's eyelids fluttered and she seemed close to drifting off, when Louisa heard the phone ringing downstairs. Bad timing, from Elvie's point of view. Gill came to Elvie's door and whispered, 'Call for you.'

'Elvie might like another story.'

Gill took her place while Louisa took the call in the front room where, true to his word, Gill had lit a fire in the old iron grate.

'Hello?'

'Hi, babe.' It was Foster's husky voice.

She listened to his rambling explanation of his fleeting visit to Dublin. Phrases like 'business crisis' and 'quick decision' . . . she hadn't seen him for weeks, yet he seemed so close.

'You've been away too long. Maybe you haven't got time for a relationship,' Louisa said, keeping her voice even. 'If that's the case, just tell me. Better to get out now before there's any misunderstanding. Seeing you was fantastic, but there doesn't have to be any more.'

There was silence on his end of the line. For a moment, she even wondered if they'd been disconnected. The pause lasted too long.

'There's nowhere I'd rather be than with you. Hump's used to having me at his beck and call, but if us being together means me giving up this business venture, I'll do it. I mean it. The only good thing about it, is that it brought me to you. If Hump hadn't decided to set up in Dublin, and if Belly hadn't walked into your studio – well . . . next weekend. Come to New York.'

'What about my kids?'

'I want to see you here, on my ground. In Dublin, Hump is hassling me constantly. Can you get your kids minded?'

'I won't go that far without them.'

Silence from his end. Louisa waited, listened to the transatlantic hiss.

'I'm coming to Dublin, then. I'll arrange everything,' he said.

She knew she should be happy. 'Can't wait!'

They said halting goodbyes, each reluctant to be the first to hang up.

Louisa stared dreamily into the fire. When she looked up, she realized Gill had been watching her.

'The princess is asleep,' he said.

'Thanks, Gill, I really needed to take that call.'

'I got that impression. Listen, there's something I've been wanting to say.'

'Sit down by the fire.'

He seemed in two minds, then sat in the wing chair across from the sofa Louisa was on with her feet near the hearth. She stole a glance at his clear, young face and told herself to relax, although she was expecting him to say he was quitting. He'd found another job, another woman, another life, away from her domestic chaos.

Gill laid his hands palm up on the arms of the chair. 'I'm sorry about going through your photographs.'

Louisa sighed with relief. 'I've forgiven you, Gill. I thought you knew that.'

'I don't want to be forgiven. Not yet, anyway . . .'

Louisa remained quiet, waiting for him to continue.

'When I found the pictures, I was looking for you. The real you. Not who Louisa was with Ben, or who Louisa is with Foster. The real you. That one picture of you in the boots –'

'It's only a picture, Gill.'

'I don't believe that. I saw a gorgeous, angry girl, make-up smudged around her eyes, looking as though she hadn't slept or eaten in days. That was you. It wasn't heroin chic or whatever they call it. You can't fake that kind of pain.'

Louisa felt her face flushing. 'Listen, I was kipping on the floor of this photographer's studio in New York. He was quite a famous fashion photographer and I was fortunate to be his lackey, I supposed. And that's all I was, a lackey.'

'You've been places I can only imagine, Lou.'

She thought of his superior attitude when he'd returned from Africa. The chip on his shoulder. His conviction that only he had touched the darkness.

'I've given up a lot of things in my life, some harder than others.'

She hadn't noticed him carrying the picture that he showed her now: 'Milton Goodbody, Plaza Hotel, 1993'. She held it, feeling it was from another life. Europa's grimace, as she struggled against the men, shocked her. Had she really taken that picture?

'Where did you find that?'

'Ben's old study. I found it the day you asked me to pack up his things.'

'It was the party where I met Ben. I was taking pictures – I don't know what was in my head.'

'The night Ben came in on his white charger and rescued you? Brought you back to his castle in Ireland?'

'Something like that,' Louisa said.

'That's not what happened, though.'

Louisa picked at the nubby fabric of the sofa nervously.

'What happened to destroy you like that? To make an amazing woman like you bury herself in a cad like Ben Maguire? What were you running from?'

'What do you mean?'

'The children say you have nightmares.'

Louisa's heart fluttered with shame. 'Gill, I know you care about me. And I'm so, so grateful. Without you I'd be . . .' Part of her wanted to succumb, but it was Foster she was in love with.

'Without you I'd be what? Unable to go for dirty weekends with Foster Adams?'

'Honest to God, I don't want to be your next humanitarian relief project, Gill. Stop poking around in places where it still hurts. That was me then. This is me now. Two different people.'

'Only two? You're a good mother, a fantastic friend to Becca, a photographer and a lover. You put up with Ben Maguire for thirteen years and a portrait of you hangs in the Museum of Modern Art in New York – someone else entirely.'

That stunned her. 'Really?'

'Really.' He handed her an art postcard. It was a reproduction of Alice's painting of her, pale and gaunt, her body bent across a fabric-draped bench as though her spine was broken. Louisa could still feel the pain of lying there, for hours on end. She'd been powerless to resist Alice's commands.

'That's you, isn't it? The happiest summer of your life, with the great love of your life,' he whispered.

Louisa remembered lying there exposed to Alice's chilly eye, thinking of . . . what? Of being on the beach at night with Foster, the boys' voices in the distance, anticipating the party, believing her mother to be in India when she was dying at New York Presbyterian Hospital . . .

'What are you thinking?' Gill asked.

'That you mean well, but I wish you wouldn't do this.'

He touched the card. 'Who is she, Lou?'

'I hated that portrait the moment I saw it. Alice could be very cruel and this picture was sadistic. Look at me! A slab of meat. Anyone's for the taking. She saw what she wanted to see.'

'Are you sure about that? She was an artist with a reputation for seeing beneath the veneer. Like you. I think she believed she was painting the truth.'

'*Her* truth, perhaps. A message about sexual politics or something. Not *the* truth. I was only her model.'

'In the picture your famous fashion photographer took. You weren't modelling then.'

'Not consciously modelling. Passively, I suppose. Observing myself. Wanting to please. Everyone knows that models are friable.'

'Malleable, you mean?'

'That too. By friable I mean easily smashed into tiny particles then rearranged to seem almost the same, but not quite.'

'Blown to smithereens and then recreated? Is that what happened to you?'

Louisa felt suddenly so tired. She closed her eyes.

'I know how you look first thing in the morning, when you've had a bad night. I know how you look when you're waiting for him to call. I know the look on your face when you're watching the children. I know how your face shuts down when Ben comes charging in to screw you over. I know how you look when you're going to meet Foster, your face expectant and brave. I know that Alice painted *you*.'

She threw the card into the fire, where it melted and twisted.

Gill tried to lighten the mood. 'Unfortunately, I have the original,' he joked. He kneeled at her feet as she sat on the sofa. '*You* are an original. But so hard to know. You offer different versions of yourself to different people. With me, you're always behaving like a flirtatious mother. Then I see you going off to meet Foster with all the innocence of a little girl and . . . in his bed, well – I'd say you're somebody else then too.'

She let him take her hands.

'Does it make sense to you that the girl in the portrait, that girl who looks so lost and unloved, was actually in the throes of a love so true that, twenty years later, it has come back to take over her life?' he asked.

She wished she could explain, but her mind in that moment felt like blank canvas. 'Maybe you think I'm so malleable that you can put ideas into my head. Turn me away from Foster.'

Gill reached down into his motorcycle bag and pulled out

three more postcards. 'It was a series, wasn't it? When you left, she kept painting you.'

'Louisa II, 1986', a girl resting her head on a steel and formica kitchen table, her dead-eyed face turned on its side, one arm flung across the table and the other hanging limp. Louisa remembered that morning, being barely aware of Larry making tea for Alice. Had he photographed her so that Alice could cannibalize her later? Or was that another morning, with Alice breezing in and out, seeming not to see her, while Louisa stared into space, wishing she would stop breathing.

'Louisa III, 1986', a girl lying on the beach in a white bikini that's merely a swirl and fold of paint blending into her sandy body – again whites and nudes. And there, almost hidden, just a hint of a man's shadow over her.

'Nude II, 1987', a mattress in a bright, white-washed room. A scrap of dress fabric lying on the mattress in place of the body, whose indentation marked the mattress. The bottle, the snuffed out candles . . .

'You're crying,' Gill said, reaching up to wipe her tears. 'Do you know you're crying?'

She began to sob. 'Alice – how dare she? If she knew what had happened to me, or even suspected, why did she paint it like that? How could she? I stopped telling people I was related to her. I didn't want to be *that* Louisa. That's why I left.'

'Tell me about that Louisa.'

To her surprise, she wanted to tell him. She felt safe telling him things she would never have dared tell Foster. 'She was a stupid, stupid girl. She was in love with him – saving herself for him. Not like her mother, who acted like sex was a function to be separated from love. No. Louisa, silly child, wanted her first time to be like she'd read in books, seen in films, dreamed about in bed on her own at night. Foster was so good, so patient. And then she chose the time. The glass room. It was perfect. High above the house but beneath the stars. So private, yet with a view for miles. He was to meet her there after work.

There was a party in the house. No-one would notice him creeping up the stairs to the glass room. All night at the party, all she cared about was seeing him. She was so nervous and excited that she drank too much champagne, smoked too much weed, lost herself in that Dionysian atmosphere that Alice had perfected. It was only a game to Alice. That was the difference between Alice and Amanda. Poor Amanda took it all so seriously. She lived like an artist but couldn't paint like one. It was Alice who had the steel to be an artist. The discipline and self-absorption. The steel ego that no-one could get past except for one man who would do anything for her.'

'Larry Stein,' Gill said.

Louisa slumped forward and let Gill take her in his arms and she wept the tears that had waited twenty years to be spilled. Not like the tears she'd wept with Foster – tears of relief at being accepted by a God. These were tears from the very bottom of the well.

'The stupid, stupid girl lay in the glass room out of her head and waited for her boyfriend to come and give her that one thing she thought she wanted. And when he didn't show up, other boys took his place,' she wept.

'Who? How many?'

'They weren't Foster, that's all she knew. They were evil.' She began to cry again. 'Why are you doing this to me?'

He seemed at a loss now. 'Because I love you.'

'You *love* me? You call this love? You're just like *her*. Analysing me. Manipulating me.'

Gill almost seemed ashamed. 'I wanted to get past the mask.'

'Like Larry unmasking Alice, do you mean? You're wrong there. I'm merely mortal like Amanda. I'm a portrait photographer, not an artist. And you're not my psychiatrist. What are you doing? Trying to get into my head because you can't get into my pants?'

Gill held his hands up. He seemed to have made a decision. 'I'm going to stay the night in the guestroom, Lou. I'll leave in the morning. I won't be coming back – not as your child-minder anyway. I can't bear to be so near you and love you like this. It hurts too much.'

Louisa turned on him. 'So that was the plan, was it? Strip me bare and then abandon me?'

'No.' Gill smiled weakly. 'This was supposed to be the part where the hero helps the heroine to heal her soul, then she falls into his arms forever . . . It hasn't worked, obviously.'

Louisa was stunned by his naïveté. 'Do you really think I'd want a lover to know me as a piece of pulp? Like that sick little girl? Not even Foster knows what you know now. And I hope he never does because I wouldn't be able to look him in the eye, much less make love to him. You think it's sexy, do you – to imagine beasts gang-raping your woman?'

Gill seemed diminished suddenly, as though his worst fear had come to pass. 'It wasn't sex I was thinking of.' And he left the room, his feet scuffling on the stairs.

Louisa jumped up from her chair and called after him, with no thought for her children. 'No. You don't have to stay. Go now, if it's so painful to be with me.'

He stopped, one hand on the banister, and nodded. 'You're right,' he said softly. 'I don't know what I was thinking.'

Louisa's outburst woke Milo. 'Mummy!' She dashed up the stairs to find him trembling at the top. 'Come here, baby,' she said, 'It's all right. I'm sorry.'

She carried him to her bed, wrapped the duvet round them both and rocked him, 'Everything will be all right, sweetheart. Everything will be all right.' But Milo had already fallen asleep, and the tears on Louisa's cheek were her own.

25

Elvie was dancing around Lucy, desperate to try on the short white fur coat, which Lucy wore over a pair of jeans cut so low that the dragon tattoo at the base of her spine was visible. And above the jeans, Louisa saw it: a telltale bump. Lucy should remove her navel ring, Louisa considered. She made the younger woman a cup of camomile tea and put a plate of shortbread biscuits in front of her.

'Elvie? Milo? You can talk to Lucy later. Would you go upstairs and play for a bit? I need to talk to her alone for a few minutes.'

They didn't move. 'Please?' Louisa said.

Lucy offered each a biscuit. 'Please?'

To Lucy, they listened. Each took a biscuit and sped off. What was it about kids? Loyal to everyone but their own mother. 'So,' Louisa said, sitting down and offering Lucy honey for her tea, 'Ben told me you're expecting his baby.'

'I was hoping you could talk some sense into him. He doesn't want it. He thinks I should have had an abortion. I want this baby. I love Ben. I need him to take his responsibilities seriously.'

Louisa sighed. 'I spent the best part of thirteen years trying to talk sense into him, trying to get him to face up to his responsibilities. I failed, Lucy. He's not going to listen to me.'

Lucy sniffled. 'He's acting like I forced him to knock me up just to do his head in. It's his problem as much as it is mine.'

'So it is a problem, then.'

'I didn't want to get pregnant. I don't want to *be* pregnant. But I am . . . what am I going to do?' Lucy began to cry. Louisa got up and found a box of tissues. 'Cry it out, Lucy, I'm here.'

'You're such a great mother, Lou. Ben never denied that, really he didn't. Milo and Elvie are great kids. I love kids. But I wanted a career, you know? I want to do something with my life.'

'Who says you can't?'

Lucy threw her arms out to her sides in exasperation and then pointed to her belly. 'This.'

'When's the baby due?' Louisa asked.

'After Christmas, probably,' Lucy said.

'How long after Christmas?'

'First week of January – I think. Can't be sure, precisely.'

Louisa was stunned. When she'd been pregnant, she'd bloated out like a circus clown – both times. 'Are you saying that you're at least six months pregnant, Lucy?'

'Uh-huh.'

Louisa counted back the months in her head. 'Do you mind if I ask – I won't be angry whatever you say – how long you've been seeing Ben?'

'Two years,' Lucy said.

'I see.' Louisa felt calmer than she knew she should.

'I'm sorry,' Lucy said. 'More than you know.'

'Listen, we have to book you an appointment with a doctor, so you can talk to them about your options.'

'I'm not having an abortion! I don't believe in it!'

'Neither do I. I wasn't suggesting that. But there are probably certain services you're entitled to. Medical care, financial help and so on. And, if you really think that keeping the baby is going to be hard, there's always adoption.'

'You're scaring me,' Lucy said.

'Have you told your mother?'

'She'd kill me. Anyway, she lives in Spain with my stepfather, who can't live far away enough as far as I'm concerned.'

Louisa nodded. 'I see.' She had no idea whether Lucy knew that Ben was seeing someone else – if that was what the episode in the study had been about. She still hadn't got over the shock.

Stella, who had always seemed unshockable before, had visibly reacted, then fired off a letter to Ben's solicitor, applied for a court barring order and got it.

'I don't want to see Ben ever again after what he's done,' Lucy said.

'What's he done now?' Louisa asked, keeping her own counsel just in case.

'At first I thought he was one of those eejits who can't bear to have sex with a woman once he's got her pregnant – but he's got a tranny!'

Louisa bit a nail. She thought of the hefty pillow of a woman with the gold chains. A *transsexual*? 'Good God,' Louisa said.

'I didn't mean to shock you.'

Louisa got up to freshen the teapot. 'Nothing Ben does could shock me anymore. He's betrayed you, like he did me. Like he does everyone. At least now, for a while, you're in the one place where you're least likely to see him.'

Lucy crunched a biscuit. 'My biggest problem is I haven't got anywhere to live.'

'Where were you and Ben living?'

'His place. You know, the apartment he bought in the Docklands. I decorated it for him. And when I found him with that piece of trash I had to leave a lot of cool stuff behind.'

Louisa put her mug down so hard that tea splashed over the table. 'He owns an apartment in the Docklands?'

'Yeah.'

'Since when?'

'I dunno. A couple of years, I suppose.'

'And I paid for him to stay a week in the Monroe!'

'I know. It was fun!' Lucy said, then realized her mistake. 'Sorry, Louisa. I didn't know you then – like, you didn't exist. You know what I mean?'

It was karma. Lucy was her irresponsible younger self come back to haunt her. 'No hard feelings,' Louisa said. 'It's not your fault. What would you say that apartment's worth, by the way?'

'I dunno. It might stretch to a million, I suppose. It's the penthouse.'

Louisa was enraged. What a lying thief Ben was, claiming to be skint and making out he was homeless. Stella would be dispatching a letter to his solicitor first thing in the morning. But there was no point venting her rage on Lucy.

'Ben's responsible for your child, Lucy. You can't let him off scot-free. So I'm glad he's got funds.'

'Oh, yeah? If you'd had the choice all those years ago, Lou, knowing what you know now, would you have made Ben face up to his responsibilities? Or got as far away from him as you could?'

'There's only one answer to that.'

She sniffled again, so pathetic that Louisa wanted to sweep her up into her arms.

'What do you want from me, Lucy?'

'Like I said, I wanted to say I'm sorry. And . . . well, maybe I could stay here for a while. If you have room.'

Louisa thought for a moment. Gill had left her in the lurch, especially considering that she was planning to be away with Foster for two nights in a few days' time. 'I'll make a deal with you, Lucy. I'll give you a roof over your head if you'll take care of Elvie and Milo after school and for the occasional week-end – like this one. They know you, they like you. There's only one restriction: if you let Ben back into your life, you're out on your ear.'

'I'd love to look after your kids,' Lucy said. 'I can't think of any better way to tell Ben where to get off.'

'The way I see it, Ben's not going to look after your child, so at least his mother's house can be of some use to you. I never felt St Agnes's belonged to me, but now I'm coming round to the idea.'

The day before she was due to see Foster again, after nearly four weeks without him, Louisa was sweeping the infinity curve.

'So what's the story with Gill?' Paul asked.

A light had gone out. The children never stopped asking about him. Louisa was angry at herself for having relied on him too much – and he'd taken advantage.

'He's on sabbatical,' she answered.

'You two have a row?'

'I'd rather not discuss it.'

When Lucy dropped in at lunch-time on her way to get the children from school, Louisa was grateful for the diversion. 'Your cheeks are rosy this morning. Feeling better?'

'I'm just catching my breath before I walk the rest of the way up to the school. It's not far, but – wow – Dragonbaby here is getting heavy. Woops!'

'You OK?'

'He just kicked me. Likes walking, I think. Puts him to sleep. I think he's woken up again at the sound of my voice. Isn't that funny? Where's your loo?' Lucy's face, so bright with love for her growing baby, reminded Louisa of how she'd felt in those days of mid-pregnancy.

'I'll show you,' Paul said.

Louisa realized they hadn't formally met. 'Lucy – Paul. Paul – Lucy.'

'Just get me to the toilet,' Lucy said.

Paul whispered, when she had gone inside, 'I'd say she causes a bit of a stir on the school-run.'

Louisa smiled. 'She's good company.'

Lucy returned, visibly more relaxed. Paul couldn't take his eyes off her. 'You sure you shouldn't have that bump covered up in this weather, Miss?'

'Dragonbaby has his own central heating system,' Lucy answered.

Louisa had often wished she had a picture of herself as she was during her first pregnancy, as a reminder of those hopeful days. 'Lucy, I'm all set up here. Why don't you pop up on the curve and I'll take your picture.'

'Are you serious? I'm not made up or anything.'

'That's good. It's better if you're not. Go on.'

Lucy was wearing a white leather skirt below her bump, and her usual midriff-baring tiny T-shirt above it, and the red cowboy boots Louisa coveted. Lucy struggled to pull herself up onto the platform and Paul gave her a hand.

'Ooh, the lights are lovely and warm. I could go to sleep here,' she said.

'So do,' Louisa said. 'Go on, lie down.'

'You gonna take my picture?'

'Yeah, why not?'

Louisa adjusted the light, loving Lucy's curves. 'Just lay your head back, Lucy, like you're day-dreaming. When I need you to look at the camera, I'll just say the word. Don't worry about how you look.'

'Jeesh, why should I? I'm a hippo. Like, you can't do a bit of air-brushing, can you?'

That would be a neat trick. Air-brush out a pregnancy, a boyfriend, a husband, a whole life. 'No, I'm afraid you're stuck with yourself. It'll just be a private picture, for you. So Dragonbaby can see what he looked like in his Mama's tummy.'

Lucy was relaxed and uninhibited. A young Amanda, Louisa imagined, slightly feckless and overawed, though settled in herself. But if Lucy had been receiving no support from Louisa or anyone – as had been Amanda's predicament – she might easily be stressed and anxious now instead of merely apprehensive. Under pressure, her eccentricity could become something troubling.

Babies eat you alive, Louisa recalled Amanda saying. Alone and unsupported, that must have been what it felt like.

Louisa started shooting, and, as she focused on Lucy's lovely face, she forgave her own mother.

'Why are you looking at me funny?' Lucy asked.

'You remind me of someone I used to know.'

Lucy lay back and looked up at the high ceiling. 'I suppose every portrait is a self-portrait, really, isn't it?'

Louisa had never been able to put it into words as succinctly as that. 'Yeah, you're right.' These would be amazing pictures: Lucy in that dreamy, wallowing state of pregnancy that made her deep-blue eyes both wise and vulnerable.

'Lou?'

'Yeah?' Louisa answered, distracted.

'Will you come with me to hospital, you know, when the baby comes? Hold my hand? Take a few pictures?'

'I'd be honoured.'

'Thanks,' Lucy answered, relaxing into herself and closing her eyes.

Louisa took a few more shots, then decided not to overdo it. Lucy had to get to the school and lunch-hour was nearly over. 'Lucy, I think we're done.'

Lucy didn't respond.

'Lucy?'

She was asleep.

Louisa whispered, 'Paul, I'm going to go fetch the kids. If the next clients come in early, wake her gently, yeah?'

'Sure thing,' Paul said, bemused.

26

The joy on Foster's face when he saw her coming towards him in the hotel lobby told Louisa he really was in love with her. During their time apart, doubt had wormed its way into her mind – aided by Gill. Now Foster swept her into a passionate embrace.

'I was going to suggest a drink. But if I don't get you into bed immediately, I think I'll die,' he whispered.

They kissed in the lift, in the corridor, inside the door of the room and on the bed, as though parting their lips would break the spell. Their bodies were so attuned now that she felt him in every nerve-ending.

Afterwards, his voice was hushed. 'I love you. With all my heart. I love you more than I ever thought it possible to love . . . I didn't know what love was, Lou.'

She smiled up at him, believing that he was her reward for getting through the previous twenty years. He was all the man she wanted. 'I love you too.'

Yet she was famished. 'I'd love an artichoke right now.'

Foster was nestled against her bosom. 'Okay then, let's go out! I'm starving,' he said.

'No room service?' Louisa pouted.

'One of the other guests told me the food's not great here. And I just want to do something really ordinary with you, like go into a pizza-and-pasta joint like normal people. Do you think we could find an Italian place that serves artichokes?'

'I know a good one,' Louisa said.

The Unicorn was bustling with late-evening diners, but the waiter found them a table. Foster picked up the menu and scanned it. 'What's Italian for artichokes?'

'*Carciofi*,' Louisa said. 'Let's live in Italy.'

'In a heartbeat,' Foster said. He asked the waiter if the chef could produce *carciofi*.

No artichokes. Louisa sighed. If Foster knew of the connection with Alice, he didn't let on.

When they'd ordered, Foster leaned across the table and held her hands in his. 'This is dangerous. I'm afraid of being so in love with you.'

'I love danger,' Louisa answered.

'And I love dangerous women,' Foster said.

'*Do* you now?' Louisa asked.

'You know the story, rose-tinted spectacles, idealizing the woman you love. There is a type of woman who can convince you that she loves you, when what she really loves is your money. I'm a sucker for it, I'm afraid.'

'Isn't everybody? I mean, how can you ever really know for certain?'

Foster looked stricken. 'You mean you're still not sure?'

'I've never been more sure of anything.'

He kissed her fingers, one by one. 'I want to make sure that every molecule of you is sure – and every atom too.'

When they had eaten, Foster leaned back in his chair. 'Listen, darling. There are a few things I have to say to you. I should have mentioned them before but . . .' He dabbed his mouth with his napkin.

Panic swept through Louisa.

'. . . I was embarrassed. I didn't want to lose face. That's the difficult thing about impressing a girl at seventeen, then seeing her again at an age when you're supposed to have lived up to your image.'

Becca's warnings that Foster wasn't all he seemed flooded into her mind. 'Go on.'

'Something you said, Lou, made me remember that I was very keen to impress you all those summers ago. And, well . . .' he cleared his throat '. . . I think you might have made some assumptions that I failed to correct. So, if we're going to be together – and I hope we will be – I don't want them to come between us.'

She had no idea what he was talking about and tried to make a joke of it, 'You're going to tell me that you're not a champion surfboarder after all?'

He laughed half-heartedly. 'I didn't go to Yale, Louisa. I wouldn't have got in and, if I had, my parents wouldn't have been able to pay for it. I went to business school.'

'I don't think you actually told me you went to Yale. You talked about being there with Hump, and I just assumed.'

'Is it important to you? Where I went to college?'

'Don't be ridiculous.'

'The second thing is, you remember I worked in the kitchens at the club. I told you some crap about how my father wanted me to experience life at all levels.'

'Yes.'

'I felt totally inadequate around people like Hump, even though he and I grew up together – in the summers anyway. OK. Here we go again. My father was never rich. He was a groundsman at the club. Not a servant, I hasten to add, more of a fixer. Other men did the grounds-keeping. My dad made sure that everything ran smoothly. He and Humphrey's dad were friends.'

Louisa couldn't believe what she was hearing. 'So it's a hereditary position, then?'

He laughed self-consciously. 'I've done better than the old man.'

'So now, you're . . . comfortable?'

'I'm self-made, Lou. If you can call hanging onto Humphrey Smith's coat-tails, self-made. His contacts helped me make something of myself, and, as I became more and more successful, he pissed away his family's money. This project in Dublin, it's kind of a last chance for him.'

'What is it, Foster?'

He sighed. 'A casino. Ireland's first. A glitzy, showgirl, Vegas-style casino with associated online games world-wide. The luck of the Irish – you know? But Humphrey, I'm afraid, was a little naïve about how easy it would be to bribe his way into the golden circle. And I was more than a little naïve to believe that a casino was all it was. It looked great on paper. Now I wish I'd never got involved.'

It sounded so tacky and brash. She didn't like to think of Foster being manipulated by Humphrey into investing in such a scheme. It was madness to think that Americans could best the Irish gambling establishment. 'Maybe he wouldn't have been so successful without you. You shouldn't feel guilty if he's blown it on a crazy idea. Maybe it's time to divorce him.'

Foster shrugged. 'I thought I wasn't good enough for you. You were the real deal, Lou. I wasn't. I'm a fake.'

She realized then, that she was giggling.

'What are you laughing at?'

'Foster, all along I thought that I was the one who wasn't good enough for *you*.'

They leaned across the table and kissed each other lightly. 'So, am I good enough for you, Louisa Stone?' he asked.

'Better than that. You're the real deal.'

They skipped dessert and coffee in favour of getting back to their room. When Foster discovered he'd left his wallet in the room, Louisa paid. They walked, hand-in-hand, along St Stephen's Green, then down Grafton Street, the old-fashioned streetlamps casting a glow.

'Your divorce,' Foster said, 'is it final?'

'These things take a little longer here.'

'I see. Well, when it is, will you marry me?'

They stopped in the middle of the pavement, outside a showcase of mannequins in designer dresses. 'I want to marry you,' Louisa said, 'but you need to meet Elvie and Milo before I can commit myself.'

'Of course.'

'Will you want more children?'

His comment spun her round. 'And if I did?'

She could tell that Foster was being cautious in answering and she feared what it might mean. 'Then I'd want children too.'

He put his arm around her shoulder as they walked, her head in a dream of what their child might be like.

She had never known a night so fervent and – part of her feared – never would again. It would be impossible to keep loving at such intensity without breaking apart and burning up on re-entry to real life. It was after lunch before they dared leave the bed and, when they did, Foster insisted on bringing her back to Grafton Street where he pulled her into Weir's jewellers, an old-fashioned treasure box with everything a girl could want, from Tiffany's diamonds to antique Victorian necklaces.

'Time to choose your engagement ring,' Foster said.

'It's too soon!'

'Your Christmas present then.'

'It's too soon for that, too!'

The jeweller laid out several velvet trays before them with a respect reserved for men like Foster, who oozed wealth without trying.

'What do you like?' Foster asked, nuzzling her ear while the jeweller kept his eyes averted and his gloved hands firmly on a tray of diamonds.

She still couldn't believe he was standing beside her – and that was enough. Although his generosity meant so much more to her now that she knew he'd earned the right. Wanting to make love to him there and then, she stealthily placed a hand on his buttock to give it a squeeze.

Her eye was drawn to a Victorian diamond-and-emerald ring. Foster and the discreet jeweller exchanged a glance. The jeweller handed the ring to Foster, who presented it to Louisa to try on. A perfect fit.

'It's lovely – but I absolutely will not allow you to buy it.' Louisa played along, knowing Foster would be back to purchase her choice.

'Okay then, I must obey the lady's wishes,' Foster said and they walked over the deep pile carpet of the shop.

When they got back to the hotel room, the bed was perfectly made and the few things Louisa had brought with her were gone.

'Where's our stuff?' Louisa asked.

'This is outrageous,' Foster said. 'I'll sort it out.'

Foster left her in the sterile room to speak to the manager. Soon he returned with their bags. 'I hope it's all here. I told them I'd sue them if it's not.'

'What happened?'

'Overbooking. They messed up with their computers and thought I was checking out at noon. When we disappeared, they had to get the room ready for someone else.'

Louisa felt unsettled and ashamed that they had been treated in that way, as though their passion had been too much for the staid hotel. Foster phoned Hump and Belly and arranged to stay with them. He dropped her at the taxi rank and handed her bag to the driver.

'I don't want to leave you,' Louisa said.

'Go home and get ready for me to meet those kids of yours.'

As the taxi drove away, Louisa felt she was leaving her heart behind.

27

The next day, Louisa looked about her home and tried not to see it through Foster's eyes. 'This is it, take it or leave it. I'm planning to leave it.'

Elvie and Milo, having greeted Foster curiously at the door, were now in the kitchen with Lucy. 'It has a lovely old-world feel to it, Lou. There are decorators in New York who spend other people's millions trying to get this effect.'

'You're being kind.'

Foster was drawn to the picture of Amanda that Louisa now kept on the mantelpiece in the TV room. 'Who's this?'

It seemed odd that he didn't know. 'My mother,' she answered.

'You're like her.'

'Am I?'

'Did I say something wrong?'

'No. I've spent too much of my life trying not to be like her.'

Lucy was making spaghetti Bolognese and garlic bread, with chocolate Rice Krispie cakes for dessert, which Elvie and Milo were decorating with mini-marshmallows. Foster pretended to steal one. 'Hey!' Milo said sternly.

'Sorry, sport. I can't resist a good marshmallow.'

Elvie looked up at Foster from under her thick, dark lashes. 'You can have one of mine.'

'Thanks, Princess.' Foster popped it in his mouth.

The meal was pleasant enough, partly because Lucy's chatty stream-of-consciousness held the children rapt and gave no-one else a chance to get a word in edgeways, although Foster seemed charmed. 'I must say, I think it's very liberal of you ladies, getting on like you do.'

'We girls have to stick together,' Elvie piped up. 'You too, Milo.'

Milo seemed to find this vaguely distasteful. 'You're not like Gill,' he said to Foster.

'Gill?' Foster looked at Louisa questioningly.

'Our friend and child-minder,' Louisa said. 'He's away at the moment.'

Elvie and Milo exchanged a look, then Elvie said, 'No he's not. We saw him in the village yesterday.'

'On his motorbike,' Milo added. 'He let me sit on it.'

Lucy glared at the pair. Elvie kicked Milo under the table, which made him squeal and cry theatrically.

'Is he back so soon? I had no idea,' Louisa said. 'Now, Milo, cut the waterworks.'

Milo looked stunned, then went to Lucy and sat on what was left of her lap. He gave his mother a reproachful stare.

'Hey, Milo,' Foster said, 'I live in New York. You're half-American, aren't you? Would you like to visit some time? We've got some cool stuff over there.'

Milo was intrigued.

'We've got the Natural History Museum – huge dinosaurs,' Foster continued.

'Do they have feathers? 'Cause they're supposed to, you know.'

'Is that so? And there's Central Park, the Empire State building, great hot dogs and pretzels. You ever eat a pretzel?'

'What's that?' Milo asked.

Louisa squeezed Foster's hand under the table. The idea of bringing her children to her own childhood haunts made her feel warm inside. She had got so used to living abroad that she'd forgotten how reassuring it was to be with a man who shared the same cultural references. Sometimes his body language or turn of phrase made him seem quintessentially American, and she felt increasingly homesick.

*

As Christmas approached, Foster started talking about getting together with Belly and Hump for the holiday. Becca had been part of Christmas for Louisa and the children ever since they had met and, deep down, she knew that Christmas wouldn't pass without Becca bouncing them all along on a wave of holiday festivity. The fact that Becca was *alive* for Christmas – and Christmases to come if all continued to go well for her – made being together even more important.

Becca must have been thinking the same thing because, on the first Sunday in December, she turned up dressed for a bracing walk along the seafront.

'It's great to see you.' They hugged, Louisa missing the slightly plumper Becca and taking note of her motorbike leathers.

'Gill's got me biking. I've just bought a Harley. Let's get going then. Dress warm. It's colder than it looks.'

Leaving the children with Lucy, Louisa wrapped up and they went along the coast road as far as Killiney Beach. 'You're fit,' she said, as she struggled to keep up.

'That's Stella's work. She has me exercising every day. She's even teaching me to play racquetball. She's moved her treadmill into my bedroom.'

'So, what does that mean?'

'We're inseparable.' Becca shot Louisa a shy smile. 'So thanks, to whatever bit of serendipity had her at loose ends in the Unicorn that day.'

'I had no idea that you and she would hit it off, but I'm delighted for you.'

'Me too. That's why you haven't heard from me. I've been in la-la land. Then I realized I was neglecting my old friends.'

'Sometimes it's good to have a little space.'

'Yeah. How are things going with Foster?'

'Better than I'd ever dreamed. I feel so relaxed with him and we have so much in common. He's doing his best to get on with the kids, which makes me happy.'

'You deserve it, Lou. Nobody deserves it more, in fact. I'm

just happy that you're happy. And only you know what will make you happy.'

They stopped at the wall overlooking the beach. 'Only Louisa knows Louisa,' Becca said. And that was enough.

'Is Gill all right?' Louisa asked.

'He'll get over you.'

'I didn't do anything to lead him on, I promise. I tried so hard to be no more than a friend.'

Becca turned, her cheeks and the tip of her nose red with the cold. 'Listen here. There's nothing you could have done to prevent Gill falling in love with you. He'll lick his wounds for a while, then get on with his life. He'll be back for Christmas. I hope you, Foster and the kids will join us. You will, won't you?'

'We'd love to,' Louisa said. 'I'll do the ham.'

'And I'll do the turkey.'

'Like always,' Louisa said. 'Will we turn round and walk back? I could use a hot drink.'

'Me too.'

When they arrived at the house, Elvie met them at the door. 'Mummy? Lucy feels funny. And she did a wee on the floor.'

'Uh-oh. Where is she Elvie?'

'On the floor.'

The women raced ahead to find Lucy on all fours, her face contorted.

Louisa knelt beside her. 'Lucy? When did the pain start?'

'Last night, but I thought it was the curry we had for dinner – *yeow*!'

'Have your waters broken?'

'I'm flooding.'

'We need to get you to hospital now.'

'I don't know, Lou, I can't move. There's too much pressure on my spine. It hurts to lie down. Hurts to stand up. Hurts to do anything.'

*

Two hours later, Lucy was lying in the maternity ward at Holles Street with a baby in her arms. 'The pushing hurt like hell, Lou.'

'I think you broke my fingers,' Louisa said. 'One more picture, then I'll leave you two alone.'

'But we're not, are we? Alone, I mean.'

Louisa kissed Lucy's forehead. 'No, you're not. I'll always be here for you and this little angel.' Louisa couldn't resist stroking the baby's soft cheek. 'Do you want me to track down Ben?'

Lucy shook her head.

'Are you sure? The baby will want to know some day.'

Lucy's eyes filled with tears. 'Later.'

Louisa kissed the little head. 'What about your mother? Will I call her in Spain?'

'Not yet,' Lucy said.

Louisa kissed her goodbye on the forehead. 'You try to get some rest now.'

'I wish I could see Elvie and Milo's faces when you tell them.'

'They'll be over the moon.'

Just as Louisa was leaving, Paul arrived with a huge bouquet of flowers and a bunch of balloons. 'There you are!' he said. 'I came as soon as I heard.'

'How did you hear?' Louisa asked.

'News travels fast,' Paul said.

He sat on the edge of Lucy's bed, admiring her as much as the baby. 'So, is it a boy or a child?'

Lucy smiled at the old country expression. 'Go away out of that. It's a girl. A tiny, perfect, little witch of a girl.'

'I thought you weren't due until January?'

'She was always a little fuzzy about the dates,' Louisa told him.

'I'm glad it didn't happen on my watch.' He turned to Lucy. 'You thought of any names?'

Louisa left them murmuring to each other, thinking of all the gorgeous, single, child-free bridesmaids who had thrown themselves at Paul's feet, when all along what he'd wanted was the motherly type.

28

Ben shuffled through the heap of wrapping paper beneath the tree and asked Louisa, 'What did I give Milo?'

Louisa was already sorry she'd let him in the door.

'A train set,' she said, shortly.

'And Elvie?'

'A ham radio, because you thought she was too young for a mobile phone.'

Ben's head bobbed. 'You're kidding.'

'Yes I am. You got her a Walkman.' She paused, then said. 'Come on Ben. You've seen the kids, now it's time to go.'

'You're not even going to offer me a drink?'

'Sorry, no time. Gotta run.'

Christmas Day was planned down to the last minute. She'd stage-managed Ben's arrival for an hour when Lucy and baby Penelope were out with Paul, and Foster had shot over to Hump's, thereby eliminating one source of conflict for the day. The other had been Foster's insistence that they 'drop in' on the Smiths, since the twins were his godsons and he couldn't ignore them on Christmas Day. With Christmas dinner arranged for Becca's at two, Louisa would have to meet Foster at the Smiths as soon as she could. She didn't know when she'd be able to relax into the holiday spirit.

Preoccupied, she hardly listened to Ben's tale of woe.

'Lou, this is my childhood home. I've got memories here of poor Mam.'

'I'm not your mother.'

'What do you say we sell it? Fifty-fifty split.'

'Talk to my solicitor.'

'Ah, Lou. Come on. This blabbin'-through-solicitors-shite is costing us a fortune.'

'Small price to pay,' Louisa said, pulling the plugs out of the wall behind the Christmas tree so that its lights went out. 'Milo? Elvie? Get your coats, we're leaving now.'

'Where are you going?' Ben demanded.

'None of your business.'

He rocked back on his heels and dug in. 'You have a man living here.'

'I have the mother of your child living here too.'

Ben gave her a look of pity. 'When are you going to stop taking in strays? Is it that hard to fill the space I left behind?'

Elvie and Milo were in the hall and Louisa didn't want them to hear an argument, so she ignored him and went out to help them with their coats. 'Say goodbye to Dad. You'll see him again soon.'

They looked up at their father with incomprehension. Louisa wished she understood how they viewed him.

Ben slunk off to a waiting car, which sped off when he got into the passenger's seat. That was him all over, playing the abandoned son when all along there was back-up out on the street, she thought. She and the children drove to Foxrock. Along the way families were packed into cars, all headed some-where – to proper families, she suspected, rather than the patchwork of friends to whom she felt a duty. The diamond-and-emerald ring on her finger caught her eye as she steered the car down the motorway. Foster had given it to her that morning, slipping it onto her finger as she slept.

When she'd awoken to find it glittering on the third finger of her left hand, she'd felt a girlish delight. It wasn't the same one she'd seen that day in the jeweller's, but it was close enough and she decided she liked it. Of course she did – she loved it! What was she saying?

She had given Foster a print of the picture she'd taken of

him in the glass room, when she was seventeen. 'I'm glad it was you who took this,' Foster said, a little embarrassed at the sight of his twenty-year-old body. 'Otherwise people would think I was doing gay porn.'

They'd snuggled in bed as long as they could before the children woke up to see what was under the tree. 'Anyway, how about it?' he'd asked, kissing her.

'I love the ring, but it wouldn't be right for us to be engaged yet. My divorce hasn't come through and the children need time.'

'They'll accept what comes,' he said gruffly.

'They're part of this too.'

'They're kids.'

Louisa hoped she hadn't hurt his feelings. 'I want to marry you, some day, but not yet. Can this ring be a promise instead?'

'You just want more rings.'

'Come here, you bad boy. You can't get everything you want the minute you ask, you know,' she'd said, and hoped she could heal his hurt feelings for it with her body.

Now she drove into Hump and Belly's road, lined with identical houses, trying to guess which was theirs. 'There they are!' shouted Milo. The twins were standing outside the door in their pyjamas, looking bored. She pulled the car into their driveway, then her own children tumbled out.

'Say "Hell" ,' Elvie commanded the twins.

The boys looked at each other quizzically, then back at her.

'Go on,' Milo ordered.

'Hell,' said the twins.

'Lo!' Elvie shouted.

Foster appeared behind the boys, rolled his eyes and pushed past them to kiss Louisa. 'What took you so long?'

'You OK?'

'Right as rain – isn't that what they say over here?'

Over here reminded her again that this side of the Atlantic was alien territory to him and she felt the tug of *home* again, not knowing quite where home was but certain it wasn't at the Smiths' house.

They went in, the twins bickering over the gifts that Elvie and Milo had brought them. Foster consigned the children to the TV room, which wasn't the family approach to a Christmas visit that Louisa would have liked, but at least it kept her own two out of Belly and Hump's way. The house smelled unpleasant and Hump seemed two sheets to the wind already. Immediately she regretted coming.

Belly's extreme housekeeping had teetered into neglect since Louisa last visited. 'Foster was never one for kids,' she whispered to Louisa. 'That was why his last marriage broke up. She wanted kids. He didn't. And she had kids of her own as well. You'd think she lived in a trailer park, not Beverly Hills.'

Louisa handed her the gift she'd brought, a set of Irish crystal goblets.

'Nothing for you I'm afraid,' Belly told her. 'Shopping privileges revoked.'

Louisa shivered and pulled her embroidered vintage shawl around her shoulders as she entered the cold sitting room with its unlit plastic tree. They must have forgotten to turn the heating on. In a tone of haughty apology, Belly said, 'I was going to light the tree with those dinky little candles you can buy in Germany, but Humphrey here says the plastic would go up like a torch.' She threw a log towards the cold grate and missed. The log rolled from the hearth onto the carpet. 'How do you light one of these things, Foss?'

Foster shrugged. 'No idea.'

'Oh, fiddle,' Belly said.

Louisa could feel Belly appraising her and remembered a time when the other woman's interest had seemed like a gift.

'I need another drink. Can I get you one?' Belly asked.

'A cup of tea is fine. I'm driving.'

'Champagne for Louisa!' Belly shouted at Hump, who was

now in whispered consultation with Foster at the other end of the room.

He pulled back from Foster and beamed at Louisa. 'Did I hear something about a ring?' He stepped over to Louisa and took her hand. 'They're engaged, Belly! What did I tell you? Time for a celebration!'

Belly grappled Louisa's hand from Hump and stared at the ring. 'Don't know how he could afford it. Must have won it at cards. I love that phrase. At cards. Life's such a crapshoot, really, isn't it?'

'Shut up,' Hump hissed.

Louisa looked helplessly at Foster, hoping he would explain. When he remained silent, she said, 'We're not engaged yet. My divorce hasn't come through. This ring is more of a promise.'

'A promise!' Hump said. 'That an Irish thing?'

'Marriage is only a matter of time,' Foster said.

'It had better be,' Hump said gruffly, then softened, 'you two were meant for each other.'

How kind of Hump to be so concerned, Louisa thought sourly.

Belly was taciturn. 'Whatever you say, Hump. You're the matchmaker, not me.'

The shrill squabbling of the children in the TV room gave Louisa an excuse to leave the room. 'I'll look in on them.'

Her children were watching the twins battle each other on the Playstation. The pair seemed to do little else. Elvie and Milo were huddled into opposite corners of a couch. 'This is boring, Mum. Just like any other day,' Milo complained.

He was right.

Belly appeared with a bottle of champagne. 'There you are! Hiding out with the kids – very sociable.' Her face was rubbery and her voice slurred.

Foster's face appeared over Belly's shoulder. He mouthed, 'Love you,' and grinned. She smiled at him. He was magnificent, standing there in his white polo shirt and navy cashmere sweater, cream trousers worn casually with leather loafers. When they had their own home, Christmas would be like the ones she had wished for as a child.

Belly wriggled her copious bottom against Foster's thighs. 'Let's go find the mistletoe,' she said. Foster's face disappeared.

'Belly,' Louisa said. 'You're not doing yourself any favours acting like that.'

'You should talk, Miss Diamond Ring, leaving hotels with the bill unpaid. Of course, you weren't to know, were you? Foster got out of that one by the skin of his teeth.'

Louisa froze. 'What did you say?'

'I said, your fiancé is bankrupt, baby. Nix, nada, zilch.'

Belly handed Louisa the champagne bottle – a supermarket brand – and disappeared into the lavatory.

Louisa steeled herself to face Foster and Humphrey – Belly's whispering campaign was over. She wanted the truth now, if only to stop Belly's goading. But as she was about to re-enter the drawing room, she instinctively hesitated in the hall outside the door. They were talking about her.

'How long is Louisa's divorce going to take?'

'I don't know,' Foster mumbled, a schoolboy to his head-master.

'Why can't she get a quickie somewhere?'

'It's none of your business,' Foster said.

Dead right, Louisa thought proudly.

'This is a desperate situation, Foss. You of all people know that. When are you going to hand over the money like you promised you would? I don't look good in cement shoes, man.'

Louisa froze. She strained to interpret what Humphrey was saying. 'The Irish authorities are on to us, thanks to your buddies in the Federal Reserve. As for those loan sharks that call themselves a bank –' Was Humphrey insisting that Foster pay him back for the hotel bill? Or was it even worse . . .

She heard Foster's voice then: 'You deal with your own shit for a change. I'm not going to do it. Louisa's mine, not yours.

She's my escape from you. I'm out for good. I love her and I'm not going to betray her again.'

Hump sounded furious. 'What do you know about love? Louisa's mine as much as she is yours. We're in this together, just like we always were.'

Foster's voice was steely. 'Not anymore. Louisa and I are together now and you can get lost.'

'I don't think you're in any position to play the hero now, do you? All I have to do is tell her, Foss. Two little words: glass, room.'

Louisa felt weak and goose-pimples spread over her entire body.

'You wouldn't dare!' Foster warned.

'I would. What have I got to lose? I've lost everything. And you – you had nothing much to begin with. What would you have been without me?'

There was a silence then, as Louisa tried to calm her breathing.

'Happy,' Foster said quietly. 'We would have been so happy.'

Hump laughed. Louisa heard their voices rising and falling but she could take in no more.

'There's only one way out of this, my boy, and you know it,' Hump said.

Foster's voice rose: 'I told you, there's nothing left. I've given you everything.'

'Not everything.'

'Good luck, Hump. Do what you want. That's the last you're getting from me because I won't hurt Louisa again. You'll think of something. Hell – go back to Vegas. You and I are finished.'

Louisa, overhearing 'Vegas', thought for some odd reason of Foster's ex-wife, dressed in a tassled gold evening gown and dripping in jewels as she gambled away her fortune. But had she gambled it all away? Or had *they*?

And then, with a clarity that felt like a knife in her heart, she remembered: *Again*? He said that he could never hurt me *again*.

325

When she heard Foster say, 'I'm getting Louisa. We're leaving,' she flitted across the hall towards the TV room.

'Lou?'

She turned to see his face full of a kind of desperate hope. 'I love you, baby. Let's go. Wherever you want. I've had enough.'

She let him put his arms around her and felt again the warmth and security of a man who, she felt, had loved her for who she was. 'Foster,' she whispered, 'what's going on between you and Hump? What's all this about money?'

'I'm tired of floating his schemes, that's all,' Foster said. 'It's over between him and me. Let's go.'

His reassurance convinced her that the atmosphere in the house had infected her: she was being paranoid. Foster was doing exactly what she had wanted him to do – making the break from Humphrey. She decided to put her suspicions to the back of her mind and accept Foster's explanation that he'd been generous towards his old friend, but now needed to pull out. *I've got nothing left to give.* She was proud of him, laying it on the line like that. This was a start. They began looking for their coats.

Humphrey appeared. 'Louisa, you're not going to rely on Foster's financial advice, are you? He has nothing left to give. He said so himself. If I were you, I'd knock down that old wreck of Alice Stone's and build a dozen houses – the sort of thing West Coasters like. Lots of bathrooms. I'd say you could easily profit by fifty million – maybe that's a conservative estimate.'

Foster paled and Louisa pulled away from him as he attempted to help her into her coat. 'What's he talking about, Foster?'

'He heard a rumour in New York. He's obsessed with money, that's all. Don't think anything of it.'

Louisa's blood rose. 'I didn't know you knew about Alice.'

Hump chuckled. '*I didn't know you knew.* Which one of you is more stupid? Of course he knew.'

'It was a lot to keep from me, don't you think?' Foster asked defensively.

Louisa recalled Stella's advice not to breathe a word to anyone. 'There was nothing to keep from you. It could be years before I see a penny – not that it should matter.'

Belly was grinning at them from the kitchen end of the hall, her face smugly triumphant. 'And you'll be long married by then, won't you?'

'Let's open that champagne!' cried Hump.

Louisa allowed Foster to take the champagne from her. He gave it to Hump as though he'd changed his mind about leaving. She followed him into the drawing room, where Belly sat down by the hearth, preparing to enjoy the show.

Hump gripped the champagne bottle and prised the cork out with his thick fingers. 'Some champagne, then a few boyhood reminiscences to share about our Foster.'

'I want to go now,' she said to Foster. 'You said we were going. You and I need to talk – in private.' Thank God she was promised, not engaged, and certainly not married. The love affair she thought she'd been living now felt like a stone in the pit of her womb.

Foster's face had aged in the past few minutes. He looked at her with dead eyes.

'Oh, but you mustn't go!' Belly said, face hard in her role as diabolic hostess. 'The ham's nearly ready. I've put it under the grill to crisp it! And we must have a toast!'

Louisa had no intention of staying for ham. She only wanted to get her children and get out of there. Hump stopped her. 'You're sitting on quite a nice parcel of land there at Amagansett. Remember the glass room? It blew off in a storm a few years ago. Left the roof wide open. Alice didn't seem to notice. If she hadn't been so damned rich somebody would have called in the social workers, I reckon. She died of starvation, they say.'

'Who are *they*?'

'People.'

'I hope "people" are aware of how hurtful that sounds.'

Foster was glaring at Hump. 'I think we should let Louisa grieve her aunt in her own way, don't you?'

'It's none of your business either,' Louisa snapped.

'Hey, it's OK, Lou, drop it,' said Foster soothingly. 'Let's not upset the kids.'

He was just like Ben, making out like she was being unreasonable.

Hump poured the champagne into four glasses. 'Sit down, Foster. We're going to celebrate your *promise*.' He made the word sound like an obscenity.

Louisa refused to take the glass he offered her. She was trying to figure things out. Hump's conversation with Foster kept running through her head. This wasn't the Foster she knew. When she looked at him now, she saw a defeated middle-aged man, going soft around the middle.

Belly wobbled to her feet. 'I'd like to propose a toast. To Alice!'

Ignoring her, Foster and Hump stared each other down, Foster's eyes were full of fear as Hump gloated.

Suddenly Louisa was coughing – and saw a wisp of smoke. Dazed, she watched it thicken, then she leaped into action. She pushed past Foster – 'Out of my way' – and followed it to the kitchen. Smoke and flames were pouring from the grill. Belly had closed the oven door on it when she should have left it open. Coming up behind her, Hump moved to open the oven door. 'Don't!' she shouted, grabbing his arm. 'If you open the oven door you'll let oxygen in. The whole thing could go up.' The steel oven was too hot to touch – she couldn't turn off the burners. 'Where's the main supply?'

Hump looked at her stupidly.

'You idiot, somewhere there's a switch or a lever or something! Get the children out.'

She wet a T-towel and put it over her face so she could breathe, then threw more wet cloth towels over the oven door. She found the switch and turned it off, then she shoved open a window to get some fresh air in. The danger over, Louisa wiped sweat from her face, while Hump lurked a few feet away, smirking, unconcerned for the children or anyone else.

'You're the Girl Scout, aren't you, Lou? I always said I should have married you instead of Belly.'

He strode forward and put his arms around her.

'Get off me,' she warned.

'You know I got what Foster didn't, don't you? You loved it, Loopy-Lou. The boys loved it too.'

She froze. Just like before, her body let her down. Into her ear he hissed, 'Foster let me have first bite of the cherry, didn't he? Foster used to do anything I told him. Then he had to go and fall in love with you. Bitch.'

Foster pounded into the kitchen and punched Humphrey, then he grabbed his arm and twisted it behind his back. 'You bastard. You *sick* bastard!' Foster shouted. He wrestled Humphrey to the floor and kicked him in the groin, the stomach and then the head.

'Foster stop! You're going to kill him!' Louisa cried.

Through the open kitchen door she saw Belly run into the TV room and slam the door behind her.

Foster was rigid with anger. 'He's lying, Lou. It was nothing to do with me, nothing. He was out of control. I had no idea!' He held her by the shoulders, trying to convince her. 'Don't listen to him,' but she pushed him away.

Hump was dragging himself to his feet and hissed. 'Now, I'll bet you're sorry you pulled the plug on me. Huh? How many times did I bail *you* out, huh? Look at you. You and your fucking *love*.' Hump shoved his face up against Foster's. 'Fuck you *boy*. And fuck *her*.'

'Lou, don't listen to him. He's crazy. He's mad at me 'cause I pulled out of the investment. I'm sick and tired of floating his schemes, playing the soft touch.'

Louisa looked at him numbly. 'You came back sniffing after my money. No other reason.'

Foster whimpered, 'It doesn't matter anymore. At least it brought me back to you. I love you now. I want to spend the rest of my life with you. I'll sign a pre-nup, if that's what you want.'

Louisa felt herself so distant from him that she no longer cared. 'And why would you want to do that?'

'To prove to you I love you for you, not for your money.'

Suddenly her mind cleared. 'I was always currency to you, wasn't I? That night you were to meet me in the glass room. You stood me up deliberately. You handed me to *him* like a piece of meat. That was your little deal, wasn't it Foster? You sold your soul to that bastard just so the groundsman's son would be accepted in polite East Hampton society. How many other girls did you do that to? How long have you been Humphrey Smith's pimp?'

'You're wrong,' Foster yelled. 'I'm the success – not him. He used me. He's the one who would have been nothing without *me*.'

'How many others have there been, Foster? How many women have you set up? How many *girls*?'

The truth crystalized around her heart like ice. She was speaking aloud to herself now, as much as to Foster: 'Why did I think it was friends of Alice's all these years? Strangers taking advantage of a drunken girl? No-one could have found a way into the glass room by accident. They had to know how to get there. And they had to have been told I was there – and only one person knew . . .'

Louisa stared at Foster and held herself together by sheer willpower. 'You set me up, Foster. You didn't turn up in the glass room that night because Hump told you not to. Did you know he'd bring his friends? Huh? That turn you on?'

Foster disintegrated as she watched, like nitrates exposed to light.

In a voice so cold that it didn't seem her own, she said, 'I'd trust that evil scum before I'd ever believe another word you said. Was the pay-off, worth it? Huh? Did the poor grounds-man's son get rich quick? Did he make a few bob on the market? And what happened then, Foss? You gamble it all away again? How many other women have you conned to fund your little gambling problem? Or is it Humphrey's problem? Why am I even bothering to ask. You two are one and the same.'

Foster tried to put his arms around her. 'Ssh, baby. Nothing he says is real.'

'Get off me! I can't believe I ever let you touch me!' She shoved him away and over his shoulder, saw Humphrey, her rapist, grinning at her slyly. She held his gaze, staring him down.

Foster's grovelling was annoying her now. 'I'm sorry. Please –'

She flung out an arm and knocked him to the floor, her eyes flickering between Humphrey and Foster as she spoke. 'There were never any goddamned letters. That's why I never got any. You never wrote them. You didn't give a shit about me as long as you pleased *him*.'

'It wasn't like that,' Foster begged. 'There was nothing I could do to protect you from him. He would have got you anyway.'

'Protect me from *him*? You're worse!' She ripped off the ring and threw it at Humphrey, 'Hump's the one you should be married to, not me.'

On his knees, Foster begged her forgiveness. 'I love you. Don't leave me. Please don't ever leave me.'

Hump laughed to himself until Louisa turned her rage on him. 'You're the one who raped me, you creep. And then you got off on watching your friends stirring the porridge. That's what scum like you call it, isn't it? You sick psychopath.'

This knowledge – which she should have seen all along – came flooding from her very core. She resisted an urge to kick Humphrey's face in. 'The only reason I'm not killing you now is I have two children who need me. But watch out, *baby*. I'm such a rich bitch now I'll be able to pay someone else to kill you. You'll be looking over your shoulder for the rest of your short, pathetic life.'

After her outburst, Louisa felt preternaturally calm. All the pain had gone. She walked down the hall to the TV room, kicked open the door and said, 'We're going. We've stayed here way too long. Becca will be wondering where we've got to.'

Elvie and Milo jumped up with evident relief and pulled her towards the door.

'Louisa!' Foster whimpered after them as they got in the car. Louisa slammed the door closed in his face and shouted at the children, 'Fasten your seat-belts!' Then she reversed, catching sight of Belly and the twins' faces pressed up against the window. She put the car into gear and drove. As the road unfolded before her, she felt herself floating away into the deep orange and blue Christmas afternoon sky.

'Slow down, Mum!' Elvie shouted.

Louisa barely heard her. She wanted to end the pain. The car hit seventy miles per hour.

Hump's voice was in her head. *First bite of the cherry.*

'Mum, *slow down*!'

'Mama!' Milo screamed. 'You're scaring us!'

His voice brought her to her senses. She slammed on the brakes and skidded to a halt on the side of the road, then laid her head on the steering-wheel and wept. 'I'm sorry, I am so, so sorry.'

Elvie and Milo were so silent and still in the back of the car, that it dawned on her they might be hurt. She turned to see them staring at her blankly.

'I'm sorry. It's OK, now.' She wiped her hand over her face, found her phone in the battery charger beneath the dashboard and punched speed dial.

'Lou?' It was a reassuring male voice. 'Lou? Is that you?'

'We're on the N 11. Come and get us. Please.'

'Don't move.'

She didn't know how long it took him to get there – it might have been minutes or months. Eventually the sound of the motorcycle engine was roaring up behind the car, then idling by the passenger window. The sweetest sound she'd ever heard. Gill peered into the back seat, assured himself that the children were safe, then ran round to the driver's door and yanked it open. Louisa reached up and let him pull her out. 'I'm so sorry,' she said again. 'I'm sorry.'

Gill embraced her gently, as though she'd break if he didn't hold her together. She was aware of him escorting her to the passenger side, and buckling her into the seat. Then saw his face in profile as he talked to the children, their faces responding to him with relieved smiles. It didn't matter what he was saying. All that mattered was that he was there. Gill steered with his right hand and clung to Louisa's hand with his left, letting go of her shaking fingers only to shift gears, then he was with her again, keeping her grounded in the present. *Don't ever let me go*, she wanted to say. *Don't ever let me go again.*

Becca and Stella were waiting outside Becca's house.

'Come see my Christmas tree,' Becca called.

Louisa followed as the children muddied the acres of white carpet, black on white, like footprints in snow.

'Sorry, sorry, sorry,' Louisa said lamely. It was the only word she seemed able to say.

'It's only a carpet, love.' Becca said, then spoke quietly to Gill.

Louisa let him settle her on a sofa by the fire, while Becca introduced Milo and Elvie to her Christmas tree – pure white, with crystal decorations and tiny white lights.

'The Snow Queen's tree!' Milo exclaimed.

Elvie touched one of the glistening baubles. 'Are they real ice?'

'No, thank goodness. Look under the tree, why don't you? There might be something there for you.'

'This is a real Christmas house,' Elvie said. 'Not like the twins'.'

When the children were occupied opening presents, Becca crept over to Louisa and bent down to her level. 'What happened?'

Louisa couldn't speak.

'That's fine. You can tell me some other time.'

Stella handed Louisa a glass of brandy, while Gill wrapped a blanket round her shoulders. 'You're shivering,' he said.

He sat beside her and she leaned her head on his shoulder, not wanting to move. Not ever.

Somehow, Becca, Gill and Stella understood. They jollied the children along, pulling crackers and wearing paper hats, reading the jokes that tumbled out of the crackers on tiny slips of paper and laughing. Between them, they tried to eclipse earlier events with Christmas joy. The children fell asleep between Stella and Becca on the sofa and Louisa knew she would never have to explain if she didn't want to. All that mattered to her family – for that was who Gill, Becca and, now, Stella were – was that she had been deeply hurt but had now returned to them, come what may.

29

That night, Gill took Louisa and the children home to St Agnes's and never left. After the children were asleep in their beds, he knocked on Louisa's bedroom door.

'Come in,' she said, sipping the cup of camomile tea he'd brought her earlier.

'Only checking to make sure you're safe,' he said. 'Can I get you anything else?'

'Sit by me,' she said.

He sat on the edge of the bed and slipped his hand into hers. He took the tea-mug from her and put it on the bedside table, and when she shivered, he laid an extra blanket over her.

'Go to sleep. I'll be in the guestroom if you need anything.'

She closed her eyes and the day flashed back. 'Gill?'

He was still there, watching her. 'Yeah?'

'Hold my hand.'

He sat beside her on the bed, making himself comfortable with pillows plumped behind his head, then stretched out on top of the duvet. He took hold of her hand again, 'This feel OK?'

'Perfect,' she said. 'Gill?'

'Yeah?' He switched out the light.

'Never let me go again.'

He lightly stroked the back of her hand. 'I never did,' he answered.

By the end of January, Louisa's separation had been formalized and everything was in place for the divorce in a year's time. She cursed the slowness of the Irish legal system, but Stella managed to uncover Ben's financial trail and Louisa pressured him into giving her St Agnes's.

At Easter, Paul and Lucy were married in a quiet civil ceremony. Louisa gave the bride away, then cuddled Penelope while Paul and Lucy exchanged vows. Becca held the reception at her house, decorated for the occasion with pink roses round the door. A few minutes before the bride and groom, with their baby daughter, were due to leave for their honeymoon in Venice – a present from Becca – Louisa found a chance to talk to Paul. 'I nearly forgot to give you my present,' she said, and handed him a large envelope.

He broke apart the sealing wax that held it closed, and pulled a sheaf of documents half-way out. He only needed to read the first line or two. 'You've given me the business?' he asked her in disbelief.

'I guess so,' Louisa said. 'It was always as much yours as it was mine. But you now own the building, the equipment and the right to make as much money as you have time for. Just promise me one thing.'

'Yeah?'

'Keep doing what you're doing and you'll be all right.'

He held her close and whispered, 'You're always welcome to come back.'

But Louisa knew she never would.

'I think this is the first time I've ever actually enjoyed a wedding,' she said to Gill when he appeared at her side.

'And it had better not be the last,' he answered, and gave her bottom a polite little squeeze. They watched the ebb and flow of guests as they spun and stumbled to the Dolphins' Barn Salsa Band, friends of Paul's. 'Have I mentioned, Miss Stone, how edible you look in that naughty dress you're wearing?' he asked her.

'No, Mr Lynley, but if you were to mention it, I would have to say that your rather sexy tuxedo shirt shall be ripped of its buttons by eleven o'clock this evening.'

'I'll consider that, Miss Stone, before I speak my piece. As long as you promise, once I've ripped the dress asunder, that you will continue to wear those rather fetching come-to-bed shoes.'

Louisa leaned against him and giggled shyly. He put his arm round her to pull her closer and kissed her on the top of her head. It occurred to her then, how wrong she had been to think that it mattered that he was ten years younger than she. In so many ways, he was decades wiser. I can trust this man with my life, she thought. And my children's lives.

'Say cheese!' Elvie called to her mother and Gill.

Click.

'Gotcha!'

In May, Louisa turned thirty-eight. Gill rented a small boat and brought her to Dalkey Island. She sat on the craggy hill that she had watched from her bedroom window for so long, and saw St Agnes's staring back at her darkly. The thirteen years that Ben stole seemed small enough to hold in her hand. She let them go. 'I've stepped out of one life and into another . . . in this life I want to see people as they really are, not as I want them to be,' she said.

'To this life, then,' Gill said, raising his water bottle.

Louisa smiled inside.

He turned to her. 'I love you, birthday girl.'

'But I don't love you. I haven't figured out what love is yet.'

'Do you like me?'

'Very much.'

'Then be "in-like" with me. It feels good. One day, maybe, you'll love with me.'

'It's scary to make love to someone you like . . .'

'I know.'

They walked a distance to the Napoleonic tower that Louisa had gazed at for years from her bedroom window. Then they sat on the stones of the tumbledown house, which turned out to be St Begnet's, a seventh-century church. 'St Begnet was a virgin saint,' Gill offered, 'an Irish princess, others say. The Christians had to make her a saint because the locals adored her.'

'I'd rather be adored than be a saint,' Louisa said. As they were leaving, she laid her cheek against St Begnet's cool stone wall and said goodbye.

The summer in Ireland that year was the most glorious anyone could remember, which was ironic, Louisa considered, as she, Gill, the children and her lawyer, Stella, flew over the Atlantic on their way to New York. All the arrangements were complete: she had only to sign some documents and attend a few meetings with lawyers, which, Stella said, would all be conducted more efficiently if Louisa appeared in person. There would be a press conference – art journalists only. The enormity of what she had inherited was only beginning to dawn on her. There was the property, of course, but also the vast art collection. She had it in mind to make Paradise a sort of retreat for women artists. She wanted to build a handful of family cottages, so that their children could stay with them, and lay on activities during the day. Many women had given up the time they needed to fulfil their dreams not just because they had to make a living, but because they couldn't leave their kids.

Alice's studio would become hers.

Louisa was in control of her life for the first time. There was more to it than having financial independence unexpectedly thrust upon her by her aunt. She felt she had choices now, as though she was starting out on life. Humphrey had, perversely, given her this second chance by reuniting her with Foster and dragging her back to the glass room where a secret part of herself had lain forgotten. She chose to be thankful for that: now that she had fought her way out of it, she was free.

Gill held her hand as he listened to his iPod and napped. Looking out at the passing clouds, Louisa thought how strange it would be to arrive back in the States after so long. Would she recognize it? Or even belong anymore?

A manila envelope lay in her lap. Stella had given it to her just before they boarded. 'I had a sleepless night or two, wondering whether to give you this, Lou. At times, I thought you'd be better off without it. Becca convinced me otherwise. She tells me I'm too prone to playing God.'

They'd been in the air for three hours when Louisa found the courage to open it. Inside, protected by two pieces of cardboard and filmy sheets of acid-free paper, was a photograph.

A baby girl, not quite a year old, sat on Amanda's lap in the chaotic Manhattan apartment, the crammed shelves and crookedly-hung paintings just visible in the background. Amanda was a beautiful teenager, looking far younger than twenty. The baby was smiling joyfully, reaching for the camera as though it was a toy, while Amanda – proud but uncertain – gazed longingly at the camera.

Looking for an explanation, Louisa turned the picture over. On the back it said, 'My Daughter and Amanda, 1969'. And it was signed, *Larry*.

Acknowledgements

My thanks to Kirsty Crawford and her sympathetic third eye; to my earthly angels, Cathy Kelly and Dolores McCarthy; to Christie Hickman and Hazel Orme for their expert reading and criticism; and to my supportive friends and colleagues in *The Irish Times*.